THE
ADVENTURE

Lucy Coleman

www.ariafiction.com

About *The French Adventure*

Suddenly unemployed and single, Anna escapes to her parents' beautiful house in France for a much needed recharge – and to work out what she wants to do next with her life now her carefully mapped out plan has gone out the window.

Anna gives herself 6 months to recuperate, all the while helping renovate her parents' adjoining Gites into picturesque b&b's. But working alongside the ruggedly handsome Sam on the renovation project,

she didn't expect for life to take an unexpected, if not
unwelcome, twist…

In memory of Lilian. *Always* by my side and *forever* in my heart.

May

The L Word

Two weeks today will be the first anniversary of our first *real* date. Being wined and dined in a chic little French restaurant was a gigantic step forward; it signalled the beginning of a new era in my relationship with Karl. Even though at least half of the meal was spent talking about work, his intentions were clear – we were no longer simply colleagues and romance was in the air.

Since then, Karl must have told me that he loves me more than a thousand times. You might think I'm exaggerating, but I can assure you that's not the case. He usually manages to slip it into the conversation at least three times a day. The first time he said the *L word* to me, it slid off his tongue so easily I could almost have missed it. It wasn't a *staring into each other's eyes* moment of discovery, just a casual 'love you, babe'.

As the months rolled by, I pushed aside my growing fear that it was only a word to him. Because it means so much more to me, I freeze whenever he tacks it onto a sentence.

And, yes, I'm very aware that my air of disapproval does make me sound ungrateful and undeserving. But it's all about self-preservation, you see. I'll never utter that word again until I'm one hundred per cent certain that the man I'm saying it to believes I'm their soul mate too – the perfect fit.

The last time I uttered the *L word*, was six years ago. It was to a guy I'd known since childhood and the man I genuinely believed I would marry when the time was right. He was handsome in a rugged way, fired up with ambition and exciting to be around. Sadly, everyone we knew thought we were the perfect couple too, except the guy in question, as it turned out.

Will arrived in my life when I was a very precocious pre-teen and counting down the days to attaining that revered status. I had this fervent belief that overnight my whole life would change. And it did when Will and his family moved into the house next door. It seemed living proof of that fact because in a ridiculously short space of time he became everything to me. The first glance that passed between us was magical and the best birthday present I could ever have been given.

As classmates, we were best friends throughout those traumatic school years when your hormones are changing you in ways you don't always understand. With it comes a rollercoaster of incredible highs and devastating lows. Dictated by important events in your life like whose party you are invited to and which group you hang around in, you

need one true friend. Will was mine and I was his –
life couldn't get any better. But it did… until the day
he broke my heart.

The Dilemma

I'm conscious that Lizzie is staring at me across our regular table in our favourite little coffee shop. With the mismatched, scrubbed pine tables and the eclectic mix of upcycled chairs, it's cosy. You feel like you are sitting in a farmhouse kitchen and there's always a warm welcome. But then we do spend quite a bit of time here.

Once again, we're discussing the dilemma that constantly haunts me these days. Namely, how healthy is a relationship that is based on a lie?

'Of course he loves you, Anna,' Lizzie responds to the question I blurted out without thinking. With our first anniversary looming Karl doesn't seem to be signalling any major move forward in our relationship.

But you need to experience the pain of love's disappointments to be able to understand why it leaves a scar on your heart. Lizzie is very happily caught up in a relationship approaching its second anniversary; and she's sporting a gorgeous, bought-with-love engagement ring. Daniel is her first and only love and he's a keeper.

'You two are always together and Karl dotes on you,' she offers, emphatically, unable to understand what ails my fragile heart. When I don't respond she raises her eyebrows, clearly exasperated with me.

'The move to your new house – it wasn't a test? Tell me it wasn't.' Her jaw drops a little in dismay.

I hang my head. I'm usually an open book to Lizzie, who has been my best friend since I returned to Dursley after university. The fact that I'd fooled her, too, reflects how much effort I've put into making my recent decisions seem purposeful and empowering. I wanted Karl to see that I, too, had plans for the future, because that was the truth, even if he wasn't entirely sure about where we were going as a couple. Waiting around to see what might happen seemed like treading water. But I knew that deep down I had an ulterior motive.

'He didn't say a word. It's a great little house and I love having the extra space, but I really hoped it might make Karl think about what he wants for the future, too.'

'You wanted him to say he'd move in? Or hand you a key to his place? Oh, Anna, maybe it's simply too soon for him.'

I feel like letting out one long, agonising scream to defuse my mounting sense of frustration. Another year of my life has passed and I really thought this was going somewhere. I hoped that this time it was for real, but as each day passes I'm simply feeling more and more confused. Karl's lack of interest in discussing our future sucks the joy out of every day we're together. On paper, he's perfect; we're probably *the* perfect couple. So why do I have this overwhelming feeling that something is wrong? Is this history repeating itself?

'Or maybe he likes his life the way it is,' I remark, trying to avoid eye contact with Lizzie as I know she has a soft spot for Karl.

'Talk to him; tell him how you feel. I've heard him say he loves you, he does it all the time.'

And be on the receiving end of that embarrassed smile, the one that signals you are addressing the elephant in the room? If he hasn't already sensed my growing discomfort about our situation then he doesn't know me at all. I notice every single time he utters the *L word*, not for the usual reasons, but because I've never once said it back to him. And he has never once noticed that omission. That's precisely why it worries me.

'I'll think about it.'

Lizzie is a close enough friend to know that's a firm *no*.

'Look, if this is really still about that guy Will, then you have a major problem, Anna. You told me he broke your heart but you aren't still in love with him, are you?'

I look at her aghast. 'No, of course not.'

'Then aren't you being a little unfair, doubting Karl's intentions?'

My shoulders sag and I can see she isn't going to let me skate over this.

'It's time you told me exactly what happened with Will, Anna. How else can I be a good friend and understand what's really going on inside that head of yours?'

I gaze down at my half eaten purple berry with sparkling vanilla frosting, cupcake. It's delicious but my appetite seems to have suddenly disappeared. I look around and today only half of the tables are occupied so it's not as if anyone can overhear our conversation. With that, I take a big breath and begin.

'As you know, Will and I were really close friends all through secondary school. When he told me he, too, had accepted a place at the University of the West of England, I was over the moon. I knew his father wanted him to go to Reading and with two firm offers I assumed he'd bow to family pressure. I could hardly contain my joy, even though we were still only *friends* at that point. Will standing up to his father was a shock and, silently, I loved him even more for it because I thought he'd made that decision so we could be together. I was facing the future confident that our relationship would develop on a more personal level.'

I notice that Lizzie too, has now stopped eating. She waves to the waitress to order two more coffees and I find myself shifting around in my seat, uncomfortably. Reliving this incident isn't easy, even after all this time.

'Over the next eighteen months our friendship developed into a passionate love affair and we became inseparable. Always together, always having fun and always at the centre of what was happening. We were the couple our friends envied, as they went through the trials of falling in and out of love.

'Will often joked about the pressure on guys to make a huge deal over the proposal; he warned me not to expect any more than flowers and a Chinese takeaway. We laughed about it and even talked about finding our dream flat overlooking Bristol Harbourside once we had both graduated.'

'Ah, that's heart-breaking, Anna. So what exactly happened to make the relationship fall apart?' Lizzie looks at me anxiously and I can't bear to see the sadness she's feeling on my behalf.

'Something changed between us and I found myself looking for any reason at all to avoid facing the truth. I told myself he was under pressure with a project he was working on and that's why I was seeing less and less of him. I believed his excuses.'

Lizzie stares at me, letting out a gasp. 'Oh no—'

I nod. 'I realise, with hindsight, that there were three of us in the relationship at that point. The third person was a girl named Cassandra. She was always around us and it had been that way more or less since we'd arrived on the campus. It was understandable in a way, as she was on the same course as Will. Or, at least, that's what I told myself.'

'Why didn't you tell me there was someone else involved? I just assumed it fizzled out between the two of you. Honestly, Anna, it's not good to keep a hurt like that a secret.' Lizzie's reaction makes me feel guilty for holding this back.

I shake my head, busying myself putting sugar in my coffee to avoid eye contact.

'I was young and naïve; I just didn't see it coming. One Friday night we ended up tagging along with a large group of friends to a wine bar in Clifton, in Bristol. We were celebrating the start of the Christmas holidays. Will had been in a bad mood all day and started drinking quite heavily early on in the evening. I was finding him increasingly more difficult to read and physically it had been weeks since we'd shared a bed. Eventually, there were only eight of us left. I was sitting directly opposite Will, deep in conversation with a girl named Sally. She was on the same course as me. Suddenly I heard raised voices and when I turned to look across at Will, I saw that Cassandra was sitting next to him and his eyes were blazing. She put a hand on Will's shoulder in an attempt to calm him down and keep him seated, but he struggled to his feet. Heads were starting to turn in the direction of our table as people began to wonder what the noise was all about.

'His words were slurred, "You don't think I've had enough of this pretence?" but clear enough. Even above the sound of the music thumping away in the background everyone around our table heard. And realised what was going on. Heads then turned in my direction as faces fell. I watched in horror as the little scene played out. Will stomped out of the bar, without a backwards glance. Cassandra looked around at our shocked faces and her reaction was one of total disbelief. For a few brief seconds she closed her eyes and when she opened them again she stared straight at me. My jaw had dropped and I felt as if I was frozen to the spot. All eyes were on the two of us and I struggled to keep my composure.

'Suddenly she jumped up, muttering "I'm sorry," as she chased after Will. The truth had surfaced and I was devastated. Cassandra was in a long term relationship with a guy from her home town. I thought she was lonely and didn't mind her tagging along. It never crossed my mind for one second that there was anything going on between her and Will. As it turned out, they'd been sleeping together for a while and he was pressing her to break up with her boyfriend. I wasn't even his first concern and I have no idea when he would have told me what was going on. The only way to move on from that humiliating episode was by promising myself that when it came to affairs of the heart I would never take anything for granted ever again.'

'Oh, Anna – now it all makes a lot more sense! You must have felt so humiliated, being strung along like that.'

Lizzie looks appalled.

'Karl saying the *L word* in such a casual way all the time sets alarm bells ringing for me. He's never declared his love; I mean, told me *why* he loves me. And doesn't he wonder why I don't say it back to him? Everything else between us is perfect; well, except for the lie we've been living, of course.'

Lizzie sighs. 'And I was just happy for you to have found someone at long last! No wonder you have trust issues, Anna. But then, having to keep your relationship a secret doesn't help, does it? I can now fully understand your concerns.'

'The truth is that I wouldn't normally have accepted the situation but when Karl asked me out we'd been working in the same department together for almost five months. Friendship sort of slid into dating so it all felt rather natural and, I suppose, comfortably safe from my point of view, given my understandably cautious instincts. I began to think that we were destined to meet and that maybe this really was *it*. Here was a man I already admired, who was both charming and reliable. Someone I could finally trust. He knew what he wanted out of life and was determined to get it; it's a quality to which I seem to be irresistibly drawn. He wasn't afraid of saying the *L word*, either, and I wanted to believe him – really I did. But he doesn't talk to me about our future together as a couple, it's always about work and the team hitting those targets.'

'This *no fraternisation* policy in your contract is a big deal, isn't it?' Lizzie's voice is full of concern.

'Yes, because Karl is my line manager and Creative Connect Advertising's terms of employment are clear. When he first suggested we keep our relationship a secret he said it would only be for a little while. I know, it's crazy and I should have said *no* but Karl said we worked well together and that true professionals should have no problem whatsoever in keeping their work and their private lives separate. The company are focusing on the ethics of the commercially sensitive information we often deal with. Now I'm beginning to feel increasingly uncomfortable about it. Karl dismisses my concerns with a wave of his hand but it all feels very wrong – emotionally, morally and contractually. Doesn't every woman want the man who proclaims his love to her to shout it out to the world proudly?

When you find your soul mate that should be a life changing event, shouldn't it? I've been waiting with bated breath to hear Karl say that it's time to tell HR that we're together and face the consequences. I'll probably be the one who is moved out of the department, not him. What I fear is that I mean more to him as a member of his team, than I do as a partner.'

Lizzie reaches across to pat my arm. 'You can't possibly go on like this indefinitely, Anna. You must understand that Karl doesn't know what you've been through, though, or how anxious you are. He won't have any idea about your concerns over whether this is some excuse or not, but you can't assume he has a hidden agenda. You're a sensitive soul, my friend, and yet you're so careful to hide that from the world. It's not right to hide it from Karl if you think he's the one. Not being straight with your employer is out of character so that tells me he's special to you.'

It's time to head back and when we hug goodbye I'm glad that Lizzie finally knows everything.

I drive home wondering whether a part of me didn't want to tackle the issue head on with Karl. Do I want to commit to a man who puts his career before us? If I make a fuss then maybe he will come clean but what if I only think I'm in love with him? Is it only my gutting disappointment that he's happy to continue to live a lie that keeps me from giving him an ultimatum?

A Case of Less Meaning More

'Hi, lovely lady. You look amazing in that dress.'

Karl appreciates detail. He's attentive and demonstrative; handsome and successful in a way that other people often envy. At six foot four he has presence; he's also a man who works at keeping himself in shape and well groomed. Dark, almost navy blue eyes and that jet black hair certainly have my heart skipping a beat. He's a catch and he could probably have any woman he wanted. *Enjoy it while it lasts, Anna*, I say to myself as I let him kiss my cheek. He lingers, his lips brush the tip of my ear and he whispers, 'I love you, lady'.

As usual, I smile and hug him, then pull away. I imagine the chalk board and the scraping sound as I write #1; maybe today he'll eclipse his record. Or maybe this is the day when he'll stop to explain *why* he loves me and what exactly I mean to him. And then tell me how desperate he is to hear me say those words back to him; to know that I feel the same way. Or maybe this will simply be yet another day in our cosy relationship that doesn't really move us forward at all.

'I hope this film is as good as they say it is,' he remarks casually. The awkward moment passes, seemingly without him noticing and he takes my hand in his, urging me forward in the queue.

As we take our seats he checks that my line of visibility is clear and fusses over folding my coat and placing it on the empty seat next to him.

The film is a comedy I've been looking forward to seeing, but I'm not in the mood because I can't switch off my thoughts and relax. Instead, I keep glancing at Karl's profile, watching his face in repose and instinctively smiling when he breaks out in peals of laughter.

When we first arrived, I noticed at least a dozen women in the seats behind us watching his every move. But I'm the woman on his arm, so why do I feel so insecure? He's a man of many words, but I'm not convinced about the depth of emotion some of those words carry. It's easy to say the things people want to hear, isn't it? And it's easy to hear something and read more into it than actually exists. I've been there once already and the scars take a long time to heal.

*

Karl sidles up to me. Nestling his body up against my back, he wraps his arms around my waist to give me a hug. I continue to unwrap a few cheeses and lay them out on a platter, laughing as he buries his head in my hair. We always come back to my place after a night out. He lives like a bachelor and his fridge is never stocked.

'You're very quiet tonight, Anna. Anything I should be worried about?'

I tried to join in with the spirit of the film but with my head filled with so many conflicting emotions it was hard to concentrate. I'm on the brink of challenging him about our situation and telling him how unhappy I am with the way things are. Tonight, all I could think about was how I would begin that conversation. But there's an underlying problem. Assuming that Karl immediately wants to do the right thing and make me happy, rather than risk losing me, what if I don't suddenly feel my life is complete, after all?

What if things don't fall nicely into place? It's like I have this disconnect. I want to love him; I want this to be right. However, I can't engage until he's proven beyond any doubt whatsoever that he loves me. Only then will I truly know how I feel and hopefully be able to say that back to him.

'I'm... tired. That's all.'

'Hey,' he turns me round so he can stare into my eyes. I have a cheese knife in one hand and a piece of kitchen towel in the other. 'I don't like to think of my girl overdoing it. If you need to take some time off the boss is saying *yes*.'

When he looks down at me with that look on his face it's a different Karl I see. There is a vulnerable streak there, a softness to him that never shows at work.

'I'll be fine. It's only that… sometimes I'm not sure what the future holds.'

Damn it, Anna, why do you have to soften it? Ask him outright! Or are you scared you won't get the answer you think you want?

'The future is bright, I can promise you that. We're going to be trail blazers, Anna. You're going to love being driven around in a Porsche and taken to the best restaurants. And it's not just my success we're talking about here, Anna, we're a team. Your parents are going to be very proud of their daughter's achievements.'

I stare back at him, trying hard to hide my bitter disappointment.

'I just want to be happy, Karl, and have a good work/life balance. Work is only a part of it.'

He looks at me and emits a slow sigh.

'I see this as a start and my aspirations go way beyond that. I don't want a mediocre life, I want it all – for us. One day I'm going to run my own company and prove to my father I have what it takes.'

I met Karl's parents once and that was enough. I felt uncomfortable in their company, as if I wasn't good enough for their son. Which was bad enough, but the way his father treated him was appalling. He kept asking questions and challenging every single little thing. I knew Karl was embarrassed and we hardly spoke a word on the journey back home.

'Money and material things don't necessary bring happiness, Karl.' I catch his eye, even though I can see he doesn't want to listen.

'I don't intend settling for mediocrity, Anna. It's not my style. And you deserve more. Why wouldn't I want to give you a wonderful lifestyle? I love you, babe. And don't forget that our first anniversary is nearly here and we need to do something special to mark the occasion.'

He tucks his head into my neck and kisses my ear lobe. My heart skips a beat knowing that he's remembered and that means something, doesn't it?

'Together we are unbeatable, Anna. We won't always have to be so focused on work. There will come a point when we can take time out to enjoy the fruits of our success. If you could go anywhere in the world, where would you go?'

He swings me around and I catch my breath, wondering what damage a wavering cheese knife could inflict if he doesn't stop. I look up at him, smiling. When he isn't trying to impress anyone at all and he's just being himself, I like the person I see. He's warm and caring when he isn't wearing his work hat.

'Somewhere quiet; some island where the water is crystal clear and you can see the fish just swimming around. Tall palm trees overhead and no Wi-Fi.'

He stops and looks at me. 'No internet, you are joking.'

'No, I'm not joking. All I need is a hut with a bed and a net to keep out the bugs, some sunscreen and my Kindle. Oh, and a rather handsome man at my elbow to make me cocktails.'

Karl gazes off into the distance for a moment or two.

'Done. Just give me a little time to get everything sorted and I'll whisk you away to the island of your dreams for a belated anniversary celebration. I promise. In the meantime, I have a little pre-anniversary present for you in the boot of my car. Wait here.'

I turn back to the countertop and finish loading up the platter, then get some plates and head for the dining room.

'Are your eyes closed?' He calls as he walks through the hallway.

'Yes, they're closed. I'm in the dining room.'

I hear his footsteps and a funny noise indicating hands grasping cardboard and now I'm curious.

'Put out your hands. No, not like that – as if you're going to stop someone.'

I swivel my hands back round and tip my palms upwards, like someone doing a silent mime. He shuffles forward and suddenly I feel a box; rather a big box.

'Intrigued? Do you want to guess what it is?'

I let my hands wander to either side of it, estimating it's at least three feet wide.

'I don't have a clue. Can I open my eyes now, please?'

He laughs. 'You're spoiling my fun, but yes, you can.'

The box is big and heavy, probably about six inches deep and four feet long. Karl carries it over to lean it up against the wall and then begins unpacking it. It ends up being a team effort and he holds the contents while I pull the box away from him. It's well packed, that's for sure and polystyrene beans cascade down over the floor.

And there it is – a beautiful oval Victorian mirror; not a reproduction but the real thing. The silvered, plaster frame is very ornate in style with acorns and leaves intertwined in sharp relief to the smooth background surface. The glass has a slight grey cast, mottled by typical black spots where the silver mercury backing has broken down with age. It's simply beautiful.

'I love it! And the frame is in such great condition. And look at that glass. You simply can't compare it to anything modern at all. Doesn't the vein-like mottling to the silver make a reflection look softer?'

Karl comes to stand next to me as we stare down at the mirror which is now lying on the sofa.

'If you say so; or we could both be breaking out in spots. I knew you'd love it, though, the moment I saw it. Well, it was between that and a silver statue of a stag. I was torn between the two but I could just imagine you checking your make-up in it while you were waiting for me to pick you up.'

I throw my arms around him and am touched that he picked such a thoughtful gift. I have dragged Karl out to tour antique shops several weekends in a row now. I've been looking for items that will hopefully begin to make this house feel like a home. More space seemed like a good idea, but then I was hoping it was going to be space for two.

'I have some olive ciabatta warming in the oven. Are you hungry?'

'Starving. Shall I open the wine?'

His arms are now around me and he lifts me off my feet as if I'm as light as a feather. Then he lowers me back onto the ground so that he can kiss the top of my head.

'Can I stay over tonight? I'll head off early in the morning to go back home and change.'

'Of course. I love having you here.'

If only he would move in a few items and take over one of the wardrobes, maybe the idea of living here permanently would grow on him. That would be a good sign, a sign that he's thinking about making a commitment. But instead I have to settle for having him in my bed tonight. That's no hardship as it's wonderful to fall asleep wrapped in his arms. When Karl is here, he acts like my protector. That makes me feel special and wanted. But when he's gone it's like the illusion is over and I know that something is missing from our relationship. I think about him when he isn't here but does he think about me?

Good News Travels Fast

You know that moment in life when you can almost feel your heart missing a beat, but not in a good way? I look down at my phone in utter disbelief and re-read the text for the third time.

Hey, babe. I'm on my way to Robert's office right now – this could signal some very good news! It looks like that promotion he's been talking about might actually become a reality and the offer could be on the table today! If I'm right and he calls you in, too, then just follow my lead and be very careful what you say if he asks about us – remember, they can't prove a thing. Looks like all our hard work might be about to pay off. Love you, babe x

I'm stunned. *They can't prove a thing?* Was it only ever about the promotion that Karl has had so firmly in his sights ever since we began working together? He wouldn't even have been in line for a promotion if it hadn't been for the successes the team have achieved in the last six months. We're both aware of my key role in that and how uncomfortable I've been living a lie to keep him happy. So, it seems he expects our relationship to continue on in secret and that's a major blow for me.

I can see now that the damage has already been done and he can't afford to be seen in a bad light. What a fool I've been!

The phone on my desk rings and I jump involuntarily, despite the heads-up.

'Anna? Are you free to pop down for five minutes?'

You don't refuse when you get a summons from Robert Carson.

'Of course, Robert. I'm on my way.'

I throw my mobile back into my handbag and ease myself out of the chair. Running my fingers through my sleek, dark brown bob, I straighten my skirt and slip on my jacket. Am I being unfair? Is he really the only one guilty of seeing our potential and what we could achieve together professionally? If that's the case, Anna, then why aren't you punching the air with excitement?

As I set off my stomach begins to churn. Karl has just asked me to lie about *us* again, but this time it's one denial too far. We're so good together and if he truly loves me, as he says he does, then surely he'd want to resolve our problem? Yes, I'm in shock still from his text and I'm feeling hurt, but it also means someone has been talking about our relationship. As I walk through the main, open plan admin area I can almost feel a pair of overly made up eyes watching my every step as I enter the lift and the door closes.

Serin and Karl only dated for a short while but they had nothing to hide as they didn't work directly together. It's painful knowing that their relationship was common knowledge but ours is a secret. And she's a threat that never goes away. *I know you're watching me, lady, and you'll stop at nothing to win him back.* Serin takes every opportunity she can to fawn over him and I've overhead people gossiping about whether they will eventually get back together again. And then I realise that's why keeping our relationship a secret hurts so much, because Karl is in no hurry to tell the world he's taken. Serin has obviously seen us alone together somewhere and read the signs. She'd love to step back into his life and see him push me aside.

I swallow hard before knocking on Robert's door: this is it, the moment of truth. I have no idea what exactly I'm walking into and my pulse begins to race.

'Morning, Anna. Please, take a seat. We've just been talking about you and the amazing sales figures following the very successful Port-a-Vac advertising campaign. We have one very happy client and Karl, here, has been telling me you came up with the original premise.'

I'm sitting directly across the desk from Robert and my eyes briefly flick over to Karl, who is sitting to my right. The look on his face makes my stomach churn. He's sitting there beaming from ear to ear as if he's won the lottery, after calmly texting me to be careful about what I say! Karl might be able to take all of this in his stride, but I'm worried sick and would prefer to come clean and face the consequences before we go any further.

'It's a very good product and a household essential. People already knew what it does so I simply felt that focusing on lifestyle and image was a better way to engage the customer.'

Robert nods his head, a fleeting look passing between him and Karl.

'Great stuff. Anyway, the reason I've called you here this morning is to inform you that we are restructuring the department. Karl is going to be heading up a new section to focus on our biggest accounts. We want to give our valued customers a more personal service and, in much the same way as you turned the traditional thought processes upside down, we're re-thinking customer care.'

Karl is now starting to look a little nervous. His body language is saying one thing, but I know him too well and I can see that nervous tic at the side of his mouth.

'Instead of clients coming to us when they have a new product all ready to launch, we'll be sending in an advance team for early discussions way ahead of that stage. We feel it's a win-win scenario. We're more likely to pick up the new business because we'll already have worked up some early branding ideas. And the added bonus is that the process itself might also influence the client's decision making at design stage. Karl said that as a direct result of the Port-a-Vac ad the company actually expanded their colour range.'

He's looking at me for a response and I plaster on my work smile, maintaining eye contact.

'It was an obvious progression and makes them stand out from the crowd.'

Robert laughs. 'Excellent. And that's precisely why we're offering you a promotion to step up and become Karl's second-in-command, deputy manager of the new Customer Focus team. If the trial is successful we'll be looking to expand this side of the operation very quickly. And you guys will set the bar when it comes to rolling out this initiative. To begin with it will entail you working side by side and covering virtually the whole of the country. We're going to target six key accounts to begin with, but within a year we hope to have a growing team of account executives to mirror the model you guys will be trialling. By then we see you taking on more of a mentoring and developmental role. We would like you to become trouble shooters, if you like, overseeing the set up and possibly leading to further promotion. Our company values people with drive and vision; for they are crucial to our survival in today's market place.'

Now it's my turn to feel uncomfortable as two pairs of eyes are trained directly on me. I know Karl is holding his breath. Robert, as usual, is impatient to get things moving along.

'How does that sound, Anna? HR are putting together a package for you to look at and it will be on your desk within the next hour. Obviously, it will mean a lot of time on the road travelling, but I assume that won't be a problem for you? But before you give me an answer, there's a little issue we need to address.'

He turns his head to look directly at Karl. My heart is thumping in my chest as I watch them making eye contact, Karl trying to remain cool and composed under Robert's scrutiny.

'There have been rumours circulating for a while now and I can no longer turn a blind eye. Everyone in the company is aware of how closely you guys work together and I've appreciated that, because it's been productive. The results you've produced have inspired this whole restructuring and made us re-think the way we're going to handle our business in the future. That's quite something. But if you see your working relationship developing into something more permanent, then I might need to adjust the plan a little.'

Karl's smile is so fake that it's like a mask, giving away nothing of the turmoil that's probably going on inside his head right now. I look at him, hoping that finally he will do the right thing. Robert is giving him a chance to get this out in the open and maybe find a way around it.

'Nothing could be further from the truth, Robert. Naturally, both Anna and I are used to spending a lot of time together because we are both totally committed to what we do. Speaking for myself, I think we make a good team on a professional level and I like to think that it works equally as well for Anna.'

A slight frown passes over Robert's face. 'To be clear, what you are saying is that neither of you have an issue with the *no fraternisation* policy? It's there for a very legitimate reason, to safeguard both our clients' interests and those of our colleagues. Nothing divides a team more than the conflict when personal relationships complicate matters.'

Karl's face doesn't flinch. 'Understood, and I can assure you there is nothing remotely personal going on between Anna and myself. We simply make a good team and spark off each other, which benefits both our clients and the company.'

How can he sit there and say that in front of me? How can he deny *us* without a second thought – when *'love you, babe'* trips so easily off his tongue?

He's lying to Robert but the question in my mind is *was he lying to me* all along?

I'm so angry and confused that I don't know what to do. I've lived in dread of something like this happening and now all my worst fears have been confirmed. If I make an admission now then I'm destroying two people's careers. If Robert directs the question at me next, I'm sunk. I don't know if I can hold back the angry words forming in my head and it will be a brutal outpouring. I'll leave him in no doubt whatsoever about what's really been going on. I take a deep breath, not at all sure what I'm going to say until the words are suddenly there.

'Actually, Robert, I'm making some major changes in my life at the moment and it was my intention to hand in my resignation this morning. I'm sorry that the timing of this isn't the best, but I'm sure you'll easily find another candidate who can assist Karl in this exciting new challenge. Someone who isn't sleeping with him but then that doesn't really appear to mean anything, anyway.'

The silence hangs uncomfortably between the three of us. It's not only Karl's jaw that has dropped as they both stare back at me in total disbelief. I can only hope my own face isn't giving anything away, because I'm equally as horrified as they are by the words that have just slipped out of my mouth with no prior thought whatsoever.

Karl begins speaking, his eyes flicking frantically between Robert and myself.

'Anna, I was only trying to protect you... Robert, this was a situation we were going to resolve, I can give you my utmost assurance of that.'

Resolve? How? I've not even left the room and he's already focused on damage limitation, first and foremost. When I turn and walk towards the door I push back my shoulders and straighten my spine. One thing no one can accuse me of is being a coward when it comes to drawing a line. And the line has now been drawn.

One Moment of Glory and Then Reality Dawns

The sense of elation is momentary; a transient feeling of power and being in control. A natural reaction, I tell myself, considering the way Karl has treated me. But even before I get back to my desk I'm tearful and panicky. I have one month to sort out my life and find myself another job. Was making that impulsive decision to resign worth it?

Yes.

My email to HR is brief and I don't offer any form of explanation. Less than twenty minutes later their acknowledgement informs me that I am being granted thirty days paid *gardening leave* to commence with immediate effect. After which, my employment with the company will cease. The HR manager reminds me of the commercial-in-confidence clause within my contract and informs me I have until the end of the day to clear my desk. It's like a slap in the face. So my hard work counts for nothing, nothing at all.

Well, at least that means I don't have to face the humiliation of coming back into the office while I'm serving my notice. Rumours won't begin circulating until tomorrow, if I'm lucky. I don't want to be around when people start asking what happened and why.

As I'm re-reading HR's email for the third time, still reeling a little, a notification alert pops up and there's an email from Karl.

Hey, babe. Well, that was unexpected. I'm not even sure I understand what happened. I didn't mean anything I said, I assumed you'd know that – it was just a way of getting around the situation. Fortunately, Robert was fine about it all after you left and said he thought it was for the best. But I was shocked and I will miss having you by my side. Still, you took one for the team and I owe you. It's full steam ahead and Robert said it was good to clear the air. When everything is up and running I'm sure I can talk Robert into welcoming you back. We can say that your plans for the future didn't quite work out as you'd hoped and that we've started seeing each other again.

Fist pumping the air! We did it and I'll soon have you back at my side – what do you say? I must go – Robert has called me into a meeting so I'll catch up with you as soon as I can. We'll sort this, don't worry. Love you, babe, you're the best!

Am I missing something here? It takes two to have an affair and yet Robert is prepared to overlook Karl's part in this deception. That's unbelievable, given that first of all he was my boss and secondly, he stood there and blatantly lied to his face. I stand up and tell the truth and I'm treated as if I was the only one breaking the rules. Talk about double standards!

Why had I let Karl talk me into doing something I knew from the start was wrong and which pushed aside my principles as if they meant nothing? Am I so desperate to be loved that I'm willing to pay any price at all? And now I have nothing. No relationship and no job. Karl, on the other hand, has a nice promotion and still thinks he can waltz back into my life when it's convenient. You've just shown your true colours, Karl, and now I know the reason I was feeling so hesitant. It wasn't my past insecurities but my instincts screaming at me that I was in danger of making a big mistake. Why, oh, why, didn't I listen?

*

I leave the office less than an hour later without attracting any undue attention. I'm often out and about so it's not unusual and the few personal things I keep in the office barely fill a small carrier bag. I feel like I'm slinking away, though, and I keep telling myself that maybe I played into Robert's hands. Karl is the one he wanted and I'm collateral damage.

For some inexplicable reason, when I arrive home I throw myself into cleaning the house from top to bottom. I suppose it helps to have something to do while I try to take it all in. I keep going over and over some of the things that have happened in the past and suddenly I'm seeing it from a slightly different perspective. Two hours pass and I'm just finishing off in the bathroom when the doorbell rings. As I open it, I realise I'm still wearing my bright pink rubber gloves.

'Babe, you didn't respond to my text. We were lucky Robert took it so well but that was a big risk you took there. Here, why are you cleaning? Let's take those off.'

Karl steps inside and immediately begins to slip the gloves from my hands, throwing them onto the console table in the hallway.

'We need to talk through what happens next,' he adds, apparently totally unfazed by today's events.

'Next?'

He turns and walks into the sitting room and I follow him, trying to keep up with what he's saying.

'… the meeting went well and things need to be put in place rather quickly now. I'm not going to be around much at the start and the panic is on to replace you. But you're a tough act to follow and it isn't going to be easy. I wish we'd had more notice as that was a bit drastic, Anna. You didn't have to resign; we could have found a way around it if you'd stuck to the plan.'

'More lies, you mean? Well, I'm done with that, Karl.'

'Done with what?'

'With *us*. It's over. The fact that you could so easily dismiss what we have when you had no idea how I'd react to that. Didn't you think I'd be at least a little hurt by what you said and maybe see that as something to be concerned about?'

The look of surprise on his face is quickly turning into one of anger. ·

'It's business, what's your problem? We did what we had to do for me to get that promotion. I was doing it for both of us and we each had to make a sacrifice. We only have to wait a short while and then I tell everyone how much I miss you, so much so that I ask you to marry me.'

From where I'm standing Karl made his *sacrifice* seem worryingly easy; too easy. And now, it seems, his plans extend way beyond a mere promotion. Isn't that something he should have mentioned before now?

'Everything that has happened goes against the grain for me. I can't go on like this, Karl. We both want different things out of life and I think that's become increasingly obvious as time has gone on. I wish you luck and great success but I can't be a part of your future plans.'

He stands there looking at me as if I'm mad.

'You are joking, Anna, aren't you? Where has all this sudden disapproval come from? I thought we were clear from day one about where we were heading.'

I turn on my heel and head towards the hallway. A few seconds pass and I'm already standing with the front door open when he eventually walks up to me.

'You're heading out of my life, Karl, and I'm going to have a long think about what I'm going to do next. This chapter in my life is now firmly closed.'

*

It's a full week before I pluck up the courage to ring Mum. The glow from the satisfaction of handing in my resignation lasted what, three minutes at most? After that it was like being on a rollercoaster heading towards the ground at a terrifying speed. I've never hit rock bottom as fast as I did later that night. Sitting at home, alone and wondering what the hell I was going to do next was the most depressing moment of my entire life. And I thought I'd already experienced that several years' ago.

'Anna, how are you, dear?'

Just the sound of Mum's voice is like the hug I so badly need right now. Warm and comforting.

'I'm good. How is life in Saint-Julien-de-Vouvantes?'

Mum and Dad moved to France ten months ago. It's something they intended to do when they retired, but when Dad was made redundant it seemed logical to bring their plans forward. Neither Mum nor Dad were happy at the thought of us being parted when the day finally came to wave them off. However, I encouraged them to go for it because the time was right. After all, I'm an independent woman and they should be able to stop worrying about me and put themselves first for a change.

Admittedly, set in the Loire-Atlantique department in western France, Saint-Julien-de-Vouvantes is about six hundred miles away from my home in the market town of Dursley, in Gloucestershire. But my life seemed to be finally settling down and we said our goodbyes the day they sold their house nearby, safe in the knowledge that I wasn't alone. After all, I had Karl by my side. Well, almost, because he lived in Stroud, about a fifteen minute drive away from the office. That was another reason why my move to a bigger house on the same new build development in Dursley was crazy. I was so sure he'd step in at some point before I could sign on the dotted line. But the disappointments just kept on coming right up to the end.

I tune back in, trying not to sigh at Mum's blissful state of total ignorance.

'– and we're already fully booked for the entire summer season. It's marvellous, isn't it?'

This is great news, but it takes a lot of effort to make myself smile enough to lift my voice.

'That's wonderful, Mum. Is the house totally finished now?'

'Oh, yes. Dad's done well and it's been a blessing, as you know, having English builders virtually on our doorstep. The Callaghans have become great friends. Neil and Sarah have been so supportive and their son, Sam, is still working here. He recently began renovating the first of those two dilapidated stone buildings in the orchard that we're planning on turning into gîtes. It's all so exciting seeing our dream coming alive.'

'Things really are moving along nicely and I'm thrilled for you both.'

'Ah, thanks lovey. Neil obtained the *permis de construire* for us and we had the mayor, Bastien Deniaud, to dinner to talk about our plans for the gîtes. Many of our bookings came from Bastien's referrals and we're turning people down for the peak weeks on a daily basis. How we're going to cope with all the rooms full, I have no idea, but Sarah has offered to help out.'

It's lovely to hear her sounding so happy. When they bought Le Manoir d'Orsenne it was in a relatively good condition, just needing general redecoration and a new kitchen. But there was a lot of work to do to turn it into a bed and breakfast business. The biggest problem was the plumbing, which was never designed to accommodate multiple en-suite facilities. On my very first visit I was shocked to hear my father, one of the most patient men I know, swearing under his breath as he struggled with a labyrinth of old pipework. The solution was to install a new system alongside the old one, rather than to try to utilise what was there and overload a system that worked well within limits.

'When I was there last your guests looked very happy, despite the fact that Dad and Neil were still working on the outside of the property. It must look so lovely now.' I can't hide the wistful note in my voice.

There are a few seconds of silence before Mum jumps in.

'What's happened, Anna? I can tell something is wrong.'

I clear my throat, uneasily. Crunch time.

'I handed in my notice and I'm looking for another job.'

The sharp intake of breath is as clear as if Mum is standing in front of me.

'Oh, Anna. Is this about Karl?'

I nod, then realise she isn't here in the flesh.

'Yes. I was offered a promotion but things became complicated. Karl wants us to focus on our careers—'

My words dry up as a feeling of hurt, combined with a sense of abject failure, threatens to overwhelm me. I mustn't start crying as that wouldn't be fair on Mum.

'My poor, darling, girl. Maybe it's for the best… oh dear. I'm sorry, I shouldn't have said that. It's only that I want to see you happy, lovely girl, because it's what you deserve.'

I can hear the concern in her voice.

'What will you do?'

I try my best to sound upbeat. 'I'm in the process of applying for a job with another agency and it would be a step up – sort of on a par with the promotion I was offered.'

Mum isn't fooled.

'Your heart's not in it, Anna, I can hear it in your voice.'

The seconds roll by as I try to pull myself together and lighten my mood, as Mum continues.

'Anna, I know you, my love, and whatever has happened between you and Karl has hit you hard. I'm not trying to interfere, but if it really is over then you're going to need some time to pick yourself back up. You deserve better and you must never forget that, Anna. Why don't you come and spend a little time here? It's such a wonderful time of the year and it's very warm.'

'Oh, Mum, if only life was that simple. I've not long moved into the new house and I simply can't afford not to work. I guess it was a bit cavalier of me, handing in my notice when I've so recently taken on an even bigger mortgage. Bricks and mortar might be a good investment but they're also a heavy burden.'

I can hear Mum whispering, no doubt her hand is only partially covering the mouthpiece of the phone and she doesn't realise I can hear them talking. Dad has probably been listening in, concerned by her responses. There's a rustling sound, then Dad's voice comes on the line.

'Hi, Anna. Listen, honey, we have plenty of work over here, whether it's helping in the house or getting your hands dirty on the renovations. We'd really appreciate some help as it's hard to find casual workers. You could earn some money, and it would be a blessing to have you here as the pressure is on.'

Aww, my heart feels heavy when I hear the love and concern reflected in his voice. He's trying to convince me that they need me, rather than it being the other way around.

'It's not that simple, Dad. I wish it were.'

'Then make it simple. Rent the house out for six months. Lizzie is in the lettings business and she'll sort it out for you. Come out and earn a little money

44

while enjoying a break away from it all. Anything is possible if you put your mind to it, Anna. I'm only cross I didn't warn you about that Karl Radford.'

'Geoff!'

Mum's voice sounds scandalised and I can visualise them jostling over the phone.

'Don't listen to your dad, Anna. If things aren't really over between the two of you and this is just a temporary... blip, then we want you to know we are here for you no matter what happens.'

It all goes silent as, no doubt, Mum gives Dad one of her infamous stares to put him in his place.

'It's truly over, Mum. When I made it clear that we were personally involved, Karl told Robert Carson he'd lied in order to protect ME. What sort of man does that? And to add insult to injury, after I left Robert told him my leaving was *for the best*. Karl's promotion is still on the table as if everything was my fault!'

'Oh.'

The line goes ominously quiet and I wonder if Mum is wondering how I could be foolish enough to let it happen to me for a second time. Am I one of those people who are always destined to keep making the same mistakes over, and over, again? I thought I was protecting myself this time around. But if that's true then why does it still hurt so much?

Her voice breaks the silence. 'Selfish people only ever consider their own agenda.'

I've never heard my mum say a mean word about anyone before and her words take my breath away. Loving someone means that when *they* hurt, *you* hurt. I realise that my gut instincts have been desperately trying to attract my attention since day one with Karl. The only person I can blame for ignoring their rumblings is myself. Time to stop dreaming your way through life, Anna, and get real.

'I'll ring Lizzie and see if she can find me a tenant. Maybe a working holiday is precisely what I need. Tell Dad that if he has any walls that need knocking down to wait until I get there and have the sledgehammer ready. I have a lot of anger to let out and smacking a stone wall is going to be therapeutic.'

'That's my girl. Life is all about how quickly you can bounce back, not how many times you get knocked down.'

*

'You're *what*?'

'I'm going to rent out the house and go to France. Mum and Dad need some help and you know how I like to get my hands dirty. There's nothing more relaxing than wielding a paint brush.' I'm trying my best to put a positive spin on this, even though it

46

feels like total defeat. I never, ever dreamt that I'd end up living back under the same roof as my parents with no clear plan for my future.

'This sounds like running away to me.' Lizzie's words come out in a half whisper and I don't think she really meant to say what she was thinking out loud. She knows me too well and her thoughts mirror my own.

'I'm going to be fine, I promise. Maybe I need to concentrate on having some fun and forget about that elusive Mr Right. Besides, the new house is a constant reminder of how silly I've been. I'm keeping my fingers crossed the rental income will cover the mortgage. I need to break even to make this work. Can you do your thing and find me the perfect tenant?'

I'm half tempted to make a joke of it and add that if she can find me the perfect man, too, it might save me from getting myself into a mess again. But something has changed in me over the last couple of days and I feel as if a huge burden has been lifted from my shoulders. Okay, so everyone I know is either in a long term relationship, engaged, or married. I need to face the fact that it just isn't happening for me and I'm twenty-six-years old, single and free as a bird. I'd become a woman obsessed with this... need. I was way too young when I thought I'd found my soulmate. I can now see that I became fixated on this rosy picture of the way I saw my life unfolding in front of me. Karl has been the wake-up call I needed. It's a big, wide world out there and this is the time in my life when my commitments are few. I'm going to count my blessings and embrace the luxury of pleasing no one but myself!

'It won't be a problem. The house was a good investment and the rental market is brisk. This is just so unlike you, though, Anna. I thought you loved your job and to walk away from it because—'

'Karl has done me a favour, Lizzie, and this is the right thing to do. In six months' time, I'll review my situation and I'll probably be heading back to the UK for a fresh start. But for now, the thought of spending time helping my parents is rather appealing.'

She gives a light-hearted laugh, mirroring my attempt to be up-beat.

'Well, I can't say I'm not the teensiest bit envious at the thought of your little adventure. A beautiful little village in France is going to be the perfect place to re-boot your life. And I'll find you a great tenant for the house, don't you worry.'

'You're a good friend, Lizzie. I'm going to miss you.' It's true, because she's always been there for me.

'Oh, you'll be having way too much fun to think about me and rainy old England. But I expect to be kept up to date with all your news. You know what a Francophile I am and I only wish *my* parents would suddenly announce they're selling up and heading in that direction. Devon is wonderful, but France is the dream!'

'You and Daniel will have to come and visit. Mum says the house is fully booked for the summer but work has begun on the first of the two stone gîtes. I'm going to help out with that as it represents an important part of their future income. Every extra euro they can earn will help to secure their long term financial position. I'll make sure you are the first to know as soon as it's ready.'

She sighs.

'Oh, that would be wonderful. We haven't booked a holiday yet, so I'll tell Daniel we're on standby.'

'Sounds like a plan to me!'

I have almost three weeks to pack up the contents of my house and put them into storage. More importantly, it will be uninterrupted thinking time now that I don't have to keep going online to check out job vacancies. It's time to re-think my life and figure out what I really want to achieve in the future. Sometimes things really do happen for a reason, even if at the outset it doesn't appear that way. I wasn't truly happy; I just didn't know why.

June

New Day, New Me

I decide to stay overnight in Folkestone so that I can catch the 6.15 a.m. shuttle train through the Eurotunnel. However, now I'm here alone and the reality of what I've done is hitting me, panic has set in.

For all my bravado about coping with the huge changes in my life and the work involved in getting the house ready to let out, my heart weighs heavily in my chest. Who am I trying to kid? If I couldn't run away to France and have a reprieve from this latest round of humiliation, it would probably push me over the edge. But what does that say about me?

Even though it's nearly eleven at night I phone Lizzie.

'Hello?' There's a yawn. 'Is that you, Anna?'

'Yes. Sorry, I hoped you'd be awake.'

'Hey, don't worry. I'm here for you and that's what friends are for. I was half expecting a call.'

She sounds more alert now and I'm grateful she understands.

'Talking is good,' she says, softly.

I breathe out and the sound is dejected, reflecting how demoralised I feel.

'You were right and I am running away because I don't know what else to do. My confidence is well and truly dented. I've run out of energy, well, not *energy* as such but motivation, I suppose. I can't believe I walked away from a job with such great prospects because of Karl. Why do I let guys trample over my life like that? Twice now I've been used in a very unfair way and I let it happen. I'm lucky to be able to run away to France but at my age it makes me feel that I'm a total failure.' I'm angry with myself and tearful. The next part of my life's journey will only serve to remind me how gullible I've been playing into Karl and Robert's hands.

'Listen, my lovely friend. You just happened to stumble across two very manipulative guys. Not all men are like that – look at my Daniel, for instance. I honestly think it's been a part of your fate and who can second guess what that throws our way? Maybe your destiny is to get all the bad stuff out of the way early on in your life. This could be a turning point, one you'll look back on gratefully because it took you where you were always meant to go.'

I know Lizzie means what she says but she's also trying to comfort me because she knows I've reached rock bottom. I wonder what a total stranger would say to me right now. That I'm a quitter? That I make lousy decisions and poor life choices?

Lizzie begins talking again, still softly as if she's fearful of saying the wrong thing and feels she needs to tread carefully.

'If you were a hard nosed career woman instead of someone who is trusting, even if a little naïve at times, we wouldn't be friends. And you wouldn't be YOU, the Anna we all love. Don't let this knock you back and destroy your self-confidence, or alter the way you look at life. If this hardens you then that's worse than any heartache this has caused. I know that it's easy to say, but don't waste time looking back. Hindsight is a wonderful thing but it won't change the past, so let it change the future. This time for good.'

I pause to collect my thoughts before I can reply. 'But starting again from scratch, Lizzie, it's demoralising. Running off to my parents is the safe option and a coward's way out. I feel like I'm going home to hide away from the world and what if when I return I can't get a proper job? I'll end up losing the house and the equity I have in it won't last long. This could literally wipe out everything I've worked for and my dreams for the future are already in tatters. I'm assuming that after a break away I will be able to come back with a fighting spirit again. What if that isn't the case?'

I hear a sigh and guilt begins to eat away at me. This isn't a conversation I should be having with

Lizzie at this time of night and on the eve of my departure. I don't want to unduly worry her any more than I already have.

'I know you, Anna. Nothing can keep you down for very long because you do have a fighting spirit. No one knows what life has planned for them and all you can do is make each decision based on the circumstances at the time. I'm being very honest with you here. If you stay and launch yourself into another job I don't think you're in the right frame of mind to do it justice. It's time to be kind to yourself, Anna, and look at this time with your parents as a bonus. You can regain your strength, prepare to shake the world again, while helping them out in their new venture. It's not as if you're going to be lying around in bed being waited on like an invalid. I know your parents and they're workaholics, too.'

Finally, that raises a smile.

'Thank you, Lizzie. That helps more than you can know. This is such a huge decision for me and it's scary because I can't think ahead at the moment. I don't know what I want out of life any more, to be honest with you.'

'Don't fret about that now, just focus on tomorrow and the next stage of your journey. Maybe fate will throw some gorgeous French guy in your path and you'll end up living in a sprawling old stone cottage with five kids. At least your parents would be on the doorstep and handy for babysitting duties!'

We both start laughing. 'Now there's a thought that hadn't occurred to me. However, I think I'll start buying a Lotto ticket each week as the odds will probably be about the same.'

'Travel safely my dear friend.'

'Goodnight, Lizzie, and thank you for being there through my ups and downs. You are a life saver.'

*

It's an early start, but with a seven hour drive from Calais it will probably take me about nine or ten hours in total, with comfort breaks. The journey is one I know well from my childhood holidays. It's a drive I've probably done at least half a dozen times sitting behind the wheel, but it's only the second time I've made the trip alone. The first being a few months after Mum and Dad's big move. Karl said he was too busy to come with me, but in hindsight I think he knew my parents had reservations about him. But it's an easy drive and aside from the busy bit when leaving the terminal, where you need to keep your wits about you to make sure you don't miss the turn offs, it's reasonably straightforward.

Fuelled by excitement for my road trip after the disappointment of the last few weeks, I have new energy. Where there was an emptiness there is now hope. For what, exactly, I don't know. Maybe an end to the nagging little worries I can never succeed in pushing out of my head. Acceptance is a big part of moving on and it allows me to enjoy the journey ahead with an uplifting sense of freedom.

I love the route via the shuttle through the Channel tunnel; it's surreal and the thirty-five minute ride passes so quickly. When it's time to drive the car down the ramp to leave the train, I slide in a CD, thinking that John Newman is going to be the perfect companion for the next leg of my journey. As the opening bars of 'Love Me Again' strike up, I realise I'm an incurable romantic at heart. It's about a guy asking his ex for a second chance after cheating on her, when he realises he's made a huge mistake. The words are hauntingly beautiful. The passion in his voice is so incredible it rings true and that's what touches me every single time I play it.

As usual, the first few kilometres are pure concentration. I don't use the satnav because it spoils the ambience and I know the route pretty well by now, anyway. Once I'm onto the toll roads I can cruise along at speed, crank up the volume and sing my heart out while enjoying the scenery. I'm on French soil now and so the adventure begins.

I stop for breaks at my favourite places – Abbeville, Rouen, Le Mans and Angers. It divides the journey up rather nicely and allows me to stretch my legs and have a drink and a snack. In between stops the route is scenic for the most part, although there are parts of the journey with roundabout after roundabout, where you need to follow the signs carefully or risk going wildly off course. But the French countryside is wonderful and never more so than at the beginning of June.

Flicking the switch to lower the window a little, I let the gentle breeze caress my hair as I savour the sweetly scented air. I'm driving past fields of wheat, some strewn with red poppies; the sun is still quite low in the sky and its rays catch what's left of the early morning dew on the tender young plants, glinting as they wave gently in the breeze. In front of me the almost straight road stretches out endlessly, the tarmac shimmering slightly as if the sun has turned it into liquid. Putting on my sunglasses I feel in holiday mode and already my body is beginning to feel less tense, my anxieties melting away like wax in the warm sun. A few cars pass me going the opposite way, heading back towards the coast, but it's mainly quiet with long stretches when I'm literally the only one on the road.

I'm reminded that France in the summer is a delight as I drive past colourful fields and orchards, interspersed with villages. Some are no more than a tiny cluster of buildings hugging an intersection or a roundabout. As I slow the car, the detail on some of these old well worn but well loved properties is often both a surprise and a delight: intricate stonework fit to grace the grandest manor house and yet a stonemason laboured over embellishing a modest home. Their love of the trade is shown in the detail and it reflects a real sense of pride in their work. Oh, how the world has changed and at this moment I can't help thinking that it isn't necessarily for the better.

Saying goodbye to my new house was easier than I thought. I realise that the reason why so many of my things still remained in cardboard boxes was because it had never felt like home. But Lizzie was right and it was a good investment. Not only will the rental income cover the outgoings, it's going to make me a small profit on top. Together with my savings that means that while I may be unemployed, I'm not penniless. Suddenly all my doubts evaporate. I'm going to have to be careful about what I spend, but hey, there's only me to consider and for the first time in ages I'm feeling lucky. Lucky to be looking forward to a new adventure and lucky to be alive on such a glorious day. I can't remember the last time I felt this positive and so optimistic about the future – and this time I'm not going to let anyone spoil it for me.

A Working Holiday

The moment I turn into the drive and catch the first glimpse of Le Manoir d'Orsenne, a little thrill courses through me, making my senses tingle. My working holiday is about to begin and once again my parents have been instrumental in helping me at a time in my life when I needed a little redirection. I shake off the thought that at twenty-six years of age I shouldn't still be making monumental mistakes that knock me off course. But that was in the past and now it's time to ditch those old, bad habits and move forward as the person I want to be. In future, I'm going to listen to what my gut instincts are telling me and when something doesn't feel right, I'm going to act accordingly.

The moment my parents hear the scrunch of tyres on the gravel the front door is flung open and even before I have a chance to turn off the engine, Dad has the driver's door open. He leans in and virtually scoops me out of my seat.

'Safe and sound. And what a sight for these tired old eyes.'

His hug lasts only as long as he can continue to keep Mum at arm's length, because she wants to step in.

'My dear girl. Such a long drive.' Mum's hug is something else. She exudes this energy and when her arms are wrapped around me I feel a sense of healing. Our eyes meet and in that split second she understands there's nothing to worry about. 'Come inside, the kettle is on.'

As we approach the front door I stop and gaze up at the façade of this beautiful building.

'I'd forgotten how imposing it is, Mum. It really is a mini-château.'

The grey stonework of this three storey building is softened by the oversized front door and matching window shutters painted in a very soft blue. With two large dormer windows in the roof conversion giving unobstructed views out over the open countryside, the overall impression is one of elegance and symmetry.

On the ground floor, large French windows lead into two of the reception rooms. Above that, at first floor level, there are a total of four shuttered windows, beyond which are the front-facing guest bedrooms.

What was once an overgrown mass of indistinguishable foliage in front of the property has now been lovingly pruned and is sporting the new season's growth. Gone is the ugly woodiness of that first drastic cutting back. The deep reddish purple leaves of a glorious climbing rose contrast nicely with the young green shoots on the old wisteria, which will hopefully produce those abundant, pendulous lilac blooms next year. Standing proud against the trellis work at the side of the front door is a sprightly winter jasmine, no longer in flower but sending out a myriad of shoots that will bear next year's blossoms.

'I can hardly believe you've been able to rescue so much of what was here. I was convinced you'd end up having to replant but this looks manicured already.'

Dad is busy ferrying my luggage from the car into the house, but stops to call over his shoulder. 'Nothing that a bit of tender loving care and nature couldn't sort out.'

Mum smiles at me. 'This house wanted to be loved and now it's rewarding us for all our hard work. Wait until you see the inside.'

As we're about to step over the threshold a van pulls up alongside my car and two men get out. They head off in the direction of the rear garden. One calls out and the other raises his hand in acknowledgement.

'We're back. Problem solved.'

Mum waves in return, smiling.

'I'll take you out to see Neil and Sam in a bit. I don't think you've actually met Sam, as he was working on another job when you came to visit. Are you hungry?'

'No. I stopped several times on the way down. I would love a cup of coffee, though.'

We cross paths with Dad in the hallway. 'You show Anna around, Viv, and I'll sort things in the kitchen.'

My eyes are taking in every little detail now that the house is dressed and the first handful of guests have come through the doors. My first visit here was when most of the interior work had been done and the new en-suite bathrooms were being fitted out. But at that point there was little by way of furnishings. The plumbing saga was a protracted one, and ran on long after my visit, according to Mum's updates.

'I love this light fitting.' Mum and I gaze up at the intricate metalwork of the large lantern gracing the hallway.

'We've spent quite a bit of time travelling to flea markets and *vide grenier* sales, the French equivalent of a car boot sale, for miles around. There's enough to make it feel furnished, but it's still very much a work in progress. The problem we have is that now we have paying guests it's not quite so easy to take a day off to go in search of new treasures. We're still only offering breakfast and not an evening meal but it doesn't seem to have put anyone off. They're all out for the day and probably won't return until this evening. Naturally, a lot of guests will head to the coast for a day at the beach. La Baule is a very popular resort with eight kilometres of sandy beach. We prefer Pornic, which is a delightful little fishing village and is about the same distance away. You probably remember it from your childhood, Anna. Or they head inland to explore some of the surrounding towns. Angers, Nantes, Rennes and Chateaubriant of course, and the markets at Cande and Pouance are nearby, as you know.'

Suddenly, I hear a loud *meow* that sounds uncannily like 'now', as a little cinnamon and brown ball of fur comes running in our direction and literally launches herself into my arms. I'm almost bowled over by the force with which we collide and hold onto her tightly while I regain my balance.

'You missed me then?' I whisper into her fur.

Now Bengals are known for being very vocal indeed, but Ziggy's response is a long one that seems to go on and on. I imagine it's along the lines of 'Where have you been? No one does a tummy tickle quite like you and it's unfair to make me wait so long.' Or maybe she's just complaining that she's hungry and telling me off for not heading straight into the kitchen.

I've missed her so much, but Karl is allergic to cats and it was yet another moment in my life when Mum and Dad saved the day and took Ziggy to France with them. It was a huge wrench, as she's my little star, but at two years old I figured she was young enough to cope with the upheaval. And I was right, because according to Mum she spends most of her time exploring the neighbouring fields and is a diligent mouser: frequently leaving presents outside the back door.

How ironic that Karl is now firmly in my past and yet it would be unfair of me to expect my darling girl to be uprooted again. At the time, he couldn't understand how upset I was to be parted from her.

'She's just a cat. Animals re-adjust very quickly. She'll soon forget you and learn to love whichever hand feeds her.' His comment had stung. I remember thinking that this was a man who wasn't brought up with animals. They never forget someone who has shown them love – ever. Suddenly I feel a sense of peace washing over me – I'm *home* and yet this has never been my home, as such.

As we mount the stairs I love the creaks as the well trodden wood beneath our feet gives a little at every step. There's a sense of comfort and homeliness, despite the small scale grandeur of this house. I notice that Ziggy follows us for a while, then disappears having found a suitably cool place to hide away.

We can only tour four of the eight guest bedrooms, as the others are currently occupied. The rooms are light and airy, the bedding crisp and white.

The original dark oak floors are well preserved for their age; wide boards that you just don't see any more and every dent and ding is a little testament to the long history of this house. Together with the matching architrave set against white walls, it's a perfect backdrop for some beautiful old pieces of furniture.

'Most of the beds were very dark wood, so Dad and I bought a paint sprayer. It didn't take much work to do a quick sand, spray on a few coats and then get the distressed look.'

Shabby chic looks so good in this setting and I can tell that Mum is enjoying every aspect of her new life here.

'And how do you feel now that you have a steady flow of paying guests?'

I search her face, wondering whether now that the dream has become a reality it's as good as they'd both hoped. Her eyes crinkle up in a warm smile, the soft brown glow from her lightly tanned skin making her look younger than her fifty-one years.

'I feel that every single moment has been worth it. The times when our muscles ached so much we groaned as we climbed into bed, this was why we kept going. And we now have a proper bed, not just a mattress on the floor. In fact, we have ten proper beds!' She grins back at me and I reach out to pat her arm, thrilled that it's everything they'd hoped it would be.

As Mum swings open the door to the first of the attic bedrooms, I step inside and feel that I'm in an advert I saw on TV many years ago. Long white voiles at the window waft gently in the breeze, casting intermittent shadows and dappled sunlight onto the stripped oak floorboards.

The wall behind the bed is covered in silver grey and white wallpaper depicting trees and birds with a subtle hint of blue. The same blue that is picked up in the scatter cushions, the fabric on the chaise longue and the chair in front of the dressing table.

'Mum, this is simply beautiful.'

'A beautiful room for a beautiful daughter.'

As if on cue, Dad enters with two of my suitcases.

'Do you like it?' His eyes are filled with pride and happiness.

'I love it! You guys are amazing. I'm so proud of you both and what you've achieved. Dare I look at the en-suite?'

'Please do.' Dad swings open the door and my hands instinctively fly up to my face.

'A slipper bath! It must be antique – I love the lion heads on the claw feet.'

'A special find. Only a few of the baths are reconditioned originals, as we ran out of time to source them. Still we've had a lot of fun, haven't we, Viv?'

Dad sidles up to Mum and slips his arm around her waist.

'We did. And off season we'll be visiting all of our favourite little places again in the hope of finding a few more bargains.'

'Anyway, coffee is waiting, ladies. Then I'll take Anna out to inspect the gîtes and look at the pool now it's back in working order. It's so good to have you here, Anna. The three musketeers are reunited!'

Dad's reference harks back to my childhood. Whenever I had a problem we'd put our heads together and just like the three musketeers I'd watch on TV, we always came up with a solution.

'It feels like coming home, how silly is that?'

Mum and Dad look at each other, smiling, and I know that when it's time for me to head back to the UK the parting will be difficult. But there are a lot of memories to be made in the meantime and this is one summer I know we're all going to remember forever.

Getting Down and Dirty

By the time I've had a tour of the garden Neil and his son have already finished for the day. Mum informs us that dinner will be ready in an hour and leaves Dad and me admiring the pool. With a brand new cover and the fencing around it replaced, an eyesore has been turned into an asset.

'You've done a great job getting it back up and running, Dad. Is it all compliant, now? And how are the solar panels working out? Was it worth the investment?'

I knew Mum had her doubts about it as there were so many demands on their budget but a pool is quite an asset and it was in good condition. It just hadn't been in operation for a few years. The soft blue tiles give the water a lovely colour and it does look inviting. It would have been a headache to fill it in if they'd decided to give up on it.

'Yes. A friend of Neil's came over and talked me through the current safety regulations. I think it will be worth the investment we've put in to it and I like to think your mother feels the same way, too. Obviously, it will take a couple of years for us to recoup the initial outlay. If it continues to run without a hitch then maybe we'll look at the feasibility of installing more solar panels to supply the electricity for the house as well.'

'It's been a real journey for you both and a steep learning curve, that's for sure!'

I'm rewarded with a tender smile and we turn to make our way back up to the house. I am beginning to wilt a little, but the excitement of being here rules out any thoughts of a pre-dinner nap. Instead I run a relaxing bubble bath. As I slip into the heavenly scented water, hints of geranium, lavender and rose fill the air around me.

I stare up at the vaulted ceiling, which is probably only about nine feet above me as I'm literally in the eaves of the house. The old beams are original and they take their shape from the tree, rather than the modern equivalents which are uniformly cut. I'm lying here thinking that everything feels distinctly surreal. I think about the office and going home after a hard day's work. Instead I'm here, as if by some sort of magic. All it took was one single decision to change everything and make this break happen. Is life really this simple? It feels as if I've stepped off the treadmill and I wonder if there's a lesson to be learned here. If every day becomes an uphill climb then you are doing something wrong and it's time for a change.

Lazily drifting off, the bath water is still warm when I reopen my eyes, but it's enough to take the edge off my tiredness. When I reappear in the kitchen Dad is busy laying the old pine table.

'We usually only have our breakfast in here on rainy days, but it's been a long day for you, so Viv thought a simple dinner would be more relaxing. We'll make up for it on Saturday night.'

I'd forgotten what it was like to have family fussing over me and I lower myself rather gratefully into one of the old, shabby chic chairs. As hard as I'm trying to fight the tiredness, it's now coming over me in waves after that warm bath. When my phone buzzes I'm almost tempted not to dive into my bag to retrieve it, but I'm conscious it might be Lizzie with a question from the tenant who moved in yesterday.

I'm sorry – things have been hectic. I was heartless. I can see that now. I called round to your house but a stranger told me you'd gone away. Where are you? Please get in touch. I miss you. x

My heart slows to a dull thud in my chest for a moment, before returning to its normal beat. As I look up, Mum is gazing down at me.

'Problems?'

'No. Everything is just fine.' I switch off my phone without a moment's hesitation. Too little, too late.

'Morning, Geoff.'

The guy repointing the back wall of the gîte stops work to rub his hand on his trousers, cleaning it off so he can extend it towards Dad. They shake hands warmly.

'Sam, this is my daughter, Anna. She's here until the end of the summer and she's going to be helping out.'

He nods and I note the firm, albeit dust covered, hand shake. His eyes flick over me, as if he's weighing up how useful I'm going to be.

'Nice to meet you, Sam. You're doing a great job there.'

'Thanks. Repointing is painstaking, but it's going to add a lot of charm to the inside of this rustic little building.'

I stand back in the centre of the open space, sizing it up. What was once a home for a few sheep is going to make a perfect little holiday cottage. There's nothing inside yet apart from coils of wire here and there, and the bare bones of the pipework in situ for the plumbing.

'It's only that back wall being tidied up so it can be left exposed. Sam will plasterboard the rest and then the space will be partitioned. There's going to be one double bedroom, a small kitchen area, a shower room and a sitting room with a sofa bed. It will sleep four, maximum.'

I rub my foot on the dusty concrete floor. Sam looks down, watching the aimless movement.

'It will be tiled,' he confirms. 'It was originally a dirt floor.'

'How long will it take?'

'Well, now my dad is on another job, twice as long as we'd hoped.' He shrugs his shoulders.

'Neil and Sarah will be coming to dinner tomorrow night to help us celebrate your arrival,' Dad informs me.

I feel myself blushing as two pairs of eyes stare back at me with interest.

'Dad… it will be lovely to meet people, but it's not a celebration.' I laugh, feeling more than a little self-conscious.

'Well, if it means I have some help with this place, then that's cause enough to celebrate,' Sam throws into the conversation. 'I know the pressure is on to get both gîtes up and running as quickly as possible. I'm off on holiday on the tenth of July and so this place has to be finished before then. I wish I could say the Côte D'Azur wasn't calling me, but it is and I'm in need of a break.'

He smiles at me, a lop-sided sort of grin that suits his guy next door face. His hair is extremely short on the back and sides, but worn a little longer on the top. He's probably only a couple of inches taller than me, with a typical builder's physique. Strong legs and arms; you know the sort.

'We appreciate everything you're doing for us, Sam. There's quite a waiting list already and I can't pretend the additional income won't be very welcome. Anyway, the introductions are over. I'm off to repair the fence at the end of the garden to stop those damned sheep getting into the vegetable garden again. I'll see you at lunch.'

'Thanks, Dad. Catch you later.'

I'm left to survey Sam's back as he returns to the job in hand. Now this feels awkward. Obviously, I don't have any building skills whatsoever, although I did help Dad when he was renovating their last house in the UK. But that was mostly general redecoration after he'd taken down two walls.

'Watch what I'm doing and then you can take over, if you like. Ever worked with mortar before?'

I shake my head. Paint, filler and a drill, yes, but mortar, no.

'This tool here is a hawk. You can only mix up one bucket of muck, as it's referred to, at a time. It takes a while to start going off but once it's on the wall it dries much quicker, of course, because it's spread more thinly.'

He works quickly, making it look effortless. Using a trowel to slide the grey mortar off the hawk, with a few deft sweeps of his hand it sits nicely in the joint between the stones. He repeats the process and then goes back to his first infill to tidy it up.

'I like to use this little tool. It's part of an old bucket handle and if you drag it lightly across the surface of the mortar once it starts to harden a little, it will give it a nice curved effect.' He demonstrates on a row of stones above where he's working and I can see how easily the slightly drier mortar responds.

'Then you take this brush here and gently flick the bristles over the entire face of the stonework to remove the excess mortar that forms on the edges. There's nothing to it, really. If it gets a little dry when you're working on an area you can moisten it with a wet brush. Everything you need is on the tarpaulin.'

I swallow hard. This guy makes it look easy because he has the knack.

'Great. I'll… um… make a start, then.'

'There are some overalls over there and some gloves. This stuff will ruin your hands unless your skin is already like leather. I can start putting up the studding ready for the plasterboard on the other walls. I'll be in and out measuring and setting up the circular saw outside to cut the timber, if you get stuck.'

That must surely be the shortest lesson ever. He takes a notebook from one of his tool boxes and the pencil from behind his ear. I appear to have been dismissed, and by the time I've pulled the overalls up over my leggings and donned some heavy duty gloves, I'm rather glad he's nowhere to be seen. I feel like I'm about to weld something.

Oh dear, even lifting the hawk in these thick gloves is difficult. It's a very heavy tool even before I begin ladling on the mortar. Then the stiffness of the gloves makes it extremely difficult to use the trowel with any degree of accuracy. I seem to be getting a lot of mortar on the front of the stones and very little in the actual joints. I work in silence, the effort and concentration making me break into a sweat.

'Arrgghh, this is stupid!' I mutter, wiping my arm across my forehead to mop up some of the sweat. In the process, it sends dollops of grey mortar in all directions. I throw the hawk down on the tarpaulin and yank off the gloves. Then I slip out of the overalls and head into the kitchen.

'You look a bit hot and bothered.' Mum looks me up and down and I realise the mortar went even further than I'd thought.

'Do you have a plastic knife and a spoon, by any chance? And I'm looking for something oblong, like the top of a sweet tin. Metal if possible, so it's durable. Oh, and some thin, disposable gloves if you have them.'

Mum's eyebrows shoot up. 'I thought you were having a go at repointing?'

'I am. Just humour me.'

Mum disappears into the pantry and returns, a warm smile on her face. 'Here you go.'

'I might end up working my way through the whole box of gloves,' I warn and can't resist a chuckle. I leave her standing there with a distinctly puzzled look on her face.

Fortunately, Sam seems to have disappeared and by the time he returns I've managed to repoint half a row. Considering the wall is some forty feet in length, I'm rather pleased with myself. Until I see his face. He's staring down at my tools, as I'm using the long-bristled brush to dust off a few stray bits and tidy up my efforts.

'What on earth?'

He moves his eyes from the floor, to my face and back again. Then he walks along the length of the wall. I stand back, trying to look at the results of my efforts objectively, and comparing them to the top third of the wall.

'That's not a bad job, but I have to see this in action.'

The disposable latex gloves allow me to easily slide the mortar off the lid of the tin with accuracy, as I hold it against the joint to be filled. I scoop it into the void with the plastic knife and because the blade is a small surface it packs the stuff in quite nicely without getting very much on either side of the face of the stones. I work along the gap quite quickly, then change tools, picking up the plastic spoon. I use the handle, which is bevelled in a similar way to Sam's old bucket handle, but is a better fit, to glide along the irregular surface. There isn't much left to clean off once it's a little drier and I stand back, watching the expression on Sam's face.

'Well, I'm actually almost speechless. And it's not a bad job, at all.'

'You're happy for me to continue?'

'Yes. I can't guarantee not to laugh, though, if I walk through the door forgetting what I've seen. And if my dad appears, you make it clear that this,' he points to my tools lying on the floor, 'wasn't my idea.'

I feel weirdly elated as if I've achieved something.

'It really isn't a bad job, is it?' I can't help crowing a little as I scrutinise the wall. Although I say it myself, if the new mortar was dry I don't think I could tell the difference between what Sam has done and where I've taken over.

As he walks out of the door carrying a long piece of wood marked ready to cut, he throws a laugh over his shoulder.

'I hope Viv has a large stock of plastic cutlery. I don't usually work at the weekends but I'm working tomorrow if you're up for it. I need to move things along now.'

'Great.' Well, my head says *great*, but my arm muscles are saying something else entirely.

Welcome to the Village

At the end of the second day of working alongside Sam, I need a long soak in the bath to ease my sore muscles. Even with my improvised tools, the fact that my arms have been working at shoulder height for two whole days has been a shock to the system. I'm sure the muscles I usually use at work are grateful for the rest, but I can't recall ever aching quite so much.

When I eventually manage to drag myself out of the bath and dress I do, at least, feel refreshed. I heard car doors slamming outside about half an hour ago and hope no one is put out that I'm arriving late to my own celebration dinner. Although it's a buffet, I believe. Mum wouldn't let me do anything at all to help, even though she spent virtually the whole day in the kitchen. She said that Sam's mum, Sarah, was also bringing food, which is rather concerning. How much do they think six people can eat?

I throw on some skinny jeans and a summery top, give my hair a quick brush and put on a slick of lip gloss. This is rustic living and I'm sure I'll do. Besides, it's nice to feel relaxed and not to have to dress up, even if every single arm movement produces a groan.

As I descend the final flight of stairs I can tell by the volume of noisy chatter coming from the dining room that this is no intimate little buffet supper. As I push the door open a few inches and try to slide into the room unnoticed, I can't believe what I see. Fortunately, the first pair of eyes that flash in my direction are Sam's and he grabs a second glass of champagne and walks towards me.

'You look shocked. What were you expecting?'

I wince as I raise my left hand to take the glass he offers me.

'Well, not half the village, that's for sure.'

We exchange smiles over the top of our champagne flutes.

'Let me guess. Arm muscles are in revolt. I should have warned you, I'm sorry. But you have to be pleased with what you've achieved these last couple of days.'

I nod, trying not to make eye contact beyond Sam's line of vision, but suddenly Dad spots me and raises his voice to shush everyone.

'At last! She's here.' He heads straight towards me, Mum is close on his heels. Sam rather diplomatically stands to one side, a momentary look of commiseration on his face.

'This is our lovely daughter, Anna.'

There's shuffling as everyone turns to look in my direction and I can feel myself shrinking.

'Hello.' My voice has never sounded quite so small but it doesn't seem to matter because Dad immediately takes over.

'Can I ask everyone to please raise their glasses to toast what is a very special occasion for Viv and me. Having Anna here for the summer means so much to us, as do the wonderful friendships we've made since we arrived here. To family and friends, à votre santé.'

A chorus of voices chime in and, to my relief, within moments the room is once more full of general chatter. Mum turns to give me a hug.

'Mum, you didn't tell me you were inviting so many people. I would have made more of an effort if I'd known.'

'You look fine,' she whispers into my ear. 'Perfect, in fact. It really is so wonderful to have you here with us, Anna. This was always our dream.'

'Viv, shall I start handing out plates?'

Mum gives me a warm smile before heading off towards the buffet table with Dad. I look at Sam and he strides across to stand with me in the corner.

'You can't hide here all night, you know. You will be expected to talk to everyone at some point.'

'But I don't know anyone aside from you and your dad. And my French is patchy to say the least.'

He opens his eyes wide, feigning surprise. 'And I thought you were a woman of unlimited talents. Everyone here speaks at least a little English, so you'll be fine. The tall, wiry looking character standing to the left of your mum is Monsieur Bastien Deniaud and next to him is his wife, Agnés. He's the mayor and you should head in his direction first. It'll score you a lot of points.'

Sam winks at me and I stifle a laugh. His eyes move on to a much older woman who is in conversation with another couple.

'That's Madame Allard, she's your nearest neighbour. She lives in the little cottage on the left just before you turn into the drive. She's eighty years old but don't be fooled by her meek and mild manner. She can be formidable from what I hear, but I don't know her very well. The couple she's talking to are Claude and Inès Gaubert. Come on over and I'll introduce you.'

As we approach they all turn to look at Sam and he does a brief introduction.

'Anna, Monsieur Gaubert here runs the village boulangerie and you won't taste finer bread or croissants anywhere. Madame Gaubert runs the little épicerie next to the bakery and it's the place to go to find out what's happening in the village. I'm sure you will have noticed Madame Allard's charming little cottage on the opposite side of the road.'

I receive a very warm reception and I briefly wonder what Mum and Dad have been saying about me.

'My husband prefers fishing to making baguettes these days,' Inès Gaubert informs me with a scowl. Claude is quick to respond.

'Maybe it's because I like a little peace and quiet.'

They aren't arguing about that fact, merely acknowledging the truth of their situation. Inès shrugs her shoulders.

'The world goes on around you, Claude, and you never know what's going on. That's why people come to me.' She laughs and he gazes at her, the bond between them is quite touching and their easy banter has no edge to it at all. 'Don't you agree, Madame Allard?'

I don't really catch the response as it's in French and spoken very quickly, but everyone begins laughing.

'Madame Allard said that she's simply grateful for the most wonderful croissants in the whole of France. And fish is so easy to digest.'

Now I understand the laughter.

Sam suggests we top up our drinks and I give a friendly nod of acknowledgement as we all part company. 'It's lovely to meet you all.'

I lean into Sam, keeping my voice low as we walk away.

'Thank you. Your help is much appreciated. It's all a little… embarrassing. I mean, coming back to live with my parents for six months, could be viewed as—'

'Uh oh, prepare for the next assault.' Sam grins as a couple approach us, smiling broadly. 'Anna, this is my mum, Sarah, and you already know my dad, Neil.'

Neil gives me a nod and a smile. 'We met when Anna came over for a few days earlier in the year.'

I step forward, honouring the French tradition of *la bise*, the air kiss. Thankfully I get it right, turning my cheek three times and reciprocating; often in the UK, people only turn their cheeks twice. Sarah follows it with a welcoming hug.

'It's so lovely to meet you in the flesh, at last, Anna. I've heard so much about you.'

Inwardly I groan. Having proud parents who insist on singing my praises, even though my life is in a complete and utter mess, makes me feel like a bit of a fraud.

'And Sam says you're a quick learner and the repointing is coming along nicely. He was very impressed and it's wonderful that you can be here to get involved. Neil is so busy and turning work away. After helping your dad with his plumbing problems, he's running way behind. It's such a shame, though, as it's not ideal to have major building work going on when paying guests are around.'

'Don't worry, Ma. I'll get it sorted as quickly as humanly possible.'

'I know you will, my son.' Sarah places her hand on Sam's cheek, a loving gesture that doesn't seem to embarrass him in any way and I like that.

'Sam's a good teacher, even if he did make repointing look a whole lot easier than it is when I gave it a try.'

'Fair play to you for having a go,' Neil lifts his glass in my direction. I lift mine back at him and, forgetting about my arm, let out an involuntary groan. Sam and I exchange glances and start laughing.

Mum and Dad join us at that precise moment, wondering what the laughter is all about.

'I seem to have discovered some muscles that I haven't used in a long while. Okay, maybe never. Guess I'm not quite as fit as I thought I was, but it won't stop me, I promise.'

'I'll hold you to that,' Sam grins at me over the top of his glass and I notice a small smile creeping over Mum's face. Now that's something I need to make very clear to her. He's not my type, but it's also going to be a long time before I commit to a full-blown relationship again. Besides, I can sense that he hides more than he cares to share and the last thing I need is someone whose life story is more complicated than my own. He is attractive but my head is now ruling my wayward heart.

The fact that every time I pick up my phone I end up deleting a string of texts from Karl, is a sharp reminder of how messy things can get. From now on my gut instincts are in charge and they're telling me that I'm safe around Sam because he has no agenda. No agenda at all, so it seems, other than heading off on holiday before too long.

And as for my own agenda? Well, I spend most of Sunday resting up and thinking about the future, mulling over the ideas I've spent the last month thinking about. It's time to begin formulating a plan because procrastination is beginning to feel like merely a delaying tactic. When I go back to the UK I'm going to set up my own business and in future no one is going to be the boss of little old me.

Baa Baa Black Sheep

On Monday morning, Sam is back at work and he's on good form. The studding for the plasterboard is flying up around me as I continue to work my way along the wall, one painstaking row at a time.

'How long do you think this is going to take me?' I talk to Sam over my shoulder, grateful that the run I'm currently working on is lower so isn't quite such a stretch for my arms.

'Probably a week, if you can keep up that pace. I'll be honest with you, it takes a certain mindset to deal with a repetitive task like that. Some people would find it boring and lose interest.'

I stop and turn to face him.

'It doesn't bother me. In fact, it's rather therapeutic and I find it relaxing. If only my muscles would stop complaining I'm sure I could work a little quicker.'

'You're the sort who prides themselves on finishing what they start, then?' He looks up at me from his kneeling position as he marks off another line to cut on the timber in front of him.

'Always. Can't stand loose ends. And you?'

He sits back on his heels, resting the palms of his hands on his knees.

'Me? I'm the black sheep of the family which makes life a lot simpler. I guess no one really expects me to tie up anything, anymore. My role is to make my brothers look good and that's something I seem to excel at.' He laughs, but I realise it's to himself, rather than something he's sharing with me.

I raise my eyebrows, surprised by his words. 'I find that hard to believe. I wasn't the only offspring enduring an outpouring of parental pride on Saturday night. Your work ethic is impressive and I can't believe you are almost ready to start putting up the plasterboard. This is going to go from a shell to a blank canvas in no time at all.'

This time his laugh is abrupt, more like a self-deprecating snort.

'I'm not a builder really, just a builder's mate. I have no formal training. I learnt by watching my dad and working alongside him.'

I reluctantly turn back around, conscious that the mortar is drying and I can't really stop and chat.

'How long have you been living in France?' I call, over my shoulder.

Sam, too, continues with what he's doing and is already making his way to the door.

'Three years, nearly. But I'm still living my life one day at a time.' With that he disappears and it's clear the conversation is over.

Admittedly, this is a strange life for a single guy who is probably not much older than I am, so maybe twenty-six or twenty-seven years old. Everyone I've met so far are Mum and Dad's generation, or older. It's a great place to settle if you're in a permanent relationship, or have a young family, and finding a job isn't going to be an issue. Or young enough to make a new set of friends while learning the language, so that you don't become isolated. But Sam must have the same problem that I would face if I moved here. Having your family around you is one thing, but when you have your whole life ahead of you the opportunities in this rural village are rather limited. I guess with his skills he's always guaranteed work, but doesn't he miss city life and socialising with his friends?

The morning passes with very little chatter between us. After lunch, I clear away my tools and sweep up, ready to help Sam carry in the sheets of plasterboard. They're more awkward than heavy. I'm tasked with holding each piece in place while he screws them to the wooden studding. By the end of the day over half of the three walls have been plaster boarded and my exposed stone wall is starting to look like a real feature. I haven't been able to repoint as large an area as yesterday, but enough to feel I've continued to make some progress.

Rather unexpectedly, Ziggy appears and runs straight up to Sam, totally ignoring me. I stand with my hands on my hips looking indignant. Well, I guess I really am a part of the fixtures and fittings now and the novelty of welcoming me back has worn off already.

'What?' Sam exclaims. 'We're old friends.' He looks at me askance.

'Yes, but she was originally my cat and I deserve at least one meow and the chance to smooth her back, before she streaks past me. Hey, I've just realised that you both have green eyes!'

My remark makes him smile.

'Ooh, and now the *green-eyed* monster raises its head, Ziggy. Are we scared?' With that his hand deftly sweeps along her entire back and her tail – the thing she loves the most – and then she begins to purr. Loudly.

'Traitors!' I exclaim. I turn my back on them and finish sweeping up, almost ready to quit for the day. Sam picks up the last of his tools, placing them in a crate.

'Right, I'm done. Thanks for your help, Anna. Appreciated. Are you okay to help again tomorrow so I can finish getting these walls lined, or do you want me to see if I can get someone in so you can crack on with the repointing?'

'No, it's fine. It's nice to do something different. I think I'll sleep well again tonight, that's for sure.'

He grins up at me for a second or two before putting away the last of his tools for the day.

'One thing I know for sure, though, is that I won't be giving up the day job.' That makes him laugh. Then I realise I don't have a day job any more, which kind of turns a smart comment into a joke of a very different kind. As Sam leaves, Ziggy follows devotedly in his wake – *really?*

*

Two of the couples staying here have children and tonight they are back early, taking advantage of the pool. Mum suggests we have our evening meal in the secret garden, which is a little corner tucked away out of sight of the house in the rear garden. We carry everything down on trays, passing through the rose covered archway and settling ourselves quite comfortably on the weathered, but fully functional, wooden table and chairs.

'This is beautiful, guys. And I couldn't have ordered better weather.'

Dad pours the wine while Mum and I uncover the plates and lay out the cutlery.

'How did it go today with Sam?' Dad's still working on sheep-proofing the fencing and this is the first chance we've had all day to catch up.

'Good. I spent the afternoon helping him with the plaster boarding, but aside from that I'm not unhappy with how the wall is coming along.'

'You don't have to work constantly, you know.' Mum settles herself back in her seat and frowns at me. 'This is a working holiday. Notice that *work* isn't the only word in that phrase.'

I nod, my mouth full of sweet young lettuce leaves from the garden.

'I'm happy and I like to be productive. My focus is getting that wall finished so I can help Sam when it's time to start the painting. He's a hard worker, that's for sure.'

'I'm glad the two of you are getting along. He's a nice young man and I know he needs the money, but he has really put himself out to help us. The clock is ticking and we need those gîtes to be rented out. He usually works alongside Neil, so we have him to thank, too.'

We eat in silence for a few minutes. Even though we're a long way from the front of the house I can hear the children's excited screeches and laughter carrying on the breeze. Other than that, it's mainly bird song and the occasional bleating from the sheep in the field behind us.

'Sam has settled here permanently, then?'

Dad stops eating to take a sip of his wine and glances across at me.

'You must get him to show you his project some time. He bought a wreck of a barn and he's turning it into a home.'

'He said he's been here for three years. Why isn't it finished by now?'

Dad looks at Mum, who looks back at him with one of her warning expressions.

'He works on it when he can between the day jobs, darling. How's the fish?'

Well, that ends that line of questioning. From what I've seen so far, I can't see why Sam would think he was such a disappointment to his family. Anyway, Mum is making it clear it's none of my business and she's right. I know she's close to Sarah, but I doubt Mum would have told her the details of my sorry little tale, either.

'Wonderful. You really should offer dinner to your guests, Mum. Your cooking is on a par with any restaurant I've eaten in and it would increase your income.'

'I've been telling her precisely the same thing, Anna. Admittedly, we'd need some help in the kitchen, but when all eight rooms are let with potentially sixteen adults and maybe half-a-dozen children between the two *family* rooms, we'll be able to afford to bring in some help. However, letting out the gîtes will give us a safety net and we're hoping to be able to top our savings up for a rainy day.'

Mum glances across at Dad and then her eyes alight on me.

'I'd forgotten what an effective team you two are when you're in agreement about something. I am listening and maybe. We'll see. Anyway, Anna, I don't suppose you've heard from Karl at all?'

I hesitate for one tiny second but recover well.

'It seems no one wants to speak to me, not even Lizzie. Still, that means the tenant will have settled in without any problems, so it's good news in a way.'

Technically I haven't *heard* from Karl, I've just scanned his texts with increasing irritation.

I love you, babe. Nothing will ever change that fact.

I know you are angry but please just let me know you are OK.

I'm in Edinburgh and it's raining and I miss you.

Just let me explain, please. Don't cut me off like this.

'Well, I think you are well rid of him. I never liked him from the start. Overly confident, if you ask me and smug with it.'

'Geoff! No one asked for your opinion and I think that's something best kept to yourself. Anna, don't take any notice. We hardly knew Karl and what matters is what you feel about him.'

Mum is now glaring at Dad, worrying that now he's put his feelings out there it places me in an awkward position.

'Actually, I agree with Dad. I am just as ambitious as Karl, but if I truly loved someone they would come first, every time. You guys have set the bar high, relationship wise, and I don't intend to aim for anything less.'

Mum's eyes suddenly begin to glisten and I change the subject by suggesting that we clear away and then have a look at today's progress on the gîte. I think they are both in for a very pleasant surprise. At least that's something I can feel positive about.

New Life, Old Wounds

Day four on the job and I'm up early. I start working on the wall before Sam arrives. The problem I have is that at one end there are some rather large gaps where, over the years, individual stones have fallen out. On Sam's suggestion, I've been rooting around outside as there are pockets of stones in several places around the garden. Most have fallen out of the boundary walls, but it's a case of finding the right shape and size to fill each hole. Gradually though, I'm making progress and if I can just stop worrying so much about the spiders who live in the larger crevices it would probably become quite a pleasurable task. It's very much like putting a jigsaw together and you know when you have the right stone. As you set it into the mortar, it either looks at home, or it looks wrong. It's a question of trial and error.

As I gingerly push my gloved hand into the next void to scoop out any loose rubble, my hand brushes against a flat edge. I manoeuvre my fingers around the object and yank, but it won't budge. Taking a screwdriver from one of Sam's tool boxes in the corner, I chip away at a couple of pieces of rubble that are holding back some of the crumbling mortar.

Bit by bit I can work my hand further inside to scoop out the loose debris surrounding the object. Finally, a piece of stone that seemed to be wedged in front of the object releases and suddenly there it is in my hand – a small wooden box. It's probably six inches square and it's very old. The lid is too warped to prise open. I rub my gloved hand over the top of it but the dirt is caked on and will require some work to clean it up. I wonder why someone would shove this into a hole in the wall. Shaking it, it's hard to tell if there is anything inside so I guess my curiosity will have to wait until later.

I place it on the window sill and get back to clearing out the hole, ready to fit a new stone and line it with mortar.

'Hey, what's this? Are you trying to show me up? How long have you been here?'

'Not long. What do you think?' I stand back, one arm folded across my chest and the other one raised as I cup my chin in my hand. It's my thinking pose. Having just filled probably seventy-five per cent of the biggest hole I'm trying to assess my work with impartial eyes.

'You haven't done all of that this morning, have you?' Sam looks at me incredulously.

'No, of course not! After dinner, last night, I spent ages wandering along the boundary wall in search of suitable stones until it was too dark to see.'

A smirk makes its way over his face and I instantly react.

'What? I'm loving this time with my parents but they do need a little quality time alone together. And I'm not used to having all of this spare time on my hands.'

As Sam begins to unpack some of his tools ready to start work he flashes me a sympathetic look.

'There isn't much to do here in the evenings except walk and you're very welcome to join me tonight if you want.'

Karl's latest text flashes through my mind.

Call me, let's talk. Please. I can make this right, I promise you.

It's a kind offer and I do need to keep myself occupied at the moment. I try not to read Karl's texts before I delete them but sometimes I can't help myself. He's trying to make me feel that I owe him the chance to explain himself. Nothing will change how I feel, though, and being coerced into talking to him is the last thing I need right now. 'Okay, sounds good. What time?'

'Seven thirty. Now, sorry to drag you away, but when you've finished using up that mix can I borrow those strong arms of yours? If we can finish the boarding today then tomorrow I can begin filling and applying the tape to the joints ready for plastering.'

Typically with Sam, we exchange more words in that first five minutes than in the whole of the rest of the day. We work together in companionable silence, going back and forth with the plasterboard sheets. He likes to concentrate on what he's doing, only breaking the silence to give me directions. Although I don't get time to do any more repointing, it's another very satisfying day.

When it's time to finish, Sam walks over to perform a quiet inspection of my repointing before packing everything up. He seems content with what I managed to achieve first thing, as I watch him out of the corner of my eye.

'Right, I'm off to eat, shower and change. See you later.'

Dad and Sam pass in the doorway and I notice he gives Sam a grateful pat on the back before walking over to me. Ziggy puts in a brief appearance but disappears when I collide with the bucket and a trowel hits the floor with a loud clatter.

'Poor Ziggy, a building site isn't the best place for her but she likes to know what's going on. It's looking good, girl. The holes are nearly gone and you're doing a great job. Mum's worried you're overdoing it, though. You were pottering around out here until late last night and up way before everyone else. Is there anything in particular worrying you? Or is this just general anxiety because you are at a crossroads? How are you doing for money?'

'Dad, I'm a grown woman. I'm doing fine. I'm settling in, that's all. It's such a huge change for me and I'm happy to say I'm enjoying it. I just need to adjust to my new routine. Besides, my head is working on my plan of action for the future and gradually it's coming together, but that's not always conducive to sleep.'

'Well, if you need anything, even just a listening ear, I'm here. I know you don't like to worry your mum. I'm sorry if I was out of order about Karl. If he is the one for you and you end up going back to him, he might even redeem himself. Either way, I promise I'll keep my opinions to myself.'

Dad places his hand on my shoulder and gives a gentle squeeze. I know that must have been so hard for him to say.

'I appreciate your honesty, Dad. As for Karl, I think I'm guilty of seeing what I wanted to see, rather than what was really there, to be honest. I feel like I've been duped in a way. That's why being here right now is so good for me.'

He nods his head, clearly relieved to see I'm not upset.

'You're no fool, Anna, and whatever you decide to do will be for the right reasons. Now, Mum sent me over to ask what time you want dinner?'

'As soon as possible. I'm going for a walk with Sam tonight.'

Dad raises his eyebrows. 'Mum will be pleased.'

I roll my eyes. 'It's not like that, Dad. I need to get back in shape and walking is gentle exercise. I can't end up going home with arms like Arnold Schwarzenegger and legs like a sparrow.'

He laughs and we link arms as he walks me back to the house.

*

I close the passenger door, turning to Sam as I do up my seat belt.

'I thought you said we were going for a walk?'

'Yes, we are, but this isn't the best place to take a stroll at night as there aren't any pavements. It's only a couple of kilometres away and it's worth the drive, plus you'll get to see the sunflowers as it's a track around a field. Much safer when dusk falls.'

He has a point. The sun is sinking in the sky but there's plenty of time for a good walk before the darkness descends.

'I'm taking you to one of my favourite viewpoints. Was Geoff pleased with what we achieved today?'

'He was delighted. He said he's going to start clearing out the second gîte tomorrow. It's packed full of old furniture but after poking my head in to take a quick look, I doubt anything in there is salvageable. There are too many spiders around for me to give him a hand, though.'

Sam's side profile reflects an instant smile which he immediately tries to hide. He stopped short of laughing out loud, so that's something, I suppose, but I can't help my phobia. I notice that we turn right at a signpost marked *Erbray 6km*.

'They were both in pretty much the same state. People tend to hang on to everything until one day all it's good for is firewood.'

'Oh, I found a box. I forgot to mention it to Dad. I can't get the lid off, because it's warped. It was stuffed into the wall.'

'Interesting. Maybe it's full of gold coins. Now wouldn't that be a nice little find?'

'I expect it's empty, but if there was anything valuable inside it, then it begs the question about who put it there and why hide it in the first place?'

'I'm pretty sure you could lay claim to it. Buying property means you buy it as it stands and that includes useless old furniture, as well as precious finds.'

I laugh. 'Well, perhaps we can try to open it tomorrow.'

'I have a six millimetre chisel that might ease it off. Right. This is it.'

Sam parks up on the verge alongside a field of sunflowers. The small heads have all closed and are bowed after a day spent gazing at the sun. In a few weeks' time, this crop will be towering way above us, but today the sturdy stems barely reach my hip. We follow the narrow track around the outskirts until we reach an old wooden stile. Sam extends his hand to help me over it and we skirt around the edge of yet another field; this time it's corn and there's a rustling sound as the plants wave gently back and forth in the breeze. It's not the easiest of walks as it's slightly uphill, but we round a large copse and suddenly the land falls away in front of us. We are standing on the brow of a hill and the view is amazing. Less than half a mile away are three enormous wind turbines, standing like sentinels over the landscape. One is stationary, but the other two emit a low hum and a loud whispering sound as the blades turn and glint in the light of the glowing sunset.

With the sun low on the horizon behind them and the silvery blue sky streaked with a deep crimson pink, it looks more like a painting than a real life scene.

'Impressive, isn't it?' For one moment, I'd forgotten Sam was standing next to me.

The sun shifts slightly and now there's a huge ball of light being funnelled between two trees way in the distance. It sends a shaft of light across the field in front of us.

'That's quite a scene.'

'Here, hop up onto this wall and we'll watch the final rays before the sun slips below the horizon.'

We sit in silence for quite a while, watching as the ball of light becomes smaller and smaller. Time seems to stand still and suddenly my head is empty of all thoughts. I turn to glance at Sam, a look of pure concentration is on his face. He's a very attractive guy and there are moments when he makes my pulse race. Like now, for instance.

'Some people think wind turbines are a blot on the landscape, but I guessed you wouldn't be one of them. You're a thinker and you take pleasure in the aesthetics of life. A part of that is caring about the environment.' He turns to look at me and I nod gratefully.

'It's taking me a while to unwind and let go of a few things. But I'm getting there.'

As I turn to look at him what I see on his face is empathy and maybe a tinge of regret, reflected in those mysterious green eyes flecked with a hint of grey.

'Sometimes life's hurdles aren't easy to jump. It's a case of learning how to survive the fall really.'

There's sadness and pain in his voice.

'Was it that bad?'

'Bad enough. Anyway, it's time to head back or we'll find ourselves walking in the pitch black.'

We hardly speak on the journey home and I can see that he's deep in thought. I give a final wave goodbye as Sam pulls the van off the drive, wondering why such a sensitive guy has chosen to turn his back on life. Yes, I know I've more or less done the same thing, but it's only for six months. After that I'll pick my old life back up again, just in a new way. I wonder why Sam can't do that, too.

The Discovery

I hop into bed, waiting for Ziggy to decide where she's going to settle before picking up my phone. I do so with a sense of something akin to dread. I don't want to cut myself off from everyone in Dursley, or the friends I made at work, but being here seems to make my old life seem unreal. Nothing matters in quite the same way as it did back home; I don't feel an urgency to respond and get drawn back into it because I'm moving on. Living in France is a temporary thing, but when I go back everything will be different because I'll be starting over again.

My inbox sends an automatic reply telling people I'm on holiday and will get back to them when I can as I have limited Wi-Fi access. Yes, that's a cop out and I know it, but I figure I deserve a real break. I scan down the long list of emails, noting there are messages from several people I used to work with and the usual social media notifications. Then I find one from Lizzie:

Hey, Anna, I will call you at the weekend but I wanted to give you a few days to settle in. The tenant is fine and loves the house. He says the location is perfect for him as it's close to where he works. When the tenancy is up he will be looking to buy something in the area. I know your long term plans are a bit up in the air at the moment, but having had a long chat with him, this guy is serious. He's keen to talk to you before you think of putting it on the market, if that becomes an option. Anyway, hope the weather is wonderful and you're enjoying yourself. Speak soon. L xx

I read it twice and find myself absentmindedly chewing my lip. I don't know how I feel about this because I keep telling myself I have plenty of time before I start thinking about my next step. But selling the house wasn't on my list of options, that's for sure.

I scroll on down and Karl's name is suddenly staring back at me. In the subject line it simply reads "Please don't ignore this". As I click to open it I can feel a knot forming in my stomach as my muscles tense.

Anna, nothing is working here. I'm going through the motions and hating every minute. You're supposed to be here by my side as we're a team and I've forgotten how to function alone.

I thought you felt something for me but to up and leave like that, without even a goodbye! I can't believe this is happening. I thought this was the start of getting to where we wanted to be and that meant doing everything together.

107

We can still make things good between us, Anna, but you need to talk to me. Please, just talk to me. I love you, my darling. Karl x

I throw the phone down on the bed in anger and Ziggy rolls over, temporarily disturbed. My reaction is partly due to the fact that my eyes are filling with tears. I don't want to cry for a guy who can't understand that what *he* wants isn't what *I* want. I even gave up my beloved cat baby for him and Ziggy was my only comfort during some very emotional times. Everything still centres round work for Karl and I know how his mind operates. Knowledge is power to Karl and it gives him the edge. Well, perhaps unwittingly I gave him the edge. People laugh at the old phrase *pillow talk*, but when two people who work in the same organisation are sleeping together they talk about everything, whether it's confidential information or gossip. I realise that I'd stopped trusting Karl a while ago and looking back there were even times he accused me of withholding information from him. I'd simply held things back, not out of self-preservation and the fear of people realising how close we were, but because I'd begun to feel used.

My dreams are troubled and the dawn chorus is a welcome sound, a distraction from the turmoil inside my head. Maybe selling the house is worth consideration as then it means I can start over again in another city and cut all ties.

*

When Sam arrives, I'm perched on a stool and scraping the last of the mortar mix off the tin lid and into the gap in front of me.

'Ah, stool height already. Impressive. Is that better on the arms?'

I nod, stifling a yawn.

'Yes, but I think my leg muscles are going to be challenged when I'm on the bottom three rows. It will be either bending or kneeling and that's sure to hurt.'

We exchange smiles.

'You sound like you didn't sleep well. Everything okay?'

'Fine, just one of those nights. That was a great view, by the way.'

'Some people hate wind turbines but I find them fascinating. I love that gentle swoosh, it's calming. And there's a majesty about them, plus of course it's a green way to generate electricity. Where's that box of yours?'

I'd totally forgotten about it again and I walk over to the window sill to retrieve it. I hold it out to Sam, who picks it up and immediately tries to prise off the lid with his hands.

'Ah, you're right. The wood is warped. It's clearly very old and the carving is quite intricate. It smells musty but it's made of hardwood – maybe oak – so it hasn't rotted and it's probably been in that wall for a long time.'

He shakes the box but I can't hear anything moving inside as the wood is so solid.

'Well, it's not full of gold coins because it's not that heavy. I can probably get the lid off with a chisel but it might damage it. What do you think?'

I bend to wash off my tools in a bucket of water, ready to think about making up a new mix of mortar. I squeeze out a cloth and hand it to Sam.

'Here, give it a wipe with this and go for it. It will probably end up on the fire with the rest of the furniture Dad's going to be burning today. It's a pity the damp has got into it, though, as it's a pretty box.'

By the time I return carrying a full bucket of mortar mix, Sam has started work. I glance across to see he managed to get the lid open and has placed it on the stool.

'It seems you have found some treasure, after all. And the box isn't in that bad a condition after I scraped the muck away. If you look closely, I think you can make out the initials *M* and *L*, carved into the top among the scrolls. It might even be valuable if the jewellery inside is the real deal.'

I pull off my gloves and pick up the open box. There's a delicate, gold coloured brooch inset with tiny pearls, a silver locket, two hat pins and a beautiful ring.

'Do you think that's a diamond?' He sounds a little excited about the prospect.

I hold the ring up to the light and it sparkles. The stone in the centre is probably the biggest single stone I've ever seen up close. Around it are four smaller stones forming a cross.

'It looks old, maybe Victorian, even. I'm not sure though; I'm no expert when it comes to jewellery.'

'No engagement rings in your past, then?'

Sam's throwaway comment makes me look up. 'No, and there probably never will be.'

He immediately spins back round to continue running some tape down the joint between two sheets of plasterboard. 'Sorry, it's none of my business.' He throws the words over his shoulder as I slip the contents back into the box.

'Time to get back to it. This wall isn't going to repoint itself.' I know I sound a bit moody but that's one topic I won't get drawn into discussing.

I head out into the sunshine again to get some water to clean off a few of the stones before I continue with the repointing. I can't help wondering why anyone would need to hide away something so beautiful and, no doubt, meaningful. Time to do a little research I think, as clearly this property has a past and someone round here must know something about it.

Ziggy appears, slowly making her way down the path towards me. She stops to sniff every single flower and watch every bee buzzing around the blooms. Then she finally offers up her back for a stroke and I can't help smiling. When humans are stressing you out, or work seems like a chore, an animal is there to remind you that life is only as hard, or as complicated, as you choose to make it.

When I go back inside we continue to work in silence. It's quite a relief that Sam doesn't want to talk all the time as I like to concentrate on the job in hand. Physically it's tiring, but my mind is beginning to feel a lot less cluttered. Even Karl's constant texting is no longer a cause of stress. I didn't respond to his email yesterday and this morning there wasn't anything new in my inbox. Perhaps it's beginning to sink in at last that whatever we had is over.

Our lunch break is a short one. We sit in the garden with Mum and Dad to eat cheese filled baguettes and the first of the greenhouse tomatoes. Mum makes a jug of freshly squeezed orange juice and sparkling water that is really refreshing. In between eating I tell them about the discovery of the jewellery box and start quizzing them about the previous owners. The property was purchased from Monsieur and Madame Allard, but as Monsieur Allard died during the process, Mum and Dad were unable to find out much about the place. Madame Allard speaks very little English, as I've witnessed, having relied upon her husband who seemed to have been quite fluent. The house had been empty for a while after being let out for several years, when it suddenly came up for auction. Monsieur Allard bought it, hoping to persuade Madame Allard to move in. He eventually gave up on the idea and decided to sell.

Once we get back to work, I can't stop thinking about the mystery of the hidden jewellery box and eventually I turn towards Sam. He senses me watching him and stops what he's doing.

'What is it?'

'How's your French?'

He shakes his head. 'I knew you'd ask me that. You want to speak to Madame Allard, don't you? Well, it's pretty good but she's a very private woman and I'm not sure how she will react if we descend upon her.'

'Leave that to me. What are you doing this evening?'

Sam continues to skim the trowel over the surface of the wall. 'OK. I'll pop home to change and then I'll head back here.'

'Dinner will be on me, after we've spoken to Madame.'

*

I hear the scrunch of tyres on gravel and look out to see Sam parking up. He isn't driving the van but a beaten-up old Citroën. The pathway to Madame Allard's stone cottage is immaculately swept and there isn't a weed to be seen. As Sam leans forward to raise the lion's head door knocker, I hold the small basket of freshly picked tomatoes in front of me.

'Bonsoir, Madame Allard. Anna vous a apporté un petit cadeau du jardin.'

Sam doesn't sound that comfortable speaking French, although his accent isn't bad.

'Bonsoir Sam, bonsoir Anna.'

She looks a little hesitant, although she seems to be delighted to see us. I present the basket to her and she smiles warmly back at me.

'Pour moi? Vous êtes très gentille, Anna, merci. Entrez, entrez.'

She holds the door open so we can enter. It's dark and very cool inside, but she ushers us on through and out into the back garden. She indicates for us to take a seat underneath a large apple tree.

Sam and Madame Allard exchange a little conversation that I can more or less follow. She's saying we should call her Honorine and I nod and smile so she's aware I understand what's being said.

Sam starts to explain about the jewellery box and I pull it from my handbag to show her. She raises her eyebrows, nodding in acknowledgement of such a fine item. He explains that I'd like to return the box to its rightful owner, if I can locate them. Then he asks her about the initials carved into the top and whether it means anything to her.

I will admit that Sam loses me as they both speak too fast for me to catch more than a few phrases that mean anything at all. He's very gentle and respectful as they converse and it's rather touching.

As Honorine talks she keeps engaging me, as if we are the ones conversing, so she understands that Sam is asking on my behalf. He turns to me to interpret.

'Honorine says that the previous owners were Tony and Yvette Waverley. Tony was English but Yvette came from Lyon. They lived in the house alone together for about six months before a young boy arrived. He was about eight at the time, she thinks. His name was Thomas and people assumed he was a Waverley. He was privately schooled by one of the local teachers and it seems he spent a lot of time with Honorine. She became very fond of him. He told her once that they weren't his parents and that his mother had died. She says he mentioned his mother's surname, but she can't remember it.'

'What happened to them? Did they all move away?'

Sam turns in his chair to face Honorine and continue the conversation. When he turns back there's a frown on his face.

'No, it seems that when Thomas was sixteen he went away. She said he suddenly disappeared, but I don't think she means in a suspicious way, as in the police being involved. A few weeks later the Waverleys moved away, too, and the house was let for a couple of years. When it came up for auction it was a surprise. Her husband bought it because it was cheap. She said he always had an eye for a bargain. It remained empty for a few years before Honorine managed to persuade him to sell it. He tried to convince her to move there but she said nothing was going to make her give up her home of many years. She wasn't at all happy about the idea of cleaning a large, empty house that she didn't want at her age and said he was a silly old fool. Unfortunately, as we know, he died while the sale to your parents was going through.'

'Well, that's something. But it's a little sad. I wonder if the boy was the couple's grandson?'

Sam thanks Honorine and she reaches out to take my hand. Her fingers are chilly, despite the balmy evening, but her eyes are full of warmth.

'A good boy. Kind boy. Sad. They were not loving people. You speak Bastien Deniaud. I had card a few years ago.' She impresses the words upon me, not letting go of my hand.

'I'll try to find him. Thank you, Honorine, every little piece of information is a great help.'

She moves closer, takes both my hands and raises them to her lips. I'm touched and can see that this boy meant something to her.

Don't We All Have At Least One Little Secret?

As Sam and I walk back to his car he turns to look at me, his forehead knotted into a deep frown.

'Why did you say you'd try to find him? He could be anywhere.'

I shrug my shoulders. 'A young boy comes to live in a foreign country with a couple who clearly aren't his parents. And I seriously doubt an adult would hide some valuable jewellery in a hole in the wall. What if the box belonged to his mother? It might be all that he has left of her.'

Sam stops and turns to face me, his eyes searching mine.

'Now that wouldn't even have occurred to me. So, what's the next step?'

'Well, according to Honorine, I need to speak to Monsieur Deniaud, so that's what I intend to do. I chatted to him briefly at the party the other night and he seemed very approachable. And his English is much better than my French.'

'Well, good luck with that. If there's a secret here then maybe it's not a good idea to start digging up the past. If you do find this guy, it might resurrect feelings he's finally managed to distance himself from. No amount of money can compensate for reliving painful memories. Look, I know you're only trying to do what you think is right, Anna, but be wary of getting pulled into something you don't understand and making it worse.'

I can tell from Sam's warning that it's obvious this touches a nerve with him for some reason. Truthfully, I wish I hadn't discovered the box. But I did and my instincts are telling me that it means something to someone and maybe, as time went on, whoever owned it simply forgot where it was hidden.

'Point taken and I'll tread carefully. Now, where are we going for dinner? As I said, it's my treat.'

He smiles, swinging open the passenger door so I can slip into the seat.

'I have just the place in mind. A friend of mine owns a rustic little restaurant overlooking a lake. We'll get a discount, so it won't break the bank.'

Out of the blue, an image of Karl's face appears in my head and I'm whisked back in time to a romantic dinner to celebrate our six month anniversary. Everything was perfect that night. No expense was spared and he made me feel that I was everything to him. Am I blaming Karl for my own insecurities? Was I the one putting up barriers and now I'm trying to put the blame on him for yet another of my failures? I shake off the thought by thinking about Thomas Waverley.

*

Rustic is rather special when your table looks out over a beautiful lake surrounded by tall trees, filtering the ruby red rays of a beautiful sunset. Inside it's like a big log cabin. There's a wood burner in the corner, but today the windows are open wide and overhead fans help to dispel the heat a little.

We both opt for the *prix fixe* menu. With a *petite tarte flambée* to begin, so light and crisp it melts in the mouth. The *moules frites* are accompanied by chunks of crusty baguette to mop up the sauce. The air is filled with the aroma of sweet onions, intermingled with the tang of fresh mussels and a slight smokiness from the white wine which has a hint of oak. I pass on the dessert options but Sam happily tucks into baked peaches with ice cream. It does look good but I'm full.

'That was delicious but I feel bad we didn't pay the full price,' I admit as we wander outside.

'It was payback time, so don't worry about it. *Mates rates*. I do a bit of work for them and it's only money, so I never charge them the full price. Do you fancy a walk along the beach?'

'Yes, that would nice.' I look at Sam, thinking that when he's relaxed he's easy to talk to but when the subject strays onto something personal it's not long before he clams up.

'This is a great little resort,' he offers. 'People stay in cabins dotted around the site and there's plenty for families to do with nature trails, horse-riding and various water sports. They organise a lot of activities in July and August, so it's popular with the locals, as well as tourists.'

'You do a lot of work here?'

He nods. 'Quite a bit.'

I slip off my shoes, letting my toes wriggle around in the sand. A large group of adults are clustered around a barbecue. Within shouting distance, their children are dashing about throwing balls up in the air and taking great delight in kicking up their heels as they run to catch them.

'This area is a wonderful place to live and bring up a family,' I comment, thinking out loud.

We amble back to the car, side by side.

I remember Mum mentioning he'd bought what she described as *a wreck of a barn*. Why is he willing to do work for someone else where he isn't able to charge them the full rate? Sam's quite a conundrum at times.

'Mum said you had your own project you're working on. How's that going?'

He glances my way, but his eyes are back on the road before I can interpret the look.

'It's between here and St-Julien. It's very much a work in progress.'

'So, living here was a part of your plan, too?'

Another fleeting, sideways glance.

'There are worse places to live.'

Ooh, was that telling me to mind my own business, I wonder?

'A lot of British people fantasise about moving to France and renovating a property. The reality is it's a lot of hard work and then there's the problem of how you earn a living. I really hope Mum and Dad can earn enough to keep their dream alive because it would break their hearts to have to head back to the UK.'

Sam doesn't reply and he drives on in silence for a few minutes before suddenly pulling off the road and driving a few hundred feet up a narrow track.

'Welcome to my little piece of France,' he declares, turning to stare at me as I try not to look surprised.

In front of us is a huge stone barn, sitting like a dilapidated blot on the landscape. It's surrounded by a well kept grassy area and there is a tired looking caravan standing alongside.

'This is home.'

It looks nothing at all like a home.

It wasn't quite what I was expecting. Clearly, he lives in the caravan and while the barn has obviously had a new roof, the two wooden doors forming the entrance are so old they're almost falling off the hinges. It's the only opening and there are no windows on this side of it.

'The sheep still come up to the garden wall wondering why they've been evicted.'

I'm almost rendered speechless by the state of this sadly neglected building and can find nothing to say for a moment. The impression I get is that financially Sam lives from day to day. It's going to take him years to make it habitable and it will, no doubt, cost a small fortune.

'It's a lovely setting.' I've broken the silence and he seems pleased.

'At last, someone who doesn't think I'm totally mad. Let me show you around.'

He yanks open one of the barn doors.

'You don't keep it locked?'

He laughs. 'There's nothing to steal.'

The inside is in a much worse state than Mum and Dad's second gîte, which hasn't even been touched yet. If I thought the repointing job I'm doing is big, the task here is huge. The barn still has the original dirt floor and it's just a massive open space right up to the wooden trusses supporting the new roof. But, surprisingly, most of the rear wall has been taken out and I now see why there's no need to lock the door. Sheets of plastic tacked on to wooden strips cover the wide opening. But once you look past the grimy film, what you see is a totally unobstructed view out over fields and beyond that a vast swathe of trees.

'It's beautiful, Sam. This view is absolutely stunning.' Even in the fading light, it has a presence.

'I know it doesn't look much now but it will look great, eventually.'

I'm thinking fifty thousand pounds plus later might make for a rather distant *eventually*. Sam turns on a row of three LED floodlights on a telescopic tripod.

'This is a long term investment. Still, being in the trade makes it a lot less daunting, I suppose.' I'm thinking out loud and then realise that might sound a little negative.

'No, not really; it's still daunting. But when I arrived here I didn't have much money and this was all I could afford. I came here because I'd had a nervous breakdown and before I left the UK I racked up a lot of debt that needed repaying. When you lose everything and completely mess up your life, anything you can hold onto is a bonus. At least I'm not living with my parents and the caravan is adequate. I know you're only here for the summer, but it isn't easy, is it? Once you've had your freedom it feels like a backwards step to go home. With my parents now virtually on my doorstep it's only natural they want to be involved in my life. Parents tend to cling on and feel it's their job to save you from yourself. But I don't need saving as I'm happy enough as I am.'

There's hurt behind those mysteriously deep green eyes of his. I wonder what it is he's running away from, because to me the life he has here makes no sense. Why did he have that breakdown and why did his life suddenly fall apart? He's going to be living in that caravan for a long time to come. And yet it doesn't seem to bother him, as if he has accepted this is all his life has to offer him. He's obviously a guy with a lot of different skills and a sharp mind; to me it seems like a waste, but then ambition is a key motivator for me. Once I've recharged my batteries, I'm going to seize every opportunity that comes my way. When I start my new business, nothing is going to stop me.

'I'm sure it will be a wonderful home once it's finished.'

'Well, if you get a chance to repeat that in earshot of my mother, I'll buy you a drink. She says I've given her more grey hairs than my other two brothers combined! It's frustrating not having the cash to make a real start and the progress is slow. I don't want to borrow any money from anyone, though, as being debt free is important to me. But there's plenty to do to keep me busy and fill all of my spare time. The trouble is the jobs are those which require a lot of effort and don't really alter the look of the place. I'm working on digging out the trenches for the services at the moment.'

As we make our way back out of the barn we share an uneasy smile. I guess we both feel the guilt of being offspring who are a constant worry to our parents.

The Way Forward

When I walk into the kitchen the next morning, both Mum and Dad have already been up a while by the look of it.

'Morning, Anna. Did you have an enjoyable evening with Sam?'

Mum passes me a cup of coffee as I move the plate in front of me to make room on the table. I need a moment to consider my answer, so I take a huge bite of croissant. She's watching me intently, but Dad is too busy reading the newspaper to notice.

'Sam did me a favour and in exchange I said I'd buy him dinner. Besides, he's been a very patient teacher. We went to that little restaurant by the lake and on the way back he showed me his barn.'

Mum shakes her head, sadly.

'This is just between *us*, Anna. His parents fear he'll lose what little money he has and that it will never be finished. They've offered to help fund the work, but he's stubborn and will only go at a pace he can afford. Personally, I think he's rather a lost soul; he works non-stop but a lot of that is helping out other people. I know he needs the money but there are a few small businesses around here he often helps out for free. But spending a couple of hours of his time to fix a water leak in return for a meal isn't helping his own cause. It's all rather sad. I'm only telling you this because you're spending a lot of time with him and you need to be aware of the situation.'

'Aware of what?' I'm not sure where Mum is heading with this.

'I simply mean… Sam's fragile at the moment, Anna. I know it annoys you when people waste their God-given potential, but he has his reasons. It isn't that he lacks motivation but he puts other people first and I'm not sure that's solely about his lack of funds for his own project. What was the favour he did for you?'

Am I quick to judge? I suppose I might be on occasion, although I don't mean to be. I still can't fathom out why Sam is settling for the quiet life, when there are so many other options out there. Maybe he just wants to take things easy and have as few responsibilities as possible, which isn't a crime. But it is a waste when he's obviously capable of so much more.

'We popped in to have a chat with Madame Allard and Sam acted as my interpreter. I thought I'd try to track down the people her husband bought this place from. I had a quick look online and I think that just the ring alone is worth a lot of money, mainly because of the stones. Judging by the style and setting, it's early Victorian.'

'Was Honorine helpful?' Mum asks, clearly interested.

I nod, finishing a mouthful of croissant and homemade strawberry jam.

'Yes. She told us that the previous owners were an Englishman and his French wife. A young English boy came to live with them. He wasn't their son, though. His name was Thomas. She told me to speak to Monsieur Deniaud.'

'Really? Geoff, what do you make of that?'

Dad immediately turns his head and I can see his attention wasn't on the paper in front of him.

'I suppose it can't hurt to ask a question or two, but I can't see what Monsieur Deniaud could add to what Honorine has said. I think you might have to accept defeat on this one, Anna.'

Defeat? Me? Never.

'But what if the boy was the one who hid the jewellery box there? I'm curious about why he would leave behind something valuable and, possibly, of even greater sentimental value.'

With that my phone kicks into life and all three of us stare at it in total shock. I grab it, flicking open the cover and mutter with relief, 'It's Lizzie. Excuse me.'

I get up from the table and walk out through the hallway as I talk.

'Hey, Lizzie. Lovely to hear from you. I've been meaning to call you to thank you for your email.'

'It's good to hear your voice. It feels like you've been gone forever.' There's something in her tone that makes my heart begin to race.

'Are you okay?'

I listen, holding my breath as she clears her throat and I start meandering down the garden, heading for the vegetable patch and a seat under the old oak tree.

'I was until I arrived in the office ten minutes ago. I don't know where to start really and you aren't going to like this. I'm fuming, too.'

I can't recall ever hearing her sound this mad and I don't even try to interrupt her.

'Karl has texted me a few times, asking for an address for you. He said he wanted to send flowers. I ignored him and assumed that eventually he'd give up. I was out showing a customer around a property late yesterday afternoon and I've just been informed by our newest member of staff that while I was gone your tenant called in. He asked for your address as he told her he had some mail to forward on and she fell for it. When she described the guy it was Karl all right. I'm so sorry and if she wasn't still learning the ropes, this wouldn't have happened.

'We simply don't give out any information whatsoever about our clients. I know that sorry is a totally redundant word here and I realise how much trouble this could cause you.'

130

My head flops forward, chin resting on my chest as I let out a deep sigh.

'It's partly my fault. I should have warned you that he's been texting me every day and has sent me a few emails. I almost feel like I'm being stalked, which is crazy considering how devastated I was when he put our relationship on hold. He lied to get the information he wanted, so the only one at fault here is Karl.'

'Well, she's learnt an important lesson the hard way, but if you weren't a friend—'

'But I am.'

'It's kind of you, Anna, and if you'd been angry it would have been more than justified. But Karl, well, he's certainly determined to win you back and he's prepared to do anything to achieve that. Nothing's changed at your end, has it? I sort of thought this might demonstrate that he has always loved you. Isn't that all you really wanted to know? Or is it too late for that, now?'

Now she's gone full circle and once again, Karl is looking like the hero. But he was a villain just a few moments ago.

'I really can't get my head around this change in him, Lizzie. He can't do that to me and then expect me to run back to him because he's sorry for putting his career before *us*. If he'd simply sat down with Robert and explained the situation at the start, this wouldn't have happened. I know how important it was to him and his career. Okay, he would have been away travelling quite a bit, but we could still have moved forward as a couple. And I'd still have a job. Instead, I sacrificed my financial future to guarantee his – he knows that wasn't fair.'

I wish I could see Lizzie's expression to gauge her reaction.

'Well, at least you are aware he has your address and I hope that doesn't cause any problems. How's it going over there?' She poses the question tentatively.

'Great. I'm helping with the renovation work on the first gîte and settling in quite nicely. It's very quiet here and I'm determined to enjoy every moment of this break so I can come back refreshed. I might even opt for selling the house, as when I get back I'm going to set up my own business. I have this idea of targeting people with a smaller budget who need someone to create a brand for them and either set up a new website from scratch, or improve the one they already have. I would offer set packages at fixed rates, so the client is clear about the overall cost.

'One thing I've learnt from this is that I don't want to have a boss in the equation. I thought as a starting point I'd talk Mum and Dad into letting me redesign their promotional materials and website. I'll be setting up my own website, too and hopefully I'll have that all done before I head back to the UK. Then

I really will be able to hit the ground running. All I can say is, watch this space!' Maybe I'm faking my level of optimism here, because up to now this has just been an idea that I've been mulling over in my head. But it's a lifeline and the only option I have at the moment. If I don't latch onto something soon I'll find myself six months down the road and no further forward.

'I will admit that I was a bit worried there for a while. Knowing that you have a plan means I can relax. Daniel told me you'd come back even stronger once you found your feet again.'

That does make me smile and if I can convince Lizzie I'm pulling myself together then maybe I can convince myself, too.

'He's a great guy and you two are so perfect for each other. I am envious, I will admit, but any romantic thoughts that pop into my head in the foreseeable future are going to be very quickly swept aside. Once I've established myself, then and only then, will I ease up.'

'Wow, you really are back on form! Must be all that fresh air, or maybe it's the wine. So, are you actually getting your hands dirty with this renovation work?'

'I'm repointing a wall and when I've finished that I'm going to learn how to tile a floor.'

I hold the phone away from my ear a little as Lizzie bursts out laughing.

'Don't knock it. It's fun and it's giving me plenty of time to think. And that's just what I needed. But first I have a little mystery to solve. I'll tell you all about it when you and Daniel come to stay.'

'Oh, sounds too good to be true. Anyway, I must go as the other phone is ringing. Take care, lovely friend, and watch out for your dreaded stalker!'

What Sort of Boy Touches So Many Hearts?

When I go back inside, I use Lizzie's call as the opportunity to tell Mum and Dad about my plans for the future. It helps to explain away the length of the call and I leave out any reference to Karl, as I don't want them to be concerned. It's probably better to let them think that we've had no contact at all. They are thrilled at my offer to sort out their promotional materials and Dad is clearly relieved, as designing a website from scratch with no previous experience hasn't been easy for him. And, sadly, it shows. His computer skills are good, but limited. Besides, it's something I can do in the evenings to keep my mind occupied and I'll enjoy doing it.

However, I'm shocked when Dad suddenly announces that he has phoned Monsieur Deniaud. We have both been invited to afternoon tea, at four o'clock today.

'Oh, thank you, Dad. Will I need to dress up?'

'It's quite an honour to be invited to the Mayor's house, Anna. And so very kind of Monsieur Deniaud and his wife.' Mum's tone is serious and I take that to mean I should wear a skirt and a top, or maybe a dress.

I make my excuses and head out to join Sam, who has been here a little while by the look of it.

'Sorry I'm late. I had a call from the UK.'

'Problems?'

'No, nothing I can't handle.'

'Good. My heart stopped for a second there, as I thought you were going to say you were heading back home. The timetable to get this finished is rather tight and it's going to need two people to get it done.'

'How long do we have?'

'Three weeks.'

As I mix up the first lot of mortar for today, I look up at him.

'You can count on me and if you think that's long enough to get it done, then I'm sure we can do it.'

He swipes his arm across his forehead, wiping away some little drops of perspiration. Even with the door and windows wide open, it's stuffy in here today.

'Five days in a villa in Cannes is too good to turn down. Jack's family are loaded and it's an offer I can accept without feeling awkward. He owes me a few favours. It isn't just a free holiday, it's also a reunion with a group of friends from my uni days.'

'What did you study?'

Well this is a surprise.

'Architecture at Greenwich University but I dropped out. As I said, I'm the black sheep of the family.'

He comes to an abrupt halt and heads for the door. I'm left with no clues at all about what went wrong.

By the middle of the afternoon I'm sitting cross-legged on the floor on a cushion and making good progress. There are only three rows left to do and as I peer up at the wall above me, I feel a real sense of satisfaction. I'm almost loath to quit for the day but I'm conscious I can't be late for Monsieur le Maire. When I tell Sam about Monsieur Deniaud's invitation, he makes me down tools immediately and says he'll clear up, so obviously it is a big deal.

*

Madame Deniaud ushers us into a large room that looks like a formal study. Two of the walls are lined floor to ceiling with books and it has that distinct smell of aged paper and well-worn leather. Monsieur le Maire rises from behind a huge, dark oak desk and walks towards us. He shakes hands with Dad, patting him on the back and then we air kiss and I turn my cheek three times.

'Bonjour, welcome. Sit, please, sit.'

He nods to his wife, exchanging a smile.

'Merci, ma chère. Nous vous rejoindrons dans le salon en une demi-heure.'

Half an hour? So, this isn't going to be a five minute chat before we have tea, then.

'Monsieur le Maire, it is very kind of you to agree to talk to me. I wish my French was more fluent.'

'Is not a problem. Your father has told me about the find. Can I take a look at it?'

His accent is thick but his words are clear and well formed. I pull the small box from my bag and place it on the desk in front of him. Sam managed to sand down the inside edges of the lid so that it now fits quite snugly.

'Ah, merveilleux! This is old. And valuable. How can I help, Anna?'

Dad leans in to give my hand a reassuring squeeze, as I consider how I'm going to phrase my question.

'Madame Allard told me what little she knew about Tony and Yvette Waverley, who lived at Le Manoir d'Orsenne before Monsieur Allard purchased it at auction. I wondered if you knew whether they went back to the UK and what happened to Thomas, the young boy who came to live with them? Madame Allard said he disappeared, quite suddenly, shortly before they departed.'

Monsieur le Maire is sitting with his elbows on the desk and his fingers locked, resting against his chin. He's a tall man, probably in his sixties with a wiry build. His demeanour and general manner command respect. So much so, that I feel I should weigh up every single word I say, for fear of saying the wrong thing.

'By law whatever is in the property belongs to your parents now.'

This isn't going to be easy and I can tell from his tone and expression that he, like Sam, can't see the dilemma.

'I understand. Do the initials ML mean anything to you?'

Monsieur le Maire's face doesn't give anything away. He considers my question and takes a few moments to respond.

'Such a sad story. Monsieur Waverley originally lived near London, I think. Madame Waverley was Thomas' aunt and she had temporary custody of him. Her maiden name was Laurent. I do not know her late sister's Christian name. When the boy suddenly appeared, some in the village were curious. It was my duty to see that all was well. The Waverleys showed me his passport. He was born in England, where he lived before coming here, and he was a British citizen. The boy was accepting of the arrangement. His mother had died the year before. The couple were very private, but the boy made friends with everyone. He was bilingual, so there was no barrier for him. When he was sixteen his father, he came one day and took him away. Soon after the Waverleys left and the house, it was let out for several years.'

'Do you know if Thomas went back to the UK with his father? Madame Allard said he had a different surname.'

Again, same pose and he's considering his answer, looking at me with a frown creasing his brow.

'Alors,' he sighs. 'Parker-Laurent. I don't think the Waverleys made that common knowledge. The boy loved animals. He wrote to me once, about five years ago, from the École nationale vétérinaire de Toulouse. He asked about Madame Allard and whether she was still alive; he wanted me to let her know that he had achieved his ambition and that he hoped to come back to visit. When he left here with his father he went on to do a two year baccalauréat scientifique before he began his veterinary studies.'

'So, he's a vet and if he studied at Toulouse he may even be working in France now. I am so very grateful to you for trusting me with this information. It's not my intention to pry; but if, as now seems likely, this could have been given to Thomas by his mother, I will try my best to track him down.'

Monsieur le Maire nods his head and stands.

'My wife she waits and so does the delicious gâteau she has made for us. Come.'

*

After dinner I retire early, keen to get my laptop set up in the bedroom. I want to start gathering ideas for Mum and Dad's new-look branding. It will mean taking lots of new photos of the house and gardens, as the ones currently in use are already out of date.

The first thing I do on my return is to Google Thomas Parker-Laurent, but all that comes up is a stream of entries relating to Thomas Parker, which seems to be quite a popular name. Searching for Thomas Laurent merely throws up pages of entries about a famous racing driver. Realising that I'm going to have to look elsewhere for clues, I check my inbox and my heart sinks when I see there is yet another email from Karl. I'm half tempted to delete it, but my finger hesitates for a second and I instinctively end up clicking on it. I recoil in horror as I begin reading.

Dear Anna,

I know you are angry but after a year of being together you owe me a chance to explain. All I'm asking is that you call me and listen to what I have to say. I can change; I will change. Please don't make me fly over and turn up on your doorstep uninvited, because that's what I'll have to do if you keep ignoring me. And I know that will make you even angrier.

Please give me one more chance, that's all I'm asking.

Karl x

My jaw drops. What on earth would I do if I opened the door to find Karl standing there? I close my inbox with shaking fingers, as if simply reading the words will make him suddenly materialise. Now is not the time to be thinking about him. I don't want to spend the night tossing and turning with Karl in my head as I need to be up early and ready for a full day's work.

Damn Karl. Why can't he just leave me alone? Is this merely a fit of pique, wanting what he suddenly feels he can't have? If that's the case, then this is still all about him and nothing really to do with *us*. If there ever was an "us". But this also sounds ominously like a threat and I don't want my quiet life here disturbed in any way. I hear a rather lonely 'meow' as Ziggy jumps up onto the bed. Suddenly it's easy to push all my worries away and the last thing I remember before falling asleep is stroking her back and the loudest purring I've ever heard.

Sending a Message

The next morning, I take my croissant and coffee up to my bedroom, on the pretext that I have a few promotional ideas I want to get typed up before I head out to the gîte. It's partly true, but I know at some point Mum will sense something is worrying me and, right at this moment, I'm too angry to talk about it. I feel that Karl's behaviour is a little threatening and I'm not happy that he's trying to force his way back into my life.

When I'm ready to start work I manage to slip downstairs unnoticed. I'm quite content to sit on the squishy old cushion, muttering away to myself under my breath. When Sam arrives he's just as subdued and instead of our usual opening banter we simply exchange a brief 'good morning'. It isn't until lunch time that my mood lightens. I head into the kitchen to collect the sandwiches Mum prepared for us before Dad took her off to the Friday market. It makes me smile, as she's left everything laid out on a tray covered in a white linen tea towel. I'm so lucky that they are both fit enough to enjoy this time in their lives. When many choose to begin slowing down, they seem to be speeding up. I simply can't imagine how devastating it must be to lose your mother at a young age, as poor Thomas did. I make my way to the secret garden to join Sam, picturing a lonely young boy being handed the only link he has left to his mother.

Sam takes the tray from me, places it on the table and then sits back in his chair with a low groan. I watch as he eases his shoulders back, stretching out his right arm and rotating his shoulder.

'Muscular problems?'

He grimaces.

'Nothing serious. I need to get a new mattress really. There just doesn't seem much point in spending money on the caravan, though.'

I'm tempted to point out that he won't be moving into the barn any time soon, but that would be stating the obvious. He's such a nice guy but Mum is right and he does seem as if he's lost his way when it comes to sorting out his life. And yet when he's working, he's focused and happy. Why didn't he choose an easier project, something he could do up and sell on to make a profit? He's a mystery, that's for sure.

'Your mum is a star. I did tell her she doesn't have to feed me every day but she wouldn't listen.'

I uncover the plates and pass one to Sam.

'You've been good to them. Do you miss working alongside your dad?'

A third of Sam's sandwich disappears in one bite and I wait patiently as he chews his way through the food.

'In a way, as we work well together and I can do most of the labouring for him. There are a few guys he employs as and when he needs them on a job, but the language is sometimes a bit of a barrier. And he likes things done his way. He's old school. He'd be horrified if he saw you working out there with a plastic knife and a tin lid. But when he sees the quality of your work, he'll be impressed. I guess we all like to think there's only one correct way to do something, when often that isn't true at all. Anyway, the first gîte should be finished by the beginning of July and then that just leaves the second gîte before my work here is done. I made a promise to your parents and I intend to keep it. Are you still enjoying it, or is it turning into a bit of a nightmare? After all, you did say this was a working holiday and yet you don't seem to be in a holiday mood, at all.'

I guess my demeanour this morning warrants that comment.

'I'm fine with it, really. I'm a workaholic by nature and I like to be busy. I had some bad news last night and it's playing on my mind a little this morning.'

Sam finishes off his first sandwich and sits back, looking concerned and waiting for me to explain.

'My ex is threatening to turn up on the doorstep.'

His eyes narrow a little. 'Is this some form of intimidation?' His tone has changed and that laid back air of his has completely disappeared.

I need to get myself out of this quickly.

'No. It's fine, really. I wasn't implying that I'm scared, but... it's over between us and he's having difficulty accepting that. I can't imagine for one moment that he would suddenly turn up, as he's just been promoted. He wouldn't be able to drop everything just like that, even if he wanted to. I'm sure it will all be fine. It was a bit of a shock when I read his email, that's all.'

'People say stupid things when a situation gets out of hand. Look, if you ever need someone to intervene on your behalf, you only need to say. I'm sure he's an intelligent guy and it wouldn't take much to make him see the error of his ways. Intimidating someone isn't the answer to anything.'

It's a bit of a surprise to hear Sam taking this very seriously, considering he's only known me for a few weeks.

'Thank you, but I don't need any help. I intend to spell it out to him today.'

'I wasn't trying to undermine your ability to handle this, Anna. Don't think that for a moment, but sometimes it's quicker and easier if a third party steps in. The offer stands; you only have to say if you need my help.'

I feel uncomfortable and desperate to talk about other things. A sudden movement makes both of our heads turn and Ziggy skips down the path. Her cinnamon coloured coat sparkles with tips of gold as the sun catches it. Suddenly she jumps about a foot in the air, as if she's been stung, but then bats her paws at a large bumble bee in front of her. She misses, thankfully, and immediately continues on her way as if nothing has happened, even though the hunter has lost her prey. Fleetingly, I wonder if that sums up the life of a cat. They don't carry baggage around with them like humans tend to; dragging the failures in our lives around with us like badges of defeat is like wearing a millstone round our necks. Cats just accept that you can't win every battle and move on. Diplomatically, I decide to change the subject.

'Monsieur le Maire was very understanding yesterday.'

Sam picks up another sandwich and looks at me with interest, his mood instantly changing.

'He had some answers?'

'Well, he was able to tell me that Thomas is now a qualified vet, having studied at Toulouse. His mother was French and his father lived in London. As Honorine mentioned, Thomas' mother died before the boy was sent here. Monsieur le Maire confirmed that the Waverleys had custody of him. Yvette was his aunt. And he confirmed that Yvette's maiden name was Laurent.

'He said that people here were naturally a little suspicious when the boy turned up quite unexpectedly. He satisfied himself that everything was above board. He told me that the boy's surname was actually Parker-Laurent as he had been shown his passport. It seemed the locals simply assumed his surname was Waverley. I wonder if his aunt wanted people to believe Thomas actually was their son? He didn't know the mother's Christian name, but it's looking increasingly likely that the *ML* ties it back to her.'

Sam nods, as he continues eating.

'Thomas made contact about five years ago, after he'd qualified and he wrote to Monsieur Le Maire, asking him to pass on a message to Honorine. When she was talking about Thomas it was so touching to see that she felt such an attachment to him.'

'It seems he settled into the village well, then.'

I'm barely listening, reflecting on the fact that Laurent is quite a common name, though, so it isn't going to be easy. Not knowing his mother's Christian name is going to make the search a lot more difficult.

'Hey,' Sam interrupts my chain of thought, 'Honorine said he was schooled at home. Do you want me to pop in and ask if she can remember the name of his teacher?'

'What a good idea. I'd totally forgotten about that. Anyway, thanks Sam, that would be great if you don't mind, as while Monsieur le Maire was helpful I felt there was information he didn't feel at liberty to share.'

'No problem. I'll pop in after work. I'm going to start putting up the studding for the partitions next, so I won't need your help until that's done.'

'I can't imagine what it's going to look like divided up into rooms. I quite like the sense of open space, even though I realise that would be impractical.'

I watch as he puts his plate back on the tray and I notice how strong his hands are and yet there's a gentleness to him. That's partly why his reaction to what I said about Karl was so surprising.

'In the barn I'm going to have the downstairs as open plan as possible. There will be a cloakroom on the ground floor, but the kitchen and living area will be one big space. On the first floor, there will be two bedrooms with en-suite bathrooms. Well, that's the long term plan, anyway.'

A moment of sadness washes over me. His dream is well beyond his reach in terms of both time and money at the moment. It's too much for one person when he also has to earn a living. If he could afford to hire a digger, I'm sure those trenches he's working on could be dug out in a weekend. That would really get his project moving forward. He gives me an ironic smile.

'We need to get back to work.'

'Yes, I'll just take the tray up to the house and I'll join you.'

He heads off and I follow a few paces behind. The sun is hot overhead, but it's partly cloudy today and there is a slight chill in the air when the sun fleetingly disappears. I wonder if Sam minds working inside at this time of the year because it's much pleasanter outside when it's cooler.

None of the guests are around, so I slip into the kitchen and pop the tray down next to the sink. Turning on my heels, I hear a knock on the door and redirect my footsteps in the direction of the hallway. Surely Karl wouldn't just—?

'Bonjour! Des fleurs pour Mademoiselle Lacey?'

'Oui, merci.'

I reluctantly take the large bouquet of roses the woman is holding out to me, while trying my best to raise a pleasant smile. My mouth is suddenly very dry. I walk back into the kitchen, laying them down on the table so I can rip open the small, white envelope. It carries the logo of *Erbray Eternelle, Fleuriste.*

You are in my thoughts, always. Please forgive me.
Karl x

I take a moment to pull myself together, then search around for some scissors. I chop the flowers up roughly, making a quick trip down to the composting pile. When I return to clear up the debris I rip the card into bits, dropping them in the bin on my way out to join Sam. Suddenly his offer of help doesn't seem quite so unnecessary. If I was here alone today it would play on my mind about what I'd do if Karl turned up. I know that I can't just continue to ignore this and before too long I'm going to have to talk to him.

Realisation Dawns

I can see that Mum isn't happy that I'm trying to rush through dinner, but even though I disposed of the flowers I still feel unsettled. The sooner I'm head down, working on the laptop the better, as keeping busy is the only way to keep my thoughts at bay.

'Darling, you really do need to learn to relax a little. You can't spend every minute of your life working on something or other. It's not healthy. I nearly forgot, Dad has a little something for you.'

Dad has just walked into the room and he looks across at Mum, questioningly.

'It's Friday, Geoff.'

Dad's eyes light up. 'Ah, yes. Pay day.' He sifts through a pile of paperwork Mum left on the counter top earlier. 'Here it is, your first pay cheque.'

He walks towards me with two envelopes in his hand.

'One for you and the other is for Sam. Are you seeing him over the weekend? Viv usually sorts this before he leaves for the day. I feel bad because we were back later than we planned and missed him.'

'I wasn't expecting to, but I could pop in to see him tomorrow. He was going to call in to ask Honorine a question for me on his way home. I'd like to know if he discovered any more about Thomas so I can plan my next move.'

'You're not giving up on that, then?' Judging by his tone, Dad thinks I'm wasting my time.

'No.' I tear open the envelope and then look up at Mum, then across at Dad. 'I can't take this, guys. I'm working here because I want to and I'm living free of charge. That's payment enough.'

'Now we don't want you making a fuss, Anna: it won't break the bank. If you weren't helping Sam out then we'd be paying one of his builder friends. It's a tax write-off and a legitimate business expense.'

Mum has her serious head on and Dad nods in agreement.

'It feels wrong. You have both done so much for me over the years and I like to think that finally I can do something in return. And I know things are still tight at the moment.'

Mum takes the seat opposite me at the table and extends her hand to cover mine.

'We love you so much, my darling, so please let us do this our way. We can see how hard you are working and that touches our hearts, because you understand that this is our dream. But eventually all of this will be yours.'

A cold sensation hits the pit of my stomach.

'Please don't talk like that, Mum. It sends a shiver through me.'

She smiles, her eyes full of love and pride. 'I understand, but if you should decide to make this your home too, nothing would please us more. No pressure as we understand that this life might be a little too quiet for you. But it's something we felt needed to be said, just in case.'

'I can't stay forever, Mum. I have big plans but one day, who knows?'

We both know that I'm trying so very hard to be positive about the future because the reality is that I'm starting all over again. If I can't make it work then knowing I can come back here is a comfort but we both realise that would mean my efforts had failed. Not that I'm undermining the wonderful job they've done in creating their new business here, but I need my independence.

The silence is heavy and I swallow the lump that has risen in my throat, then quickly change the subject.

'Are you still happy for Lizzie and Daniel to be the first guests in the gîte? Sam says it'll take about three weeks to get everything finished.'

Mum and Dad seem relieved that the awkward moment has passed.

'Of course, they'd be welcome to come and stay to try it out. They can give us feedback before the paying guests arrive. Seems we need to be thinking about sorting the furniture very quickly, Viv. And maybe we should start contacting the people on our waiting list, now we have a completion date. It will be good to get firm bookings in the diary, at last.'

'Thanks, guys. It will be nice to have some time with Lizzie, although I think she'll be keen to show Daniel everything that's within a day's drive. What date is the first Saturday in July?'

Mum goes to fetch the bookings diary and I make a mental note to set her up with an online version. She leafs through the pages.

'It's the first. I'm so glad you're here to help Sam, as he would have hated heading off to Cannes if it wasn't all finished.'

'When's he due to leave?'

'I have it marked down as Monday the tenth of July. You should take a week off, too. It will be a nice break before he gets back and work starts on the second gîte.' Mum looks at me, pointedly.

'Maybe. I'll think about it.'

Mum and Dad exchange glances and I pretend not to notice.

*

Tonight, the first job on my action list is an email that's extremely hard to write. I sit in front of the blank screen for quite a while before my fingers finally begin to move around the keyboard.

Hi Karl

I've had a lot of time to think about what happened between us and my reaction now makes a little more sense to me. This isn't about how you feel, but about me not facing up to how I feel.

That's not what you want to hear, but it's the truth.

Maybe when I return in six months' time our paths will cross again, who knows? But I don't want you to put your life on hold for me, because as it stands we are over. I've let you go and now you need to accept that fact.

You can't make someone love you, just because you think you are in love with them. That's a lesson I learnt a long time ago.

What I'm asking is that you respect my honesty and privacy. It's time you began to move on with your own life, as it's way too short to waste it trying to fix something that's broken beyond repair. You once said to me that success was all about knowing when to give up on a bad idea and begin looking in a new direction. That's what I've done and now you need to do that, too.

Take care, Anna.

The deed is well and truly done. I press send and as it disappears so does a lot of my anxiety. Only a loser, or a maniac, would ignore that message and Karl is neither of those things. Maybe I should have sent that email a lot sooner, but it's taken a while to get to the root of my problem and accept that my hesitancy wasn't just about Karl's blasé attitude.

Now, as I work on redesigning Le Manoir d'Orsenne's website, my head is full of ideas for my own new business. Suddenly, any mental barriers have finally been broken down and the future is starting to excite me once more. I hear a scratching at my bedroom door and on opening it, Ziggy flounces in and jumps straight up onto the bed leaving little room for my legs. But it's a comfort having her with me and I don't care if that means having to sit with my legs bent awkwardly. I feel calmer and more at peace whenever she's around me, so it's a small price to pay.

Before I go to sleep, I email Lizzie, as if she and Daniel can't make that week in July I will be so disappointed. I miss the buzz of having friends around me and I even, sort of, miss the working environment. There was always something happening at home, whether it was a party, a concert or just the day to day general interactions in the office. Then I realise that what I also miss is the gossip and that's something I find surprising. Ziggy twitches in her sleep, her whiskers moving vigorously, as she's no doubt chasing something in her dream.

When I finally lie down and turn off the light a feeling of blissful tranquillity settles over me. Soon sleep begins to weave her veil around my thoughts, shutting them down. A feeling of well-being consumes me as if a line has been drawn and I'm now free to move forward.

Settling for Tranquillity

Turning up at the barn unannounced, I'm not sure what Sam's reaction will be.

'Morning. This is a nice surprise.'

Sam saunters towards me as I slam the car door shut and greets me, French style.

'Mum felt bad they were too late back yesterday to give you your cheque.'

He takes the envelope I hold out to him and nods gratefully.

'You needn't have driven over, but it's kind of you. Now you're here do you have time for a coffee?'

'I don't want to hinder you if you're working.'

He's dressed in his usual work wear of old jeans and a faded t-shirt splattered with everything from paint to cement.

'I'm always working, but weekends it's at a slower pace as I'm limited by what I can afford to buy. Anyway, I need the caffeine.'

His smile is warm and I can tell he's pleased to see me. I wonder if he ever feels lonely and isolated at weekends with few people of his own age to mix with. There's only so much time you can spend with your parents and their friends. It's not like there's a venue close by where he can go to see his favourite band, or dance the night away after a beer or two with his mates. Although I suspect there may be a few local guys he can share the odd pint with on occasion. He mentioned working alongside a couple of guys from the village when his dad has a big project on the go.

'Come inside, it won't take a moment.'

The inside of the caravan's not quite as bad as I'd feared at first glance. If you can ignore the seventies curtains, which could almost pass for fashionably retro. I start laughing and he turns on his heels, mugs in hand, to look at me in surprise.

'What's so funny?' He's amused by my amusement.

'You could probably sell these curtains on eBay to an avid seventies collector. Orange circles and brown squares aren't actually too bad when they're… nicely faded. Vintage is all the rage these days.'

That makes him chuckle out loud.

'Sugar?'

'No thanks. This is rather nice – *you* making *me* coffee for a change.'

'I guess I do owe you a few cups. Shall we take it out to the barn?'

'Good idea. The view's stunning from there.'

He picks up both mugs and I follow him outside. As soon as I'm safely down the rickety wooden steps he hands me a mug.

'Thanks. You can talk me through your plans. Last time I was here it was rather late in the day and everything looks different in the sunshine.'

He glances sideways at me, as if surprised by my interest. I can understand that he's cautious, after all, we aren't friends as such. Just two people working together for a short period of time. It's not as if we singled each other out in a crowd. I fleetingly wonder if that could have been the case, though? Maybe in a different time and a different place. Although these days I don't really recognise myself anymore; I'm changing and that fiercely independent, over-achiever is mellowing. I don't know if that's a good thing, or not.

'Sorry, I'm not used to anyone showing any real interest.'

'How many people have you invited out here?'

He laughs. 'Erm, I guess that could be the reason, then.'

The double doors to the barn are open wide and I can see that Sam has shifted a whole stack of oak floorboards he's recycling. There's a long piece of partly sanded timber supported at each end by heavy duty sawhorses.

'This is a good sized space; not so big that you feel overwhelmed but not so small that it will disappoint when it's finished. It's going to have the wow factor, isn't it?'

'That's the idea. I'm going to partition this end off and there will be a cloakroom, a utility room and a large pantry. It will come to about here.' He marks a line on the dusty floor with the heel of his boot. 'The rest will be open plan living, with the kitchen units and integrated appliances housed on this back wall. Above this area will be two bedrooms, each with an en-suite bathroom.'

'That view is going to be stunning from the bedrooms, looking out over the fields and the tops of the trees. It's going to be something very special, Sam.'

He seems pleased that I can appreciate his vision.

'Both bedrooms will have vaulted ceilings to give an added feeling of space and it's going to have a contemporary feel. The furniture will be minimal and the windows won't have anything at all to obscure them. The glass will be tinted to act as a filter to prevent glare from the sun and also reduce the amount of heat build-up. The idea is to use materials that are energy efficient and keep running costs down.'

'How wonderful to wake up each morning to be greeted by nothing but green fields and the odd sheep, or rabbit, who happens to be passing by.'

We stand, coffee mugs clasped in our hands, looking out at the field beyond the boundary wall. It's a little piece of heaven; a place where you can pretend that no one else exists, because all there is as far as the eye can see is nature at its best. Apologies to the sheep who are too busy grazing to notice us, but I'm talking about humans here, the beings who make life complicated and screw things up.

'It's a good investment. What's your timeframe for completion?'

I take a swallow of coffee, peering at Sam over the top of the mug. He doesn't take his eyes off me.

'Now that's where you and I are very different. It will take as long as it takes.'

His tone is slightly defensive.

'But you must have some idea. Months, years—?'

'Why?'

I'm beginning to wish I hadn't asked the question.

'Okay, are you likely to still be living in the caravan in five years' time?'

Now I'm beginning to lose my patience. If this is how he reacts to some friendly interest in his project, then I can see why he isn't keen to ask people around.

'You've missed the point. Living here means choosing a different lifestyle. There is no big life plan as I don't think like that anymore. It's not an "investment" because this is where I'm going to be spending the rest of my days. I'm happy enough in the caravan and if I started setting myself targets it would turn this into work, not pleasure.'

I listen to what he's saying, but I can't comprehend his attitude.

'Now that sounds a little crazy to me, as clearly you know exactly what you want to achieve here. When you're doing the day job you have no problem setting yourself deadlines. Without a plan of action days will turn into weeks and months into years. Aren't you worried you'll end up wasting some of the best years of your life? The years when you are supposed to be setting things up for a better future for yourself?'

He looks down at the floor, feigning a sudden interest in the layer of dust beneath his feet.

'You can't understand because you're ambitious and you want more. More than you have right now. I already have everything I want, so why should I stress myself out working harder to earn the money to speed up the process? Can't you see that's a vicious circle? We get trapped into believing we need more and more and more. The truth is that we need a lot less than we think. I could up my hourly rate and stop doing favours for people but that's not the way I operate.'

He makes it all sound so simple, but life is anything but in my experience. It's wonderful to do a good deed and help someone out but it's almost like he regards this as a penance. Who could he have possibly hurt so badly that he feels he can't put his own needs first at times?

'You're either a genius or a man destined for disappointment and I can't make my mind up which, at this precise moment. All I know is that settling for so little could never be a life I would choose and yet, despite what you might think, I don't regard myself as obsessively materialistic. Yes, I want a nicer house and money in the bank as a measure of security for the future, who doesn't? I see that as the minimum to aim for, rather than an unnecessarily ambitious goal. But for me it's also about the satisfaction of rising to a challenge; succeeding at something that makes me grow. Achievement isn't a dirty word, Sam, and whether you like it or not, your project will be just that. The fact that you're not doing it to make money is your conscious decision.'

I think my honesty has shocked him a little. We continue to stare at each other in silence for a few seconds.

'Let's have this conversation again in thirty years. Make a note of it in your diary. I know I'm not a genius and I hope I'm not destined for disappointment. Only time will tell.'

He smiles at me, his eyes crinkling up and his face relaxed. My words haven't upset him and I'm relieved, as that wasn't my intention. Without knowing his past it's impossible to know why he dropped out of university, or what triggered this major re-think of his life. At some point it seems that he had a plan and it's abundantly clear he has a passion for architecture and design. I wonder where it all began to go wrong for him?

'Did you manage to talk to Honorine?'

He raises his eyebrows. 'Smart move; that conversation was going nowhere fast. Yes, I did. She gave me the name of Thomas' teacher but unfortunately she now lives in Rennes. Honorine thinks she also knew Thomas' mother. I made a few notes and they're in the car.'

I perk up, after starting to feel rather down about a conversation that was getting a little out of hand. Although I don't think I was judging Sam any more than he was judging me.

'Oh, great, thank you. And as for the other matter I think we are going to have to agree to disagree on that one.'

He reaches out to take the empty mug from my hands. 'Spoken like a true diplomat. You should be in politics. Now let's get that address and you can decide what your next move is going to be. That's another skill you can add to your list – budding detective.'

Now he's getting his own back and I can't say I blame him. It's not as if my life is a shining example of how to achieve true happiness, is it?

'Look, if you want to talk to this lady then I'm happy to interpret. It's probably just over an hour's drive and I could take you there tomorrow if you fancy a trip out.'

It's a very kind offer and I realise that no matter what our differences, we respect each other's choices.

'That would be great, thank you, Sam. I'd be delighted to take you up on that offer.'

An Afternoon of Discovery

As we head towards Rennes, where Thomas' teacher now lives, Sam brings me up to speed on what Honorine was able to tell him.

'Elise Moreau taught English at the local school and Honorine believes that she knew Thomas' mother well. Why she thought that, though, was rather vague. Her memory wasn't very clear but she repeated it several times. Elise moved away the year before last and I thought at first this was going to be a dead end. But then Honorine rang Inès Gaubert.'

'The baker's wife I met at the party?'

He nods. 'Claude's wife. She runs the little épicerie next door to the bakery and she knows everyone and everything that goes on in the village.'

I bet she doesn't know much about Sam.

'And Inès knew Elise's address? Does that mean they kept in touch?'

Sam shakes his head. 'They are cousins, apparently, and she sends her a card every Christmas. You might want to speak to her yourself, at some point. I'm sure she'd be delighted to tell you what she knows.'

I wonder if I should have done that anyway to save the trip but Sam seems happy enough to be involved and it's a lovely day for a ride out.

'Well, thanks for gathering the information and let's hope this lady is at home and is receptive when she's faced with two strangers.'

'She's bi-lingual, so that's half the battle and Honorine was our contact, so we can mention her name. This seems to have really touched her heart and I think if you can return the jewellery box to Thomas it will mean a lot to her. She is eager for further news that he's settled and happy.'

We're cruising along a straight road that seems to go on forever and I can't believe how relaxed I feel. Sam is good company and our frank exchange of yesterday hasn't left any ill-feeling between us.

'That's good to hear and I hope at the end of this search we can perhaps reunite them. I wonder why he has never come back to the village, even just to see Honorine?'

Sam shrugs, not taking his eyes off the road ahead.

'Too many mixed memories, maybe. It's funny, but I've never had much to do with Honorine and yet, over the course of the last few days she's come to feel very comfortable around me.'

He seems pleasantly surprised by this and I wonder why. You have to make time to get to know people, or they will always be strangers to you. Obviously, living here, he doesn't really have an active social life and maybe you don't notice when your little world begins to shrink. He interacts when he's at work and with his parents, but then he goes home to his little plot of land in the middle of fields and forest with only the animals for company.

'Your mind is whirring again, I can almost hear it. Is this an ominous silence?'

I smile to myself. 'No, just surprised that you don't feel isolated out here at times.'

He turns his head to look at me for a brief second.

'You have to stop analysing everything all the time and treating what happens as if it's a part of a puzzle that needs solving. I like my life just the way it is, Anna.'

It's a reprimand and I realise I was thinking aloud and that was wrong of me. Some things are better off left unsaid.

'Sorry, that slipped out without thinking.'

'Well, as we're being personal can I ask about this ex of yours? Has he gone quiet now?'

Oh, I guess I can't really dodge this one and I know he's trying to make a point here.

'Yes. I think it's finally sinking in that I've moved on. Although in practice he was the one who put our relationship on hold.'

I have a feeling Sam isn't going to settle for that as an explanation and I'm right.

'Why would he do that?'

I run my left hand through my hair, tucking a few strands behind my ear – a sure sign that I'm uncomfortable. But Sam could be the sounding board I need. Even Lizzie isn't impartial, as Karl charmed her from the moment I introduced them. And Mum and Dad, well, will anyone ever be good enough for their only daughter?

'It's a long story.'

'You have my undivided attention. I'm a captive audience for the next hour at least.'

I sigh, leaning my head against the window as I continue to stare straight ahead. I don't want to get emotional and yet, even now, it still hurts to acknowledge that for the second time in my life I made myself so stupidly vulnerable.

'Karl says he loves me and yet his career always comes first. He was my boss and we had to lie about our relationship as I was a member of his team. Contractually that wasn't allowed. So even when we began seeing each other it was never going to be a normal sort of relationship. In private we became very close but it didn't seem real somehow, having to conduct our relationship behind closed doors. At work, we were dynamic together; people could see that and then the rumours started to circulate.'

'Couldn't you just have owned up to it and maybe worked with another team, instead?'

I sigh, emptying my lungs and feeling as deflated physically as I do mentally about the situation.

'Karl is no fool. He needed someone with sound organisational skills who would help pull his team together. There are times when he can be difficult to work with, prone to losing his temper if things go wrong. He's charming when he wants to be but he has a tendency to talk to management very differently than he does to his staff. He used me to get where he wanted to be: in control of a team that was the envy of the organisation because we pulled together and he succeeded. He was given a big promotion and I was asked to step up and be his deputy.'

Sam frowns, but he doesn't reply.

'The question came up about the company's *no fraternisation* policy. He denied any personal connection whatsoever between us as if our relationship meant nothing at all to him. I blurted it out and ended up resigning. He told his boss he was simply protecting me. Afterwards he said we could pick back up where we left off at a later date.'

Sam emits a scandalised, 'Huh! Unbelievable! No wonder you walked away.'

'At first it hurt, then I realised that I'd been fooling myself from day one. Karl is charming and his commitment is an inspiration, but his focus never wavers and work is always number one on his agenda.'

'I hate to say this, but that's sort of how I perceive you.'

Well, that feels like a bit of a slap in the face! Sam pulls the car into a lay-by, turning off the engine. He reaches onto the back seat to get a couple of bottles of water.

'Here you go.' I take the bottle and he grabs his phone. 'I'll check the satnav quickly before we go any further as I'm not sure where we need to turn off. I wasn't trying to be offensive with that remark, but it's true. You come across as being very focused and knowing exactly where you are going and what you want to achieve in life. What I can't understand is how you could get yourself into that sort of situation in the first place. It doesn't seem to make any sense.'

I gulp and it isn't just to ease the water down my now dry throat.

'I was confused.'

He looks at me and raises both eyebrows in surprise. 'You were confused? About what? The motives of a man who doesn't want the world to know he's in love with you?'

'Now who's the one analysing every little thing? You don't understand the situation we were in and Karl is a man who is going somewhere. It was a

173

sacrifice for *us*. I thought I wanted to settle down and now I find that isn't the case at all. It was a momentary aberration.'

He smiles, but I can tell he is suppressing a laugh. 'Ah, tall, dark and handsome, was he?'

I'm so furious with him that I open the door and climb out, walking around to the rear of the car. He makes no attempt to follow and when curiosity gets the better of me I peer inside and see he's still looking at the satnav on his phone. I wait for a few minutes until I'm more composed before sliding back into the passenger seat.

'Second turning on the right and then it's only about two kilometres from that point. Are we ready to go?'

He acts as if nothing has happened and I go along with it for the sake of keeping the peace. I don't know what I was expecting anyway, as Sam isn't someone whose judgement I'd trust because, let's face it, I hardly know him. And it's becoming abundantly clear that he finds my lifestyle choices almost as bizarre as I find his.

We end up driving around in circles for a while before we realise we've passed the house several times. It turns out to be a cottage in the grounds of a church. As Sam pulls into the car park there are quite a few people milling around and it's obvious there has been some sort of service or celebration going on in the church.

There is a gate set into the car park wall and beyond that a path that leads up to the cottage. It's very pretty and very old. As we're walking along in single file, a voice calls out from behind us.

'Bonjour. Puis-je vous aider?'

We turn and the older woman who is walking towards us has a pleasant smile on her face.

'Bonjour, Madame. Sam Callaghan et Anna Lacey. Nous recherchons Elise Moreau.'

She stares at Sam in surprise, before glancing in my direction.

'Ah, English. I am Elise Moreau. How can I be of help?'

Sam indicates for me to take over the conversation.

'We have come from Saint-Julien-de-Vouvantes. My parents now own Le Manoir d'Orsenne, Madame Honorine Allard told us that you used to teach Thomas Parker-Laurent. We are trying to trace him, so we can return what we believe to be some jewellery belonging to his late mother.'

Her smile disappears for a moment as if she's recalling some memory from the past that invokes sadness. Then she nods and walks ahead of us in the direction of the front door, indicating for us to follow her. The house is very comfortably furnished with dark wooden furniture which has that wonderful patina only age can lend it. The pieces have probably been handed down from generation to generation. The general décor though is light and bright, giving the old stone cottage a warm feel.

We follow Elise into the kitchen and she pulls out two heavy, rustic chairs from around a long, dark oak table.

'Please, sit. I'm sorry but I have only a few minutes. Today is a special celebration and there is a party. I came away only to fetch the cake. It has been quite a few years since I last saw Thomas so I'm not sure how I can be of help.'

Sam and I exchange a brief glance of disappointment, but if we can obtain any information at all about Thomas' story that will make this trip worthwhile.

'Honorine said that you knew Thomas' mother well? I wonder if you have ever seen this before?'

I pull the jewellery box out of my handbag and as Elise reaches out to touch it a brief 'Ahh—' escapes her lips.

'Yes, it was given to Thomas after his mother died. Where did you find it? It was the boy's treasure and he must miss it so. That and a few photos were all he had to remind himself of her.'

She doesn't open the box but holds it within her hands, as if it's a delicate object and not a sturdy wooden box.

'My parents have recently renovated Le Manoir d'Orsenne and we found this hidden in a stone wall in one of the outbuildings. All we know is that since leaving the village, Thomas studied at Toulouse and is now a vet. His story is an unusual one and we would be grateful for anything at all you can tell us that might help us discover his whereabouts.'

Elise places the box on the table and lowers herself onto the chair next to me.

'Such a sad story. Michelle Laurent, Thomas' mother, and I grew up in Lyon. We went to school together and remained good friends, even when our paths went in different directions. I met my husband and we moved to Saint-Julien-de-Vouvantes shortly after we were married. Michelle was in London at that time and had just become engaged to Richard Parker. Her life was a whirlwind and so very different to the life she'd had before. She was so happy when she found out she was having a son but after Thomas was born she wrote to me to say she longed to come home. As Richard's business interests grew she was not happy and she complained he was always working. She longed for her son to have the sort of childhood she'd had.'

Elise lowers her head for a moment and as I look across at Sam he shakes his head to discourage me from speaking.

'People assumed having a big house in London and a successful husband to provide for her meant she was happy. But in her heart, she longed for her son to be brought up in France. Thomas was six years old when she was diagnosed with breast cancer. She had treatment and was constantly back and forth to hospital. I think by then she knew it was a battle she wasn't going to win and that she was not long for this world. But it wasn't until the very end of her illness that she told Richard of her wishes.'

Hearing this, and the catch in her voice as she talks, makes me think of that small boy and the way his life changed virtually overnight.

'Is that why his aunt and uncle moved to Le Manoir d'Orsenne?'

'Yes,' Elise nods in confirmation. 'Richard was intent on honouring his wife's wishes, even in his grief. I have no doubt he would have preferred to keep his son by his side. But he knew that was not practical. He was away on business frequently and I can imagine that the house no longer felt like a home without Michelle's presence. When he contacted me, of course I agreed to help him. Michelle's sister, Yvette, and her husband, Tony, said they would look after Thomas, and Richard purchased the house for them. I was teaching at the local school and it was very convenient. The arrangement was that I would school him at home and keep Richard updated on his progress and well-being. However, Yvette became a very jealous and bitter woman as the years passed. Unable to have children of her own and feeling that her life in general could have been better, she became cold and unloving.

'Little Thomas, well, he grew close to Honorine as she gave him the love his aunt seemed unable, or unwilling, to give. Tony was good with the boy, though, and I was there not just to teach him but to talk to him about his mother. I tried to help him hold onto what memories he had of her and we talked a lot about her childhood. He was a loving boy and people took to him easily. You say he is now a vet? Ah, I'm not surprised. Even as a child he was drawn to animals. He was a good boy, always, but our paths never crossed again after his father took him away.'

She glances up at the clock on the mantelpiece above the original kitchen fireplace and Sam stands.

'We appreciate your time, Madame. And thank you. Every little piece of information we can gather helps and we won't give up on our search.'

I swallow hard, trying to dispel the lump in my throat. It seems that Thomas touched the heart of everyone who knew him.

'Thank you. Hearing that makes it even more vital that we find Thomas and return this.'

I put the little box back into my handbag and offer my hand to Elise. We shake and as we do she looks deep into my eyes, a frown creasing her brow.

'Thomas' father's business had become very successful almost overnight and he had to be based in London. His visits were rare, although they kept in touch by phone, but that hurt Thomas a little. I think the truth was that Richard never recovered from his loss because he didn't have time to grieve. He never lost interest in the boy but it was a difficult situation.'

I place both of my hands over hers and nod, momentarily unable to speak.

'Of course, Madame.' Sam answers on my behalf and Elise turns to lead us out.

As Sam and I head back towards the car we exchange a brief glance as I try to shake off my sadness.

'That's quite a picture building up of this Thomas. All the women around him, except for his aunt, seemed to want to mother him and his uncle was the only male influence active in his life at quite an impressionable time.'

I frown. 'I know; it's so sad.'

'No wonder he reached out to Honorine and she must have felt that they had a very special relationship.'

What child wouldn't crave love when his mother was no longer there for him? The boy must have felt he had been abandoned in his hour of greatest need and maybe his father couldn't see that. He'd honoured his wife's wishes and had done everything he could to provide for Thomas; but my heart feels heavy knowing that an eight year old boy wouldn't have understood the complexities of the situation.

The Surprise

Heading back in the car we are both feeling a little subdued. After a few kilometres, it's Sam who finally breaks the cold silence between us.

'This is turning out to be some story, isn't it?'

I don't respond.

'Look, earlier on I think maybe I was being a little unfair to you. Hearing what Elise had to say reminds me that everyone's situation is different and it's easy when you're not affected by something to make a quick judgement. I was out of order questioning you about Karl. Anyway, perhaps you and I can stop judging each other and throw our energy into tracking down Saint Thomas.'

I give him a friendly scowl, but I'm relieved and more than a little surprised by his peace offering. And his attempt at injecting a little humour.

'I think that's a great idea, Sam. Somehow the more we discover, the more important it becomes to do this. I can't find anything online about a Thomas Parker-Laurent, or even a Thomas Waverley, but I did find a Richard Parker who had a son named Thomas. He's the managing director of Joie de Vivre International and there's a lot about him online. What's rather strange is that Elise didn't offer any information about him. She must know that would be our quickest option, unless she didn't think he would necessarily know of Thomas' whereabouts. Or maybe he's not the easiest person to talk to.'

'I was thinking the exact same thing. And I'm surprised that Honorine didn't seem to know more about Richard Parker, either. It's not exactly an unusual name, so how can you be sure you have pinpointed the right guy?'

I find myself absentmindedly chewing my lip as I admit to Sam what I discovered.

'I found an interview he did shortly after his wife died, so I know he's the right one. I was just surprised to discover he's the man behind Joie de Vivre. I mean, jewellery and perfume, who would have guessed?'

Sam seems as shocked as I am and I'm a little surprised he even recognises the company name.

'What?' He glances sideways at me, wondering why I'm surprised. 'You think I've never bought jewellery or perfume as a gift?'

I hesitate; assuming he wouldn't recognise a designer brand was rather rude of me and I need to get myself out of this one quickly.

'Sorry, I was surprised myself when I made the connection and I thought you would be, too.'

'If you're correct, that is.'

I nod. 'That's why I think none of them have had anything to do with Thomas' father. I seriously doubt he'd be on the other end of that phone number, anyway. It will be answered by some PA or assistant and it will be hard to get to talk to the man himself. I also wonder if there was a reason why it was more convenient to let people think Thomas was a Waverley. Maybe his father felt he was safer having complete anonymity. There are some ruthless people out there and he was at a very vulnerable age. Imagine the horror if Thomas had been taken and held for ransom? It's not beyond the realms of imagination when the death of his mother would have been covered in the tabloids, no doubt.'

I sit back, allowing the head rest to ease some of the tension in my neck.

'Sorry, Anna. I've been a bit off again today and you're just trying to do the right thing. Look, all we're getting is snippets of information about Thomas' childhood and what we really need is to find someone more likely to know his whereabouts now. If he's a practising vet and still living in France, then maybe we can track him down via that connection and take it from there.'

Now I feel guilty because I know I have this tendency to become preoccupied with an idea. As an obsessive starter/finisher I hate giving up on anything.

'Thanks, Sam. I really do appreciate everything you've done. Teaching me some new skills and being patient as I learn. Helping my parents means turning other work away. And now, letting me drag you into something that might be going nowhere fast. Maybe Thomas isn't the only saint around here.'

That makes him laugh and the tension between us dissipates once more. Why is there this sense of friction between us that is always so close to the surface?

'Me? A saint? Ha! Ha! No one has ever called me that before. Not even my dear mother. In case you haven't noticed, not a lot happens around here and you've turned into a distraction.'

He reaches forward to turn on the radio and I get the message that the conversation is over. So, I'm a distraction… but from what? He says he's content with his life as it is but I don't believe this quiet life is enough for him, even if that's what he's telling himself. Why else would he offer his time to help me search for clues about Thomas' whereabouts?

I let the music clear my head of thoughts and the rest of the journey passes quite pleasantly. When we arrive back at Le Manoir d'Orsenne Mum greets us, saying she hoped we'd be back in time for lunch. Sam doesn't really get a chance to decline as we're immediately enlisted to carry trays of crockery and glasses out into the garden.

'Sorry, Sam. I hope you didn't have other plans.'

He smiles, raising one cheek in a lop-sided grin.

'You and your mother are quite a force to be reckoned with. My mum knows to expect me when she sees me, so no harm done. Besides, Viv is a much better cook but don't repeat that to anyone.'

I mull over his words, reflecting that Sam displays a sort of unfiltered honesty at times. In a way, I suppose it's rather refreshing and I'm wrong to let it annoy me. We set the table and shortly afterwards Mum and Dad appear with trays laden with a mouth watering buffet. I can see Sam is delighted and as Mum plies him with food he's eager to fill his plate.

'Was it a productive trip?' Dad asks.

I screw up my face, nodding my head from side to side in a so-so manner.

'We're learning a lot about Thomas' childhood but few have had contact with him since he left the village. Sam's idea is to try to trace him through the veterinary link and I agree that's our best bet now, even though I've been online and his name just doesn't come up.'

Sam seems pleased I've acknowledged that and he nods in agreement.

'Oh, I nearly forgot—' Mum suddenly jumps up from the table and disappears back into the house, returning with a small FedEx parcel in her hands.

'This arrived for you earlier this morning, Anna.'

As she hands it to me across the table I try not to look flustered when I see the return address staring back at me. It's from Karl. I put it down on the floor next to my chair.

'Thanks, Mum. Great food, as usual.' Three pairs of eyes are on me and I feel distinctly uncomfortable.

'Aren't you going to open it, dear?' Mum thinks any parcel is bound to contain something exciting and now I feel awkward and uneasy.

It's not like it's my birthday or anything, and I can't imagine what I left behind that Karl would feel he had to go to the trouble of sending to me. But everyone has finished eating and is looking at me expectantly. Even Sam.

Reluctantly I stoop over and pick it up, thinking how light it is and hoping it isn't a bra, or some other item of underwear Karl discovered in his sock drawer. I slide my knife along one edge of the oblong box and tip the contents onto the table. There's something about eight inches in length wrapped up in tissue paper and a much smaller package wrapped in silver paper. I rip off the packaging around the larger item first, to find it's a white silk rose. I frown, wondering what's going on. As the paper falls away from the second package, Mum sucks in a breath as I stare down in horror at a small, white silk padded heart attached to which is the most ostentatious diamond and platinum engagement ring tied with a red bow. Even the birds have fallen silent.

'Um… well. That's a surprise.'

Mum and Dad exchange a worried glance as I look across at them.

'Were you expecting this?' Dad asks, trying his best to sound neutral, despite the look of total shock he's unable to hide.

'No, of course not. This is ludicrous.'

Mum squirms in her seat and poor Sam is sitting there watching our discomfort and not sure what to make of it.

'I'm not getting engaged and I wasn't expecting this, or anything at all from Karl. It's over and I've made that very clear.'

I know it's rude, but I stand up and hurry towards the house feeling mortified and foolish. When I get to my room I grab my phone and check my emails. Sure enough, there's one from Karl and several from ex-colleagues with congratulatory comments in the subject line. I click on the one from Pam Michaels, the friendly lady from accounts who was always grateful to have a little chat. She wasn't a gossip, but was a very genuine person and we got on rather well.

So very thrilled to hear the news, Anna! Karl can't wait until you get back and he's planning a big party. Enjoy the rest of your holiday and congrats, lovely!

Best regards, Pam

There's another email from Lizzie but the subject line simply reads: *Whaaattt???*

Anna – have you seen Karl's Facebook post? I'm assuming it isn't true as I know you would have warned me, but it looks so real. Everyone is talking about it. Please reply when you pick this up as I'm worried.

Lx

I sink down onto the chair in front of the laptop and click it out of sleep mode. Unbelievably, it seems Karl has blocked me and I can't access his Facebook page. I call up Pam's page and sure enough, she's shared his post.

Thrilled to announce my engagement to the lovely Anna and can't wait to plan the party on her return! I'm one lucky man.

He's posted a photo of the rose and the ring lying on the silk heart next to it. He hasn't even tagged me, just used my Christian name so it looks like he has – I assume he blocked me so I can't deny it. There are already over forty congratulatory comments and nearly twice as many *likes*. I feel myself crumbling

189

inside, as if the wind has been knocked out of me. I ring Lizzie, willing my hands to stop shaking. She answers almost immediately and launches into a torrent of words.

'What on earth is going on? I couldn't believe it when I saw the post. Did you have any warning about this? Everyone seems to think it's true!' At least she doesn't sound angry with me.

'I had no idea and absolutely no warning at all. He sent the ring by FedEx this morning and I've only just opened it. In the last communication we had I made it very clear we were over. And now he's blocked me on Facebook so I can't deny it. What should I do? My parents are shocked and I denied all knowledge, of course, because that's the truth.'

Lizzie makes a noise like a grunt, but I'm simply feeling numb and totally confused.

'I don't think there is anything you can usefully do given the circumstances. In fact, if you do nothing then it's going to make people start to wonder what's going on. I can't be the only one who noticed he didn't tag you properly and now I understand why. Maybe keep off social media completely until things die down. But what are you going to say to him?'

As the enormity of what he's staged is starting to sink in, anger is beginning to rise up. Karl is trying to take over my life again, but this time I'm not there to see what's going on.

'I don't know yet. If you hear anything else can you text me? I have an email from someone I used to work with, who I know I can trust. I'll find out what's going on in the office and what exactly he's telling everyone.'

Lizzie sighs and I'm grateful for her concern, and the fact that she knew there was no truth in this.

'I'm so sorry for you, Anna. He isn't the man I thought he was and now I can see why your dad took an instant dislike to him. Unlike the rest of us, he saw Karl's manipulative nature. I'm only angry with myself that I fell for his charismatic charm and let it colour my judgement. Not much of a friend, am I?'

'Nonsense!' I exclaim, hating the thought that Lizzie thinks she's let me down in any way at all. 'He's good at manipulating people and you have a trusting nature. Remember, I fell for all that too. Just ignore him if he gets in touch while I decide what to do next. I hope this will be old news by the time you come over, so don't worry.'

Working as a Team

When I eventually calm down enough to feel in control, I make my way back downstairs again. Sam has already left. Mum makes us all a cup of tea and I tell them what little I know. We all agree it's probably best to let things settle and hopefully people will soon realise something isn't quite right. The fact that I have no voice at all in what's being said is bound to make people wonder what's going on.

When I'm stressed or feeling frustrated with life, my coping mechanism is to bury myself in my work, and that's precisely what I do. I spend the late afternoon taking photos of the house and gardens, then spirit myself away to my room to begin the makeover of Le Manoir's website. After a couple of hours Mum appears with a tray of sandwiches and a hot drink.

'I won't disturb you, darling. Just remember Dad and I are here for you if you feel like talking.'

'Thank you and don't worry, Mum, the only one who is going to end up looking like a fool is Karl.'

But as she closes the door behind her I wonder if I'm kidding myself and when it's time to go back home will all of this really be forgotten?

'Morning, Anna.' Sam gives me a sheepish look, then turns his back while he sets down some tools on the floor.

'Morning. Sorry about yesterday and walking out on you like that. I did make my way back down to say goodbye and to thank you for taking me to meet Elise Moreau. But coping with anger is best done when one is alone, I find.'

He straightens and as our eyes meet I see concern etched on his face.

'That was quite something,' he admits.

'I know. Worst of all it's all over Facebook, well, that's what it feels like. I've decided to do nothing and see what happens next. The parcel will be on its way back to the UK later this morning.'

I didn't add that it had taken me ages to deconstruct the silk flower into a pile of little pieces. I don't do fake anything and Karl needs to be very clear about that.

Sam's jaw drops a little but he doesn't say a word. He stands there studying my face as he realises I'm just a victim of this nonsense.

'People are bound to wonder why there's no photo of the happy couple and hopefully notice the absence of any comment from me,' I explain.

He nods, pursing his lips and then finally says something.

'I haven't been on Facebook since… well, for a long time. Social media is great for keeping in touch and sharing stuff, but some bits of life need to be kept behind closed doors. I'm sorry you've been put through this and I think you're handling it rather well. That was one expensive looking ring, though, so maybe it's only now he's realising what's really important to him.'

Why do people look for the good in the bad, every single time?

'I'm not into playing games, Sam, and that's what Karl is doing. He had his chance but thankfully I came to my senses just in time. Buying me a flashy ring only goes to show that he doesn't understand me at all.'

The frown on Sam's face doesn't quite cover the underlying look of confusion. Do men really think that spending a couple of grand on a diamond ring is all that's needed to get a woman to say, 'I do'?

'Right, well, guess I'd better start work. There's a lot to do.'

'I'll finish off this bottom row of stones and then I'm all yours. I quite fancy starting on the tiling if you show me what to do.'

He smirks. 'Tiling? You're getting adventurous. Maybe that's something we need to do together, what do you think?'

'Sounds good to me. How long will it take?'

'There's a bit of cutting to be done, so maybe three or four days. Gérard is coming in to sort the electrics this week, so we might have to work around him. Then it's skirting boards and architrave, hanging the doors and your next task will be painting. I'll be plumbing in the bathroom and the kitchen while you do that.'

That sounds like a lot of work.

'And we'll get all this done in just three weeks?'

'I'm feeling confident. With a reliable painter doing a passable job, it's do-able.' He gives me a meaningful stare. 'When are your friends arriving?' His cheeky grin is back.

'Saturday, the first of July.'

'You'd better get your parents moving on that furniture, then. I might even have time to make a start on the second gîte before I go away.'

And this is the man whose own house is going to take years by the look of it. How can he bear to live in that caravan with no end date in sight?

*

Sam is true to his word and although it's almost seven o'clock on Thursday evening, we're standing looking at the freshly tiled floor with a sense of satisfaction. It took me a while to get the hang of it but although I was appreciably slower than Sam, he even allowed me to take on some of the cutting.

'Is it okay to step on the floor?' We spin around to see Mum and Dad standing in the doorway behind us, looking very pleased indeed.

'Yep. It's all done.'

They walk through the sitting room area and turn right, into the bedroom.

'It flows nicely considering there's a lot packed into this space,' Mum comments.

'Once the doors are hung it will feel a little smaller. The shower room works well, but the kitchen is rather bijou.'

They saunter back out and walk across the open space to poke their heads into the two small rooms on the other side of the front door.

'I see what you mean, but it is nice to keep it separate from the sitting room and you've done wonders, you two.'

'Gérard is coming in tomorrow and we'll get those electric radiators hung. He'll be here on Saturday, too, but I won't be around.'

I glance at Sam in surprise, as I assumed he'd be working here. Guess I have the whole weekend off, then. Maybe on Saturday I'll contact some veterinary practices to see if I can track down Thomas.

Sam and I end up sitting in the secret garden to eat a meal Mum insists on preparing for us. We're both tired and dirty but very hungry, eating our food far faster than is good for the digestion.

'So, you have plans this weekend? I hope you're doing something nice and not just more work.'

Sam doesn't look up. However, as I say the words he stops spearing pieces of chicken onto his fork.

'It's an anniversary.'

There's a cold tremor in his voice and something tells me not to say any more. He's picking at his food again but still hasn't looked up from his plate.

'I thought I'd spend Saturday morning ringing around a few vets' surgeries and run Thomas' name past them in case anyone has heard of him. Then I'm going to do some more work on Le Manoir's website.'

Sam suddenly goes very quiet and the look on his face is almost morose. As soon as he's finished eating he bids me goodnight. After three very pleasant days working shoulder to shoulder together, with a lot of laughter and a lot of chatter, suddenly he clams up just like that. Oh, Sam, whatever your problems are if you don't talk about them the pain will never ease.

A Purposeful Life

After breakfast, I head out to start work and am surprised to see that Sam and the electrician are already on site.

'Morning.'

Both guys are on ladders at either end of the sitting room, yanking at a wire.

'Hi, Anna. This is Gérard. Anna is Monsieur et Madame Lacey's daughter, she's been helping out,' he explains to Gérard.

Gérard nods in my direction and flashes me a smile before tugging once more on the wire.

'That's it.' Sam gestures to Gérard, who mutters something in French that means nothing to me.

'Problems?' I ask, sensing Sam isn't happy.

'One of the coils of wire isn't long enough and it's going to be a nightmare re-threading a new piece.'

I think that given it's already been a hard week, tiredness is adding a little extra pressure to the frustration. Maybe today it's best if I make myself scarce rather than risk getting in their way.

'I'll leave you to concentrate on getting the wiring sorted and the radiators up. If you reach a point sometime today when I can start painting, just let me know. Good luck with that.'

Sam stops what he's doing and looks down at me.

'Sorry, Anna, but I think that's maybe the best idea. I think we'd end up being in each other's way and the air might get a little blue. Gérard's brother ran the wires for him and now he's here to do the actual connections, he isn't happy. I can only hope we don't end up having to cut out bits of plasterboard to re-site stuff.'

'I hope it doesn't come to that. See you later.'

He grimaces and even though I'm not sure Gérard can understand word for word what Sam is saying, he lifts his eyes to the ceiling to endorse his own irritation.

I check in on Mum to see if there's anything I can do to help, but she tells me to go and relax, so I head up to my bedroom.

Checking my emails there's nothing from Karl, although he will have received his return package by now. I open Pat's congratulatory email and consider how I'm going to respond. I sit with 'Hi Pat' on the blank email in front of me for a good five minutes before my fingers are ready to type again.

Hi Pat,

Thank you for your email, so lovely to hear from you. I know you won't mind if I tell you in confidence that this news came as a huge surprise to me. I've had little direct contact with

Karl since I left and thoughts of getting engaged couldn't have been further from my mind.

I'm trying to find out what's going on, but as you can imagine that's rather difficult to do, given that I'm in France for a while. I don't want to drag you into this, but if you do feel you can give me any information whatsoever about what's happening with Karl and the work situation at your end, that would really help me decide how best to handle this.

We were a couple and I think Robert suspected that, but Karl and I are over. When I do get back, I'll probably move out of the area so I can make a fresh start.

Anyway, hope things are good with you.

Best regards

Anna

I press send without giving it a second thought. There isn't any other way to put it and I don't want to give her the wrong impression, so it's better to be open and honest.

Next on the agenda should be the website but instead I search online for some numbers of local veterinary practices. It's hard making the calls when, invariably, the person on the other end of the phone doesn't speak much English. Thomas Waverley's name doesn't spark any recognition at all from the first three numbers I ring. I widen my search and decide to centre it around the Toulouse area, thinking that maybe he joined a practice local to where he studied. There is quite a long list of practices and pet hospitals within a reasonable distance, so I choose one and dial the number. The receptionist can't understand my question but she does hand me over to a colleague who speaks nearly perfect English. Then it occurs to me that while he might have been known locally as Waverley, I need to mention both surnames.

'I'm sorry to trouble you but I'm trying to trace someone by the name of either Thomas Waverley, or Thomas Parker-Laurent, who studied at the École nationale vétérinaire de Toulouse. I have no idea if he moved away from the area, so I'm phoning around in the hope that someone will recognise the name.'

'I know a Tom Laurent. Lovely man and so compassionate. He runs several practices, but they are rather scattered. His work is mostly of a charitable nature for people who can't afford to pay vet bills. I'm sure one of his staff would know of his whereabouts, but the last I heard he was working abroad. Let me find some contact details for you.'

I'm still in shock, having told myself that this was such a long shot it was unlikely to throw up any information at all. So, he's a Tom now and he's dropped *Parker* from his surname. I wonder if he fell out with his father after he left Saint-Julien-de-Vouvantes?

When I ring the number I'm given, the receptionist doesn't know when Tom is going to be there. She explains that he's mobile, working the odd day here and there to help out at his various practices, but he does a lot of charity work abroad. She gives me yet another number to ring. He has five practices in total and she explains that while they do charge people who can afford to pay, those who can't have their animals treated for free.

I ring the number she gives me and eventually get through to someone who seems to know his whereabouts.

'Tom is travelling, as usual. He is due back here at this clinic sometime around the middle of next month. He blogs and that's probably the best way to find out where he is, at this particular moment in time. Just type in *Le vétérinaire ambulant* and his blog will come up. He has a Facebook page, too.'

'Thank you, I will. He doesn't know me but I have something of value to return to him and I'd rather do that in person as it's irreplaceable. Where are you based?'

'We're in Nîmes. Do you want to leave your contact name and number?'

'If you don't mind, that would be great.'

This person has been extremely helpful and even before I put the phone down I'm typing with one hand and up comes the travelling vet's blog. I click on the translation button, as it's in French.

Oh, my goodness, Tom's face is staring back at me. Tousled brown hair, streaked by the sun and a tan that goes with the outdoor life he seems to lead. The home page is literally covered with photos of his travels and his work with animals. I click on the most recent blog post and discover that he's currently working as a volunteer in an African wildlife rehabilitation centre. There are some harrowing pictures of a group of men rescuing an injured lion believed to have been shot by poachers. But equally there are some very positive photos of monkeys, antelope, reptiles and birds being released back into the wild.

I sit back in my seat feeling rather overcome by what I've seen. I don't know what I was expecting, but the reality is that Tom has become the sort of man of whom his mother would have been very proud indeed. It's clear he loves what he does and obviously money is not an issue for him, running practices here in France and being able to donate his time freely abroad. What jumps off the screen is his sense of caring and, at the same time, adventure. He is living his dream by the look of it. He has a kind face and bright, smiling eyes. This is a man who wouldn't be content to sit behind a desk, but who needs to be active all the time.

A notification flashes up on my screen and I see it's a reply from Pat. Reluctantly I click on it, eager to read what she has to say, but rather loath to take my eyes off Tom now I finally have a face to go with the name.

Oh, Anna! I had no idea.

Karl is saying that when you return to the UK there will be a big party. He's telling people that you guys didn't realise how close you'd become until after you left for France. He made it sound like quite a love story. There are going to be a lot of shocked faces when the truth comes out.

Karl is back in the office for a while as his project is on hold. He hasn't been around much but whenever I saw him he wasn't his usual self; I think he felt a bit lost without you here. Anyway, there are big changes coming and he's been working long hours. One of the directors left rather abruptly after an argument at the last board meeting. There have been a stream of conversations going on behind closed doors and Karl seems to be spending a lot of time here with Robert these days.

I don't really know what to say to you, but it's obvious to everyone Karl misses you. He isn't having some sort of mental breakdown, is he? I mean, announcing his engagement to you like that is shocking after what you've told me. How on earth he's going to get over this, I don't know, because he really seems to believe it's going to happen.

If there's anything at all I can do, please just let me know and I'll be in touch if I hear anything further that I think might help.

Pat

What a nightmare! And most annoying of all, Robert seems to have totally absolved Karl of any blame whatsoever with regard to our blatant breach of contract! Perhaps Pat's right, and he really is having a breakdown, or he's delusional. Either way, what am I going to do about it? I grab my phone and dial Lizzie.

'Morning, I have an update.'

'This is early for you to ring. Why aren't you working on getting my gîte ready?'

She laughs, totally unaware that today's little hitch could be a real setback.

'There's a lot going on today with the electrics and I'm surplus to requirements. I'd only get in their way as my next task is to tackle the painting.'

'Sounds good; two weeks and Daniel and I get to sample some of that peaceful existence in rural France. I simply can't wait. So, what's the latest on Karl?'

A sigh escapes my lips of its own accord and I realise I really have no idea what to do next.

'I spoke to Pat back in the office; she works in accounts, and I told her the truth. She said that Karl's project is on hold and he's back in the office. He's told everyone we're engaged. They've been told that he's planning a party to celebrate our engagement on my return. It seems Karl is spinning some sort of story about realising how we felt about each other after I left for France. He's trying to smooth the path ready for my return so that it looks like a genuine excuse to appease Robert and the board. She was totally shocked when I explained the situation.'

'It's almost unbelievable. I mean, Karl is such a professional and this is… weird. And he hasn't been in touch, even though you sent the ring back?'

'Nothing. What do you think I should do next?'

The seconds tick by and I know Lizzie is as lost for words as I am.

'I don't even know what to suggest. I know you don't want to hear this, but if you were back in the UK this would be a lot easier to handle. For a start, he wouldn't be able to make rash claims like this as you'd be there to refute it.'

Oh no, Lizzie thinks I should go back to sort this out.

'I can't go back at the moment, Lizzie. I have things going on here and I don't think I have the emotional energy to deal with it. Karl made this mess and I feel it's up to him to sort it out. Do you think there's any harm in just waiting to see what happens?'

There's a little laugh full of irony.

'Well, eventually the truth will come out when you don't turn up and fall into his arms. Anyway, what's going on at your end, other than renovation work?'

'It's a long story and I was saving it for when you arrive. But I found a box with some jewellery in it, hidden in a wall I was repointing, and I'm hoping to return it to the owner. It turns out that he's this amazing guy; he's a vet and he also does volunteer work in animal conservation. He's in Africa at the moment teaching at an animal rehabilitation centre but I've been told that he's due back in France sometime next month. The jewellery belonged to his late mother.'

'Ah, Anna, that's a totally unexpected surprise. You sound smitten.'

I gulp. 'Oh, I... um, well, I've been reading his travel blog and the life he leads is so inspiring. When I think of Karl who's so self-centred, yet this guy,

Thomas, who had a really rough start in life, has made his life really count for something.'

'I'm guessing he has the rugged, outdoorsy look to go with it?' She sniggers.

'Well, he looks easy on the eye in his photos, I will admit. But that's not what this is about. As a young boy, a lot of people here grew close to him. What I've been told leads me to believe there is a lot of sentimental attachment to the items I found. When I hand the jewellery box back I have a lot of messages to pass on to him from people I've talked to.'

'He sounds interesting. At least it's something to take your mind off Karl's antics. Listen, if your gut instincts are telling you not to do anything about all that right now, then leave it alone. It's up to Karl to contact you to explain himself. I certainly haven't heard from him, so maybe reality will dawn and he'll come clean. At the very least he owes you a massive apology. I must go or I'll be late for my first appointment. I'm counting the days until our trip. Take care, Anna, and speak soon.'

It's Not Easy to Shake Off the Past

Work on Le Manoir's website is going well, although Mum clucks around me like a mother hen when I insist on eating lunch in my room. By mid-afternoon I'm more than ready to stretch my legs and enjoy a little company, so I head downstairs. It's deserted and I saunter out into the garden. I can hear hammering and sawing noises coming from the gîte. I walk purposefully past the front door without turning my head for even a glance. I can hear the murmur of voices coming from the secret garden. Sure enough, when I pass beneath the rose covered arch there appears to be a tea party going on.

'Ooh, those scones look good! Hi, Mrs Callaghan – this is a surprise!'

'Sarah was passing and called in to see Sam and to take a sneaky peek. However, we weren't in there for more than a minute because they're having a few problems and we thought it was best to make ourselves scarce.'

Sarah and Mum exchange a meaningful glance.

'That's exactly what I thought this morning. It's such a pity as things were going so well.'

'Now you're here, sit down and have a scone. I'll go and make some more tea. I was hoping Dad would join us, but Honorine's lawn mower isn't working and he's popped over to have a quick look at it.'

Mum disappears leaving just the two of us.

Ziggy suddenly bounds across the garden, intent on escaping from of the intensity of the heat and seeking the shade of a large, leafy bush. I'm wilting a little myself, but with her, albeit beautiful, fur coat this heat must be almost unbearable. The sound of Sam's mum's voice breaks the silence.

'How are you enjoying your stay, Anna? And please do call me Sarah.'

I can see up close, that Sam has her eyes and yet in other ways he's undoubtedly his father's son. They are both stocky, hearty looking men whereas Sarah is a very slim and elegant lady.

'It's a wonderful break and I'm enjoying the physical work. But it has been fun working on the new website, too. It's nearly finished and I'm also designing some new leaflets. Mum and Dad haven't seen any of it yet, so I only hope they will be pleased.'

Sarah smiles, her eyes scanning my face with interest.

'Sam has been enjoying your company and he tells me you're very driven and focused. I think that scares him a little, to be honest with you.'

We exchange smiles. She's wondering what I think of him.

'He's an interesting guy. I'm still trying to fathom him out.'

She crooks an eyebrow.

'Well, when you do, please do enlighten me!'

That raises a laugh that I can't hold back and I immediately feel the need to explain myself.

'He's quite complicated, isn't he? I mean, at work he's focused and time driven. He doesn't waste a moment. But I've been up to his barn and it's like he's a different person entirely. Maybe it's too much to spend seven days a week doing the same thing?' I add that by way of an excuse, rather than saying what I'm really thinking: that he lacks focus when it comes to his own project. Well, it's not so much *focus* as it is to face the fact that he, too, needs help and not just the little community around him.

She lifts her eyebrows, a frown settling upon her forehead.

'I can't argue with that, I'm just amazed you can read him so well. It's not breaking any sort of confidence to admit that Neil and I are very worried about him. That's what parents do and he's well aware of our concerns. Our hope is that eventually he'll be in a better place mentally so he can then accept our help.'

I'm surprised she's being so candid, but then it's not like talking to a total stranger. I'm now beginning to suspect that Mum has shared one or two things about me with her. I realise Mum needs an outlet for her concerns and they have become great friends.

'He's a good teacher and very patient; he just doesn't say a lot. Well, most of the time and then when he does it's a surprise. Until it comes to an abrupt halt.'

'Ha! Ha! Ha! That's my Sam.' Her laughter quickly fades and her mood becomes sombre. 'He wasn't always that way, Anna. He was a very sociable, outgoing young man. His life hasn't been an easy one and I miss the old Sam. I just hope that meeting up with his friends in Cannes isn't going to be a mistake.'

I can feel that she wants to tell me what happened but we can both hear Mum calling out to Sam and Gérard that she's leaving them mugs of tea. And now she's on her way back to join us.

'Here you go. Earl Grey this time; it goes perfectly with scones and jam. There's lemon or milk.'

I can see that Mum instantly picks up on the silence between us and she's understandably curious.

'I was telling Anna how impressed Sam has been that she's prepared to tackle anything. It's looking good, isn't it? Have you sorted the furniture yet?'

Sarah deftly manages to draw Mum into a different sort of conversation and I smile at her over the top of my cup.

'Not yet, but tomorrow Geoff and I are off to Tours to do some shopping, which includes a visit to the large antiques market at Rabelais on Sunday. I'm hopeful we'll find everything we need. We already have a new fridge in the garage waiting to be installed and a drop-leaf oak table I bought ages ago. At least that's a start.'

'I went through some of those old boxes Dad pulled out of the other gîte. There are some rather wonderful iron grilles I put to one side. I was thinking of wire-brushing off the rust and giving them a polish. They would look amazing as wall art against the exposed stonework. What do you think?'

'I wondered what that little pile was at the side of the garage. It seems to grow by the day,' Mum smiles across at me.

'I found a few old door knobs that could be used as light pulls in the bathrooms to replace the plastic ones. Just to add a bit of character. And did you see that old wine crate? It wouldn't take much to turn it into a nice little bookshelf. There are—'

Suddenly the sound of door chimes fills the air as the wireless receiver sitting on the tray kicks into life.

'Now who can that be, I wonder?' Mum immediately makes her way back up to the house. The moment she's gone Sarah turns to me.

'How long do you think you will be staying, Anna?'

'I've let out my house for six months and after that I'll head back. I'm probably going to move again so I can start over afresh.' I have no idea if Mum has told her about Karl.

'I'm asking because... because Sam needs a friend. Although he doesn't say much, I can see you've made him think about a few things in a different light. That trip to Rennes, for instance. That was so out of character for him but it gave me hope. Maybe he's ready to start living his life again but to do that he needs a stimulus. Helping you to track down Thomas has made him break out of his comfort zone a little. Please don't mention that we've discussed this and maybe we can talk some more when it's convenient.'

I can see how anxious she is and I take the piece of paper she hands me with her mobile phone number written on it. Mum appears with her arms full of flowers and I quickly nod in Sarah's direction before lifting the teapot to offer her more tea.

'Anna, these are for you.'

I stare at her and then at the roses. There must be fifty of them. All white. She hands me a small card.

I love you with all my heart. When you come back things will be different, I promise. And the ring will be waiting for you, my darling. K x

'Unbelievable!' My anger instantly makes my face flame. 'Will nothing stop him?'

Sarah looks shocked and Mum's face has fallen.

'It's her ex. He's refusing to believe their relationship is over,' Mum explains.

'Or that our so-called engagement is in fact a hoax! Oh, Mum, what should I do? It's all over Facebook and he's told everyone I used to work with that there will be a big party when I get back.' For the first time in this sorry little episode my eyes begin to well with tears.

Mum dumps the flowers down on a chair and comes to throw her arms around me, while Sarah looks uncomfortable.

'Darling, you should have told me it wasn't just a case of receiving that ring in the post. This isn't normal behaviour, Anna, he's almost become a stalker. We have to do something to stop this.'

I pull myself together, cross that it's brought me to tears.

'Sorry, I've spoilt a lovely afternoon tea session.'

There's a cough and we all look up to see Sam standing there with two empty mugs in his hands. He looks a little lost for words and gestures towards the teapot.

'Sorry to interrupt, but we wondered if there was any more tea? We've finally resolved all the problems—' His words trail off and I'm in no doubt at all that he's trying to pretend he didn't hear what was being said.

Mum fills the mugs and he beats a hasty retreat. I wipe my eyes on my sleeve and sniff.

'Let's not get this out of perspective, Mum. I let it get to me for a moment there, that's all. We're talking about my ex-workplace, so there's no real harm done. And I'm here for another five months so by then, even if I do nothing, everyone will realise there is no engagement. I put the last lot of flowers in the compost bin. This time I'm going to cut them up into little pieces and send them back to him. Maybe that will deter him from wasting his money in future.'

Mum and Sarah exchange worried glances, but say nothing. Let's be honest – however I react to this is going to be perceived as slightly odd, as it's a bizarre situation to be in. So, maybe some amateur dramatics are precisely what's called for.

A Friend in Need is a Friend Indeed

I spend a sleepless night, thoughts of Karl going round and round inside my head. What if he genuinely believes he can win me back? After all, he spent the best part of a year telling me that he loved me every single day. I just didn't believe him. Perhaps I'm the one with the disconnect issue? Maybe I'm incapable of trusting anyone again when it comes to my heart? Is that why my reaction is off the scale? I've decided to wait and see what happens when he receives that next FedEx parcel.

This morning we enjoy a leisurely breakfast together before Mum and Dad head off.

'You really don't mind covering things, here, Anna? It's just easier to get everything sorted in one go.' Dad is such a worrier at times.

'I've arranged for Sam to come and stay overnight and asked him to do the breakfast. I know cooking isn't your thing and it's unfair to expect you to cook and serve. Now don't give me that look. I can't go off with an easy conscience if I felt you had to cope on your own.'

'Really, Mum? Sam's a builder, not a chef. Okay, so I'm an advertising executive and I'm not exactly qualified either, but I'm not that bad… am I?'

Dad is trying hard not to laugh and I stare at him in disbelief that he isn't backing me up.

'What? I'm just remembering the bacon that jumped off the plate. Worse than bullets, as it shattered.'

It was only once. Burnt bacon that was way beyond crispy and almost inedible. I admit that I'm used to eating out and I do tend to regard a bowl of cereal as a meal when I'm at home alone. So what?

'And Sam cooks?' I raise my eyebrows questioningly.

'Actually,' Dad interjects, 'he does. He cooked a meal for Neil, Sarah and us once. Jolly nice it was, too. Chicken in red wine and it wasn't Sarah's recipe.'

Good looking, can renovate pretty much anything and he can cook. 'Well, I can't imagine he's had much practice in that caravan of his.'

'Anna – that was a mean thing to say.' Mum sounds disappointed.

I hang my head because she's right and I think of the paper with Sarah's number on it tucked into my purse. But I still think Mum should have run this past me first.

'You're away one night, Mum, and it's one breakfast. I could have managed, believe me.'

'Well, it's done now and if there are any domestic emergencies at least you will have a builder on hand. Everything else I know you'll be able to cope with but please, be nice to Sam and don't hold it against him that he's a better cook than you are.'

I almost choke on my toast.

'He'll arrive after lunch as he's going to hang the doors in the gîte and get the architraves up so that it's ready for you to begin painting on Monday.'

'Well, that at least makes a little more sense now.'

'That's my girl. When Sam offered to do the breakfasts, I thought that it was a rather nice gesture. He doesn't know you aren't good in the kitchen, so it's not like I've been telling tales.'

And that's supposed to make me feel better?

When I wave them off it does though, suddenly seem rather deserted as all the guests are out for the day. The house always creaks, but I guess I didn't notice quite how much when there were other people around.

Grateful for a distraction and feeling rather curious, I ring Sarah's number.

'Oh, hi, Anna. Thank you for calling. Give me a moment and I'll wander out into the garden.'

I can hear voices in the background and I wait a few moments until Sarah begins speaking again.

'Sorry, Sam's just signing for a parcel and I'd rather he didn't hear us talking. I'm not sure he'd approve, you see. It's only that Sam lost a very close friend and it's coming up to the seventh anniversary of her death. Before you arrived, I thought he was... slipping back into his old ways. Oh, it's difficult to explain as it's a long story. He's been better and finally I thought the worst was over, I mean, grief can't go on forever, can it?'

I feel she's talking to herself, rather than to me, and when she stops I say nothing, I just hold the phone close to my ear and wait.

'The psychiatrist warned he might relapse but this time we thought... hoped, it wouldn't come to that. I wanted you to know that if he acts strangely in any way there is a reason for it. I don't think he'll turn to me this time and I wondered as the two of you seemed to be getting along so well—'

'If he decides to talk to me then of course I'll be as supportive as I can. I am sorry to hear about his loss, Sarah, and how deeply it's affected him. It must make you feel rather helpless at times. He's a sensitive guy in many respects and it's at odds with his almost offhand approach to his future. I knew something was troubling him, so it does help to know that. No wonder people are more important to him than anything else, that must have been quite a blow. I'll be careful what I say and mindful of this and I'm grateful for your trust. Sam's been a wonderful help to my parents and if there's anything at all I can do, then I will.'

'Thank you, Anna. This isn't a conversation I ever thought I'd have because Sam is such a private person. But being around you has given him a lift and reminded him that life goes on, I think. I simply wish it wasn't that time of the year again, as it always brings him down. Thank you for understanding.'

Even after we say goodbye I can't switch off my thoughts as I think of the moments when I've been in Sam's company and his mind has been elsewhere. I try to shake off the sadness I feel and spend the remainder of the morning finishing off the changes to the website. Then I focus on the new brochure. After lunch, I take a lot of photos of the garden, which is now burgeoning with colour. Out of thirty shots I choose four which capture the ambience of the setting perfectly. I really hope Mum and Dad will love what I've done and then it will be on to working on my own brand for my new business.

Sam arrives, seeking me out in the garden where I'm working on the iPad. He's dressed in his usual work gear.

'I put my holdall up in the room, is that okay? Viv gave me a key for the front door and the key to room five. It's going to take me a couple of hours to hang the doors and sort the frames. Is it all right if I make a coffee before I start? Would you like one?'

I've already forgiven Mum for extending her invitation to Sam and realise that this is a rather isolated location, after all. Having someone whose French is vastly superior to mine in case of an emergency is probably a wise move. And, besides, Ziggy seems to appear every time Sam is around regardless how hot it is, so that's a bonus.

'Help yourself and yes, thank you. I'm working on the new brochure for Le Manoir and it's going to take a while to load up the photos and get the copy sorted. It's rather pleasant working out here. Do you need any help with those doors, because if you do I can break off at any time?'

'No, I'm good. Nothing I can't do in my sleep, really.' He smirks and then heads off back up the path to the house.

*

Wouldn't you know it, but late afternoon the lock jams on a guest's bedroom door and Sam seems really pleased to be able to jump in to save the day. In fairness, it's something I couldn't have sorted myself. He had to take it apart and fiddle with springs as it's an original lock. But the way he interacted with the older couple was like seeing another side to him again. He was at ease, charming and chatty. No wonder his mother is so worried about him.

I half consider suggesting I'll cook an evening meal for the two of us, but reluctantly acknowledge that everything Mum said about my culinary skills is true. Instead, I offer to take Sam out for a meal. It's the least I can do, especially now I understand what a tough weekend this is for him. However, I have my fingers crossed he will offer to step in and cook, especially when two of the families who are staying ask if they can use the barbecue. Sam – bless him – sets everything up for them while I arrange some crockery, condiments and cutlery.

'We need to stay just to keep an eye on things,' he informs me, although I feel he's also being a little diplomatic. It's kind of him, as I wasn't really happy about leaving the guests to sort themselves out; just in case something went wrong.

Swinging open the refrigerator door, I gaze inside.

'How about I sort the starter and the dessert, and you do the main course? There's a choice of steak or chicken. There's probably fish in the freezer if you want to take a look.'

When I spin back around to face him he has a broad smile on his face.

'Chicken will be perfect,' he replies but he's still smiling to himself and I think it's at my expense.

I can't possibly mess up pâté and lightly toasted slices of baguette, or a dish of strawberries and ice cream.

We work alongside each other and it only takes about half an hour to get everything ready. With the chicken fillets in the oven, we head off to the formal dining room so that the guests can have the run of the kitchen. There's a lot of noise coming from the garden but it's mainly the kids playing ball and everyone seems quite happy.

We sit opposite each other and Sam immediately tucks in, buttering a slice of toasted baguette and covering it with a thick layer of pâté.

'Everything is ready for you to prime and paint, now,' he says between mouthfuls.

'Great. I might even get a few hours in tomorrow.'

'I've left out the brushes and several tins of paint. There's a primer to paint over any knots in the wood, some filler for any cracks, then an undercoat and a top coat. Personally, I'd give it two undercoats and one top coat. There's sandpaper but I did do a quick once-over myself.'

'Thanks. At least this is a task I know how to tackle. The pressure is on now to get it finished ready for Lizzie and Daniel.'

'Piece of cake. We have it under control.' He's blasé, even though he has a small kitchen to fit out and a bathroom to plumb in.

We continue to eat in silence and I think about how hard Sam works and how well he plans everything. I feel he is always one step ahead and we've never had to down tools and wait for materials to arrive because of his organisational skills. That's quite something.

'I thought you might be a little annoyed your mum asked me to come over to help out. I'd hate to upset you and she meant well.'

I shrug. 'Proves she was right, as there's one fact I can't dispute – I can't mend locks. Oh, but I have some information about Thomas! I've found him.'

Sam wipes his mouth on a paper napkin and pushes his plate aside.

'You have? Well, that's a surprise.'

I talk him through the phone calls and how I tracked him down and pull out my phone to show him Tom Laurent's blog. He can see how impressed I am.

'You favour guys who aim big, don't you? I mean, this Karl, he's a high achiever, too. And quite romantic, from what I've seen.'

I look at him, my face deadpan.

I shake my head from side to side and sigh. 'I can see why you think that, Sam, and I guess Karl has his romantic moments. But sending that ring was no romantic gesture, because to get engaged to someone you have to ask them first. In person. And they are required to give you an answer, whether it's *yes* or *no*. It's not a one sided thing, so how can that be regarded as romantic in anyone's eyes?'

Sam scrunches up his face and nods in agreement.

'I see your point. I guess I just saw what looked like the gesture of a guy trying to convince you he thinks you're the one for him.'

'That's understandable, I suppose. But he's convinced quite a few people that it's true and that we really are engaged. Thankfully, when I go back I'll be starting over somewhere new and setting up my own business, so no lasting damage will have been done. The stand I'm taking is that Karl made this mess and now he has to clear it up.'

Sam grimaces.

'You're one tough lady. But you are controlling your anger surprisingly well. So when will you be meeting up with this guy, Tom?'

'Apparently Tom's back the middle of next month and he'll be in Nîmes for a few days. I'm hoping to go and visit him there.'

Sam is watching me, intently.

'Nîmes, you say? That's only a couple of hours' drive from Cannes.'

I shrug; I haven't had time to consult a map yet so I wasn't aware it was going to be such a long journey.

'It's just a thought… risky, I know, as I seem to keep putting my foot in it with regards to Tom. But,

I'm heading off on the tenth for this five day trip and you are very welcome to join me. Jack's parents' place is huge and it has stunning views, a great pool and a hot tub. There will be people there I haven't seen in years, but there will be lots of organised things to do, too, I suspect. It would be nice to have some company on the journey and on the day trips I'm sure Jack will be planning. Nîmes will also be a great day out. What do you think?' We've both finished eating and Sam checks his watch, then pushes his chair back. 'The chicken will be ready. I'll take out the plates, you sit and relax. It will only take me five minutes to reduce the sauce.'

I'm glad of the thinking time as I mull over his suggestion. I've never been to Cannes before and a break would be nice. But it's a risk as I have no idea what his friends are like, or whether we'd have anything in common. And, besides, I hardly know Sam. I only know the little that he's chosen to tell me and what Sarah felt she could share with me.

'Here you go. Chicken fricassée with asparagus and new potatoes.'

The creamy wine sauce smells heavenly and I get a whiff of onions, slightly caramelised and with a distinctly buttery overtone.

'This looks amazing, Sam, thank you. You don't really want to go to Cannes, do you?'

He sits down, leaning back in his chair and resting one arm on the table. His body language is open.

'No. I don't. But if I don't do this trip then I can't lay the past to rest. I'm not doing it for me, but for my mum. But don't feel obliged to take up the offer as I'm going anyway. Sometimes you have to make yourself do the thing you least want to do.'

I don't know whether to feel alarmed, or saddened, by his words.

'And while we're on the subject, did my mum talk to you about me the other day in the garden?'

I clam up, my face freezes as I try not to give anything away.

'No. Why?'

He narrows his eyes as he peers at me.

'You're an awful liar, Anna, and it doesn't suit you.' But then he begins laughing. 'She thinks you are a good influence on me; that being around someone vibrant, motivated and forward thinking will turn me around. She means well, but whatever she said, please remember there are times when everyone's parents embarrass them.'

'Like my mum asking you to babysit me?' We both burst out laughing. 'What are we, twelve year olds who need watching?'

'One day you'll be doing the same to your kids, just remember that.'

That's a bit of a statement. 'What makes you assume I'm going to have kids?'

'You're the sort, Anna. It's not a criticism and I'm surprised you feel it might be. I suppose it's not quite politically correct these days. But if you said I was the bachelor type I wouldn't take offence at that.'

This is getting just a little more personal than I'm comfortable with and we both pick up our knives and forks to resume eating.

Time to Relax

'I know you're doing a lot of work on the internet in your free time but I wondered if you fancied a quick dip in the pool, as a nice way to end the day?'

With the dishes all cleared away it's true that I was intending to head off upstairs and jump online. It seems rude, though, to reject his offer when he's here doing me a big favour.

'Sounds good. I'll meet you out there.' Obviously, Sam is in need of a little company tonight.

We head off in different directions and once I've changed I grab a couple of large towels. Thank goodness I have a bikini that doesn't look too bad on me and as I approach the pool I'm pleased to see I've beaten him to it.

The solar lights are plenty bright enough to give a lovely warm ambience to the setting and as I slip into the water it doesn't take long for my body to adjust to the temperature.

I lie back, drifting around lazily and watch Sam as he walks towards me. His navy blue swimming shorts reveal just how fit and muscular his body really is and this matches my expectations. I find myself fighting a rather naughty smile. It's a pity we aren't the type of people to throw caution to the wind but then we aren't here alone and it wouldn't be the right thing to do. Imagine how awkward the morning after the night before would be. I start laughing as he eases himself over the edge of the pool.

'What's so amusing? I was counting on you to bring the towels.'

He thinks I'm laughing because he forgot.

'I'm that predictable, am I?' Maybe not quite as much as you think. Sam, if you could read my mind. Shame on you, Anna, this is a line of thought you don't want to venture down.

He stands to stretch out his back, extending his arms and twisting his head until there's an ominous crack. I watch as he turns in the other direction and grimace when I hear an even louder one.

'Ooh, that doesn't sound good.'

'When I'm working and doing a lot of lifting the stress tends to build up in my neck which leads to muscle spasms. It pulls on the vertebrae and stretching it out corrects the balance. It sounds bad but ten minutes in the pool and I'll be as good as new.'

We circle around each other and I'm glad I took up the offer as it is soothing and it does feel a little decadent in the gathering darkness. The pool is Dad's pride and joy and its maintenance a labour of love. Earlier on I noticed several of the guests out here with two of the kids excitedly splashing around with a ball. We both head towards the side of the pool and I hitch my arms up over the edge, letting my legs float up to the surface of the water.

'So, what do you think about Cannes?' Sam prompts me about his offer, which I thought I'd managed to side step quite nicely.

'Am I going as a friend, or as a plus-one?'

'There isn't a catch to this offer, Anna. I'll introduce you as you, not as my girlfriend and you'll have your own room. I will admit it would make the trip a little easier for me, for a number of reasons; not least because most of the other people there will probably be couples. It's just an annual meet up, but this is the first time I've accepted the invitation. Hence the hesitation.'

'Can I give it some thought? It would solve a problem for me but I sort of assumed I'd do the trip to Nîmes and back in a day. Hmm... but it is Cannes. I don't know, let me sleep on it.' I look at my feet, thinking it's time I replaced that nail polish and quickly slip them back beneath the surface of the water. When I look up I see that Sam is checking me out and it flusters me.

'Good. You can let me know what you decide in the morning.'

With that he turns away, stretching his arms out and pushing his feet against the side of the pool to glide off through the water with ease. It takes him no time to travel the length and return; I watch him as he swims effortlessly back to my side.

'Do you ever get lonely, Sam?'

He runs his hands over his head and down over his face, wiping away the drips of water.

'It's not as simple as that for me. There are times I look back on the life I had but so much has happened since then that I'm not the same person anymore. I made some bad decisions and I wasn't the only one who was affected by the fallout. It taught me that spending time alone is like being free. The only person it affects is me and I'm fine with that.'

He sounds accepting, as if that's a normal response. I can't even think of how to respond to that.

'Oh, did you mean do I miss being in a relationship?' He swivels around to face me, raising his eyebrows and clearly not at all concerned if that was where I was heading. 'If you like. Having someone special in your life is a big part of it.'

My back is now up against the side of the pool; Sam moves around in front of me, easing forward until he has one arm each side of me resting on the tiled edge. Our faces are no more than eighteen inches apart.

'Women are trouble,' he smirks and begins laughing.

I stretch out my hands either side of him, raising them up and then bringing them down to splash him.

'That's a sexist remark, Sam Callaghan.'

He backs off for a moment, then leans back in towards me, holding onto the tiled edge again. There is a twinkle in his eyes as they wander from my face down over my body.

'Okay. *Some* women are trouble. Maybe you aren't one of them.'

The way he's looking at me makes my stomach begin to flutter. His face is so close to mine and his mouth looks like it's waiting to be kissed. I wonder what he's expecting, if anything. I hold my ground even though a little spark of excitement is beginning to course through my veins. Could I do this? Could he do this?

A one night stand with no strings attached. Is that the question I can see behind those eyes or is it my imagination?

'I think it's time we went back inside. I expect all the guests have returned by now as it's getting late.'

For one brief second, he did edge a little closer but then he suddenly drew back just before he spoke. I wonder how I would have felt if he had kissed me, or if I had kissed him? He says he's not lonely but I don't believe that at all. Two lonely people comforting each other wouldn't have been such a bad thing, would it?

*

When we head back up the garden it's obvious the kids are all in bed and only two couples are still in the sitting room playing cards.

Sam and I say goodnight and I lock up before going upstairs. When he leans forward to kiss my cheek, it throws me slightly as I was prepared to do the air kissing ritual. I recover well, though, and accept that we are more friends now than mere acquaintances. Of course we are.

I hop into bed to check my emails and my heart plummets when I see there's one from Karl. Ziggy's head peers around the open bedroom door and I knew she wouldn't be far behind me. However, when she lies at my feet she doesn't seem her usual self and has trouble settling as I reluctantly begin reading. She seems to sense when I'm unsettled and hearing from Karl has that effect on me.

Dear Anna,

I admit I can get a little carried away sometimes. I have good news and... well, I can't go into that now but it means nothing if I don't have you by my side. I thought you'd rush back here the moment you opened the package and saw the ring. Then when it came back to me I realised that it meant nothing because I need to ask the question in person.

I've taken the post down from my timeline on Facebook and admitted to everyone at work that you haven't given me your formal response yet. That took a lot of guts, Anna, so I hope you can see that I regret what happened.

However, please say you'll marry me and I promise to ask you properly and in a fitting style if you will only give me the chance.

I'm going to be in a position soon to offer you everything you could ever want. You won't even have to work and we can sell your little house and buy something in the country. But it must be in the UK, so you need to come back home.

I'm here for you, my darling, and I'm prepared to be patient and wait until you are ready.

Love you always, Karl x

I throw the phone down on the bed out of pure frustration. Now he's trying to convince me it's true love. But why am I not feeling it, when I suppose this is exactly what I'd hoped to hear for so long? Ziggy pops her head up to look at me and emits something akin to a growl – well, that's a first, and I wonder if she's endorsing my own feelings.

I clamber out of bed and sit in front of the laptop.

'This needs two hands on the keyboard, Ziggy, and it will involve some pounding of keys. Don't worry, I've no intention whatsoever of letting him back into my life.'

She looks at me with those green eyes of hers and melts my heart, then she nestles back down, seemingly content.

Karl,

Tomorrow morning you will receive a box full of rose petals that have been cut up into tiny pieces. If the message isn't clear enough, then I'll say it once more: I'm sorry but I'm not in love with you.

This whole episode has been embarrassing. You cannot announce to the world that you are engaged when you know full well that I've made it very plain that 'we' are over.

I hope your good news allows you to start afresh and realise that I'm not a part of your future any more. I want to make it very clear that even when I do come back to the UK I have no intention of meeting up with you.

For your own well-being please now draw a line under this whole sorry episode. I wish you well, but I hope this is the last communication between us.

Anna

I don't even re-read it for typos, I just press send as I feel so deflated. When you realise what you once thought you wanted means nothing to you at all, it's like a void has suddenly opened up in your life. I love having someone else's energy around me as it inspires me to greater things. But choosing a life partner is about two people who complement each other perfectly. Each has their own individual strengths, but together they are so much stronger. Even in that apparently heartfelt letter, Karl's intention is to take over 'our' lives and be the person who drives our future forward. He doesn't want someone he can respect as an equal, but someone who looks up to him and to me that smacks of a one sided arrangement. And a superiority complex.

When sleep eventually overtakes my mind, I dream I'm back in the office and when I walk into the kitchen to get a coffee everyone goes silent. I end up leaving the room in tears, the whispering growing louder and louder with each step I take until the noise fills the air around me and I begin to run.

Sunny Side Up, Please Chef

Poor Sam; Mum offers a full breakfast menu, as that's a part of the attraction for guests, until she's staffed to offer evening dining. Then, hopefully, she'll be able to get away with a simple continental breakfast with a small bespoke list of items to cook. The list I have for Sam has everything from waffles to a full English, as well as French toast and crispy bacon. Rather impressively, he doesn't look panicked but tapes the list to the wall above the range cooker, where he already has bacon and sausages lightly browning.

'Is there anything I can do to help? The toast is under control and everyone has tea and coffee.'

'You could watch over these waffles if you don't mind. Give them three minutes and then check them every thirty seconds until they're brown.' He ladles batter deftly into the waffle iron and closes the lid.

It's warm outside, but in the kitchen the heat is already really beginning to build up. I think Mum and Dad are going to have to consider investing in some sort of fan, as August is supposed to be even hotter and it will be unbearable in here with the range going.

But within an hour everyone is served and the breakfast room is empty. The guests seemed happy enough and the half full parking area empties within minutes of breakfast being over.

'Listen to that,' I say, turning to Sam as I place the last plate in the rack.

'What?'

'The silence. Everyone has gone.'

'Now, what do *you* want for breakfast?'

'You're kidding me. I'm not washing up anything else so you can't make any more mess.'

He frowns.

'Um, you can't actually cook without making a bit of a mess. Okay, you make two coffees and I'll throw some fruit and yoghurt into a couple of dishes. Minimal damage.'

We spend a relaxing hour in the secret garden chatting away after breakfast has long gone. Ziggy puts in a brief appearance, allowing Sam to stroke her until a passing fly has her chasing down the garden after it.

'I need to go, too,' he smiles. 'Only because I'm cooking dinner for my parents. I've stripped the bed and left the sheets in the laundry room. You're welcome to join us for dinner if you want.'

It's a kind offer but I need to be here just in case anyone comes back early and wants something.

'Reluctantly I'll have to pass, but I will take you up on your other offer. It's the least I can do as you've spared me a lot of stress this morning. I couldn't have coped with that. And I will really appreciate it if you can spare a day while we're in Cannes to take me to Nîmes to visit Tom. I hate loose ends and it's a particularly touching story, so it's lovely to know there might be a happy ending.'

He smiles and reaches out to touch my shoulder.

'You're welcome. I enjoyed the company and thank you. See you in the morning, then. Ring if you need anything in the meantime.'

I nod. 'I'll be painting. Mum is going to be impatient to get her newly bought furniture installed now.'

'I'll be here bright and early, promise.'

*

Explaining to Sam about the situation with Karl gave me the confidence to send that email last night. It was as if saying the words out loud made it sink in, at last, that I was the innocent party. And today I feel lighter, happier.

When Mum and Dad return they seem surprised to find me alone, painting the gîte.

'Where's Sam?' Dad asks, popping his head through into the bedroom which is now a very pristine white.

'He went home mid-morning. Breakfast went well and he is a pretty good cook. You were right, Mum. And he mended the lock on room number two. Aside from that it was quiet, really. How was the buying trip?'

I bundle up the brushes to take them into the house to wash and put the lids back on the tins of paint. 'I'm done for the day. I think it's time for a cup of tea and I want to show you both the new website.'

'We bought a bed and some beautiful old bedside tables. Oh, and a pair of rustic chairs for the small dining table. And I managed to get some bedding; white background with a pattern of simple green leaves. Was that it, Geoff, or have I forgotten anything?'

Dad gives it some thought as we head across to the kitchen.

'The lamp.'

'Oh, yes, a rather beautiful standard lamp. You'll love it.'

Dad takes the brushes from me and I go upstairs to wash my face and change. Collecting the iPad, I return to the kitchen and as I walk in they immediately stop talking.

'What is it?'

Dad looks uncomfortable and Mum looks worried.

'It's just this business with Karl, Anna. We're both rather worried about it.'

I hold up my hand. 'Go no further. I want you to read the email I sent him last night.'

I take a chair at the kitchen table as Mum carries the mugs of tea and places them down in the middle. I click the iPad into the slot on the keyboard and open up my inbox.

'Here, I don't think I could have been clearer, do you?'

They both stand behind me and lean over while they read my words.

'Well done, that woman. You certainly told him.' Dad sounds pleased. Mum seems to be mulling it over.

'It won't inflame the situation, will it? I mean, he is stable, isn't he?'

'He's manipulative, Mum, that's all. He's used to talking people into doing what he wants and now he'll realise I'm not going to be talked into anything. So, you can relax, really you can. By the time I go back to the UK he will have found someone else.'

She sighs and shakes her head. 'Such a sorry state of affairs. Anyway, was Sam happy when he left?'

I start giggling. 'If you're checking that I didn't upset him in any way, then you can rest easy. We had dinner here last night. And he left in a good mood. Oh, and I'm going to Cannes with him.'

Mum is sitting opposite Dad and they stare at each other in surprise.

'Well, we weren't expecting that. I mean, we're obviously pleased you are going to have some time off. I certainly didn't realise you two were getting on that well.' Mum sounds incredulous, but I thought she'd be happy.

'Well, we're only going as friends, Mum. But there's another reason. I've tracked down Thomas, he refers to himself as Tom, now. Wait a second, I can show you his photo.'

I call up his blog and once more, Mum and Dad come and stand behind me while I show them some of the photos.

'He has certainly done well for himself,' Dad comments.

'He's in Africa at the moment, but coming back next month. Sam is going to drive me to Nîmes so I can hand over the jewellery box to him. Stay there… and this is your new website.'

Mum's hands fly up to her face and Dad chuckles.

'Oh, my word! It looks so professional!' he exclaims.

'Um... Dad, it's what I do, remember? I might not be able to cook but I know a bit about advertising.'

'Well, well, well. You've done us proud, darling. Time for a group hug.'

I stand and we throw our arms around each other. This last few weeks have served to remind me that family is everything. And Sam was right; I want a successful career, of course I do, but I also want to find my soul mate and settle down. I want to put down roots and, at some point, I want children.

'What's going on in that head of yours, now?' Mum stares into my eyes, looking for clues.

'I was just thinking how lucky I am to be able to come here and unwind. Not only am I feeling more relaxed, but working on this little re-branding project for you has given my confidence a boost. With your permission, I'd like to use it as the first case study on the website for my new business.'

Mum's eyes are shining. 'There you go, Geoff, I told you that nothing would keep our daughter down for long.'

'Well, if we ask around I expect you could get quite a bit of work just in the village alone. The B&B network we belong to has a lot of members who are struggling with websites they've set up themselves. IT related issues are permanently on the agenda of every meeting and many problems go unsolved. People play around but often they have no idea what they're doing. If you want us to spread the word, you only have to say.'

'Thanks, Dad. I'll bear that in mind. I'll finish off your new brochure tonight and once I have my website up and running too, maybe I'll see what help I can be. While I'm here I won't need to charge anything, but it would be good to have a gallery of projects I've worked on.'

When I climb into bed my head is buzzing with ideas. When sleep eventually overtakes me, I swear there's a smile on my face and no hint of a nightmare anywhere. Only the soft purring of the furry little ball curled up against my leg breaks the silence.

It's a Bright New Day

I was hoping to start work before Sam arrives as I'm first up. I tiptoe out of the house at just after 6 a.m. But when I see that the door of the gîte is open, it's quite a surprise.

'I know you said you'd be here bright and early, but this is just a wee bit earlier than I expected. And here she is – Ziggy, you deserted me!'

They both spin around to face me. Sam gives me a big grin and the first thing I notice is that he has a clean t-shirt on. It isn't an old one and it doesn't have any holes, or builders' debris on it. He ignores my stare and turns on his heels to continue marking up the back wall of the kitchen. Ziggy deigns to come over for a stroke but it's only the one and then she saunters back to sit next to Sam.

'I'm building the units this morning and will be installing them from midday.'

'But I haven't painted in there yet. I should have thought of that and painted the shower room and kitchen first. What an idiot.'

'Well, I thought the same thing but I wasn't going to say it. Can you work around me?' It's good to hear his banter.

'No problem. As soon as you've finished marking the position of the units, I'll work in the kitchen until you're ready to install them. In this heat, it will only take an hour or two for everything to dry. I can do the top coat after you've finished installing the cabinets. Then I'll work in the shower room so we won't be in each other's way.'

'Hey, you're even thinking like a builder's mate now! Did you mention to your mum and dad about Cannes?'

I'm loitering in the doorway, watching as he moves the tape measure along the wall.

'I did. Does it matter if I paint over those numbers?'

'No, I'm just working out how much of a gap I'll have left over. There you go, all done. So, what did they say?'

There's something different about Sam this morning. He's chatty and pleasant, rather than his usual early morning, rather reserved manner. Or maybe it really does mean something to him to take someone to Cannes, even if it's just a friend.

'They thought it was a good idea and they were pleased to hear the news about Tom.'

'Bet you showed them his blog.' Another grin.

'And I showed them their new website as well,' I say, sounding a little defensive even to my own ears.

He leans back against the wall.

'Ah, so now you are all fired up with enthusiasm for your next project. Well, congratulations and whatever you set up, I know it will be a success. Maybe some of that will rub off on me, during our road trip.'

As he walks off to the garage to start unpacking the kitchen units, his remarks leave me feeling rather speechless. That isn't a Sam comment at all. I shrug it off, thinking that he was probably being a tad sarcastic but disguising it behind a semi-positive tone.

'Success doesn't just rub off,' I shout after him, 'it's the product of hard work.'

Then I remember that it's only just after 6 a.m. and everyone else is still fast asleep.

*

By the time Sam returns with his arms wrapped around a sturdy looking base unit, I'm already working in the shower room.

'How's it going? Is it all dry?' His head appears around the side of the unit trying to gauge how much space he has either side to get through the front door. I rush over and help take the weight of the front.

'Left a bit. Okay, you're through. It was touch dry half an hour ago. You've been a long time. Have you built all the cabinets?'

'I have, but I had some company for a bit. Your dad brought me a coffee and we had a chat.'

I bend a little to help lower the unit onto the sitting room floor. When I straighten I throw him a questioning glance.

'He thanked me for helping out, that's all. Why the suspicious look?'

'I'm not the only one who isn't a good liar.'

His face remains blank but his gaze immediately moves away from my face to settle on the back wall of the kitchen. He's trying to be dismissive but I'm not falling for that as I know the wall is perfect.

'It was nothing. Don't be so paranoid.'

With that he heads back to the garage to get another unit.

If Dad has mentioned… no, he wouldn't do that to me. Nobody talks about Will. His name was banned when he broke my heart, but that was a long time ago. Sam is right, I'm being paranoid. I'm sure Mum and Dad know me well enough to understand that Sam can only be a friend. We'd drive each other mad, as we're two very different people. To be honest, I think both my mum and his mum would like me to try to bring him out of the shell he seems to have crawled into. Well, that might happen I suppose with this impending road trip. Maybe I can make him see that a future without plans is no future, really. But if that happens, great, all I can do is be myself and hope he continues to open up.

Today, though, I'm feeling free at last. No worries and no concerns. Life doesn't get much better than this.

*

It's a long day again and as soon as dinner is over I head up to my room. I open the window wide to take advantage of tonight's breeze, even though the air is still warm. Just the rustling of the leaves on the trees is relaxing. The heady perfume from the climbing rose wafts through the window tickling my nose and making me sneeze.

It doesn't take long to finish the brochure for Mum and Dad, then I turn to Tom's blog to see what he's up to today. It's written almost like a diary and it's fascinating. Then I notice there's a contact page. When I click on it there's a simple form to fill out with a name, email address and a message box.

I hesitate, then click away and decide instead to *like* his Facebook page, as there's a link in the side bar. He probably doesn't respond to messages anyway, as clearly his days are full and there does appear to be rather a lot of travel involved over some extremely rough terrain. He needs to go where the animals are and wherever there's trouble, I suppose.

Today he's been helping to rescue an antelope caught in some barbed wire. There's a video link to some footage and they end up having to sedate the animal to free it and then get it into the truck.

Annoyingly, I find myself finding fault with the structure and navigation of the website. My fingers are almost itching to do a re-design. It's rather basic and yet it could really jump off the page. But this is man versus the environment stuff and it isn't about presentation, but content. I notice there's no advertising at all for Tom's veterinary practices. All that jumps out at me is his passion for animal conservation and the way he seizes life, determined to make a difference. He could easily add a donation button to one of the wildlife rescue funds. I wonder fleetingly why he hasn't employed someone with the requisite skills to raise the bar, considering he's also a business man. I call up his practice website and am appalled. It's even more amateurish than his blog. Okay, it gets the message across about what they offer and the charitable side of their work, but the layout is awful and some of the photos are grainy.

I go back to the contact page and fill in the form. Clicking in the comment box I type away for a minute or two and then re-read the text.

Hello,

My name is Anna and my background is in advertising and media support. I'm just about to embark on a freelance career and am looking for a few clients whose websites I can re-brand at no cost. In return, I'd like to feature them on my new website to showcase my work. I would love the opportunity to re-design both your amazing blog and your veterinary website. The content is great but I have a whole raft of ideas that could be easily implemented to make both more visually attractive to the visitor. As the charity side of your work seems to be very important, I can easily add donation links to the key organisations in your field of work.

If you are interested and would like more information, please don't hesitate to email me.

Thank you.

Next, I look at the Saint-Julien-de-Vouvantes tourist information page and there's only one word to describe it and that's awful! It must be one of the first free templates ever issued and there's not a single redeeming feature. No photos, no links, awful fonts and dowdy colours. The only thing that jumps out is the crest they've used, which has been inserted into a header and appears to be a part of a castle. As the header is landscape and it looks like the original photo was portrait style, it's been cropped so that all you can see behind the shield with the crest is an oddly squat door flanked by mullioned windows.

It's going to be easy for me to effect a complete transformation. If I can redesign maybe a dozen websites reflecting a wide range of business areas, that would give me some eye-catching case studies to showcase. Okay, that's quite a bit of work but now is probably the only window of opportunity I'm going to have to do work for free. Once I'm back in the UK, I will have overheads again so this is probably my one and only shot.

I switch the laptop into sleep mode and jump into bed, having to encourage Ziggy to one side. She looks like she's doing a superman impersonation and is fully stretched out diagonally, front paws together as if ready to fly. She lets out a little whimper of protest, but can hardly open her eyes as she's so sleepy.

Lying there in the dark I mull over ideas for how I want my new website to look. It's exciting having a free rein as usually I'm working to a client's brief and can only throw in ideas. Now I'm starting with a blank page and it's heady stuff. The name 'Brand New' jumps into my head and while it's rather basic, the more I think about it the more I like it. I'm imagining the word 'brand' in upper case, followed by the word 'new', which would be double the size in lower case in a soft flowing font simulating an elegant, hand written style. BRAND *new* it is, then!

Feeling Energised

'What's up with you today? That humming is irritating, if you don't mind me being honest with you. I have a radio in the van and I'm quite happy to bring that in if you're in the mood for music. And what is that song you're murdering, anyway?'

I ease the roller in my hand away from the wall and turn around to face Sam. He's learning against the door frame of the kitchen and already the heat is beginning to get to him. There's no breeze at all today and I suspect we are both equally hot and bothered. It's difficult to get a solid night's sleep in this heat. Ziggy appears briefly in the doorway but slinks off when she realises it's probably hotter inside than it is outside.

'It's Queen.' I replace the humming with some words. 'You know the song – 'Don't Stop Me Now'.'

Sam winces. 'Worst rendition I've ever heard. You're strangling it. Singing is not one of your skills. So, what's put you in such a good mood today?'

'Oh, well, I love it when a plan begins to come together. A few things clicked into place last night and now I know what needs to be done it's just down to the execution bit. I don't suppose you know anyone who has an antiquated website in need of a free facelift?'

'You're working for free, now, are you? Doesn't sound like a very sound business plan to me. I thought the whole point was to make a living and get that flash car and dream house.'

Now that *is* sarcasm.

'I need to showcase what I can do and maybe help a few small businesses along the way. It's a win-win situation and the building blocks of my new business. I can only work for free while I'm here, so if you know of anyone this is a one time only offer.'

'If you're serious, then Dad doesn't even have a website and I keep telling him that's a big mistake. Would that be too much work for a freebie job as it's starting from scratch?'

Sam is serious and for some strange reason I feel rather flattered.

'It's easier in one way but it's all about content. Does he have any before and after shots of any of the jobs he's done?'

He pauses and then nods. 'I'm pretty sure he has and I know I've taken a few on my phone. Would those be good enough?'

'Yes. Phone shots are often very good quality. I could set something up for him quite quickly but I'd need to know exactly what copy he'd want included –

contact details, a suitable blurb describing what the business offers etc. Does he have a logo?'

'He has a letterhead that goes out on the invoices. I guess I could sit down with you and we could pull something together. Dad wouldn't have a clue, to be honest.'

'Well, as long as someone can give me the info I need then, yes, I'm up for that. There will be a small ongoing cost for a domain name and a website host, but it's minimal. Ask him if he's interested and we can take it from there.'

Sam heads off to get the radio from the van, leaving me deep in thought. My head is buzzing and doing this physical work leaves me free to harvest ideas. How ironic is it that what I considered to be one of the worst days of my life was the catalyst that turned me in a completely new direction? I would never have considered setting up my own business in the past, but now it's probably the most exciting thing that has ever happened to me. I'm humming again and I force myself to stop before Sam returns and I start driving him mad again.

*

It's a busy day all round with the furniture Mum and Dad bought at the weekend arriving in several deliveries. I help Dad stack it in the garage, making sure Sam can still get to the mound of boxes containing the sanitary ware for the shower room, the worktops for the kitchen and the tiles for the splashbacks.

'Nearly there,' Dad nods in the direction of the boxes. 'Every day it dwindles a little more. Then we will have to buy it all over again for the second gîte. I can't say I'll be sorry when it's all finished, as it feels like it's been a long old haul to get to this point.'

'Everything takes time, Dad. But I know what you mean, you've both been constantly on the go and you never get to sit and enjoy it. It is beautiful here and the time will come when you can chill out in the garden for the afternoon and marvel at what you've achieved.'

'I don't think we're wired that way, sadly, Anna. We don't do relaxation, do we?' He winks at me and I guess he's right. I'm not happy unless I'm doing something productive and I'm not sure if that's a good thing, or not.

'You and Sam are getting on well and that's good to see. You've really worked together as a team. Sarah and Neil have been so worried about him. All work and no play isn't good for anyone but with Sam it's all that keeps him going. But he'll work for anyone, except himself. He's never going to get that barn of his done, is he?'

Dad doesn't say a lot but he notices everything.

'I feel the same way. But he isn't a totally lost cause, because I'm seeing small changes in his attitude. On the road trip, I'm aiming to enthuse him about his own project. I have a couple of ideas.'

Dad smiles at me. 'You don't like loose ends, do you, Anna? You like everything sorted and that includes people. Well, if there's anything at all you can do to inspire Sam he's one deserving cause.'

Once everything is neatly packed in, I return to the gîte and find Sam lying on the floor underneath the sink unit, swearing. I guess the heat, the confined space and a tap with a nut that won't do up is a bad combination. Mum appears a few minutes later to say lunch is in the kitchen and they're off to the shops. I encourage Sam to put down the wrench and take a break. It does the trick, because an hour later he's back on the floor and within a couple of minutes the job is done and he's onto the next unit.

While I wait for the paint to dry before I do the second coat in the shower room, I pop back into the house to wash up the dishes. Then I head upstairs to check my emails. I'm not really expecting a response from Tom but there is an update from Pat.

Hi Anna,

Breaking news today. Karl has been promoted and is now a director. It's just been announced. He's switching offices today and he's in high spirits. I wasn't sure if you were back in touch with him, or not. There's a drinks party here after work today.

I'm off on holiday next week and to be honest with you, I can't wait. There's been a lot of tension around here lately with one thing and another, and it will be nice to have a break away from it all.

Hope things are going well there,

Pat

I quickly respond, hoping she's still at her desk.

Hi Pat,

Wow, that's a surprise and I bet you are almost counting the hours to your hols.

Has Karl said anything about his engagement announcement at all?

France is relaxing and it's hot, hot, hot!

Anna

I'm in luck and there's an almost instant response.

Hi Anna,

What a coincidence we were both online! Not really, but with everything that's going on here with the changes it's no longer hot gossip. I overheard him telling someone the plans for the party were on hold, though.

I did notice the announcement is no longer on his Facebook timeline but only because I made a point of looking. No one else has mentioned it. Guess doing nothing was the right option, after all.

I wouldn't worry too much as you know how transient these things are and by the time you return to the UK, anyone you bump into will probably have forgotten all about it. People are wondering how Karl has managed to get on the board so easily and thoughts are that he just happened to be in the right place at the right time. But there are some concerns as you know what he's like and he's bound to want to shake things up and make his mark. I'm hoping it all happens while I'm away and when I get back the worst of it will be over.

Speak soon,

Pat

So, Karl lied to me yet again, selling himself in a good light when he took the cowardly way out. I instinctively knew he was unlikely to make a big announcement and risk looking foolish. But Pat has a point and besides, I'm not there to be affected by it all. Karl will be busy trying to prove his worth and impress the rest of the board so it seems I'm finally off the hook. Besides, the new bait is much bigger this time around – he's now where he always wanted to be and he'll be concentrating on making his mark.

Making Contact

Tomorrow, at long last, Lizzie and Daniel are due to arrive and I'm counting down the hours. Everything has gone according to plan; so well, that yesterday and today Sam and I are working outside. Sam is putting up a small picket fence to give each of the gîtes a bijou garden of its own. I'm in charge of planting and after two trips to buy plants, it's beginning to look rather pretty. Gone are the compacted, ugly brown patches of dirt from all the trudging backwards and forwards. Instead there's a stepping stone pathway. The building rubble was cleared by a guy from the village who spent yesterday loading it into a skip. Mum and Dad are inside setting up the bed and everything will be finished before the end of the day.

I finish patting the earth around the last plant and give it a good sprinkle of water. Sam is leant over fixing one of the uprights onto the picket fence. I stand, watching him in action and Ziggy trots up to join me.

'What?' He straightens, frowning a little.

'Nothing. We think you deserve a high five.' As if by way of endorsement Ziggy adds a *meow* before turning tail and heading for the nearest patch of shade.

I put up my hand and he meets it in mid-air. 'Why?'

'Because I'm impressed. This was a big job and you made it seem easy. One step at a time. If you can turn an old stone shed into this beautiful little house, then your barn is going to be stunning.'

He raises an eyebrow and it appears that I've said the wrong thing. He kneels down on the ground and reaches for another screw.

'Have you been talking to my mother again?' He throws the words over his shoulder, obviously annoyed.

'Hey, I was trying to give you a compliment, so you don't have to be so touchy.'

He makes a grunting sound. 'It's not rocket science,' he mutters.

This is the old Sam and I wonder if he's beginning to stress about the trip to Cannes? It's ten days away and now we're finished here he hasn't mentioned what he's doing next week. Obviously, I'm going to want to be around a fair bit to make the most of Lizzie's visit, but it is a holiday for her and she's going to be doing day trips with Daniel. If Sam decides to make a start on the second gîte, then I'll be available to help out but I don't feel it's a question I can ask. I casually threw it in to a conversation with

Mum but she wasn't expecting him to be around, so maybe he's taking a bit of time off.

But I'm standing here feeling bad as I didn't mean to make Sam feel defensive and now I can't leave things as they are.

'I don't suppose you are free tomorrow night, just for a few cocktails in the garden with Lizzie and Daniel? Mum and Dad have been invited over to Honorine's for one of her famous suppers. Apparently, she makes a wonderful rabbit stew. Anyway, I wanted their first night here to be a bit special and I'm thinking of doing a few nibbles to soak up the alcohol.'

Sam's head tips back and he looks up at me with a smile on his face.

'You're going to cook something?'

I give him a purposeful stare. 'It's not rocket science.'

'Touché. Sorry, I'm being grouchy again today. I have a couple of interesting recipes for nibbles that take minutes to put together. But as for fancy drinks, I don't have a clue.'

I grin back at him, relieved to see the awkward moment has passed.

'Oh, I know my way around a martini, or two. Sounds like we're sorted. Six o'clock?'

'That's a date.'

That's a date? I check out his expression and he's messing with me. I hope this is the fun Sam who is going to appear tomorrow night, as if Mr Grouchy takes over it will kill the entire evening.

*

It's an early finish and after a relaxing bath I settle down in front of the laptop. Ziggy insists on jumping up onto the desk and walking between me and the screen.

'Ziggy, that's not helpful. Look, you can have the bed all to yourself for a while.'

I smooth her soft coat and she arches her back, stretches and then finally leaps across to curl up on the duvet.

All of the emails in my inbox are junk; one click, and they're gone. But suddenly a new one pops up and it's a response from *Le vétérinaire ambulant.* My heart rate increases as I click to open it up.

Hi there, Anna,

Thanks for getting in touch and I'm intrigued by your offer. My only problem is that I travel around quite a bit and spend very little time at home, or at work. I know the blog is a bit of a mess and I've never been happy with the design for the practice. It's my fault as I tend to commission people to do things and then don't have the time to get involved. So, I might not be the best candidate to take up your offer, even though it's sorely needed.

Best regards, Tom

Soon my fingers are tapping away on the keys as a sense of excitement courses through me.

Hi Tom,

I wouldn't really need any input from you. If you are happy for me to 'lift' some of the copy and photos straight from the blog and the website, I'll pull a few ideas together and send you a presentation. If you like what you see, I can take it from there.

I think the charitable work you are doing is amazing and I'm not surprised you're so busy. But I really think your online presence would benefit from a makeover and gain you an even wider audience. Many, I'm sure, would click and donate to some of the causes you support if the options were there in front of them. Also, it's not clear from your blog that you run a veterinary practice, so it would be beneficial to link the two together.

What do you think?

Anna

I half wondered if I should mention Le Manoir d'Orsenne, but I decide to keep it simple. Anyway, this is something entirely separate and would be a coup for me. If I want to prove how diverse I can be in terms of ideas then this would be an exciting way to showcase that. As I'm about to put the laptop into sleep mode my inbox pings and there's an almost instant reply from Tom.

Hey, Anna,

Determined lady, I like that! Feel free to grab whatever content/photos you like and I'll be excited to see your ideas.

Thanks so much. Have a great day and I'll wait to hear from you.

Tom

I close the email and then immediately open his blog to read his latest post. It's all about a vervet monkey who was finally well enough to be released back into the wild today. There's a short video capturing the moment and for a brief second the lens focuses on Tom's face. It's a magical shot and what I see reflected in his eyes isn't just the thrill of another success, but the passion he has for what he does. He immediately high five's the cameraman and that's the end of the clip.

Seemingly out of nowhere, an image suddenly pops into my head that would be perfect as a logo. It's a chain of animals in a circle, representing the world. I visualise a monkey with one arm outstretched and one trailing behind him, linking to a lion who is leaping and covers the top of the circle. Maybe that should be balanced by a few domestic animals so that the logo would work for the blog and the website. My brain is working overtime as I click on sleep mode and slip into bed. A menagerie of animals are now jostling for my attention and if I wasn't so tired I'd sit down and begin designing the logo tonight. But my dreams are calling me and my eyelids are fluttering, despite the sound of Ziggy's gentle snores in the background.

A Few Surprises

It's late afternoon when our special guests arrive. It's so good to see Lizzie and we hug like long lost sisters. Daniel waits patiently, shaking hands with my parents and then turning to hug me, as Lizzie turns to hug Mum.

'It feels like such a long time. How was the drive?' I have a silly grin on my face but it's nothing compared to Lizzie's beam.

'It does. It was good; we stayed overnight at Rouen, so we've only been travelling for just over four hours today. We toured the cathedral there and the church of St Joan of Arc. Then we spent a couple of hours at the Muséum d'Histoire Naturelle. I had no idea it was the second largest natural history museum in France. Thanks for suggesting it, Anna.'

'Well, I'm glad you've had a good day. Mum and Dad are out socialising this evening, so Sam is coming over shortly to don his chef's apron. I thought we'd have drinks and supper in the garden later. Anyway, let's get you settled in first.'

As we walk around Le Manoir and follow the path up to the gîte, Lizzie seems overawed.

'Oh, wow! I'm not going to want to go home! Anna, how on earth are you going to be able to walk away from this? It's a little piece of heaven. And here's Ziggy!'

Ziggy runs straight up to Lizzie, who holds out her hand to be sniffed. Recognising an old friend, Ziggy immediately arches her back and angles her head, waiting to be stroked.

'Aww, how she's grown, Anna. I still remember her as a little kitten. She looked like a little cinnamon bun all curled up.'

'I know. I've missed her so much but she's very happy here.'

Mum and Dad are following on behind and as I turn to look at them they both have broad smiles on their faces.

'She loves the attention from our guests. We feel blessed to have her and to be here living the dream. Sam and Anna have done a grand job of getting your gîte ready too, Lizzie.' Dad's voice is full of pride.

'I'm glad we're going to meet Sam. He sounds like a great guy. A chef and a builder, eh?'

Lizzie turns to give me a rather meaningful stare and I roll my eyes.

'Don't start.'

She laughs and follows me inside, impatient to explore. I can only hope that Sam is up to socialising and is prepared to join in when he arrives. It's going to be a long evening if he's quiet and withdrawn.

Shaking off my concerns I help ferry the luggage out to the gîte. We all saunter back to the car to see what's left. Unexpectedly, a motorbike pulls into the parking area, sending Ziggy skittering off in the direction of the rear garden. Assuming it's someone looking for accommodation, Dad steps forward but as the motorcyclist dismounts and walks towards us he pulls off his helmet. No one is more surprised than I am to see that it's Sam.

'Hi Sam, great bike you have there!' Dad walks over to take a good look and Daniel is close behind him.

Sam smiles in our direction and I step forward. 'This is Daniel and this is Lizzie. Sam, I didn't know you owned a motorbike.' I can't keep a tone of sheer surprise out of my voice as I watch them all shaking hands.

The bike looks pristine, presumably because he rarely uses it, which means it's an asset he could sell to help fund his project. For someone who admits funds are tight, I'm rather surprised by this discovery. Daniel is crouched down next to it getting a closer look at the engine.

'Wow! You don't see many Triumph Bonneville T100's about.'

Sam nods in agreement.

'A 2004 Custom Café Racer. She's sweet to ride. It belonged to my granddad but he only rode her for a year. He was just fifty-five when he died quite suddenly following a massive heart attack. I spent most weekends with him, polishing her up and he even convinced Grandma to let me hop on the back a few times for a run out. It was his life-long dream. Neither of my brothers ever showed any interest in the bike but it was his pride and joy. He left it to me in his will, much to the annoyance of Grandma and my mum. I was fifteen at the time and it stayed in his garage until I was old enough to ride it myself. I called in most weekends to give her a buff up, check for oil leaks and start the engine to keep everything working.'

Ah, that at least makes some sense, I suppose.

Mum and I move closer. It is a great looking bike if you are into that sort of thing.

'The electric blue works great with the black. And I see you have vintage style tyres. Nice bike, mate. I have a Ducati 999R but it's going soon; the wedding fund needs a boost.'

Sam and Daniel exchange a look of commiseration.

'I rarely ride these days, but Granddad loved this bike, so I take her out for a spin every now and again just to keep everything in working order.'

Well, any concerns I had about Sam and Daniel getting on were obviously unfounded.

Mum and Dad go to get ready for their evening out and Lizzie and I stop by the kitchen to make a coffee and go and sit in the garden. We leave the two guys to talk power and torque: whatever that means.

'I feel bad that Daniel has to sell his bike but to be honest, Anna, I worry every time he takes it out for a spin. It's a fast bike, built for speed and even though I rarely go on it, I'm never happy sitting behind him. I spend most of the time with my eyes closed just praying we don't crash.'

As we settle ourselves down in the secret garden, I nod in agreement.

'I can understand that. I've never been on a motorbike, so I can't even imagine what it feels like. So, you guys are saving for the big day, then?'

'Yes. We've decided to go for it and make it as special as we can. I only intend getting married the once.' She smiles and I can see how happy she is to have found her soul mate.

I sip my coffee, wondering what that must feel like. I realise that ever since my teenage years I've had a sort of fear of being alone in life. As if I need someone to make me feel whole and without that, something is missing. Is it because Mum and Dad are always so close and loving together, that being a part of a team is my definition of normality? I'm a strong person and I don't need to rely upon anyone else, so why do I feel this sense of emptiness?

'Problems?'

Lizzie is looking at me with a puzzled expression on her face.

'No. Just envious.'

'Your day will come. It needs to be the right guy, though. It's a pity about Karl. Have you heard anything more?'

I know I look and sound jaded as I speak. 'There are big changes going on in the office and while Karl didn't admit the engagement wasn't real, it's no longer on his Facebook timeline. I emailed Pat and she told me that he did say the party was on hold, but that was about it. Unless he gets in touch I've decided to put it all behind me.'

'Ooh, is this because of Sam? You didn't say how handsome and fit he was.'

She's smiling at me cheekily over her coffee mug.

'Hey, stop match-making. We're friends but we already drive each other mad.'

'They do say opposites attract,' she muses.

'Get to know him a little and then we can have this conversation again. However, I do have someone rather interesting to show you, as I now have some more information about the guy I told you about.'

I take my iPad from the table and call up Tom's blog.

'Now this is a man who lives life to the full. Have a read.'

While Lizzie clicks away, looking at photos and reading a couple of Tom's latest diary entries, she can't stifle the "oohs" and "ahhs". Some of the photos literally melt your heart when you see sick animals restored to full health and then released back into the wild.

'He's quite a guy, all right. And you're showing me this because... you're stalking him on the internet now? You want to declare your love and hope he'll whisk you off to the jungle to see the really big cats?'

She's joking with me, of course; I start giggling and she joins in.

'Meet Thomas Parker-Laurent, or Tom Laurent, as he's now known. He's the one who lived here for a while with his aunt and uncle as a young boy.'

Lizzie's surprise turns to amazement as I tell her the whole story of the jewellery box and the trail that led me to discover Tom's whereabouts. I don't mention Cannes, or Sam, but say I intend to hand it back to him.

'You've gone to a lot of trouble to track him down. Couldn't you just send the box by recorded delivery?'

'And risk something irreplaceable going missing? That's rather heartless of you, Lizzie.'

I try to sound aghast at her suggestion but I can tell she's questioning my motives.

'You want to place it in his hands yourself and have him thank you personally. As he gazes into your eyes you'll see fireworks and in no time at all you will both be jetting off to an exotic island to save monkeys, or whatever.'

Once more she has me laughing out loud.

'One step at a time, please. Okay, so on paper he looks like my sort of guy. Interesting, ready to seize every opportunity that comes his way and motivated by the passion in his life. But all I'm doing is returning something that I believe means a lot to him.'

Lizzie stares at me.

'There's more, I can sense it.'

I shrug my shoulders.

'You know I'm starting up my own business ready for when I return to the UK? Mainly branding and setting up websites, that sort of thing.' Lizzie nods and I continue, wondering what she'll think. 'Well… I've offered to overhaul his blog and re-brand his practice website for free. A lot of the work he does is charitable, aside from his voluntary work. Of course, I'm making the offer to several businesses as I need before and after examples to showcase my work.'

She sits back in her chair, wide-eyed with disbelief.

'He looks like a well-intentioned guy and a real catch, but aren't you getting a little too involved in this? Returning a valuable item to its owner is one thing, but offering him your services for free before you've even met him... what if he's weird, or something?'

I look down at my hands resting in my lap.

'He doesn't know about the jewellery box yet. I made contact via the email on his blog and he thinks I just stumbled across it. Besides, the offer of my services for free is purely business related and mutually beneficial, so what's the harm in it?'

Lizzie finishes off her coffee in silence, then looks across at me with a slight frown on her face.

'What if he's another Karl?'

'Lizzie! I repeat – I'm not trying to get a date with him. I need projects and this one will look good as well as helping a great cause.'

As if to endorse that, Ziggy winds herself around the leg of my chair and flops in the shady patch cast by my shadow. How can anyone not admire a man who spends his life looking after animals?

'If anyone deserves a freebie, it's him.'

'And when will you tell him that you know his life story?'

I sigh because I know she's right. 'When I know him a little better.'

'Ah,' she says, nodding. 'When it won't sound quite so bizarre.'

'What's bizarre?' Daniel asks as he walks through the archway. 'Sam has some savoury things in the oven and I wondered what you ladies wanted to drink.'

I immediately jump up, grabbing both mugs off the table and disturbing Ziggy who lets out a weak *meow* of protest, but doesn't move.

'Time for cocktails, I think. And Lizzie is exaggerating, as bizarre isn't in my vocabulary.'

We all traipse into the kitchen just as the doorbell rings and it's a late arrival. Mum thought they were a no-show, but they explain that they had a puncture which delayed them for a couple of hours. I leave Lizzie and Daniel to make the cocktails while I show the guests up to their room.

When I return they've already started – without me.

'First time I've ever tried an espresso martini. It's not bad!' Sam looks up at me approvingly.

They all toast each other and Lizzie offers me a glass.

'Did you stick to the recipe? A little ice in the shaker first, then the Tia Maria followed by a shot of vodka. The espresso must go in last, before you shake, and should be cooled a little with some of the ice chips, first. Oh, and the glasses must be chilled for at least twenty minutes in the freezer.'

I take a sip and nod. 'Guess you did. No coffee beans on the top?'

'I couldn't find any,' she says, rolling her eyes.

I point to the shelf above the kettle. 'In that little tin. Dad won't drink one without, he says they add that perfect little hint of bitterness.'

Sam is bent over the range, pulling some trays from the oven. The smell is amazing. We load up a couple of platters and carry everything down to the bottom of the garden.

It's more Italian cuisine than French, the thinly cut pieces of baguette loaded with an assortment of hot and cold toppings. The cold selection of cheeses and cooked meats, olives, capers and tomatoes, make perfect finger food. The hot options include a tomato and garlic sauce, with parmesan cheese and salt cured French lardons; and goat's cheese with slices of grilled red pepper. Both Lizzie and Daniel are really impressed by Sam's culinary skills, as Lizzie reminds me of yet another of my infamous disasters. It raises a laugh from everyone and even I join in.

While we eat Sam asks Daniel about his job and we listen to a string of plumbing mishaps. Daniel explains that he never really knows what he's going to find until he's on the job. He says he has experienced just about everything. Including a bath that had fallen through a rotting floor into a kitchen.

I like Daniel. He's one of those guys who enjoys what he does, doesn't moan about his lot and is simply working hard to build a life with Lizzie. They are the perfect couple in my eyes and I love the little glances he keeps stealing when she isn't looking his way.

'Have you always been a builder, Sam?'

I tense a little for some reason. But when I glance across at Sam he seems happy enough to answer. I look down and see that Ziggy has appeared and after circling around, flops down besides his chair. She pops her head up as if she's listening to the conversation, her green eyes trained on him and watching intently.

'No. I sort of ended up here and became involved in my dad's business through mutual necessity. He taught me everything I know and he's worked hard to build it up from nothing. They bought a run-down farmhouse not far from here about eight years ago and finally moved over here permanently just over four years ago, now. They work mainly for British people who struggle with the language, which makes it hard when it comes to employing a builder. It's very different over here and it's important to understand those differences when it comes to extensions and major works. But recently he's been getting work from the locals, too, and that's great because it means Mum and Dad are now a real part of the community.'

It's an honest answer and Daniel dives straight in.

'So, have you made your home here, or is this just a temporary phase before you move on?'

Sam drains his cocktail glass, gently setting it back down on the table.

'I live in a caravan next to a barn I'm converting. It's a work in progress.'

Well, part of that sentence is correct but I haven't seen much progress since I've been here.

'How lovely; a barn conversion!' Lizzie enthuses. Her dream of living in France one day is only a glimmer on a distant horizon. But she's wearing her rose-coloured spectacles, as they say, and will be imagining a pristine and cosy little caravan. She'd be appalled at Sam's real living conditions. Lizzie thinks staying in a hotel, and even our delightful little gîte, that only has shower facilities and not a full bathroom, is roughing it.

'When do you hope to be ready to move in? It must be tough getting through the winter in a caravan. I take my hat off to anyone who is prepared to do that.' Daniel is genuinely interested.

Sam purses his lips, appearing to give it some consideration.

'Hmm… it's hard to say, really. I'm happy enough plodding along. To be honest, at the end of each day I'm content to go back and relax with a beer and a burger on the barbecue. I work on it at weekends, more intensively when I'm able to buy materials. It depends on how busy the day job is, though. Winter is harder, of course.'

Daniel seems to understand, but Lizzie is very like me.

'That's such a shame. It must be so hard not being able to just crack on with the work and get it all done. I bet it will be stunning, though, once it's completed.'

Will that be this decade, or next, Sam? I busy myself sipping the last of my martini to avoid joining in the conversation.

'I hope so. I used to live by a timetable but now life is a lot more relaxed. Besides, I enjoy doing jobs like this one for Geoff and Viv. They deserve all the help they can get. And it's been a bonus working alongside Anna, of course.'

He's throwing the conversation open because he's beginning to feel uncomfortable.

'Have you seen it?' Lizzie asks, turning to me with eager eyes.

'Yes. It's… as Sam said, a work in progress. But the views are stunning and the plans are well thought out.'

'Oh,' Lizzie muses, 'if only we could start off our married life over here instead of in a new build on the edge of a city. It's convenient for work, I suppose, and besides, the drawback is how to earn a living over here. Are plumbers in demand, Sam?'

He shoots a look at Daniel, who seems surprised at the question. I wonder if Lizzie has ever mentioned her dream to him?

'I don't know a plumber who isn't rushed off his feet, to be honest. There's a lot of old pipework in the properties being renovated. My dad is always looking for English speaking tradesmen.'

Daniel spins his head back round to look at Lizzie, raising his eyebrows in surprise.

'You'd seriously consider moving here? What about our families?'

Sam looks in my direction for help and I rise, grabbing two of the cocktail glasses.

'Anyone up for another martini? Sam, you might want to stay over and take that bike of yours home in the morning. The single room at the back that we often use for storage isn't in use and it won't take much to move a few boxes around and make up the bed. Back in a little bit, folks. Can you grab those two glasses for me?'

Sam immediately jumps up, glad of the distraction and as we head back up the garden he shoots me a sideways look that is little short of a grimace.

When we are out of earshot I explain. 'Lizzie's biological father lives over here and when she was young she spent part of her summer holidays with him, his French wife and her two step-brothers. She keeps egging her mother and step-father on to buy a holiday home over here, or do what my parents did. But they don't have the same affinity with France that she does and they are happy enough living in Devon. I'm surprised she hasn't had the conversation with Daniel, though, as he seemed rather surprised.'

'There always a little trouble in paradise, isn't there?' He looks at me with that lop-sided grin of his.

'Which means?'

'Well, they're the perfect couple, aren't they? They'll settle down, have a couple of kids and, hopefully, live happily ever after.'

It's not sarcasm in his tone, it's something else.

'And what's wrong with that?'

He sighs. 'Some people have the knack of making it all look so easy but the reality is that it's hard to get it right. Anyway, let's tackle this martini, as if I'm staying over I'm definitely up for a second before I hit the real coffee.'

Sometimes Sam is so easy to get on with and I find myself looking at him and wondering... I don't know, maybe what if one of us was a bit different? Or that we weren't such extreme opposites of the scale? One thing I've learnt in life, twice over now – to my bitter cost – is that you can't change people. I'm never going to be as laid back as Sam and Sam is never going to be as focused as I am.

But the big surprise tonight is how sociable he's being. He's already spent a lot of time talking to Daniel and I wonder if he misses the guy talk thing; the bike was a surprise but a perfect ice-breaker as it happens. It's given them something else in common, aside from work, and it makes the other differences a lot less obvious. Or so I thought, until it's time for everyone to head off to bed. I give Daniel a goodnight hug and turn to Lizzie. Sam is already climbing the stairs and Daniel is on his way out through the kitchen.

'I see what you mean,' she half whispers into my ear. 'Sam is a lovely, lovely guy but isn't it a little strange that he as good as admitted he's living from day to day? I bet you know his story. Is it a sad one?'

She looks concerned, as if she's hoping to hear some revelation that will explain the situation and indicate it's only a temporary thing. Suddenly I feel quite defensive on Sam's behalf, which is silly as Lizzie is only voicing what I felt when I first met him. And, besides, Sam and I are only friends. I don't have to make excuses for him.

'It's the way he's chosen to live his life. I think there was a time when he was under a lot of pressure and something went wrong, but I don't know what.

I've tried to encourage him a little, as he's so focused on the day job. But I guess it takes all sorts to make a world.'

She raises her eyebrows.

'Shame. He is a very good looking candidate.' She sounds disappointed for me and as she races off to catch up with Daniel, she leaves me standing here speechless. Even if Sam was looking to get involved with someone the timing isn't right for me to even consider starting a new relationship. And, besides, from what his mum told me he might have already found the great love of his life, if the person he lost was more than just a friend.

The Surprises Keep on Coming

Sam leaves shortly after breakfast and I'm surprised to find out from Daniel that, apparently, we're going to meet him later at the barn for a guided tour.

I leave Lizzie and Daniel chatting in the garden with Mum and Dad after the visitors' breakfasts have been served and go up to my room. I'm relieved to see there's nothing from Karl.

I have nearly two hours before we need to set off and I want to start putting together some design ideas for Tom's new logo. After an hour of clicking, dragging, cutting and pasting I go back to the original idea I had last night. I end up with a black and white drawing of a lion's head surrounded by a circle of head to toe animals. I add the outline of two leafy bamboo canes on the left hand side, to give it a jungle look. Then I do another one in a similar vein, but this time I use a cat surrounded by a circle of domestic animals and the outline of a daisy. Perfect, if I do say so myself. Both logos look good side by side and it's easy to distinguish them, but they are also easily identifiable as being the same brand. In fact, I'm so pleased that I immediately email them to

Tom with a little note to say it's only the first draft and asking for his thoughts.

Later I'll work on finding the right template for his blog and website. I need to be mindful that Tom needs something that's going to be relatively simple to update and load posts containing lots of photos. Because he already has so much content it's going to be easy to improve on the presentation and make everything really jump off the page. But now it's time to get ready and check out the latest progress at Sam's place.

*

'It's, um, a bit of a project you have here. Quite ambitious.' Daniel's voice is even, but he's in the trade and I can see from the look on his face that he understands how much work is required. In fact, I don't think anything further has been done since I last visited.

Sam explains his plans and then goes off to the caravan with Daniel, to show him the drawings. When they are gone Lizzie turns to me, letting her face fall.

'It's going to need a team to work on this, Anna. Sam is going to be living in that caravan for ever, at this rate. I'm really shocked!'

I shrug, feeling unable to add anything to her comment.

'Can't we do anything to help him?' She sounds sad and it's touching that she's so concerned about someone who is little more than a stranger to her.

'I haven't offered because it's a sore subject. But I know what two people can achieve when they work hard, just look at the gîte. I don't know if it is simply the lack of funds, or pride that stops him reaching out to people. I bet his dad would love to be here giving him a hand. I have to remember I'm only a friend, though.'

She nods, scuffing the dirt floor with her foot.

'I really wasn't expecting this. Daniel was rather taken aback, as well. It's not so much a dream, as a nightmare. What if it never gets finished?'

We're both thinking of the very unprepossessing seventies caravan which has seen its best years.

'What if we all offered to help out? Once he saw some real progress maybe that would give him the boost he needs. Or is that a mad idea?'

'What's a mad idea?' Sam's voice seems to echo around the empty space as the guys walk back through the door.

I swallow down a big gulp as Lizzie flashes them both a well meaning smile.

'Wouldn't it be fun if we could all help out, Sam? We're here for a week and sight-seeing is fun, but how exciting would it be to spend a few days working together on your project. Okay, I don't have the skills that Daniel and Anna can offer, but I can fetch, carry and keep things tidy. What do you think?'

If I'd just uttered those words then I'm sure Sam would have exploded. Instead, he appears to consider it with some level of seriousness, before answering.

'That's a great offer, Lizzie, and a very generous one indeed. The problem is that I'm due to start work on the second gîte this week, before Anna and I go to Cannes. Geoff and Viv are understandably keen to get the building works finished. I've told them it will all be done by the middle of September at the latest. They need to capitalise on the autumn visitors and then there's only a short break between that and the popular Christmas holiday period.'

Well, that's news to me. And Mum and Dad. We all thought he was taking a week off. Oh Sam, are you ever going to put yourself first? He seems genuinely regretful but Lizzie has spun around on her heels to stare at me.

'You're going to Cannes? You never mentioned that.'

I squirm uneasily. Sam did that on purpose to deflect from the fact that he has no intention of letting anyone organise his time, even when the offer is a genuine one.

'Sam's meeting up with some old friends and he's kindly offered to take me along for the ride. At some point, we'll take the jewellery box to Tom.'

She turns back round to scrutinise Sam, but he's giving nothing away.

'Oh, I see. That's very kind of Sam. And Cannes, how exciting.' It's obvious her interest is piqued, but Daniel asks Sam a question and thankfully the subject is dropped.

However, while the guys go off to inspect a neat stack of old timbers Sam is hoping to re-purpose, Lizzie hurries across to me.

'Are you sure there's nothing going on between the two of you?'

'Nothing except some harsh words when we drive each other nuts with our opposing viewpoints. We do have some common ground, but now you've seen how ridiculously laid back he is about his circumstances, can you imagine how frustrating I find that? I know his mother feels the same way. But you can't help someone who doesn't want to be helped.'

I think I've made my point and Lizzie accepts it with good grace.

'It's such a shame. And it would have been a real buzz to get stuck in and make something happen here.'

The warm breeze picks up and the polythene sheets against the almost completely open side of the barn begin to crackle.

'That's a lovely view, though,' she concludes.

Daniel and Sam walk back across the large open space, deep in conversation. Then Sam looks at me with a smile that seems genuine enough.

'Are you ladies ready to move on? Next you get to see a completed project. I thought you might like to look around my parents' farmhouse renovation.'

Well, that's a real surprise and I can't wait. I wonder, though, if it's Sam's way of diverting attention away from himself.

*

It's lunchtime when we arrive at Neil and Sarah's farmhouse. Sam doesn't seem apologetic for the timing and, after brief introductions, Sarah insists we stay for lunch.

Neil and Sam take us on the tour of what turns out to be yet another total surprise. Set in a clearing among a swathe of tall pine trees, the original farmland extends to the rear and right hand side of the property. Only one and a half acres still belong to the house, and this is leased out to the farmer who owns the remainder of the surrounding land.

Built on the side of a hill, the original stone farmhouse is level with the road but as the land behind it slopes gently away, the extension to the rear is one storey lower. This wooden structure is on stilts and the wall-to-wall windows give a panoramic view out over the tops of the trees and the fields, far into the distance.

'Wow,' Daniel mirrors everyone's reaction. 'This is unbelievable. I'm guessing only the farmhouse bit at the front is original?'

Neil nods. 'Yes. It had three quite basic rooms downstairs and two bedrooms upstairs. Now the old part of the building houses the kitchen/diner downstairs and a master bedroom and en-suite upstairs. The annexe has two further bedrooms, two bathrooms and a large, open plan sitting room.'

We're all staring up at the rear elevation in awe.

'How long did it take from start to finish?' Daniel asks Neil, appreciating the sheer amount of work involved.

'About four and a half years, give or take. A local French builder sorted the permits and put up the shell, as at that point we were only getting here about five times a year. I was working seven days a week back in the UK so we could then come out for a month at a time. Each of my three sons have lent a hand, but Sam was my right hand man. A lot of the ideas here are his.' He stretches out his arm to give Sam's shoulder an appreciative squeeze.

'Now I understand,' Daniel says, looking in Sam's direction. 'Something worthwhile can't be rushed.'

Neil leads the way to a wooden staircase which climbs up to a raised deck. We access the rear of the house through huge bi-folding doors, which open up almost the entire rear wall to the sitting room.

Inside the décor is simple and uncluttered. A lot of the oak framing for the new annexe has been left exposed, which adds lots of character. In the original farmhouse the chestnut beams have been sand-blasted back to bare wood and it's a joy to behold. The ground floor of the original building is a spacious kitchen/diner looking out over the front garden. But as we sit eating a delicious lunch at the long, lovingly stripped farmhouse table, the now glass–less former rear windows give a tantalising glimpse down through to the sitting room level of the new annexe. Beyond which, the eye is drawn to the amazing view. It works so well and reflects the thought and time that has been put into making this renovation so impressive.

I realise that Sam's vision for his own home will come to fruition when he's ready. Maybe the problem is that the plans he has on paper aren't quite right and that's all that is blocking his progress. Or maybe it is just the funds, in which case why doesn't he sell the motorbike? I'm sure his granddad would have understood, given the circumstances.

Anyway, it's a puzzle that's for sure and one that will remain unsolved long after I'm back in the UK, I should imagine.

We spend a leisurely afternoon taking a long walk before heading back to Le Manoir. I'm relieved that during the entire time I was never alone with Sarah. I've done all I can and now even Lizzie has tried, so she must accept that Sam is his own man. As I told Lizzie, you can't change someone who doesn't want to be changed – and why should he? The only person he's potentially hurting is himself and maybe even that isn't the case, as he seems happy enough with things how they are. But in the summer his life is bearable; winter, as he admitted, is a very different story, of course.

Reality Dawns

When we arrive back at Le Manoir, Mum is ironing bedding and Dad is weeding the front garden. I leave Lizzie and Daniel setting up two loungers in the little garden in front of the gîte for a leisurely evening, to give them some time together alone. Tomorrow, it seems, I will be working alongside Sam again, while they head off to visit Nantes. Tonight, however, I'm hoping to fit in at least five hours' work on the laptop.

When I check my emails there's a response from Tom.

Hey, Anna,

You certainly work fast! Great idea using the same logo but swapping around the animals. I can't wait to see what you come up with for the website and blog.

Today I've been conducting a tour of the facilities here, showing some well off patrons where their money is being spent. It included a very bumpy, two hour bus tour and when I say "bus" I mean bone-shaker. Still, they could see that not a penny is wasted; as long as a vehicle can get from a to b, then it's fit for purpose, out here.

Tomorrow I'm teaching some volunteers about post op animal after-care.

I'm conscious that you know quite a bit about me, but I don't know anything at all about you. Other than you are kind enough to sort out my online presence for free. And I need to talk to you about that, because that's a lot of your time you are giving up just to use me as a case study for your new business. We must discuss a fee.

Tom

Eek! I suppose it's only natural he's beginning to wonder about my background. He's assumed I found his blog and that's where my interest originated. Time to be honest with him before I go any further, I think.

Hi Tom,

Well, your days are never boring, that's for sure!

I'm helping my parents finish off some renovation work at Le Manoir d'Orsenne. That's how I came to read your blog. To cut a long story short, I found a small wooden box in one of the stone outbuildings which I believe belongs to you.

I left my contact details with your practice in Nîmes and they mentioned your blog. No fee necessary, it's my pleasure and I'll drop the box off when I'm down that way one day next week. I didn't want to risk putting it in the post.

Anyway, if you're happy with the logos I'll make up some jpegs for you in various sizes and I can then start designing a new website. My idea is that your blog should be accessible from the front page. What do you think? It would make it easier for you to have everything on one dashboard.

Best regards

Anna

I press send and cursor on down through my emails. To my dismay there's one from Karl.

Hi Anna,

I know I've messed up in just about every way possible but I'm hoping you don't delete this without reading it first.

I've been appointed as a director and this changes everything. I did it, Anna, I made the dream come true! But it means nothing without you by my side.

I promise not to send any more flowers and I admit the ring thing was idiotic. I sort of hoped you were secretly missing me and that it would touch your heart. What a fool I've been. You deserve a romantic proposal and all I need is the chance to prove to you that I'm the one for you.

Anyway, please just give it some thought. You need time to sort out your feelings and I respect that. I'll try my best to wait patiently and not to get in touch – that's about the best promise I can make, because I'm missing you so much.

I love you, Anna, and I always will.

Karl

My head tips backwards as a loud groan escapes my lips, seemingly drawn from the very pit of my stomach. Now I'm the one who feels bad because I know I don't love Karl and I never did. That was the real reason I never said those words to him, not the fact that I doubted he was for real when he said them to me. Guilt, I realise, is an uncomfortable feeling.

Dear Karl,

I'm happy for you, I really am. But I don't love you and you must accept that. I never meant to hurt, or mislead you.

This is a time you should be celebrating, so please forget about me and look to your future.

Anna

I press send without even a moment's hesitation and instantly notice a response from Tom sitting there in my inbox.

Hi Anna,

Wow – it seems fate made our paths cross! If that's the wooden box I think it is, then I'm in your debt BIG time. It disappeared years ago and I thought it was gone forever.

Great idea to put the blog on the main website. It has been a pain, to be honest. I'm flying back at the weekend, so I'll be in Nîmes next week. Talk about a coincidence. Maybe if it's all ready, you could talk me through it over lunch? When you know which day you'll be around, let me know and I'll make sure I'm free.

Take care,

Tom

My heart starts to beat just a little bit faster as I re-read his email again. Lunch? Of course, it's only to thank me for the work I'm doing for him but even so – this is exciting! All thoughts of Karl are banished as I turn to designing a website that's going to reflect the personality of a guy who seems to believe anything is possible. Good job that I'm up for a challenge!

*

'You're quiet this morning,' Sam throws the words over his shoulder.

I'm leaning against a large piece of plasterboard while he's screwing it to the studding.

'I started work on a new website layout last night and I'm not one hundred per cent sure I can make it do what I need it to. Unfortunately, I don't have enough time to code it from scratch.'

Sam gives me a look that infers he didn't understand a word of what I said.

'You can design a website using code, so like starting with a blank page?'

I nod. 'But it takes time. Or, you can start by choosing one of the endless stream of templates that can then be personalised and within a day or so you have a pretty decent looking result. As I'm doing this job for free I want the best result I can get, given the time I have in which to do it.'

He reaches into his pocket for another screw.

'And these are the case studies for your new business website? Is it that easy to find candidates?'

'Well, this one was easy. It's Tom Laurent's blog and website that I'm working on at the moment.'

Sam places the last screw and I step away from the wall. We go to get another sheet.

'I didn't realise you were talking to him. Does he know you're going to drop the box off next week?'

Oh. Awkward. I should have told Sam about this beforehand, given that he's been so involved in tracking Tom down.

'Yes, I did mention it. Which day do you think you'll be free to take me over to Nîmes? I was wondering if you'd rather I hired a car for the day and drove myself, as I'll probably need to spend a couple of hours showing him how to access the new website and load stuff.'

Sam doesn't look put out. 'It's entirely up to you but I'm more than happy to drive and I can kill a couple of hours, no problem. How about Wednesday? That way we get a day either side with no travelling unless we want to. It's going to be a ten hour drive from here to Cannes, so a day off from driving would be a bonus.'

'If you're happy to share the driving I'm up for that,' I respond. 'It might be easier to put me on your insurance for five days and I can then cover the cost. What do you think?'

'Great, thanks – I'll do that. I don't mind driving all the way but in this heat, even with the aircon going, it might be nice to hand the wheel over to someone else for a bit.'

'I'll be glad when the box is in Tom's hands, to be honest. He seemed pleased. Curiously, he said it disappeared one day and he thought it was gone forever.'

As we negotiate the doorway and twist the plasterboard panel around to swing it up against the wall, I see Sam's expression is non-committal. Why I feel awkward about this, I don't know.

'If you want to spend time this week with Lizzie and Daniel, you don't have to be here every day working alongside me, you know. Their time here will fly by, so make the most of it.'

We exchange glances.

'Thanks, Sam, but I want them to have quality time together and this way they don't feel they have to invite me along on their trips out.'

'Fair enough. Did you know Dad offered Daniel a job?'

I'm stunned and my face shows it.

'Oh, he didn't commit or anything,' Sam confirms hastily. 'But I think he's beginning to consider it as a potential option. Did you say Lizzie is an estate agent? If that's the case they could do well over here.'

As I lean against the board and Sam works his way down with the electric screwdriver, my thoughts are whirling. If my parents and my best friend end up over here then life could feel very lonely once I'm back in the UK. For a few brief moments, I feel almost panic-stricken. Is this IT – the thing that continues to hold me back? That major blow to my confidence after the most humiliating moment of my life has never left me. As strong and capable as I am there's still this little demon ready to whisper in my ear, "What if everyone leaves you? How strong will you look then?"

'What's wrong? I checked it with the spirit level and it's spot on.' Sam is looking at me intently.

I didn't realise I'd stepped away and am now gazing rather blankly at the new wall in front of me.

'It's perfect. Sorry, my head was somewhere else.'

He grimaces. 'Care to share?'

I laugh. 'I think I just had one of those light bulb moments. You know, when you realise something that was staring you in the face all along. How can anyone know what they want out of life if they don't understand who they are? I've always been a daughter, a girlfriend, a best friend, a colleague or an employee, first. Somewhere along the line I forgot that sometimes it's important to understand who *I* am, rather than what I am to everyone else.'

Sam looks at me and frowns. 'So, what's the solution?'

I pause, my hand automatically flying up to my chin as I rest my lips on my fingers in reflective mode.

'To stop using people as a crutch, or as an excuse not to face up to my insecurities.'

'That sounds heavy; are your thoughts always this intense?'

'I'm trying to be honest with myself for once. The truth is I'm scared of rejection because I need people in my life; I need to be needed and the thought of being alone terrifies me. If it's just me, what happens if I don't like the person I am, deep down inside?'

One look at Sam's face confirms I've said too much and he's shocked by my admission.

'Well, if it makes you feel any better my fear is having people around me. Sometimes they terrify the hell out of me. When I'm alone I either turn up the radio and blast out the music, or I'm head down working and then nothing else matters. You should try it sometime.'

He's trying to lighten a dark moment and I'm grateful.

'Have you finished screwing?' It isn't until after I finish speaking that I realise what I've said, but by then Sam is laughing.

'I think so; I can only hope you think I did a good job.'

He's still chuckling as he walks out the door and heads off to the garage.

Owning It

This morning is going to be spent filling gaps and making the pristine new walls as smooth as possible. Shortly after half past ten Daniel and Lizzie saunter in. It's another blisteringly hot day and even with the door and windows open there's little movement in the warm air surrounding us.

'I can't believe how different it looks already,' Lizzie exclaims, walking from the main room into the newly partitioned double bedroom. This is the smaller of the two gîtes and won't have its own kitchen, just a sitting room, bedroom and shower room.

I stand back, trying to see it with her eyes. This building is squarer and it's a real shame that none of the internal walls were good enough to repoint.

'This is the boring bit,' I reply, holding up the tube of filler and the small trowel.

'How about I take over for a couple of hours and you ladies have a relaxing coffee break to catch up?' Daniel throws in.

Lizzie and I exchange glances.

'But it's your holiday—'

'I can find out a little more from Sam about what it's like to live and work in France. Seriously, ladies.

We can take a trip out later in the day when it's a bit cooler. It's too hot to walk around in this, anyway.'

I'm more than content to hand over my tools and Sam seems happy enough. Lizzie and I go to the kitchen for a jug of water and some glasses. I squeeze in a little lemon juice, add a handful of baby strawberries fresh from Dad's kitchen garden, or *potager*, as he prefers to call it, now his French is getting quite good. As we make our way down the garden I pick a few tips of mint to finish it off.

'This is bliss,' Lizzie sighs as she adjusts her hat and sinks down onto one of the benches around the table.

'I know. It's not much cooler out here than it is inside, though. Even the slight breeze is blowing hot air. Daniel is obviously keen to quiz Sam, then.'

Lizzie's face lights up. 'I know! I can hardly believe it myself. He's gone from being shocked it was even something I'd thought about, to wanting more information. The drawbacks are big, though.' She mimics a sad face, pulling down the sides of her mouth.

I fill the two glasses, pretending to be quite laid back about the conversation, although a part of me is hoping this will come to nothing. And I know that's totally selfish of me.

'It's hard to leave your family behind, isn't it? I understand now how your parents felt, but then you had Karl and they thought you were settled.'

I avoid her gaze.

'You've heard from him again, haven't you?'

I hate being so transparent at times, but then Lizzie knows me so well.

'He was apologetic, realising the ring in the post thing was ludicrous. He's been made a director and he says it means nothing to him if we aren't together.'

We clink our respective glasses. The cool, slightly fruity water is refreshing and welcome.

'No second thoughts?'

I look her firmly in the eye. 'No second thoughts whatsoever. In fact, men are off the agenda completely, as far as I'm concerned. It's time I took a journey of self-discovery.'

'Good for you. I don't like the way Karl assumes you'll just fall into his arms and to me that's a sign of an over inflated ego. I'm still seething that he managed to charm me into thinking he was Mr Perfect. Take some time for yourself before you think about getting involved with anyone else — even if meeting the lovely Tom provides an unexpected temptation. This business idea is perfect for you, Anna, and I'm proud of you for standing up for yourself. It wasn't easy walking away from your job, but if you could do that, then you can do anything.'

She leans across to give me a hug, just as Mum arrives to see what we're up to.

'The boys said you were down here. Am I interrupting?'

We both shake our heads.

'No, not at all,' Lizzie muses. 'Daniel is grilling Sam about life in France and I'm quizzing Anna on her plans, and they don't include Karl.'

Mum drops down onto one of the chairs with a thud.

'Thank goodness for that! My opinion of him wasn't any higher than Geoff's, but I'm more diplomatic.' Mum says as she turns in my direction. 'You are your own woman, Anna, not someone's second fiddle.'

Lizzie and I begin laughing – only Mum could have put it quite like that!

*

I give Lizzie and Daniel directions to the lake and they head off shortly after lunch. Mum and Dad have their hands full today as three new couples are due to arrive later this afternoon. Sam and I spend the afternoon doing more prep on the walls and ceiling, ending up in the garage doing a sort-out and de-clutter.

'The end is in sight, isn't it? How long will it take, once we're back from Cannes?'

Sam straightens, scratching his chin. 'Three weeks max, I reckon.'

'What do you have planned after that?'

'Well, Dad's struggling a bit, to be honest, so I guess I'll get stuck in and help out.'

His own project still isn't going to be top of the list. He jumps straight in, probably realising what I'm thinking and tries to distract me.

'What are your plans?'

I stop what I'm doing and stand. Looking directly at him, neither of us blink.

'I'll do what I can to help out here when the pressure is on. I might not be able to cook breakfast, but I can wait tables. I can help with the laundry and getting rooms ready for new arrivals. Even give Dad a hand in the garden. In between I'll be on the internet working away. Having a plan is one thing, making it happen is another.'

He angles his head.

'Was that a dig?'

I smile sweetly. 'Only if you want it to be.'

'Daniel is keen to come back later in the summer to give me a hand. I have no idea how Lizzie is going to feel about that. I hope I haven't caused any problems between them. He can't believe I don't have some sort of schedule for the work. Is there anyone you know who isn't like you?'

He gives me a cheeky grin and I can see it's merely banter but deep down I think he's feeling a little cornered by Daniel's interest. Anyone would feel awkward refusing outright a kind and generous offer, but I can see that Sam isn't happy. And he isn't comfortable.

'I can have a word with him if you like and suggest he waits to see how things progress, as you have a lot of work to do with your dad. How's that?'

The smile he gives me is one of immense relief.

'Could you do that? I mean, I am grateful – really, I am. I know I'm lucky to have people around me who care enough to be concerned but if I'm not worried about anything, then I don't want them to worry on my behalf.'

'Point taken. And I'm sorry if you feel I've been pushing you. As a consummate starter/finisher I see every unfinished task as a challenge.'

'So, I'm a challenge to you, am I? Unlike Karl.'

I spin around, giving him a sharp look that wipes the smile off his face.

'Sorry, I didn't mean anything by that remark. I forgot to engage my brain and it was said in jest,' he admits. 'You deserve someone who is your equal, not someone who wants to control and manipulate you.

It was my rather inept attempt at acknowledging that I'm a sad case. Maybe it's easier for us to rub along if you write me off as a worthless cause.'

I scoop back my hair, wanting him to see the look on my face.

'You aren't worthless in any sense of the word, Sam. But maybe that's the lesson life has yet to teach you.'

We both shrug; agreeing to disagree. I thought I didn't know myself but Sam wins the gold medal to my silver one.

A Garden Party

The week flies by and before we know it it's Lizzie and Daniel's last evening at Le Manoir. With every room full there's quite a buzz with a steady stream of guests coming and going. Mum and Dad decide it would be a great idea to throw a bit of a party in the garden. Sam, Mum, Lizzie and I spend most of the day in the kitchen. I'm chief washer-upper, leaving those with the requisite skills to do the cooking.

Dad and Daniel are left to dispense invitations to guests and friends in the village, then turn their attention to setting up a buffet table and temporary gazebo in the garden.

Ironically, Sam is quite comfortable to be working as a part of a team and I realise that he's only self-conscious when he's the focus of attention. So, it's not a fear of having people around him as such, it's probably more accurate to say he has a fear of other people's expectations of him. I make a mental note to tread much more carefully around him when we're off on the trip to Cannes. After all, I'm at an age where people have expectations about me too, namely that I have a boyfriend, maybe even a fiancé, in tow whereas at this moment in time I've never been more single. That doesn't mean I'm happy about it, though, or that I haven't tried.

And now I'm giving up on trying, anyway. What happens, happens. Wow – maybe Sam's ethos is catching. But then, isn't it just a cop-out, a way of avoiding the real issue? In times of uncertainty do nothing, sort of thing? Sadly, I doubt that's ever been the answer to any problem in life because it's all about trial and error.

'You okay, Anna? That's a serious look you have going on there.'

Well, at least it's Dad who has caught me deep in thought again and not Sam.

'Do you and Mum worry about me all the time?'

Dad smirks. 'Pretty much.'

'If I was settled, you know, in Lizzie's situation would you still worry about me?'

'Yep. That's what parents do, it's called caring. There's always something to worry about, Anna. And I know you worry about us – that's a part of life.'

'But what about when I've made bad decisions in the past. I mean, you're always there for me but how do you cope when you see things going wrong?'

He sighs, placing his arms around my shoulders and wrapping me up close to him.

'Unfortunately, Anna, you are a natural born worrier too, my darling. Who is hurting now that you can't save?'

'Sam. He's a great guy but he's wasting his life.'

Dad releases me, placing his hands on my shoulders and looking straight into my eyes.

'We thought you were wasting your life spending time with Karl, but if we'd told you that you wouldn't have believed us. Sometimes in life you need the bad times to be able to move on and make the good times happen. Viv and I feel that things are changing for you now, so don't get pulled into a situation which isn't of your making. We'd all like to see Sam pushing forward and fulfilling his full potential, but he's happy in his own way. Neil told me Sam was a broken man when he arrived in France and maybe he's coping in the only way he can. It's wonderful that you care, Anna, but you can't interfere. Now, let's start ferrying out the plates and glasses. I'm really looking forward to tonight.'

*

By late evening most of the buffet has been demolished and a lot of the guests seem to be out here, too, more than happy to join in. Everyone who was invited from the village has turned up at the party, and it's surprising how long it takes to circulate and chat to the people I already know.

Monsieur and Madame Deniaud ask about Thomas and I manage to find Honorine so that I can give them all an update. Honorine looks delighted when I tell her I'm meeting up with Thomas, whom I inform them prefers to be called Tom now. Sam joins us halfway through the conversation.

'We always knew that boy would turn into a very special young man. I am not surprised to hear he is in Africa again. Exotic animals held a real fascination for him, even as a boy.' Honorine's eyes shine brightly as she talks.

Sam doesn't join in, but is content to listen as I tell them about our trip to Rennes, to meet up with Elise Moreau.

'Please tell Tom that we all remember him with great fondness,' Monsieur Deniaud adds.

'Oh, I will. I'm doing some work on his website and he also has a fascinating travel blog. It's more like a diary, really, and it's an amazing read. It's called *Le vétérinaire ambulant.*'

Sam finally joins in the conversation and he sounds relaxed, happy even.

'I'll pop in with my laptop, Honorine, so you can see for yourself.'

'I would like that. Thank you, Sam.'

'I can't believe there's only one more day until we leave for Cannes.' I turn to Sam and raise my glass. 'Thank you for making this happen.'

'I'm just the transport, you were the detective.' He smiles back at me and we all raise our glasses.

'Here's to a successful mission and the return of some very precious items to their rightful owner,' Monsieur Deniaud concludes and we all clink glasses.

*

Even though it's late when I eventually climb the stairs to bed, I feel wired and I know there's little point in trying to sleep. I have a quick shower and then sit down in front of the laptop.

As I start creating the pages of Tom's new website, cutting and pasting photos and text from the old one and his blog, I get a real feel for the life he's chosen. He's an adventurer, but one with a heart and a set purpose because it's all about the animals. There are a few photos with women who could possibly be a significant other, but it's rarely the same person. I find myself checking out his relationship status on his Facebook page and see he's single. I don't suppose it would be easy to lead his sort of life and find time to keep a relationship going. I wonder if he still sees his father at all.

It's 3 a.m. before I quit working, my eyelids drooping as I gently manoeuvre Ziggy across from the centre of the bed so I can slide in. Her whiskers are going and in her dreams no doubt she's chasing a bird or a butterfly as she dashes across the garden. Sweet dreams, Ziggy.

Partings are always sad, but it's been a real tonic having Lizzie and Daniel here, so it seems even harder. It was a reminder that I have another life in the UK, even though – ironically – it seems to have sown a seed for them about a life here in France.

Sam pops in on the bike to say a very brief goodbye and then disappears, finding it all a little awkward. I admit that both Lizzie and I feel tearful, unsure of when exactly we'll next meet up.

As we wave them off, Mum turns to look at me. 'Are you all packed for your road trip with Sam tomorrow?'

I shake my head. 'Haven't even thought about it. And it's Cannes; not sure I have anything smart enough to lounge around a pool in, let alone day wear.'

Mum slides her arm around my waist as we walk back into the house. 'Let's take a look in that wardrobe of yours. I'm pretty sure I remember hanging up some clothes that you left with us in the old house. You know, the ones you always meant to reclaim at some point when you were settled.'

I laugh. 'I know. Bet you even have my old keepsakes in boxes because I know you never throw anything away.'

'Just in case,' she admits. 'You never know what you might be glad of one day.'

In fact, she turns out to be right and I discover several items I'd forgotten I ever had. Enough to make me feel that if I need to dress up, I'll look reasonable enough and several dresses that are cool and don't crease. I throw in a couple of pairs of shorts and some tops, and I'm done.

'Well, that wasn't so hard, was it?' Mum reflects. We check that the small suitcase will close and I hold my breath. Once I've unzipped the expander, even my toiletries and hair straighteners will fit in and eventually it's done. With a 6 a.m. start I'm going to have to get as much sleep tonight as I can.

Mum heads off to the kitchen, where she's going to sort out a cool box and begin preparing some things for the journey. It's going to take just over ten hours if we make minimal stops. A lot of that will be on toll roads, which at least is an easy way to eat up the distance.

I fleetingly wonder how Sam and I will pass the time and whether there will be awkward periods of silence. Just in case, I go off in search of a few CDs and pop them into my handbag alongside Tom's box, which is wrapped in a piece of white cotton. Roll on tomorrow!

Let the Karaoke Begin

When Sam arrives, I'm relieved to see it's not his work's van, or the dodgy looking Citroën he's driving but his dad's car, which is a left hand drive, Peugeot 407 estate. In all honesty, it's going to be easier to drive, as it's probably only about two years old. I did wonder whether Sam's little run around was reliable and clearly, he had the same concerns.

For the first forty-five minutes in the car with Sam at the wheel we're both rather quiet. Mainly because most of this part of the journey is on small, often busy roads that lead to an endless stream of roundabouts. It's one after another, so it's all about concentrating, listening to the satnav and not making a wrong turn. Then we hit some roadworks and our progress slows to a crawl.

Once we can pick up some speed again, the signs indicate that we're about to join the A85 and I hope that means we will finally be able to cruise along for a while.

'That's the tricky bit over and it's an easier run now for the bulk of the journey. It's about a thousand kilometres. We'll be travelling on the A85 which is a partial toll road, for just over two hundred kilometres and after that the A71, which is also a toll road. Do you fancy taking over for a while as it's a reasonably straight run? I'm already on Dad's insurance anyway. I gave him the details you emailed over to me so he could add you as an additional driver and you're all legal.'

'Thank you for sorting that out, Sam. Just let me know the cost.'

It's thoughtful of Sam to have tackled the worst bit of the journey before offering me the wheel. We pull over and I settle into the driving seat. I regard myself as being a good driver but I'm a little nervous for some reason.

'If we only stop for comfort breaks and to get a quick sandwich from the cool box, and assuming we can keep up a good speed, we'll be there by early evening. Are you up for that?'

I nod, looking in the wing mirror as I prepare to pull away.

'That suits me. I enjoy driving anyway. There are some CDs I brought for the journey in the top of my bag. Help yourself and see if there's anything there that takes your fancy. A bit of a singalong helps a journey pass more quickly, I always find.'

I can feel Sam's eyes on me. 'Singing? You're expecting me to sing?'

'My voice is awful but that doesn't stop me enjoying a good Karaoke session. Have you never seen *James Corden's Carpool Karaoke?*

'No. And I don't recognise many of these song titles, either. 'Uptown Funk'?' I can feel his eyes studying my side profile.

'Mark Ronson featuring Bruno Mars? Bruno wears a pink jacket in the video? You must have seen it on YouTube. Just put in the disc. I know all the words so you join in whenever you hear the chorus. It gets repeated a lot, so you'll get the hang of it.'

Sam slides in the disc and I turn up the volume, unashamedly accompanying the lovely Bruno, matching him word for word. About halfway through Sam seems to pick it up and before long he's singing at the top of his lungs, too, whenever he thinks he can fathom out the words. When the song finishes, we both start laughing.

'There, that wasn't so bad, was it? Maybe let's try something a bit slower. I love, absolutely love, Adele's 'Hello'. If you don't know at least some of the words then I'll be very surprised given that you love your radio.'

'I might know a few of the words and besides, I'm a quick learner.' He sounds amused, at least.

Adele's voice fills the car and it's almost a sin to allow my appalling vocal efforts to mask even one note of hers, but it's such fun and the words are compelling. When we get to the chorus Sam immediately joins in, so I guess it's one he's heard before. I literally fight to restrain myself in order not to do any hand movements, as I've watched the video so many times I could perform it in her exact style. It's a shame when the last chord is struck.

'Your turn, what do you have tucked away in that glove compartment?'

'I have something that can't fail. U2, 'With or Without You'.' He ejects Adele and soon we are rocking in our seats with Bono. I surprise myself and find that I know almost all of the words but Sam, I notice, is word perfect.

'OK. My turn again.'

'But we did two of yours already,' Sam complains.

'Now you've warmed up let's up the pace. Put on 'Wrecking Ball' by Miley Cyrus. This one is unforgettable.'

'Wrecking ball, really? That's a song title?' He sounds amused.

'Look it up on YouTube sometime. I bet you end up watching it more than once.'

Sam catches on quickly and seems to have an ear for lyrics. Next up is Metallica with 'Nothing Else Matters' and that's one rock song I have heard before.

'Ooh, I like this one. The guitar opener is awesome. Maybe we should just listen to it as my throat is feeling rather dry already.'

Sam reaches into the back to grab two bottles of water from the cool box. He loosens the screw top on one and passes it to me.

'Thanks, I need this.' The water slides down easily, soothing my strained vocal chords.

'How on earth do singers do it? Belting out numbers all night at the tops of their voices. But it's fun, isn't it? I mean, this isn't proper Karaoke, obviously, but it passes the time.'

Sam has already drunk the entire contents of his bottle and throws it over his shoulder onto the rear seat.

'What's next?' He asks, as if I have an entertainment plan organised for the entire journey.

'OK. Question time. We each ask each other a question and we have to answer it truthfully.'

I can't turn to see his expression, but he emits a low grumble.

'You go first. Ask me anything.' Can't get much simpler than that, I tell myself. But I'm not sure he wants to play because it takes him a while to speak.

'Where do you hope to be this time next year?' He asks and it's a good question.

Hmm, thought provoking, too. 'Let's see… well, I'd like to say firmly established in a respectably sized flat in London – the suburbs of course: I'm not greedy. Maybe short-listed for a new business award and looking at taking on some staff to cover the flood of work that is coming in.'

He laughs. 'Not greedy? I'd say that's pretty ambitious.'

'My turn, now. What's the one thing in life that makes you instantly happy, no matter what's going wrong around you?'

I hear a soft groan and Sam sits for a while watching the scenery flashing by as he mulls it over.

'It has to be music. Although if I had a dog, that would make me pretty happy.'

'Why don't you get one?'

'I'm not good at taking care of myself, let alone an animal.' He tries to laugh it off, then launches into his next question.

'What's your biggest regret so far?'

That's a difficult one. 'Well, as the point of this exercise is that we're being totally truthful, I have to say there are a few and it's kind of hard to choose. But, honestly? It was telling someone I knew a long time ago that I loved him, only to find out that he didn't feel the same way and he was using me. It broke my heart and I've never fully recovered. You owe me now. That hurt. It's my turn.'

I pause for a moment wondering how to phrase the question to which I'm curious to know the answer.

'Have you ever been in love?'

Silence hangs heavily between us as the seconds tick by. I momentarily wonder if he's fallen asleep, but he moves in his seat, re-adjusting his position.

'Once. Once was enough.'

That's it?

'That's not a proper answer and you know it. Why did it fall apart?'

'Because she died,' he says, softly.

I suspected as much but now I regret having asked the question and forcing the issue. I thought that maybe it was something he might want to talk about.

'You don't know my past, Anna. Anyway, I'm better off alone.'

Suddenly he sounds almost depressed. Now I don't know whether I should ignore it and change the subject completely, or give him a chance to talk. Fortunately, while I'm still considering the options he starts speaking again.

'I get asked to this get-together every year and every year I say *no*. Until now. I have no idea if I can get through this and face the people who know what happened.'

He falls silent.

'But these people are your friends, won't they understand how you feel?'

Sam shifts his body position once again.

'Maybe.'

'So why is this year different?'

'I let Mum talk me into it. She thinks I need to face my fears, so that I'll be free to move on.'

I nod. 'That's sound advice. There's no point in running away, or trying to hide from the things that haunt us. I've probably never felt as vulnerable as I do right now, but it will pass, I know that. It will pass for you, too. How long has it been since she died?'

'Seven years this month.'

His tone alone tells me how raw his emotions still are and he must have loved her very much indeed.

I keep my eyes firmly on the road ahead, although there is little traffic around. But this is open countryside we are travelling through now and there's always the chance that an animal will dash across the road. I really want to see Sam's face, though, so I turn my head for a second before spinning it back round. He looks as though he's in shock, as if he's re-living the worst moment of his life. I wish I hadn't started this stupid game. I want to be sympathetic, but without knowing the details, or the circumstances, it's hard to offer comfort without the risk of making it worse.

'I'm so sorry for your loss, Sam. It's hard to let go of someone and even harder when they are so young. Your lives together had hardly begun.'

Out of the corner of my eye I catch the movement of his head as he turns to look at me, but I don't want to see the look on his face this time.

'I knew her friends were into drugs. She just never woke up—' His voice slows to a halt.

I focus on driving and we lapse into silence. There's still a long way to go and at some point quite soon, I'll need to stop for a comfort break. I can only hope that by then Sam has regained his composure. It's my fault entirely for asking a question my gut instincts were telling me was at the root of his problem. And I know only too well that you never forget your first love, even when it isn't reciprocated. So how hard must it be when it's mutual and the person is suddenly gone forever?

Clearing the Air

We've been in the car for almost three and a half hours now and my back is beginning to ache. Sam hasn't said anything, but he must want to stretch his legs, too. There aren't many places to stop but little roadside cafés tend to stand out. Either there's a board on the pavement to catch passing motorists' attention, or often a few bistro tables clustered around the entrance.

'Do you fancy a coffee? I desperately need the loo and this looks promising. What do you think?'

I slow down, easing the car up a small ramp and into the car park alongside the café. It has a blue and white awning shading the tables and chairs, which extends along the entire length of the front of the building. The pavement is wide, but it is a little dusty when cars whoosh past.

'I'm glad you stopped; thanks, Anna. Sorry about that, earlier. I feel bad that this trip has already messed me up, even before we've reached our destination.'

'Hey, we all have our hang-ups. You aren't alone in that, Sam. It worries me if you think you are. Everyone has a problem, it's simply that every problem is different.'

Walking in through the door I head straight to the loo, leaving Sam to order the coffees. When I return he's sitting at one of the tables outside and the drinks have already arrived.

'I didn't know whether you wanted anything to eat? They have croissants and things.'

His smile is genuine and he seems brighter already.

'No, I'm fine. I thought maybe we'd stop for a picnic in about an hour? What do you think?'

He's looking at me intently, his eyes travelling over my face as if he's studying me.

'You know, I can't think of a better companion but I hope you don't feel it's a mistake. Sitting next to me listening to my problems seems a heavy price to pay in exchange for a day trip to Nîmes.'

I shake my head. 'It's fine, really. I'm glad you shared it with me and it must have been so hard to say those words. Such a tragedy.'

His hand toys with the coffee cup in front of him. 'It hit her parents really hard. They divorced a couple of years later. Maybe it wasn't the most stable of marriages anyway, but it signalled the beginning of the end. Everyone connected seemed to fall apart overnight. It isn't simply knowing we were all there together that night before Isla died, but her brother, Harry, was one of my best mates. I know he'll be invited on this trip, too. I haven't seen him since it happened.'

'That's a tough thing to face for the first time, Sam. You shouldn't beat yourself up about getting anxious as that's perfectly understandable. But he'll be feeling much the same, I suspect. It's hard to move on when there are loose ends that need to be tidied up.'

He rubs his hands across his eyes, no doubt irritated by the gritty dust from a lorry speeding by just a few feet away from us.

'Not the best place to stop, is it?' I offer.

'But the coffee is good. Can I ask about this guy? The one who broke your heart?'

I look down, absent-mindedly stirring my coffee even though I don't take sugar.

'I was really young, very naïve and so sure he felt the same way. It wasn't just that he didn't return my feelings, it was the way he dismissed our relationship. I felt humiliated. I actually stutter if I even try to say his name and I haven't talked about it to anyone for years. How stupid is that?'

'You never were in love with Karl, then?' He seems genuinely puzzled, given the fact that he witnessed the whole ring and flowers episode.

'No. He said he loved me every single day without fail but in here,' I touch my heart lightly with my hand, 'I knew it wasn't true. Karl doesn't understand what love is – he just thinks he does.'

Sam frowns. 'Explain it to me.'

'Loving someone means that you put the other person before yourself. You would do anything for them, anything at all. Your career would never get in the way, because if you lost everything but still had each other, you could always start afresh. True love is selfless. It has no ego.'

Sam raises his eyebrows.

'That's probably the best explanation I've ever heard. Love has no ego; that's prophetic.'

'Sorry, did you say pathetic?' I look up at him from under my eyelashes and see that he's a little startled. 'I'm only joking. Although it is rather pathetic, really. Here I am, no longer that shy, introverted teenager and yet the hurt has never gone away. I don't find it easy to trust anyone, when it comes to the L-word.'

We finish our drinks and Sam nips to the loo while I head for the car. When he returns he's happy enough to slip into the passenger seat and we're soon back on the road.

It's a relief to be able to pick up speed and feel the satisfaction of making good progress on our journey. An easy silence fills the car for quite a while as we clock up the kilometres.

I realise that I've barely had time to think about Cannes, or the villa we'll be staying in. I figure it might be helpful now to encourage Sam to talk, at the same time as giving me some information so I'm not walking into a roomful of people about whom I know nothing at all.

'Tell me about the people who are likely to be at the villa when we arrive.'

'Jack's family own it and it's an amazing place – money is no object. The sort of thing you see in those glossy magazines. His girlfriend's name is Sasha, assuming it's still the same one. We haven't spoken in a long while but he emails once a year inviting me along to the get-together. As for the others, well, our circle included Chris, Marcus, Ethan, Andy, Harry, Jeremy and Pete. I have no idea who will be there and whether any of them are married now, or still single.'

'Seeing them again makes it real, doesn't it? That's why you've been putting it off. Once you've conquered this you will feel better and maybe you can then, finally, let go of the past.'

'That's what Mum said. I guess if you're of the same opinion maybe this was the right thing to do. I am glad you're here, though, I will admit. I'd already be turning back if I was on my own.'

'Well, I'm sorry my stupid game triggered some tough memories, but I'm glad to be here if it's a help. And now you, too, understand why Karl's over-the-top declarations annoyed me so much. I'm not a heartless person, I'm simply not in love with him. It was yet another one of life's rather harsh little lessons when I finally realised what a manipulator he was. I can't believe that I couldn't see how his controlling behaviour meant every situation was turned to his advantage. Or that I was gullible enough to live like that for a whole year as if it was normal.'

Sam shrugs his shoulders.

'It's easy to look back and see the mistakes we've made with shocking clarity. At the time, it's different though. Anyone can be wise with the benefit of hindsight.'

He doesn't sound bitter, exactly, but jaded – or maybe the word I'm looking for is defeated.

'You really are unemployed, then, and this new business venture has to work?'

'Yep. Or the bills won't get paid.'

'From what I've seen of your determination, Anna, that's unlikely to happen and I'm sure it will be a success. Your career is important to you, isn't it?'

'At the moment, it's all I have and I feel like everything is falling apart. It's as much about succeeding in whatever I choose to do, though. Having lost my pride once, very early on in my life, it's the thing I fear the most.'

Sam does a body twist and I can feel his eyes scrutinising me again.

'No one would ever think of you as a failure, Anna, but you can't see that. When you first arrived, I thought you'd slow me down but everything I showed you, you picked up very quickly. If you didn't push yourself so hard all the time, then maybe you'd come to understand that a knock back is simply what it says it is.'

'Now who's being prophetic? I know it's only eleven thirty, but I'm hungry now. How about you?'

He grins as I glance in his direction. 'You heard my stomach growling just then, didn't you?'

'Where are we, exactly? We've been on the road for what – five and a half hours, although minus one thirty minute stop. Maybe it's time to find somewhere pleasant to sit and eat lunch.'

Sam traces his finger down our route on the satnav.

'Well, if you take the next turn off, the satnav shows it will lead us onto the Rue du Coudet in a place called Marsat. It looks like a reasonably sized village and it's only a little detour.'

I indicate and filter onto the slip road. After a couple of kilometres, we find it. It's a narrower road and very well maintained; no litter or weeds at all and you can see the residents are proud of their village. There is a lot of greenery on display in the well tended gardens. It partly obscures a variety of rather charming, cream painted houses and bungalows with either pink terracotta tiles, or dark brown pan tiled roofs.

'This is very pretty. It all looks remarkably coordinated.'

'If you keep going we should hit open countryside very shortly and I expect there will be somewhere quiet to pull over.'

Sam is right and less than a mile outside the village there's a pull-in large enough for half a dozen cars. The road is quiet, there is only us and it feels peaceful.

The first thing we do is get out of the car and stretch our legs. The field next to us is grass and sporting a good crop of yellow buttercups. In the distance, we can see a small herd of cows. It's a lot cooler today, but the sun is still very bright and almost overhead now.

I take in a deep breath, savouring the warm air laden with the smells of sweet grass and meadow flowers.

'This is lovely. It's a pity we don't have time to explore Marsat. Shall we spread the blanket out on the grass, here?'

Sam nods and walks back to the car, returning with a tartan rug and the cool box.

We sit side by side and I pass Sam a plate. Rummaging among the neat little parcels Mum has lovingly packed for us, it's a bit like pot luck. I pull out one foil covered package and pass it to him.

'Ham and cheese, my favourite,' he grins, taking one huge bite.

'I'm looking for the pizza. If I find it would you like a slice?'

'Of course. Who doesn't like cold pizza?'

We sit and eat in silence, listening to the buzzing of the bees homing in on the buttercups in the field behind us and a small flock of birds fighting in the tree tops on the other side of the gravelled area. There isn't one piece of litter to be seen anywhere.

'What time do you think we'll get to Cannes?'

I watch him as he finishes the last of his sandwich. He brushes a few stray crumbs away from the side of his mouth. There's something about him that I can't quite put into words. I feel comfortable in his company even though at times he annoys me. Not so much now I know a little bit more about his story. I had no idea it was his girlfriend who had died and I'm pretty sure his mum only mentioned the word *friend*. That's a huge difference, though, because to lose the person you are in love with must sap the joy out of life. How do you recover from that? Well, in Sam's case you don't; you just get through each day as best you can.

'With no stops at all it would have been around a quarter to four. With two short breaks in our journey already and maybe a couple more comfort stops on the way, I'm guessing it will be around six o'clock. Which is good time, given the roadworks earlier. But we do need to get on our way.'

We pack up and return to the car. Sam puts everything into the boot while I settle myself into the driver's seat. When he returns I give him a few moments to get settled before pulling away.

'Have you visited the villa before? I mean, I know you haven't been to the reunions.'

I immediately regret not engaging my brain – what was I thinking? If he went there with Isla it will stir up memories again and I was hoping the rest of the journey would be a little more relaxed.

'Once. I went to meet Isla's parents for the first time. They were staying with Jack's parents who had VIP tickets to the Monaco Grand Prix. I got the impression the villa is either empty, or it's party time, but then it's a huge place. That's how the rich and famous live. Jack works for the family business, too, but he's not at all impressed by wealth. Well, he wasn't the last time we were together. When your family has that much clout and money, it's hard to make your mark. He said that once and it made me think. Whatever he achieves is a drop in the ocean. While he has access to, and enjoys the trappings that wealth brings, however hard he works he feels like he's just a cog in the machine. I thought that was quite sad, actually.' It's clear Sam has a lot of respect for Jack.

'He sounds like a guy who tries hard. It's easy to see why the children of the rich and famous struggle to have an identity. The expectations of them are high, but when you are a part of a dynasty it must swallow you up. How do they stay motivated, when they could easily do nothing and their lives would still go on in the manner to which they are accustomed?'

'Well said. You'll like Jack. Harry – well, if I was him I'd be carrying a grudge towards me. You expect your sister's fiancé to watch over her like a hawk. A life is precious and now it's gone.'

I don't feel at all guilty this time. There are things that Sam needs to say out aloud and maybe I'm the only person he feels comfortable enough with to do that. But his words touch my heart and if I wasn't driving I'd throw my arms around him and give him a hug.

Paradise

This road trip has turned out to be a journey of discovery. I've learnt a lot about Sam and my respect for him grows by the minute.

Have I divulged a lot about myself? Well, yes, I think I have. He now understands why I'm so sensitive about some things; why even the mention of Karl's name is a red flag for me and that I might look strong, but that's because I feel vulnerability is akin to failure.

We swap places behind the wheel and I even manage to close my eyes for an hour. When I awake he laughs, welcoming me back and I think he's missed the banter.

I dig out Meghan Trainer's 'All About the Bass' for THE most fun session of Karaoke ever and we play it twice over so that Sam can get the hang of the chorus. He asks me to explain it and when I say it's all about celebrating women with curves, he pretends to be scandalised.

'Isn't that a bit... politically incorrect, these days?'

'Um... no! It's about getting the word out there that not everyone has to be a stick thin size six. If that's a natural look, great, but starving yourself to emulate a lot of young models isn't healthy. We are all different shapes and sizes. Curves are in. I'm working on it, but I'm not quite there yet.'

'Why?' he asks and I can imagine that customary frown on his face.

'A big booty is regarded as an asset these days and I have nothing with which to twerk. Stress makes the pounds drop off me and although Karl was pleased, I don't feel happy with myself, because skinny simply isn't me.'

'Explain the term *twerk*.'

I start to giggle, thinking at first that he's joking around. Then I see he has no idea at all what I'm talking about.

'It's... um... a dance move. Remind me the next time I'm on my laptop and I'll pull up a video clip. You know, Sam, none of these things matter but it's what makes the world go round. Sometimes you just need a good laugh and *James Corden's Carpool Karaoke*, for instance, would really lift your spirits. The guy is so cool and he can sing most of the songs as well as the artists. You're missing out big time and now I feel it's my job to educate you about popular culture. It's the least I can do given that you've taught me how to re-point a stone wall and tile a floor.'

For one second we manage to exchange a brief glance.

'I'd say "thank you", but I get the feeling a lot of this might go over my head.'

I bite my lip to stop my face from lighting up with a cynical smile.

*

We swap places twice more and at shortly after six in the evening the satnav ably guides us into a driveway in front of a pair of massive wrought iron gates. It's a relief when the sound of the engine finally idles. It's been a long day, that's for sure. But one that has built some sort of special bond between us. Like conspirators hatching a plot. I'll help Sam to get through this and he'll help me to relax a little.

The driver's window slowly descends. 'Sam Callaghan and guest.'

A buzzer on the intercom bleeps and the gates slide open without a whisper of a sound.

'Looks like we're in,' Sam says, slipping the car into gear and driving into the parking area in front of a massive, four car garage.

Once inside the gates my jaw drops almost immediately as I take in the scene.

'Sam, this is unbelievable!'

After parking the car, we climb the beautiful stone steps leading up to the villa. Sitting amongst the mass of trees and beautifully manicured bushes is an infinity pool looking out over the sea. Surrounded on all three sides by an expanse of hardwood decking, the pool is enclosed by large glass panels with chrome handrails and supports. To one side are probably twenty sun loungers angled towards the view. On the opposite side are bistro tables and chairs, all in matching silver-grey wickerwork with dark grey and white cushions. A small bar in the corner is set up with glasses and an array of drinks.

At the shallow end is a two storey pool house. A row of individual changing rooms accessed from the pool side have funky coloured doors; ranging from silver-grey through to deep purple. At the end of this run of doors are two single shower rooms. With a classic shed style roof sloping upwards from the rear of the building, the overhang at the front affords protection to the decking area in front of the changing rooms.

At first floor level, the façade is faced with the same coloured wood as the decking and two large, panoramic windows look out across the pool and the bay beyond. It's quite a large building which becomes obvious as we follow the sweeping white stone pathway leading up to the main house.

I stop in my tracks. Nothing Sam said prepared me for this and already I'm feeling way out of my comfort zone. I've never been up close to this sort of wealth before. A smart looking couple are walking towards us and the guy greets Sam with a quick man shake before they throw their arms around each other and exchange firm pats on the back. He's very tall, tanned and wearing a navy blue Ralph Lauren polo shirt with tan trousers and navy deck shoes. The woman is wearing a knee length floral dress in shades of sky blue, mauve and white with strappy wedged sandals. She looks effortlessly elegant given the simplicity of the style and it's a case of the lady wearing the dress and not the other way around. It's obviously a designer label but she's a designer's dream. Her dark hair is thick and glossy, nicely offset by the merest hint of a tan; this is a lady who takes care of her skin.

'It's been too long, Sam.'

Sam nods, clearly touched. 'Jack, this is my friend, Anna Lacey.'

Jack steps forward to greet me.

'Lovely to meet you, Anna. And you've just survived a ten hour trip with this man? You deserve a medal!'

We all laugh and that includes the woman at Jack's side.

'Forgive me. This is my wife, Bella. Bella, you get to meet him at last. You've heard me talk about Sam often enough when I'm reminiscing.' He turns back towards Sam. 'So how did the two of you meet?'

I avert my gaze, trying not to stare, but I'm taking in every single little detail in awe. They are such a good looking couple. I let my eyes sweep over this gorgeous and luxurious setting instead.

'We've been working together on a renovation job.'

'You're a builder?' Jack queries, looking directly at me and unable to keep the surprised tone out of his voice.

'No. I'm in advertising and specialise in re-branding, logos, website construction, that sort of thing. Sam is renovating two gîtes in the garden of an old manor house my parents bought. I'm his apprentice for the summer.'

That makes Sam smile.

'Well, it's great that you are both here. It means a lot, my friend.' Jack and Sam exchange a look that indicates how deep their bond goes. This is no casual acquaintance, but Jack knows exactly what Sam has been through and he's at pains to hide his underlying concern. Whether he understands that it's still as big a problem as it is, is hard to tell.

'Anyway, let's get you guys settled. You must be in dire need of a drink.' Bella kindly shepherds us along the path, past the pool house and in through a pair of oversized French doors leading into the coolness of the main house.

'This is breathtakingly beautiful!' I simply can't hide how awestruck I feel, even if that's not cool.

'You'll get used to it,' Jack muses. 'Seriously, it is a great place. But do my parents use it? No. Once a year. Total waste, but it's five minutes from the centre of Cannes and my Dad's business interests mean he's heavily involved with the F1 industry, which is an advertiser's dream. It's all about image and I'm sure Anna will understand that. So Grand Prix week is party time and the house is always full.'

I feel I ought to say something and I need to engage my brain to make it sound like I know what I'm doing.

'Yes, it's all about getting the brand out there: analysing consumer behaviour and attitudes to target promotional marketing. F1 is probably one of the best examples of global brand exposure. I'm at the other end of the market though as I'm in the process of setting up my own branding agency, BRAND *new*. I almost feel like I'm starting all over again but it's exciting. This time there are no constraints and there's no agenda other than to utilise what I've learnt and keep raising the bar.'

Jack looks suitably impressed by my response. I suspect Sam will be appalled. But if I don't present myself in the right way then I'm doing myself down. However, the business circles in which Jack and his family move are in a totally different league altogether.

'There's nothing wrong with a new start and fresh ideas. It's nice to be able to walk away and have that freedom to put it all together exactly as you want it. When are you launching? You'll have to give me a contact number and I'll reach out to a few people.'

Sam and Bella are listening intently and suddenly I'm the focus of attention.

'Oh, Jack, that's very kind of you but I wasn't touting for trade.' I feel embarrassed but he puts up a hand to stop me.

'Hey, I admire anyone with a passion for what they do. I meet too many people these days who have stepped into the family business, like I did, and it's never the same. I wish it was. I'd walk away tomorrow if I could, but that's one reason why rich people have kids. It keeps the family business going because you feel obliged to carry on the tradition.'

'A bit like the royal family,' Sam winks at me.

There's a pause and then we all burst out laughing.

'And the perks aren't bad,' Jack adds, a wicked twinkle in his eye.

'Ignore him, Anna,' Bella says, raising a disapproving eyebrow at Jack. 'He likes to get his dig in about the establishment, as I refer to it. But who else would employ him? Now let's grab a drink.'

Bella turns on her heels and I follow; we head towards a terrace accessed from the other side of this vast room. Bella picks up a handset on her way through and at the flick of a switch the entire wall of glass soundlessly slides back into hidden recesses either side. Suddenly there is nothing dividing the inside and the lush garden beyond.

'Hey,' Jack calls after her. 'I heard that remark. I'm not that bad… am I?'

Sam gives him a slap on the back.

'You haven't changed a bit, Jack, and that's good to see.'

Bella leads us over to a very elegant seating area with rattan loungers and a table with a dozen chairs around it. As if they'd been expecting us, suddenly two maids in traditional black and white uniforms with crisp, white linen aprons appear carrying trays.

'Thank you,' Bella indicates for them to leave the drinks for her to serve. 'We have Sangria or Pimm's for those who like a little alcohol; or a non-alcoholic fruit punch. If you prefer a cold beer, Sam, Jack can grab one from the fridge over there. While you are here feel free to use all of the facilities and please, do make yourselves at home.'

I opt for the Pimm's but Sam and Jack head off to get beers.

'I love coming here,' Bella confides. 'It must cost a fortune to staff and maintain it all year round. How long have you and Sam been dating?'

I'm about to take a sip from my glass tumbler and I stop, in horror.

'Oh, we aren't an item. We're just good friends, which has grown from working together this last few weeks. I hope that isn't going to cause you a problem?'

She shakes her head, reassuring me. 'Not at all! That's Jack, for you. He never passes on the details. I had planned on putting you in the room above here as it looks out over the bay. It's a shame as it's the only bedroom where the view is totally unobstructed by the trees. We don't have any single rooms in the main house, but we do have two singles in the pool house. It's the quieter side of the property, anyway. If Jack is up late and his music is blasting out, you'll probably be glad to get away from the noise. He said you had about a ten hour drive to get here?'

'Yes. We shared the driving so it wasn't too bad.'

She's very friendly and easy to talk to – rather like Jack.

'You sound excited about your new business venture. If Jack directs anyone your way, jump on it. He's a bit flaky at times; he doesn't mean to be but he has a short attention span. In fairness, he's caught between an over achieving father, a scheming uncle and a lazy, good-for-nothing younger brother.'

Jack and Sam are back, beer in hand.

'Are you telling Anna my life story?' Jack questions her.

'Think I summed up your family very well. And I was generous. I held back the bit about petty jealousies and your mother's temper tantrums.'

I wince; that was rather harsh but Jack and Sam are laughing.

'I'm saying nothing,' Sam adds, confirming it's probably all true.

'I'm going to put you and Anna in the pool house, Sam. The added advantage is that you can come and go without being seen by anyone in the house.'

Jack is quick to interrupt. 'What she means, Anna, is that if you want to go skinny dipping in the moonlight after everyone is in bed, no one will bother you.'

Well, if that sets the tone for this little jaunt then it's going to be quite an eye-opener.

It isn't long until two other couples arrive. Before Sam and I go to unpack our bags a quick introduction is done for my benefit and I shake hands with Ethan and Jane, and Andy and Shellie. They greet Sam warmly. I begin to hope we aren't going to be the only singletons here once everyone else has arrived.

Bella passes Sam a key and explains that our bags have already been carried across from the car. In case there's anything else we need, she hands me a slip of paper with her mobile number printed on it, saying I should simply text her.

'We don't dress up, so casual is fine. Dinner is at eight, here. See you a little later.'

As we walk off together I nearly forget and go to take Sam's hand. Whether it's a comfort thing or not, I don't know because it was instinctive.

'Sorry! All this couple thing is a bit much. It won't just be us, will it, as the unattached ones?'

'Could be, I'm afraid. That's the trouble with losing touch with people, you forget how many years have passed and how much life can be packed into those years. Bella is a pleasant surprise.'

My phone pings, and Sam looks at me.

'It will be Dad replying to my text to say we've arrived safely. I'll call them in the morning. I need to shower and change. I'm hoping that will counteract the tiredness. You drove for longer than I did, so you must be feeling it, too.'

He shrugs. 'I'll be honest and say that it was a journey I wasn't looking forward to but now I know all about carpool karaoke I'm sorted for the future.'

I burst out laughing.

'Are you laughing AT me, or WITH me?'

'You're such a dinosaur at times, Sam. When you said you like to turn up the volume when you're at home, I bet it's all classic old rock, isn't it?'

He pretends to be upset and busies himself unlocking the door to the pool house.

It's probably three times the size of a normal person's house; well, what I consider normal. The entrance door is at the side and as it swings open there is a staircase to our immediate right. In front of us is a large open plan kitchen/dining/sitting area, looking out onto a large secluded courtyard garden. Well, it's so full of plants, trees, shrubs and pots, that it looks a bit like a mini jungle but everything is beautifully maintained and sculpted.

'This is amazing,' I can't contain my excitement and I can see that Sam is impressed.

'I didn't come inside the pool house when I visited before. I thought it was smaller, though. Or maybe it's been extended. Let's look upstairs.'

Sam indicates for me to go first and I'm surprised when the stairs lead into quite a narrow corridor. It's light, because the back wall has six windows, each with a pair of white shutters. The view out across the courtyard garden is lush and green, and beyond that are the grounds to the side of the main house. Tall trees obscure most of it, which adds to the sense of privacy here.

Just as I'm wondering whether the upstairs might be a bit of a let-down compared to downstairs, Sam swings open the first bedroom door and then all becomes clear. We both walk in marvelling at the panoramic view in front of us. We are directly above the changing rooms and before us the infinity pool stretches out with seemingly no divide between it and the blue of the ocean beyond.

'Wow. Now that is a million dollar view if ever I saw one. Are both rooms the same?' I wonder out loud.

We open another door and pop our heads into the en-suite bathroom, which is spacious and has one of the most luxurious finishes I've ever seen. White marble with the tiniest touch of silver grey running through it seems to encase the entire room, in the middle of which is a slate grey tub.

'Is that actually made of slate?' I walk in to touch it, unable to figure out whether it is stone or some man-made material.

Sam follows me over. 'It feels like stone. It must weigh a ton.'

There's a separate shower cubicle alongside a double vanity unit and toilet.

'Can I choose which room?' I ask, cheekily heading off in the direction of the other en-suite bedroom.

They are mirror images, so there's little to choose between them and the only thing that differentiates them is a splash of colour on the bedding and on an iconic reclining chair and stool, probably designed by the late Pierre Paulin and upholstered to match the theme.

'Silver grey with a pop of lime green, or silver grey with a pop of mango?' I level at Sam, unable to choose.

'That's mango? How do you know that?'

'I work with graphics, remember? Colours are my thing and it's one of the in colours. Like watered down orange.'

'Okay. I'll take the lime green. Did you notice the connecting door between the bedrooms? Thank goodness we're not sharing a bathroom.'

I spin around and sure enough, there it is. I reach for the handle and it isn't locked. There's no key.

I had already noticed the beds aren't singles, as Bella indicated, but queen size at least, maybe king size. I wonder if Bella put us here because of the connecting door?

'Can I trust you?' Sam asks in earnest, before letting out a loud guffaw.

'Harrumph. I think I'm going to sleep like a log tonight, so the answer is *yes*, you can trust me.'

'Phew. It's a fair distance to drag that reclining chair just to jam it under the handle.'

I'm trying to shake my head at him but I'm laughing too much.

'Time to unpack and I really do need to stand under an icy cold shower to wake me up.' I glance at my watch wondering if there's time to have a short nap and dry my hair. Maybe.

'I'll swap the bags over. Mine are in here and yours are in the green room. You just can't get the staff these days, they're always getting it wrong,' he mutters in jest as he carries his suitcase out through the door.

I flop down on the bed as elegantly as I can so as not to totally mess it up. The softness envelops my body and I realise how tired I am. It's been a weird sort of day, well, it's a long way. I'm used to spending the day working alongside Sam but usually we're both concentrating on the task in hand. Today it's all been personal stuff or just banter between friends.

'Here you go. I'm going to shower and have a nap. If you want to meet up before eight o'clock either text me or knock on *our* door.'

He glances at me and I can't stop my lips from curling up.

'It wasn't planned, really. I had no idea where we were going to stay.' Sam says, looking just a little uneasy.

'I know. Bella originally planned for us to share a room in the main house, until I explained our situation.'

Neither of us are smiling and I know what I'm thinking, but I wonder what Sam's thinking. Would it be the worst thing ever if—?

'Right, see you later.' He turns and closes the door on his way out and I realise I'm not even sure how to finish that sentence. What I do know is that the look Sam gave me before he turned to leave wasn't a look I've ever seen on his face before.

Time to Party

Standing under a cool shower I switch off from everything, letting the water wash away the dust and heat of the day. A quick towel dry and a blast of warm air on my hair and I'm ready to set the alarm on my phone and sink down onto the bed for thirty minutes. As soon as my eyelids touch I'm transported somewhere else as sleep immediately claims me.

When my phone begins buzzing I reach across and hit dismiss, feeling surprisingly refreshed but very, very hungry.

Unpacking my case and hanging up some clothes I'm glad that most things I possess can be rolled and don't need to be ironed. It's hotter this evening than it has been all day, so I choose a long, silky, floral dress with simple spaghetti straps. It's mainly blues and greens. Sporting quite a tan now, I'm reasonably happy with the reflection I see in the mirror. Now for my hair.

I wander into the bathroom, turning on the lighting above the large vanity area, bathing it in a crisp white glow. Oh no! Falling asleep with slightly damp hair was a mistake and my usual sleek bob is curling. It's too hot to deal with hair straighteners, so

361

instead I grab a handful of mousse and scrunch it all up, accentuating the curl. While that dries, I put on a little eyeshadow and mascara, finishing off with a touch of coral lipstick.

'Not bad.' I say to the person in the mirror. She stares back at me. 'Are you trying to impress someone tonight?' I shake my head and push all thoughts away.

Five minutes and the mousse is dry. I finish off with a shine serum, scrunching the curls in handfuls. It's a different me, one who takes the time to glance in the mirror, rather than pass it by. Will Sam notice the difference? Probably not, but I don't want to let him down in front of his friends. We aren't a couple, but the people you choose to associate with say a lot about you. So tonight, I'm going to be the party me; the mixer; the happy girl and not the worrier.

As if on cue, there's a knock on the connecting door.

'Is it okay to come in?'

It must be nearly eight o'clock.

'Yes, I'm almost ready,' I call through the open bathroom door.

I head back into the bedroom to put on some dangly silver earrings and my watch, but as I walk past Sam he does a double take.

'Um… I didn't think it was you for a moment there. You look… different. I mean, good, but different.'

He shifts awkwardly from one foot to the other as I look him up and down. He's wearing a crisp white linen shirt, open at the neck and with his cuffs folded back to just below the elbow. His trousers are a dark tan colour and his shoes a couple of shades darker. He looks cool, handsome and if he thinks I look different, I have to report that in my opinion he definitely wins this one, hands down. I realise he's staring back at me, nervous about my reaction.

'Well, look at you! Guess we both scrub up rather well. Are you nervous?'

He hasn't smiled since he walked through the door and he looks rather worried.

'Is there anything wrong? Is this too much?' I look down at my dress wondering if I should have gone for something knee length.

'No. It's perfect. You're perfect.'

We're standing no more than three feet apart. 'Are we having some sort of moment here? Because this could be awkward.'

'I know. I'm thinking the same thing. I wasn't expecting this: were you?'

I shake my head.

'Well, the only thing I know for sure at this moment is that I'm starving. How about you?'

'Agreed,' I answer, willing my voice not to waver.

Then Sam does something I wasn't expecting. He reaches out and takes my hand.

'Do you mind?' he asks.

His skin is surprisingly cool to the touch, but his hand is firm and the skin a little rough. There's a gentleness, though, as he gives my own hand a reassuring squeeze before we walk out of the room together.

It's the first thing that Bella notices and she flashes me a smile when her eyes move up from our hands to my face. Her look is one of surprise and I think that maybe she's a little intrigued. Thankfully, there are people milling around and too much going on for eyes to be trained on Sam and me. As soon as we're offered drinks Sam reluctantly releases my hand. His eyes catch mine for one very brief moment, as if to reassure himself that I'm okay, even though he can see I'm a little anxious. But I can also see that he's nervous, too, but he's trying his hardest not to show it.

Jack approaches us and taps his glass, interrupting the general hubbub of conversation.

'Hey guys. We're quite a group tonight so I'll do a quick intro or this is going to delay dinner. Newcomers to this year's gathering are Anna here, and Jane. He touches each of us on our shoulders by way of introduction. Sam and Ethan, shame on you because you have been missed. The regulars, starting from this side – Chris, Marcus and Jade, Andy and Carla, Pete and Jeremy. Oh, that made it sound like Pete and Jeremy are here together, they're not, although they might have arrived—'

Jack is rambling and he pauses, losing his chain of thought as there's a ripple of laughter.

'Anyway, that makes us thirteen in total and as those who know me are well aware – what's my lucky number?'

There's a chorus of 'Thirteen!' followed by a round of applause.

'Now everyone, please take a seat as dinner is ready and we can't keep chef waiting. The bar is over there so if you haven't already got a drink, or your glass is dry, wander over. Once dinner is done we can get the music started.'

Sam shepherds me to the far end of the oblong table where there are two seats side by side. I'm rather relieved as I was beginning to wonder whether we'd get split up and that thought is a bit daunting, given that I've only spoken to Jack and Bella so far. They are sitting directly opposite us. However, the other nine people are in between us and at least seated where we are, it's easier for us to talk quietly to each other without being overheard.

'Is this a bit much for you?' Sam leans into me, his face inches from mine.

'I'm good, don't worry. He didn't mention Harry's name. Is he here?'

'No.'

I turn to look at Sam, seeing the slight frown and wanting to smooth it away.

'I'm glad. Let's just enjoy tonight and the ambience. Relax, catch up with old friends and don't feel the need to watch over me all the time. Honestly, I'm used to making idle chatter at functions and work events. I was nervous because I didn't want to let you down and I wasn't sure what people would think… about the fact that I'm here with you.'

His gaze doesn't waver from mine.

'You could never let anyone down and everyone is wondering who you are. I feel proud sitting here with you by my side, Anna. I know this is all totally alien to us both and what we've shared today has given us a better mutual understanding, but I don't want to overstep the mark. I'll be guided by you. And, of course I'm going to be one step behind you. I know these guys of old.'

'You do know what they'll be thinking, don't you?'

I take my eyes off him, pretending to be absorbed by the beautifully presented starter that has just been placed in front of me.

'I'm not complaining. Are you?'

'No. This looks too good to eat.'

We're back to the eye contact and we smile at each other.

'Well,' he leans in even closer now to whisper into my ear, 'I hope there's more to come – later.'

I nod in agreement, then realise that I might have missed an innuendo there. This certainly isn't the Sam I know, but then I will admit that I was the one who started this back in the pool house earlier.

*

Fine dining is wonderful because it isn't heavy and each course is a delight in terms of taste and presentation. At the end of the meal the chef appears and there's a huge round of applause. I don't recognise his name but everyone is fawning over him and I gather he's one of the top names in France. I'm afraid the only chefs I know are the ones who have a TV programme.

As soon as the meal is over Jack and Bella lead us through the garden to a vast patio area surrounded by trees full of tiny white lights. At one end is a booth and the music begins almost immediately. At ground level, pale blue lighting makes the patio look like a dance floor and I realise that these are serious party people.

Once again, Sam has my hand clasped in his and it doesn't feel strange but rather comforting. I tell myself it's because we're both a little out of our comfort zone and all we're doing is supporting each other.

'Hey, Sam! My man, it's been a long time!'

I slip my hand out of Sam's clasp so that he can shake the hand being offered to him.

'Anna, this is Andy. I'm ashamed to admit that this guy bailed me out whenever I'd had one beer too many. I was a little reckless when I first hit uni.'

Andy gives Sam a bear hug.

'I've missed you, man, and I'm glad to see you looking so well. This is my extremely talented girlfriend, Shellie.'

'Lovely to meet you all.'

She's very shy and looks nervously from Sam to me and back again, not sure what to do. I step forward and we air kiss. When I step back Sam does the same and I can see she's grateful we made the first move. I don't like to dive in and ask what she does, given the way Andy introduced her, but I'm curious.

'Have you come far?' I ask her and immediately she tucks in next to me, leaving the guys to chat.

'We flew into Paris from London yesterday. We stayed overnight and drove down today. It was a long way and it took over nine hours – we're both shattered!'

'Same here! We drove down the other side of France, from the Loire-Atlantique region. We shared the driving so it wasn't quite so bad.'

Shellie shakes her head. 'Oh, I'm an awful driver and I admit that. Driving on the other side of the road would take me from bad to dangerous!'

She's a little unusual but very grounded and funny.

'Do you work, Anna?'

Guess I was being a bit cautious just now, as she is very friendly.

'Yes, I'm helping Sam renovate a gîte at my parents' place, but I'm only in France for the summer and then I'm heading back to the UK. I'm taking the plunge and setting up my own business. I focus on branding, building websites, creating logos, that type of thing.'

'Oh, I'm envious of your skills. I'm an artist and a struggling one at that. I'll probably become famous after I'm dead, knowing my luck. Andy is introducing me to people to get the word around, because gallery space is expensive and I have nowhere to showcase my work.'

Now I can either commiserate and move on, or I can offer some advice and risk sounding like I'm touting for business again.

'Do you have a website?'

'No, and I know that I'm missing a trick there but my work consumes me. Andy had to drag me here, even though the thought of Paris and Cannes were such a temptation.'

Andy and Sam join us, eager to see why we're chatting away so intently.

'It's an easy way to showcase your work,' I continue. 'And you can advertise your website via Twitter and Facebook, or any of the social media platforms. It takes a while to build your following but it's an option well worth considering.'

She turns to Andy. 'Did you hear that? I know I need a website and it's Anna's line of work. What does it involve?' She turns back to face me, her eyes bright with enthusiasm.

Andy laughs. 'It involves a lot of things you won't understand, darling, and its way beyond me, too.'

'Here's my phone Anna, pop your number in and I'll give you a call when I get back to London. I'm so glad we met tonight because I wouldn't have known where to go to get this sorted and, clearly, I need an expert to do it for me.' I take Shellie's phone and tap away.

Shellie casts a glance across at Andy, who is smiling amiably.

'I'm not a computer geek, what can I say? Okay, I'll pay for it – will that make you happy?'

She links arms with Andy. 'My hero. Isn't he just the best?'

Sam and I look on, amused. This must be the wackiest couple I've ever met, but then an artist has a very different temperament and Andy's humble, almost deferential personality, is probably the perfect foil.

'Time to get a drink I think, Anna. We'll catch you later, guys.'

Sam doesn't just grab my hand but yanks me off in the direction of the bar.

'Thank you for rescuing me,' I whisper as I tuck in close behind him.

'You're like a one woman sales team. I can't let you out of my sight. It's time to relax. Now, what are you drinking?'

We slide onto the tall stools and I survey the well stocked bar. Jack sidles up next to me.

'I came over to ask for a dance after you've had your drink. I won't ask Sam because he'll say *no*.'

The bar tender is waiting expectantly.

'Can I have an espresso martini, please?'

He looks at me without blinking an eyelid. 'Of course, mademoiselle. Is that just the one?'

His accent is meltingly gorgeous. He has the most beautiful eyes.

'I'll have one too,' Sam throws in.

'Make that three please, Anton.'

I feel like a rose between two thorns and lean back as the guys lean forward, conspiratorially, to talk in front of me.

'I didn't realise she was so high maintenance,' Jack says, looking at Sam. 'This is a first, isn't it, Anton?'

'Oui. But it just 'appens to be my speciality.'

'That's why my father poached him from his best friend,' Jack informs Sam, continuing to pass banter back and forth.

'I am here, guys, and there is nothing at all wrong with my hearing.'

Anton ignores what's going on and prepares each cocktail individually. I'm delighted to see he adds the freshly made espresso last of all, although I would have added some ice before tipping it into the cocktail shaker.

'I'm impressed, Anton. This is a drink that cannot be made in bulk.'

'Ah, mademoiselle, that is part of the secret and the espresso must be added last while still fresh and hot, only to be cooled by the ice.'

The measure of Tia Maria looked wrong to me and this could have an off putting bitter taste if the coffee isn't full bodied. He gives the mixture a few shakes, deftly using his wrist action to full effect and pours the cocktail, adding three coffee beans to the top as decoration.

'Mademoiselle.'

He places the glass in front of me and both Sam and Jack lean back to watch me savour the first sip.

'That is THE best espresso martini I have ever tasted! Anton, you are a genius.'

Jack looks delighted and Sam is trying hard not to laugh.

We stand chatting and when our cocktails are finished it's Sam who takes my hand, much to Jack's dismay, as he whisks me off to dance.

Sam steps up close and finally takes me in his arms. As he whispers into my ear, his breath is warm on my neck and it feels good to be up close and personal.

'Tell me the truth. That martini was awful, wasn't it? Nothing at all like the one you made. Even Lizzie's wasn't that bad, though.'

I tip my head back. 'I know, but the guy so wanted to impress Jack. I don't think he's ever had one, either, so hopefully he won't have realised.'

'Money can't buy everything,' Sam says, staring into my eyes. 'You look lovely tonight. It's like this isn't us at all. I mean, not the Sam and Anna who were working next to each other covered in mortar dust and plaster.'

The adrenalin is rushing around my bloodstream making my heart pound and I can only hope Sam can't hear it.

'Do we need some ground rules?'

'I was going to say more or less the same thing. But how far do you want to go?'

'We're both adults. What happens in Cannes, stays in Cannes. What do you think?'

'I think you're one surprising lady, Anna. I just want you to be sure. I'm a bit rusty… being around a woman.'

Those words are spoken into my hair as our faces touch.

'I don't want to dance any more, do you?'

Sam lets go of me, sliding his hand down my left arm to catch my hand.

'I can't believe we're doing this, but if you're sure.'

'I'm sure. Let's go, before Jack comes back to claim that dance.'

We walk as quickly and surreptitiously as we can to avoid attracting attention. It's easy enough to disappear into the shadows once you step away from the soft lighting of the terrace; we're more than happy to be swallowed up by the descending darkness.

It Feels So Good to Let Go

Once we're away from the main house we run, hand in hand like guilty teenagers about to be caught by their parents.

We stop and kiss, Sam's aftershave tickling my nose with a fresh, citrusy note accentuated, no doubt, by the heat of his body. I can almost feel the excitement coursing through his veins and I know that his heart is pounding as loudly as my own.

I don't want to pull away from him and yet it's frustrating to be standing here when all I want to do is explore his naked body and feel his hands on my bare skin. Reluctantly we draw apart, picking up the pace again until we're at the door to the pool house.

Sam fumbles to get the key into the lock, the shadows cast by the trees making it almost impossible to see anything. After a few seconds, there's a click and we're in. He reaches out to grab my hand and pulls me inside, pinning me up against the wall as he slips the thin straps of my dress down over my shoulders, while twisting his leg to push the door shut.

We're both trying to kick off our shoes and help each other get undressed but the staircase is poorly lit and we make our way upstairs as best we can, laughing and kissing and crashing into the wall with silent curses.

Sam lifts me up; his arms are wrapped tightly around me, but with such gentleness that it doesn't hurt at all. He holds me tenderly against the door so that I can reach down to turn the handle and in seconds we're on the bed ripping at each other's clothes.

We laugh and hug and stop to kiss, and it's chaotic. As each item is successfully discarded the passion mounts until finally it's just skin touching skin. Sam's head comes down, his lips touching mine briefly, before pulling away in a moment of hesitation. I curl my arms up around his neck because I want him back and this time his lips aren't going anywhere. Any awkwardness between us has totally evaporated as we lose ourselves in the fire that consumes us both. I feel the muscles in his left arm tense as he scoops me up with his other arm and eases me further up the bed. When his body finally comes to rest on mine once more, just that reconnection of skin on skin elevates our passion to another level. The level where you lose yourself and your own identity because suddenly two become one.

I don't think I've ever wanted anyone as much as I wanted Sam at this moment. He's trailing his fingers down my arm trying to slow everything down, but the urgency of his mouth on my skin as he works his way down my body is almost a frenzy. I don't want him to hold back and I relax under him, letting my body tell him exactly what I want.

Whatever happens between us in the future, Sam, we'll always have this night and I know neither of us will have any regrets. Nothing this beautiful could ever be wrong.

*

'Are you asleep?' Sam's voice is low, softer even than a whisper.

'No. I'm resting my eyes, that's all.'

'You made me feel like the old me, tonight. I thought that person was gone forever, Anna, but I was wrong.'

I lift myself up on one elbow to look down at his face, which is partly in shadow and partially lit by the huge moon now shining in through the window.

'We are each made up of a multitude of layers, Sam. The deeper we delve, the closer we get to our core, the real person we often choose to hide from the world. No one wants to feel vulnerable, or risk getting hurt, but in hiding our true selves we lose something. But that's what happens when things go wrong and it's easier to sink back beneath the surface, so people only see the façade. Sometimes, though, it's so far removed from the person we are deep inside, that even we don't really recognise ourselves any more.

'Tonight, you saw the real me, too, Sam. We put our trust in each other and it was a truly beautiful moment. I have no idea where we go from here, or what is going to happen next, but you helped me overcome my insecurities and my fears in order to let go. And in return you let me get closer to you than anyone has in a long, long time I suspect. That's special, Sam, and I wouldn't change one single thing, or give up one second of this time we have together.'

He raises his hand, letting a finger trail down my cheek.

'If we could start our lives over again right now, then everything would be perfect. This, here, now, is perfect. I don't mean the setting, I mean us. But this isn't real, is it? We both know that and yet it's going to be hard to pretend this didn't happen.'

I lie down, turning into him and placing my hand on his chest, above his heart. I know he's right. My eyelids flutter and I can't fight the tiredness any longer but I don't want to sleep because I want this night to last forever.

A Brand New Day

I wake up slowly, drifting out of a dream that feels complicated and yet all I can hold onto is the fact that I'm walking in a field. I can see bright red poppies mingling with the tall corn stalks and I'm curious about where I've been. However, the sound of Sam singing makes my eyes open wide and I realise I'm still in his bed and he's in the shower.

I burst out laughing as I hear the chorus from Miley Cyrus' 'Wrecking Ball'. Not only is his singing a little flat but I suddenly visualise Sam, naked, swinging on that ball as it sways back and forth. Miley, what have you done!

Dilemma time. Do I lie here and wait for him to walk back into the bedroom to assess any potential fall-out after last night? Or do I make a quick exit through the communicating door and jump into the other shower? Think, Anna, think. Which is going to be the least embarrassing? Before I can decide, he saunters in with a towel wrapped around him and he's looking happy. How come I worked alongside him all this time and yet I managed to keep my distance? He looks so... totally kissable again this morning.

'Hey, sorry. Did I wake you?'

'I wasn't snoring, was I?' I grimace.

'Only a little and it was cute.'

Cute?

We stare at each other without blinking.

'Best night ever?' Sam throws at me, his eyebrows lift, questioningly.

'Ever.'

'Thank God! It would have cut me to the core if you'd hesitated there. What happens in Cannes, stays in Cannes – right?'

I nod. 'Those are the rules.'

'I hope there's a huge breakfast spread as for some reason I'm starving again this morning,' he muses. 'Can't think why.'

I pretend not to notice the inference, wondering how on earth I'm going to slide nonchalantly out of bed, naked and with some sort of style. But Sam comes to the rescue and hands me a crisp white cotton robe.

'Did you know it's nearly nine, already?'

I vault out of bed, holding the robe to me to cover my wobbly bits as if that has stirred me into action. I know that I'm simply trying to avoid doing a full frontal in stark daylight.

'I'll be ready in twenty minutes,' I call over my shoulder as I head back into my own room.

*

'I looked everywhere for you last night, Anna. You owe me a dance. Morning, Sam, hope you slept well.'

Jack places his hand on Sam's shoulder as he passes behind our chairs and I get a dazzling smile. Bella is a few paces behind him and when she draws level her eyes sparkle with amusement.

'Morning, guys. Wonderful night, wasn't it?'

Sam nods, the hint totally lost on him as he tucks into a pile of blueberry pancakes. Bella and I exchange a meaningful glance over the top of his head.

There are a few other people milling around, but we are the only ones eating so Jack and Bella load up their plates and come to join us.

'We're the early birds this morning. It was a late one. I hope the music didn't keep you awake.' Jack tackles the omelette on the plate in front of him with gusto.

I threw on shorts and a little top this morning and slipped on a pair of flip flops. I'm relieved to see that Bella and Jack are both wearing shorts, too. Sam is looking super cool in cut-off jeans and a white t-shirt. I was worried about fitting in, but sitting here I don't feel the odd one out and Sam certainly looks a lot more relaxed than I thought he would.

'Harry is arriving this morning,' Jack casually throws it out there.

Sam nods, but doesn't say anything.

'The plan of action today is... I only wish I could remember. What's happening, Bella?'

Bella doesn't answer immediately and she suddenly looks rather pale. She hasn't eaten anything, and has been chasing a couple of loose blueberries around the edge of her plate.

'Excuse me, I'll go check and be back,' she exits rather quickly.

I glance at Jack and he shrugs.

'Morning sickness.'

Sam drops his fork with a clatter.

'You're having a baby?'

Jack nods. 'Can you imagine me as a dad?'

'Is it common knowledge?'

'No,' Jack shakes his head vigorously. 'Bella is only two months gone and we want to wait a bit. Besides, my mother will be unbearable once she knows, so don't breathe a word.'

I reach out and place my hand on Jack's arm, giving it a squeeze. 'Congratulations, Jack. I hope this morning sickness passes quickly so Bella can enjoy the rest of her pregnancy.'

He nods, putting down his fork and smiling. Sam offers up his hand for a man shake and they perform some complicated ritual ending with an explosive opening of the hand as if a bomb has gone off. What are they, six, or something? I can't stop myself laughing as Bella appears and eases herself back into the seat, rather gingerly.

'False alarm. It's just nausea. Jack told you, then?'

She smiles across at me.

'Congratulations, it's so exciting.'

'It only seems real in the mornings when I feel absolutely ghastly, the rest of the day I find myself forgetting and then it hits me all over again that I'm going to end up looking like a sumo wrestler!'

Sam and Jack start laughing, much to Bella's annoyance.

'It's okay for you guys; it isn't your body that goes through all this trauma. I hope it's twins as I don't think I can do this more than once.'

Jack looks shocked. 'Well, we'll find out for sure later this week. And, babe, only the one? The parents won't like that.'

'Well, I'm sure we've made the perfect grandchild, so maybe they'll be too besotted to give it any thought!'

Sam and I exchange smiles; Jack and Bella have an intense relationship full of banter and quips, but beneath all of that you can tell they are both very happy. Bella isn't overly impressed by the trappings surrounding Jack, and he needs someone to keep his feet on the ground. And that's just what she does.

'You guys looked very cosy together last night. I hope you're finding the pool house comfortable?'

It's a loaded question and Jack's head jerks upright as he looks from one to the other of us.

'I knew you guys were together. You can't fool me.'

Neither of us make a comment and it's amusing to see Jack and Bella grinning.

'Anyone for coffee?' Sam asks, pushing his chair back as he stands.

I nod, Bella declines and Jack is immediately on his feet to help Sam carry the drinks back.

'The pool house is perfect. Well, everything here is perfect, thank you, Bella.'

'The moment I saw the way Sam looked at you yesterday, I knew some alone time was a good idea. I was surprised when you said you were only friends.'

I push my plate away, my stomach happily full. 'You knew more than we did, then.'

Her eyes open wide in surprise. 'Really? Last night?'

I feel myself colouring up as a rosy glow works its way up from my neck. I can only hope that it doesn't show beneath my tan. 'It's complicated. This isn't a permanent thing.' I falter as I speak, unable to explain a situation that seems to be changing by the minute. I don't know why I feel the need to explain but I can see that Bella seems to know a lot about Sam.

'He still can't let go of what happened?' Bella sounds horrified.

That confirms exactly what I've been thinking, though. 'He lost everything and now he has a chance to build something again but he's lost heart. Caring about someone doesn't mean you can necessarily fix their problems. If only this one thing changes between us, then it won't work. Physical attraction is a good start, but you have to be ready to give someone your heart. It's clear he isn't over Isla and maybe he never will be able to let go of her memory.'

Bella's expression is one of sadness. 'Jack misses Sam. Even after all these years he feels a sense of guilt knowing how tough the mental breakdown was for him. Jack says he felt he had lost a brother when Sam switched off and to this day he still talks about the fun they used to have. You see, Sam rescued Jack, in a way. He kept him on an even keel and he wasn't interested in him because of his connections or his wealthy background. Jack says that Isla wasn't the only one dabbling with drugs, but Sam stepped in at the right time. The problem was that no one knew Isla was popping pills. I know her brother, Harry, well, more so in recent years. Isla was four years older than me so we never mixed in the same circles.'

'I didn't realise you weren't part of the uni clique.'

Bella shakes her head. 'I was the annoying younger sister of one of Jack's friends. It took a couple of years for him to really notice me and the rest is history. He has a good heart and I can see, now that I've met Sam in person, why they have such a strong bond which time apart can never dent. I can only hope that now the ice is broken they'll keep in closer touch.'

We sit staring at each other across the table and Bella mirrors my frown.

'I'm worried about today when Harry arrives,' I admit. 'They've never sat down together and talked about what happened. I'm not even sure Sam is up to it, but this year something has obviously changed in him because that's why he's here.'

'I think all you can do is see what happens. I'll make it my business to keep an eye out and there will be things going on during the day with other friends coming and going. Let's hope for the best, eh?'

'Thanks for understanding, Bella.'

'There aren't many people in Jack's life who have been a genuinely good influence and have wanted nothing from him. Sam is one of them and I really hope that this trip will re-open their lines of communication again. It would be lovely to keep in touch. Goodness, with a baby coming and the pressure this awful family will no doubt put on us both, Jack is going to need someone to confide in. And I'm going to need an outlet to let off steam.'

Money doesn't buy happiness and I find myself feeling rather sorry for them both. Imagine that.

A Waiting Game

Jack and Sam disappear and I give Bella a grateful hug before retracing my steps to the pool house.

I phone Mum and Dad, keeping it light and upbeat but focusing mainly on talking about the house and describing the grounds. They seem content, unaware that my emotions are in turmoil. After the turn of events last night, I'm dreading the effect meeting up with Harry will have on Sam today. It's weighing heavily on him, too, and I suspect that Jack's taken him off to keep him occupied.

I pull out my laptop, conscious that there are emails I probably need to answer and a whole stream flood into my inbox as I watch in dismay.

I see Lizzie's name and click to open it.

Hey, girl,

I hope you're having lots of fun rubbing shoulders with the elite in Cannes. Not that I'm jealous, or anything! I know you'll be too busy to respond but I wanted to say a huge thank you for making it such a fun break.

It was great to meet Sam and I hope that tomorrow's visit with Tom goes well.

Daniel and I had a chat with his parents yesterday about France and they weren't quite as shocked as he expected. I have no idea if it could happen, but I'm so excited just to be talking to him about it.

The company he works for are going through a rough patch and job security is an issue that worries him a lot. Once we're signed up to that mortgage there is no going back. So, it looks like our plans are on hold for a while, anyway.

Sorry, didn't mean to offload but we'll talk after you get back. Have fun, party hard and let go – I'm sure Sam will be pleasantly surprised!

Lizzie xx

Well, I've managed the *letting go* thing. Is Lizzie psychic, or did she pick up on something that had been totally lost on me?

Moving the cursor down, holding my breath in case there's something from Karl, I see there's one from Tom.

Hey there, Anna,

I'm back in the UK. I'll hit Nîmes Garons airport late tomorrow afternoon as I have a few things to do in London. It's looking good for Wednesday. I've attached the directions to the practice surgery. We're in two separate locations, as one is also an animal refuge and I didn't want you turning up at the wrong address.

If you need to, call me on the number below.

I think you said you were in Cannes so I hope you pick this up in time.

Tom

I check the date and it was sent yesterday morning, an hour after Sam and I left. I still have a few things to finish off before I sit down with Tom and to be honest, I don't feel as sociable this morning. Until Sam and Harry have had their meet-up, I'm going to be on edge.

I grab my phone and ring Sam. He picks up immediately.

'It's me. Are you okay?'

'I'm good. I'm in Jack's study and he's trying to talk me into doing a joint project. I'll explain later. Harry will be arriving early and is about an hour away. Do you want me to come and find you?

'No. I'm going to lie down and have a nap. I'm exhausted from the long day yesterday and I have a bit of a headache. So, don't worry about me. I'll resurface in a couple of hours ready to take a dip in the pool.'

I keep my voice upbeat, not wanting to let him know of my concerns. If I told him I was going to do some work he'd feel he was neglecting me. He's better off passing the time with Jack and I should imagine Jack will want to be there when Harry arrives, anyway. After all, who knows what's going to be said or how fiery either of them will be.

I take a quick photo of the infinity pool and the ocean beyond from the window and send it to Mum and Dad. I caption it "Wish you were here!"

I don't think they would see what happened last night as a good idea for me, or for Sam, if I'm honest. But sometimes in life things happen and you can't over think them.

I carry the laptop over to the recliner and prop it up on my lap. If Tom is flying into Nîmes Garons airport then I bet he's hiring a private jet. Goodness, maybe his father has his own jet. At the end of the day, though, we're all just people, individuals trying to live our lives as best we can.

I log in to the new website dashboard and finish copying across some of the posts and photos from both Tom's blog and the practice website. It's cleaner, easier to navigate and the menu includes links to the five animal charities Tom supports.

The new logo catches the eye and keeping it simple with the black and white outline drawings of the animals was an inspired idea. Even though I say so myself. It's almost noon when I next check my watch and I panic a little. I meant to head out and hang around in case I'm needed. I turn off the laptop, literally throw it on the bed and turn on my heels, going as quickly as I can without running.

It's so warm again and hurrying makes a trickle of sweat roll down my back. I'm surprised to see over a dozen people with yoga mats in the area where we were dancing last night. I don't recognise many of the faces, but then Bella said other friends would be arriving.

I can't see her, Jack or Sam anywhere.

Andy approaches and I can tell he wants to talk to me about Shellie's website.

'Hi Anna, I was hoping to bump into you. I'd like to surprise Shellie—'

'I'm really sorry, Andy, but I need to find Sam as I have a message for him. Would you mind awfully if we catch up a little later? You haven't seen him, have you?'

He doesn't look offended and spins around to scan the people milling about.

'No, and I don't think he's out here. There's a martial arts class after the yoga, so maybe that's more his style.'

I smile in his direction but my eyes are checking out the people standing behind us.

'Don't worry, I'll find him. And we will speak later, I promise you.'

I go back inside the house and stop one of the waitresses who is carrying a tray of soft drinks out to the terrace.

'Have you seen Bella, or Jack, by any chance?'

Before she can answer I catch a glimpse of Bella walking down the staircase.

'I've just spotted her, thank you.'

I rush across the vast open space and I can see Bella is already heading in my direction.

'Follow me,' she catches my arm and then walks quickly in the opposite direction, opening a door in the far corner beyond the staircase.

When we're both inside she closes the door and indicates for me to take a seat. It's quite a cosy room, with soft white leather chairs and sofas.

'Sam and Harry are still talking. They are both calm and I've just taken in a tray of coffees. Jack is there, too. He texted me and obviously it was an excuse so that I could casually pop in and see what was happening. I'm sure he wanted me to let you know not to worry.'

'What was the atmosphere like?'

Bella shakes her head from side to side.

'It was difficult to gauge. They stopped talking the moment I walked in. I couldn't tell anything from the expression on Jack's face and both Sam and Harry had their backs to me. I simply walked in, put the tray on a side table and walked back out. We all knew it was going to be hard for them both. I have no idea how long they are going to be in there. How are you feeling?'

'Nervous. I spent a couple of hours in my room but I don't know quite what to do next. My stomach is churning a little, if I'm honest. If I wasn't so on edge I'd have joined in with the yoga.'

Bella's eyes brighten. 'Yoga is wonderful for relaxing. I think it's martial arts next, then lunch. After that there's going to be a chess tournament on the terrace. Later I'm sure the pool will be popular. Have you found the hot tub yet?'

I shake my head.

'It's quite secluded. Wander out behind the pool house. In the far corner, there's a lattice screen with a huge climbing rose; it's just behind that. I go there sometimes when I want a little privacy as it's a quiet little oasis. Why don't you get a drink and go and chill out there? I'll make sure Sam knows where you are when he appears. I seriously doubt they'll talk for too much longer as they've already been in there just over an hour. Stay positive; let's hope it does more good than harm.'

Bella squeezes my arm affectionately and leads me off to the bar, forcing a Pimm's into my hands and pointing me back in the direction of the pool house.

'Go. Really, there's nothing you can do waiting around here. I'll send Sam across as soon as he appears.'

Everything Begins to Fall Apart

Bella is right and although it's only twenty minutes later that Sam comes to find me, it feels like much longer. I'm next to the hot tub, but still in my bikini with my sarong-wrap around me, just waiting. The Pimm's is on the little bistro table, untouched.

As soon as I hear his footsteps I'm on my feet, even before he appears around the side of the screen.

'I'm sorry it took so long. I know you've been worried.'

He strides across to me and I wrap my arms around him, hugging him tight and feeling him sinking into me.

'Are you relieved it's over now?'

He presses his head into my neck, saying nothing but I understand that he's all talked out. I slide my arms down his, catching both his hands and lead him across to the pool house.

'You're exhausted, Sam, and you need to sleep. Shut your mind off from everything and rest.'

He allows me to lead him upstairs and push him gently down onto the bed. I slip off his deck shoes and go over to close the shutters. The sunlight is streaming through the windows and is too bright to encourage sleep. The air-con maintains a pleasant enough temperature but now, in the shaded room, I know he will be able to rest.

I want to hang around, to be there whenever he stirs but I'm conscious of the need to keep things as normal looking as possible. I creep out through the open communicating door and half close it behind me before looking out of the window. A few people are already gravitating towards the sun loungers and I decide to go down and show my face for half an hour. I'm sure Jack and Bella will understand and appreciate the effort I'm making.

*

If I check on Sam once, I check fifty times. The afternoon seems to crawl by and it's exhausting making idle chatter, constantly excusing myself to pop back upstairs and pretending that I'm having fun.

I have a long and detailed chat with Andy, who has now commissioned me to literally set everything up for Shellie. He's even going to foot the bill for me to spend a day with her to get her started online and set up social media accounts.

'She needs to have visibility, Anna, and she isn't half as scatter-brained as she makes out. We all prefer to spend time doing the things we love, but now she needs to cultivate a business mentality. People expect you to be available and want to read all about your lifestyle, where you live etc. I keep telling her that's the way life is these days.'

I ask him if he would like an idea of cost but to my surprise he waves that suggestion away and shortly after he thanks me and goes in search of the lady herself. Bella comes across to talk to me.

'Jack spoke to him about you, yesterday. You don't recognise him at all?'

'No, who is he?'

'Andy McColl, the lead singer with Outdated Machinery. Don't tell me you didn't know that Sam played the drums with Andy way back before his uni days?'

I shake my head. There's a lot I don't know about Sam.

'Money isn't an issue for him, trust me. He'll do anything to keep Shellie happy as she's his muse. Is Sam still sleeping?'

'Yes, he hasn't stirred.'

'People are starting to pack up and it will soon be down to just the core group again. Maybe have a quiet evening here, poolside. I'll arrange for a table and chairs to be set up and when you are ready text me and I'll have a meal brought over. Tomorrow is another day and Jack is planning a coach trip for us all to Monaco. We're visiting the casino.'

My smile fades. 'I have a meeting in Nîmes tomorrow. Sam was going to drive me there. I think it's better if I head off on my own as it's partly a business meeting, anyway. Would it be too much to ask you to keep an eye on him for me?'

'Jack won't leave his side, I can assure you, if he knows you're not around. I'll do my usual standing back and only poke my nose in when I can see it's needed.'

I lean in and give her a warm hug.

'You are a very special person, Bella. There aren't many people I instantly gel with but you are one of them. I really can't thank you enough.'

'Well, it's nice to have someone normal around for a change. Some of our guests have big egos and get upset if they feel I'm neglecting them. I'm sort of like the housekeeper-cum-mum-cum-confessor at times. Now off you go, Sam is probably waiting for you.'

I turn and leave the stragglers packing up their things as the group quickly thins out. I look up and notice the shutters in Sam's room have been opened and that makes me hurry up.

'Are you okay?' I call out as I walk into Sam's bedroom, just as he's turning off the shower.

'I'm good, I'll be out in a second.'

With a towel wrapped around his waist and his damp hair standing up in tiny spikes, he looks refreshed.

'Bella suggests we don't go to the main house for dinner this evening and she's going to get a small table set up for us down by the pool. We just need to text when we're ready to eat. Are you hungry?'

'I am, actually. But first I need a hug and then I need a drink.'

He wraps his arms around me and swings me playfully from side to side. My anxiety begins to dissolve.

'I want to tell you everything, but I need a little alcohol first,' he adds, nestling his face into my hair. 'You smell so good. I guess you passed on the hot tub and the pool. Don't tell me, you've been sitting around worrying about me most of the day?'

I pull away. 'Pretty much.'

'I have to admit that my head is in a bit of a turmoil and I'm not sure how I'm going to feel once it all sinks in. Harry and I both said the things we never thought we'd say to one another. But I got through it and all I needed was a little rest to put me back on my feet. I'm not falling into a depression like I did in the very beginning, so stop worrying.'

I let out a sigh of relief. 'I'll fetch some alcohol. I'm not going to change in case we decide to use the pool later.'

He nods and then heads back into the bathroom to finish drying off.

*

The empty plates in front of us are a testament to the standard of the cuisine. I didn't even realise I was hungry after expending all that nervous energy and I suspect that Sam was much the same.

The bottle of champagne Bella insisted I bring back with me is already half empty and when two waitresses appear to clear the table they bring another one in a second ice bucket.

'Is Bella trying to get us drunk?' Sam enquires of me, after the waitresses have departed.

'I bet this stuff costs the best part of a hundred pounds, or more, a bottle. It slips down easily, I will admit, but the Prosecco I buy from my local off-licence at a fraction of the cost is, to my taste buds, on a par. Maybe I wasn't destined to have expensive tastes.'

Sam looks across at me in the fading light, the candle on the table between us sending out little flickers and the odd puff of smoke.

'I'm very glad to hear that. Thank you for today, Anna, for being patient and for caring. It means a lot.'

'My pleasure, Sam. And now, I want you to do me a favour in return tomorrow. Jack is organising a trip to the casino in Monaco. I must go and meet Tom, not just to return the box but to walk him through the new website. If I can get his agreement we can make it live, there and then, but it will take an hour or so at least. I'll leave early and I promise to be here waiting for you when the coach returns.'

He opens his mouth to argue with me, but I put up a hand.

'I did you a favour today, so you owe me one in return.'

He isn't happy but that passes as I encourage him to tell me a little more about Harry, how they met and how Isla came into his life.

Sam talks for a while, then suddenly he lifts his head to look directly at me, scanning my face. I know that something is about to happen. He's going to cross a line and he knows there is no going back.

'The guilt will never leave me, Anna, because I should have been able to save Isla and I can never forgive myself for what happened. She wasn't a heavy drinker, it wasn't her style. As soon as I saw the state she was in I should have known something was wrong. I simply assumed she was drunk and I took her home in a taxi because I'd been drinking, too. I put her to bed to sleep it off, not realising there were drugs in her system. If I'd been sober that night—'

His voice trails off and I wait until he's able to continue.

'When I woke up the next morning she was still lying next to me, in the exact same position, but when I reached out her body was cold to the touch. I ran from the room out into the street, a scream caught in my throat as I was unable to comprehend that it was already too late. I re-live that moment often in my nightmares. Why didn't I check her breathing, or her pulse? There might have been time to get her to hospital. It was my fault and I let her down when she needed me the most.' A sob rises in his throat and his voice ends in a whisper.

As tears start to fill my eyes, they spill over, rolling down my cheeks and I swipe them away with the edge of my sleeve. My heart constricts for Sam's pain: a pain that he has lived with for seven long years and the reality of what happened was more horrific than I could ever have imagined.

'If I can't learn to live my life without constant regret, then the future is always going to be uncertain. What if nothing ever changes for me?'

A Very Different Sort of Guy

I creep out, leaving Sam fast asleep but having pangs of guilt. Last night was such a waste. We drank too much and when we eventually both dropped down onto the bed the passion was there, but our heads were spinning. It would have been meaningless, maybe even unsuccessful and disappointing. We both knew that, so we stripped off and lay in each other's arms for comfort.

It's a two and a half hour drive to Nîmes and I punch in the address Tom gave me, glad that the satnav will take me straight to the door. I'm in no mood when I set off at 6 a.m. to fuss over which is the quickest route. Once I'm on the A7 I can relax and begin clocking up the kilometres.

Why didn't Sam tell me he spent the night in bed sleeping next to his dead girlfriend? He told me that Harry confirmed Isla knew their relationship had run its course and the two of them were already arguing about a lot of things. Drug taking, though, was something she hadn't shared with Sam. So, it was just one of those lust at first sight, quick fizzle things that loses its sparkle very quickly. That's another thing he never mentioned to me. I really believed that when she died he was deeply in love with her.

I think his guilt is so ingrained now that he can't even admit that to himself. What a mess! What a waste! Harry's attitude was sadly predictable. He blames himself because he knew Isla was popping pills occasionally and he blames Sam for being too drunk to take proper care of her.

No one seems to lay any blame at Isla's door and I know how harsh and maybe cruel, that sounds. But she was the one who swallowed the pills and we each need to take responsibility for the results of our actions. I know that death isn't a consequence that would cross anyone's mind – who stops to consider the worst case scenario? The coroner pronounced it an accidental overdose, but a verdict doesn't alter how people feel about the part they did, or didn't, play.

I'm too upset, jaded and confused to think about what all this means for Sam, let alone the impact of this trip on our friendship.

I do the only thing I know that will help blot out my thoughts and I slide Adele into the CD player. She's my friend in times of need and sometimes you just need to have a damn good cry.

The road is quiet; it's early on a Wednesday morning and the sadness in her voice seems to pull the sadness out of me. As the tears flow and my voice grows louder, it's like I'm expelling the stress and what has, overnight, turned into anger. I'm angry for the stupid actions of a young girl who didn't understand the risk she was taking. Angry, too, for the way her brother and Sam are now forced to carry a burden that is hard to shed and impossible to ignore.

By the time I hit Aix-en-Provence, two thirds of the journey is done and it's time to leave the A7. With just over a hundred kilometres to go, the satnav is saying I will get there about twenty minutes before my scheduled time of 10 a.m.

I eject Adele, thanking her for helping me through a difficult two hours. I pull over, idly throwing CD after CD out of my bag and into the passenger side foot well.

At last. I slide the disc into the slot and ram the car into first gear to the strains of the late, great and irreplaceable, David Bowie.

I sing my heart out, and still manage to shed a few tears at the loss of a man whose voice seems to touch my soul as profoundly as Adele but in different ways. But ultimately, you can't blast out the words to 'Heroes' without having a huge smile on your face and a warm feeling in your heart. Show me one woman who doesn't secretly want her man to demonstrate at some point that he is her real life hero. But women can be heroes too, and I hope someday to feel that sense of strength and determination that will allow me to be strong when someone else is in need.

An hour? It flies by and Sam is right. When the world becomes too much all you need to do is turn up the volume and drown out your thoughts.

*

'Anna, it's so good to finally meet you in person. How was your journey?'

Tom is nothing like the recent photos on his blog. He had a full head of hair, which was usually tied back. Now his head is shaved. Instead of cut-off cargo pants, he's wearing a tidy pair of jeans and a denim shirt which looks rather sober for him.

'Oh, the hair. It was unbearably hot so I shaved it all off last week. It's just more practical although annoyingly it does require a little daily maintenance. It grows like weeds, anyway. That's enough about me. It's rare that someone impresses me in the way you have. For a start, you tracked me down and I pride myself on being a modern day nomad.'

He laughs and we're still shaking hands, what, ten seconds on? He releases mine from his grip.

'I'm waffling. I'm like this when I return from a long spell away. It's just nice to be here where everything is so easy. We don't realise how good we have it. Running water, a cold shower when you're hot. It's always the basics that give the most creature comfort.'

He won't stop talking, but I love it. It's so refreshing. I dive into my bag before taking the seat he offers and I slip the box out of its cover to place it in front of him on the desk.

'My mother's jewellery box.' He sits, suddenly unable to speak and stares at it for a while before reaching forward to slip off the lid. The very one that Sam carefully sanded to make it a perfect fit.

Tom empties the contents out onto the leather top of the desk.

'I remember her wearing this,' he says, holding up the ring and twisting it against the light. Then he picks up the locket. 'This was my grandmother's, God rest her soul.'

He's a man of many beliefs, then.

'How can I possibly thank you? As if you haven't done enough already, you've offered to give my website a much needed facelift.'

I laugh, not expecting him to be so witty and charming. I expected someone much more serious and maybe even a little angry about his childhood.

'You made a big impression on the people of St-Julien. Goodness, everyone wanted to be remembered to you. Honorine, of course, as I think she secretly regarded you as her adopted son.

Monsieur and Madam Deniaud – oh, and Elise Moreau, who now lives in Rennes.'

Tom looks overawed.

'You're like a walking history book. Now please tell me that Inès Gaubert is still keeping her husband, Claude, in line. He's a great baker and the village is lucky to have him. The fact that he'd rather get out his fishing rod and sidle off to the lake was a constant irritation to her.'

Again, I'm laughing and he's laughing too.

'I met them at a little gathering and I loved the way they banter with each other. He seems a very serious type of man to me, but I think everyone is a little scared of Inès.'

'Tea, coffee? You deserve champagne, but it's all I have.'

He buzzes an intercom.

'Coffee would be lovely, thank you. White, no sugar.'

'Carol, my darling, I'm sorry to interrupt as I know how busy you are and how annoying I can be, but could we possibly have two coffees?'

'Sorry boss, I'm just off on an emergency dash to bring in a kitten who has been hit by a car.' Carol's accent indicates she's probably a Londoner and she dismisses Tom's request without hesitation.

Tom's face changes in an instant. 'Drop everything and go, lovely lady. I'll cover.'

He turns to face me. He really is a very charming man and quite the gentleman.

'Sorry, Anna. Walk this way, I need to look after the reception desk for a while.'

He doesn't stop. While he answers phones and books in clients, I'm dispatched to the kitchen to make the coffee. When I return he's just replacing the handset on the receiver.

'There's always a flurry of activity when Carol's not here. I'm sure she organises it to remind me how hard she works. I think I have everything under control, so shall we jump on her PC while we're waiting for her to come back?'

He manoeuvres a chair in my direction and I settle myself down.

I type in the URL and log in to the dashboard.

'Right. This is how your website will look with the new styling. Let's swap seats and you can scroll through the pages and posts. The navigation is now a lot simpler. You have the basic veterinary information on clickable tabs at the top, just here. On the right hand side the first link is to your blog, which is now a part of this website; I'll show you how to access that in a moment. Then you have links to the charitable organisations you support and when people click through there's also a pop-up donation option. Anyway, I'll leave you to have a little look around while I drink my coffee.'

I stand back and carry my mug over to the window of the waiting room, so I'm not tempted to look over Tom's shoulder. All of this is a surprise, actually. This is just like any other vet's practice I've been in over the years. Obviously, they are well used to functioning without him here and his attitude seems to be that he doesn't want to get in their way.

'All of this was your idea? Or do you work with a team, or something?' Tom enquires, sounding genuinely interested.

I walk back, facing him across the counter, coffee mug in hand.

'It's just me, for now, but I hope at some point to develop the business and bring a couple of people on board.' Well, that's the long term plan, anyway.

'What was the attraction for turning your back on a well paid job and going it alone? It's a risky venture these days.'

'That's rather a long and boring story.'

With that, Carol rushes through the doors carrying a mewing kitten in her arms, nestled in a very large blanket. Tom jumps up and before I know it, I'm the temporary receptionist.

A Real Life Adventurer

As I sit opposite Tom in a very rustic, but charmingly traditional, roadside restaurant, I can't help thinking of David Bowie singing 'Heroes'. For Tom is a genuine hero; from the animals he saves, to the people he employs, whom he treats like family, and to whom he entrusts his business interests. But it's not solely about making money and that doesn't seem to be a motivator for him.

'Anything we make, over and above the cost of the overheads and salaries, is ploughed back into setting up another practice. My staff run the show at each location and I pay them well because they are all people who go that extra mile. Besides, they have a boss who is rarely around and they are the ones who make it all happen. I swan off to foreign places because basically I'm a big kid who has never grown up. My inspiration was always Indiana Jones in *Raiders of the Lost Ark*. That film got me through a lot of difficult times.'

He eats with gusto and the portion sizes are probably suited to the lorry drivers who seem to make up the bulk of the patrons sitting around us today.

Even the bottle of red wine is free and is a part of the *prix fixe* lunch menu. What it lacks in presentation, though, it makes up for in taste and the pâté starter is delicious.

'Ask me anything you like. I can see you have questions, probably stemming from the research you did to track me down. That jewellery box means a lot to me and when it disappeared I really believed my aunt had burnt it on a bonfire in the garden. She was an angry woman, who felt life owed her more than to be the paid nanny to her sister's son. She told me that's what she would do if I misbehaved.'

I swallow hard. You don't do something like that to a young boy who has lost his mother.

'I'm sorry to hear that. It's an awful threat to make.'

He looks up, seemingly unable to understand my tone.

'I was a handful. I missed my mum, obviously, but I still had her values and her love of nature. And animals, of course. I made Aunt Yvette run screaming from the house on lots of occasions, as she hated mice and spiders, in particular.'

He grins, then finishes off his pâté, letting out a satisfied 'mmm'.

'I haven't had pâté in over a year and that was good. French lorry drivers know the best places to eat. You might not get an extensive menu, but you know that the person in charge of the kitchen is likely to have learnt from watching their own mother, probably even before they learnt to talk.'

He pours two glasses of water and leans in close.

'The wine is rustic with a capital R.'

I'm driving anyway, so I take Tom's lead and stick to the water.

We chat about the people in St-Julien he grew close to and the fact that animals replaced the affection he didn't get from his aunt and uncle. He seems unfazed when I ask him about his father and simply says that he understood that he'd done what he felt was best for Tom at the time.

'I remind him of my mother and that was tough, still is. I was with him in London on Monday as I'm one of the directors of Joie de Vivre International. I don't really do much, but it keeps him happy to think I care about his business. We get on well, but we've never been exceptionally close. I didn't blame him for that, as my mother's wish was that I had the sort of childhood she'd enjoyed. I'm sure she thought with one of her best friends as my teacher and her sister to look after me, I was in safe hands. I was, but Aunt Yvette was disappointed with her life as she set out with grand aspirations. Uncle Tony wasn't like that at all. He was a carpenter by trade and made wonderful pieces of furniture, things that became family heirlooms. My father accepts the way I choose to live my life and I respect him for that. Besides, what do I know about jewellery and perfume? It's not for me and he knows it. I have no idea what will happen when he decides to retire. I set up a foundation with the money I inherited on my twenty-first birthday from my mother's will. It helps fund trainee vets to do a stint abroad. I think it adds to their education and they learn quite a bit. Not least, how easy we have it over here.'

The *patron* speaks no English at all, but he obviously knows Tom well and they converse easily. We hand him our empty plates and he brings the main course.

'What is it?' I ask, savouring the smell of some sort of meat in a rich looking sauce.

'Today it's venison. Often, it's wild boar, or pheasant – whatever happens to be around when the hunters are up and about in the morning.'

Well, it's nice to know it's fresh.

'Anyway, Anna. You've gone to a lot of trouble to track me down and travelled a long way to get here. I owe you not only a reward for finding the jewellery box, but also for your time and petrol and your amazing branding skills.'

I feel embarrassed hearing Tom say that as I'm beginning to feel like a stalker. Given recent events with Karl, it's not a term I care to be associated with. Watching him, though, he is very attractive and a large part of that is down to his personality. But to my surprise I'm not attracted to him in the way that I'm attracted to Sam. I realise Tom is staring at me, waiting for a reply.

'Let's just say tracking you down and working on your website saw me through a difficult period. If I can feature before and after shots of your blog and website in my portfolio for my new business, that's payment enough. Believe me, as before and after case studies go, they don't get any better!'

Oh. That sounds rude but Tom laughs.

'It still feels wrong. Okay, instead I will make a donation in your name – what's your favourite endangered animal?'

'That's easy. Bengal tigers. I have a Bengal cat named Ziggy, she was one of a litter of three and we bonded immediately. She's quite a character and a very good judge of people.'

'Felines have their own type of intuition about humans and they can tell if you are a true cat lover. They seem to instinctively know how to play the cute card when there's someone around they want to know better. I have no doubt Ziggy picked you for a reason and maybe that was because you, too, are a good judge of character.'

I nod, point taken. We eat in silence for a while and it's comfortable, rather than awkward.

Over dessert, which is some sort of profiterole filled with fresh strawberries and a light, vanilla cream, Tom tells me a little more about his childhood antics. He's right, he was a handful. He mentions Honorine and I realise that he has a great regard for her.

'She isn't getting any younger and when you are around next she'd be thrilled to have a visit. You could even stay at Le Manoir d'Orsenne; my parents would love to meet you.'

He frowns. 'I'm so busy dashing here and there I forget that life is whizzing by and I'm grateful to you for reminding me of that fact. Honorine was kind and caring; the fact that she had no children of her own was something that made her very sad at times. I came bounding into her life because she welcomed me in and I was often glad to get away from Aunt Yvette. I will go back to see her and I understand what you're saying.'

'I'm so glad our paths crossed, Tom. How long are you back for?'

He looks abashed. 'Don't tell the staff, but I'm off again next week. I have a friend at one of the institutes I volunteer at in Borneo. Chelsea is working on an award winning orangutan project at the Matang Wildlife Centre. Maybe one day I might want to put down some roots and just maybe Chelsea will be at that stage at the same time, who knows?'

'I'm glad your difficult childhood didn't leave any long lasting emotional scars. You touched a lot of people's hearts and they were the richer for it. Everyone needs somebody in their lives, even if every moment of every day is filled. It must be so satisfying to be a volunteer and know that you are helping to save an endangered species.'

'Well, if you ever want to get involved just get in touch. We need everything from admin people through to veterinary surgeons. The path I've travelled brought me here, to this point in my life. I'm the person I'm supposed to be, a nomad who only needs a sleeping bag, a tent and a bottle of water to fall asleep with a smile on my face. If I'd had a normal life I'd probably be working for my father, having to spend my life juggling figures on a computer.

'Instead, I get to experience the wonders of the plains and the forests. Often, I can help bring sick animals back to good health. Sometimes it's about helping an animal to take its final breath when its injuries are fatal. Or training people up so the good work can be continued. It's a blessing, either way, and a constant adventure. I wouldn't change a thing.'

Tom walks me to the car.

'Drive safely, Anna. Sometimes when we feel a little lost for direction it's wise to take a while and think things through. Listen to your inner self and

418

when you hear its voice you know you are being true to yourself. Don't try to start common-sensing it, or applying logic – just act upon it.'

He stoops down to give me a hug and I laugh, as I wasn't expecting that.

'As for the donation – I'll make it a generous one and I'll send you a link to their website.'

*

On the first leg of the journey back to Cannes I think long and hard about some of the things Tom said. He made a lot of sense and he is a remarkable man. Coincidentally, I'd sort of reached the same conclusion, that I need to take some time to discover the inner me anyway. The timing isn't good, of course, given the events of the last couple of days. But I'm no good to Sam until I know where I'm heading. Tom is a lovely man and his blog definitely piqued my interest, but when we met all I felt was a deep respect for him. That was a bit of a surprise. There was a sexiness to his passion for his work and I wondered if I'd feel a bit of a deeper connection to him. All it did was make me realise how much I fancy Sam and that's not helpful at this point.

Adele and David Bowie accompany me for the last part of the journey. I'm almost hoarse when I finally pull up outside the villa gates and press the buzzer. I manage to shower, change and settle myself down by the pool on a lounger before the luxury coach eventually off-loads its passengers.

'Did you have a good day?' I ask Sam as he walks towards me, smiling.

'I'm not a gambler and I lost everything. The whole twenty euros.'

I laugh and it's good to hear him joking around.

'How did it go?'

I stop to consider what to say about a rather extraordinary day.

'He's a busy guy and he appreciated the work involved in tracking him down. He's off on his travels again next week. And he loved the website.'

Sam slides onto the lounger next to me.

'I was rather concerned there for a while, I must admit. I mean, he's obviously a dynamic, adventurous sort of guy who makes things happen. I wondered if you'd take one look at him and feel some sort of attraction. I mean, he saves animals – it doesn't get any cooler than that.'

My heart squishes up in my chest.

'Sam, Indiana Jones is his hero. He says he's like a little boy who never grew up.'

Sam's face drops a little. 'That's an odd thing to be discussing. So, you won't be heading off to join him and his volunteers any time soon?'

Does Sam need something to shake him out of his complacency? Could this be just the sort of threat he needs to shock him into action and, hopefully, commitment?

'He did make me realise that until I know what I want out of life, I'm just stumbling around in the dark. They are desperate for all kinds of help with that project in Borneo working with orangutans. Sometimes you have to step outside your own life to get things into perspective and I'm giving it some serious consideration, I will admit. He's so passionate about what he does and it's refreshing.'

That kills the conversation and I wonder if I've gone too far. I feel mean, but I need Sam to get a grip right now and choose me. I want to be his *one*.

Heaven and Earth

Dinner tonight is leisurely, with the house party now down to just eight of us. I get to know a little more about Marcus and Jade, and Ethan and Jane, but we seem to have little in common. The after dinner chatter is hard work and Sam and I head back to the pool house shortly after nine o'clock, saying we're heading for the hot tub.

It isn't until we're walking back that I look up and see the sky is a spectacular inky blue and littered with stars. There doesn't appear to be a patch anywhere without a myriad of twinkles bouncing off it as I spin slowly around to get a three hundred and sixty degree view.

'Maybe we really should jump in the hot tub, what do you think? It's a shame to waste that sky.'

Sam shrugs his shoulders. 'Okay. I'm up for it.'

We hurry upstairs to change and I grab two bottles of water before we head out to the hot tub.

Lying back and allowing the jets to do their work, there's nothing else to do but look up at the sky.

'When you gaze at it like this it's mind blowing, isn't it?' Sam sounds awestruck.

'I was going to say the exact same thing. What if there are beings up there looking down on our planet? I read somewhere that if you are far enough away even the earth would appear like one of those little specks up there, although it would actually be a blue dot. So maybe they aren't all stars but some are very, very distant planets, too. And they don't twinkle at all. It's the earth's turbulent atmosphere that causes the twinkling effect so only we get to see that. I think that's rather sad in a way.'

'As unmanned crafts travel further and further out into space, that was more than likely based on research. It kind of puts things into perspective, doesn't it? We're just a tiny speck in the universe.'

'Sam, would you mind if we head back home tomorrow, instead of Friday? I need some time to think and being here isn't... doesn't... I don't know. It's turning everything upside down and I feel that things between us need to settle before we decide where it's going. I hope you don't think I'm letting you down?'

I turn my head to face him and he looks sad, but his gaze doesn't waver and his eyes search mine, as if he's trying to read my thoughts.

'I have the same dilemma. There's so much going round and round inside my head that needs to be processed. I think it will all make more sense when I'm back on familiar ground.'

I'm glad he feels the same way.

'This is all lovely and I have had a wonderful time, really I have.' I hope my tone conveys that I have no regrets and I mean what I say.

Sam's arm circles my shoulders and I scoot up to fill the gap between us on the bench seat. Just the touch of his skin on mine sends a little shock wave running through my core. He rests his head against my shoulder and I allow myself to relax into him, the warmth of the water making every muscle in my body relax. Ironically, I feel I'm where I'm meant to be, wrapped in Sam's arms but it isn't up to me. Once again the problem isn't of my making.

'It doesn't have to be over, Anna, does it? We could make a new reality for ourselves.' Is this a knee jerk reaction because he really believed what I said about Tom's offer?

'Oh, Sam! Nothing can ever be as good, or as perfect as the other night. It wasn't real and we both said that at the time. We were different somehow, maybe we became the people we dream of being, because it was a night of make-believe. Time stood still and suddenly anything was possible. But it all changed very quickly, didn't it, as old habits are hard to break. We couldn't stop reality flooding back into our lives, no matter how hard we resisted it and we couldn't recreate that night together because letting go is difficult. It was like pushing our troubles aside for a while and then we stepped back into our lives.'

He turns to look at me, sweeping a wet straggle of hair away from my face with his hand. There's a desperate, haunted look in his eyes that's painful to see but I need him to be strong now, for me and for himself. It's time to show me whether the passion he feels for me can overcome his guilt for what happened.

'I don't want you to walk out of my life and yet I know you are right. I can't be the person you need me to be.' He hangs his head, unable to look at me now, because even his body language is signalling defeat. What was a firm, almost urgent, grip, is now simply two people hanging on to each other in desperation. I can feel the physical tension between us and wish that was all it would take to make everything right.

'I knew something would go wrong, it always does, Sam.' In my heart I know I have no control over how I feel about him but I can't live in the shadow of Isla.

'If we can't be the people we were that night from here on in, then one night of passion means very little. Our past helps to define us whether we like it or not, it seems. I knew when we started this trip that we could only be friends because my heart wanted to heal you and I cared about your pain. But now I understand that it's the memory of Isla that still prevents you from being free and I know that's tough. Only you can break that spell, Sam, and you're not ready. You would end up hating me because I could never give up on trying to make that pain go away and make you whole again.'

I'm crying beneath a sky lit up with so many stars that it was made for a romantic night that I know isn't going to happen; it's probably one of the saddest moments in my life so far. I continue to look upwards, begging the universe to fix this; to fix me. To fix Sam.

I remember Tom's parting words: listen to the inner you and when you hear that voice you know you are being true to yourself.

But what if Sam's inner voice is on mute? What do you do then?

*

The bags are packed, the *goodbyes* and *thank yous* have all been said; as we pull away from the drive to start our homeward journey I reflect upon the fact that St-Julien isn't my home, anyway. Last night nothing happened between me and Sam, because we parted with heavy hearts and only a peck on the cheek.

I look across at Sam as he follows the satnav's instructions, easing out into a busy flow of Thursday morning traffic. We're both still subdued and it's hard not to be. This never was a simple holiday, designed for lazing in the sun and relishing the fact that it's a break from work. The silence isn't about the sadness that it's over, but the sadness of returning to our real lives knowing nothing is sorted. Oh, we've learnt a lot about each other but that's only served to complicate matters in a way. Now we have the added pressure of not wanting to let each other down.

'Sorry, but it has to be carpool Karaoke again until we both cheer up a little, at least.' The determination in my voice is telling him he has no choice in the matter.

'I'm so glad you said that. The silence is killing me.'

Bowie, Adele, Miley, Metallica, Aerosmith... whichever disc comes to hand is honoured in equal fashion. Sam joins in as and when he can.

'How on earth do you know the words to so many of these songs?'

'I run a lot when I'm at home listening to my iPod. I always have music on when I'm in the car and there was a fair bit of travelling with my old job. By the way, I learnt something new about you, from Bella. You never mentioned you used to play the drums.'

His smile is back, and so, too, that relaxed profile I've come to know quite well.

'It was only ever a fun thing for me; more about the social side and getting to perform at gigs. Andy had a little following, even in those early days. I had fun but then my life moved on and Andy went on to do great things. I had to sell the drum kit because I needed the money and by then I'd lost interest in it. Besides, it wouldn't have fitted into the caravan. Did you learn anything else?'

A warm, fuzzy feeling hits me square in the gut and I can only hope Sam isn't having a flashback, too. We're lying on the bed and his arms are around me. We're both naked. It felt so good; he felt so good.

'Your singing is flat but you make up for it in volume. Do the chorus of 'Wrecking Ball' again, it's just unbelievably funny. James Corden would love you!'

And I think *I love you too*, but it never occurred to me that love doesn't conquer all. You were there, with me, opening up to me and letting it all go. Then you slid back down and out of my grasp. I want that perfect night, but I want it permanently – I want to be your everything, always. My inner voice is talking to me at last and I'm listening. I want you, Sam, but our love won't grow if Isla is constantly there between us. In the same way that no one can take the adventurer out of Tom; I can't take away your guilt about what happened to Isla.

Mum and Dad don't make a fuss when we suddenly turn up. Mum's simply relieved we're home safe and sound, but I can see she has picked up on the tension between me and Sam.

We hug when we part, maybe a little too long and I see Dad flashing a look at Mum as they stand behind us, ready to wave Sam off. Mum gives Dad one of her stares, probably thinking it's only natural we've become a little bit more relaxed in each other's company.

'See you tomorrow? Work as usual?' Sam inclines his head. All he has is a caravan and a shell of something that may never become anything more.

'Usual time. I'll have the coffee ready and waiting.'

But when he's gone I feel hollow inside. All I have left is a business I have yet to build and a house in the UK that has never felt like my home. Sam, you are my wrecking ball and you have, unwittingly, wrecked me.

When Normal is No Longer Enough

It's like Groundhog Day. We've been working side by side for an hour with barely a word spoken between us. As I sand and prep the walls of the second gîte ready for painting, Sam is fixing the architraves around the doorways.

It's Friday and we should be in the car travelling back from Cannes. We would have had one more night. One extra night to prove that the most perfect night of both of our lives wasn't a mistake, and wasn't a one-off. When I suggested we leave a day early, Sam didn't try to talk me out of it. Afterwards, that began to feel like a sort of rejection, which was unfair of me, given the situation.

And today, irrationally, anger starts to well up inside me. Aren't I worth fighting for? Aren't I worth getting over a tragic event that no amount of guilt will ever change? I steal a sideways glance at Sam. My heart does a somersault as he raises those powerful arms above his head to measure a piece of wood for cutting. I know the feel of that skin on my skin and how it feels to be held in his arms and lifted up.

Is this it? Is this love? Because if it is, then it hurts. And nothing prepared me for that.

I keep sanding, trying not to look distracted and swallowing down my anger. You don't deserve to be loved, Sam, if you won't fight your demons for *us*.

Dad appears in the doorway, an anxious look on his face.

'Anna, you'd better come inside for a minute.'

Sam stops work, spinning around to glance at me. I shrug and walk towards the door but Dad has already gone on ahead. I catch up and follow close on his heels as we enter the kitchen.

Mum is standing with a tea towel in her hands, looking pale. Sitting at the table is Karl. The minute he sees me he stands and steps forward, but I instinctively take a step back.

'What are you doing here? I made it very plain, Karl. I don't love you and I realise with hindsight that I never did.'

He's inching forward and I continue to edge backwards.

'Listen to me, please. That's all I'm asking. I've been a fool but I love you,' the words slip easily off his tongue as they always did.

Dad tries to step in between us. 'Karl, you're not listening to what Anna is saying.'

Karl tries to push Dad out of the way and it catches him unawares. He stumbles and I lunge forward, putting my arm out to steady him.

'This is between the two of us. It can all be sorted if you just give us some privacy.' Karl's voice is now raised and I'm in shock. He's inches away from Dad and me, and I don't know what to do.

There's a movement and it takes me a few seconds to realise that Sam is here, too, and I pull Dad with me as I take another step backwards. A fist comes flying through the air. Dad and I duck, but it glances off Sam's cheek.

He spins around and in seconds he has Karl's arm twisted up behind his back so that he can't move.

Karl's eyes are flashing with anger and indignation. After a couple of seconds of stunned inaction, suddenly he lunges back with his other arm, hitting one of the chairs sideways and it falls, catching Mum's leg. She cries out and I run towards her, ducking under Karl's arm as it flails out once again. It catches one of the shelves and sends china plates crashing to the floor.

Both Dad and Sam now have Karl pinned up against the kitchen wall and he's unable to move.

None of us know quite what to do next.

'I'll call the gendarmes,' Mum's voice is firm but she doesn't move as she's still in shock.

'Look, that's not necessary,' Karl is struggling to free himself but realises that isn't going to happen. 'I didn't come here to cause trouble but I don't intend to leave until I've spoken to Anna, alone.'

Sam laughs, it's hard and throaty. 'If you think I'm going to let you get anywhere near Anna, matey, you're a fool.'

Karl looks at Sam, narrowing his eyes.

'And you are?' His voice is haughty, dismissive and full of sarcasm.

Mum looks at Dad, who looks at me and I look at Sam.

'Sam is the man who has captured my heart.' I turn to look at Sam, who seems to be in shock. 'I love you.'

Mum looks like she's going to faint. Dad draws in a sharp breath but Sam now has the biggest smile on his face I've ever seen.

'What?' Karl spits out the words as if they are leaving a bitter taste in his mouth.

'This is a joke. He's just the builder, right and you're trying to make me look like a fool. You let me tell you every single day for a year that I love you and you said nothing. What did you expect?'

'Don't you think it's rather strange, Karl, that you didn't notice that until I sent you an email just a couple of weeks ago and pointed it out to you? Love is more than a word. You can say it as often as you like, but it means nothing unless your actions back it up. I'm not arm candy, Karl, I'm a living, breathing person. You now have that directorship. Tick. The big, executive style home will be next. Tick. Now you need a wife, someone who will idolise you and not realise that the only person you love is yourself.'

Karl is livid and begins struggling again. Both Dad and Sam are having none of it and push even harder against him. I wonder whether he would lash out at me in his anger if he did break free.

'You slept with him, didn't you?' He twists his head around to stare at Sam, then back at me. 'You slept with someone your parents are employing to work on the house. I bet he couldn't believe his luck. Well, now I'm the one who's done. Let me GO. There's nothing here for me any longer and I'll press charges if you continue to hold me against my will.'

Dad is the angriest I've ever seen him.

'*You'll* press charges, eh? Well, there's the matter of assault on my person and criminal damage to my property, first. I'm a peaceful man as I believe that violence is a sign of someone who is out of control and has no respect whatsoever for other people, or their property. You did your best to manipulate my daughter and it grieved me to see the change in her. Hearing her talk about Sam I know that she's finally found a man worthy of her and good luck to them.'

Sam and Dad are only the width of Karl's body apart and Sam turns slightly to face Dad.

'You seem to have captured my daughter's heart, Sam, and I don't think she could have made a better choice. If I wasn't holding down this idiot I'd be the first to shake your hand.'

Karl is frog-marched out through into the hallway and they don't let go of him until he's firmly the other side of the front door.

'The ground you are standing on, young man, belongs to me and my wife. You have ten seconds to put yourself the other side of that gate. If, at any time in the future you put one foot anywhere within the boundary of my property I will prosecute you for trespass.'

Mum and I are in the hallway, arms around each other as two of our guests descend the stairs to see what the noise is all about. We reassure them we're okay, but Mum is still trembling slightly and they can see Dad and Sam standing guard outside the front door.

'Has he gone?' Mum asks and Dad turns.

'Yes, Viv. He's walking down the street. I can see his car from here. It's finally over.'

'How awful, can we help clear up? You poor dears.' Our guests are taking over and guide Mum and myself into the sitting room.

'Rob, find a broom.' Nicola calls over her shoulder. 'That unpleasant young man has smashed a lot of good china. I'll put the kettle on.' Rob and his wife, Nicola, might only have been here a couple of days but they're very friendly. Thank goodness this episode doesn't seem to have unsettled them unduly.

As Dad and Sam walk in through the door, they loiter, uneasily. I should imagine the adrenalin rush is affecting them, too. We're all glancing from one to another, trying to assimilate what just happened as if we can't believe it, even though we saw it with our own eyes.

'Can I ask a quick question?' Sam's voice pipes up. 'I did hear that right, didn't I, Anna? You did say—'

'I said that I've fallen in love with you. You grew on me, what can I say?' I smile at him and he looks shell-shocked.

'But what about Tom and grabbing that experience in Borneo?'

'I was trying to make you jealous, you idiot, hoping you'd beg me to stay and let me know how much I mean to you.'

There's a rattle of cups and our guests reappear with a tea tray.

'Well,' Sam looks pleased, but still in shock. 'I guess tea is good enough for a toast.'

Mum and Dad give each other that special smile of theirs.

'What exactly happened, while you two were away?' Dad asks, curiosity getting the better of him.

I flash a look at Sam.

'I'm under orders. What happened in Cannes, stays in Cannes,' he mutters. 'But she means a whole lot to me. Everything, in fact.'

Mum pretends to look scandalised, but I can see a smile beginning to creep over her face.

All I Ever Wanted Was My Very Own Hero

At last we're alone for a few minutes and I walk up to Sam. I stare into his eyes, holding his gaze.

'You didn't hesitate; you are my hero. I know you could have had Karl on the floor in seconds but you demonstrated control and that's the sign of a true man.'

'I wasn't going to risk anyone getting hurt, whether that was Geoff, Viv or you, Anna. A man like that is quick to anger because he thinks he's better than everyone else. And then he disrespected you and I will admit I had my fist clenched and you'll never really know how hard it was to hold back. No one insults or threatens the woman I love.'

I lean into him, smiling into his eyes.

'Was it such a shocking revelation when I said those words? Didn't you have even the teeniest little clue during our trip away?'

Sam arms snake down around me, holding me just about as close as we can possibly get.

'The truth is that I didn't think I could get that lucky. I guess we were both holding back and being a bit cautious but I wouldn't have wanted it any other way. You can't just jump into someone's arms and assume it will all work out. I think we both know that we're going to work together to make the future we want and that's the only way to start a relationship that will see us through the rest of our lives.'

He plants a kiss on my forehead, which is an irritating tease, but I know Mum and Dad are in the hallway looking through the crack in the door and he knows that, too.

*

I realise that what's special about Sam is that he encourages me to be who I am and knowing he's not perfect either, there's no reason to be afraid of setbacks. And setbacks aren't failures.

But what has surprised me the most, is that I really believe he finally has the strength to change and grow, rather than standing still and wallowing in his disappointments. I can hardly dare to acknowledge that I'm the person who shook him out of his state of torpor and inspired him to live his life with passion once more. He'd been through a truly horrible experience and anyone would have been traumatised.

'The truth is that I tried very hard not to let you into my heart, Sam. I knew it was wrong to begin a relationship wanting to change someone so every time I felt drawn towards you, I pushed those thoughts aside. But now I realise that the person who had to change was me.'

'We've both changed,' Sam whispers into my ear. 'And we were both wrong about that night. We are the same people who could so easily shed what was holding us back and let go of the past. We just needed a little time to believe we really could make it work. When you fall in love with someone it isn't an instant thing, it's something that grows inside you. We unleashed a passion that comes from loving someone with all your heart and it wasn't simply that first flush of physical attraction.'

Sam had merely been taking his time to heal and that's a process that can't be hurried. What he's taught me is that sometimes all you need to do, is to be patient. It takes as long as it takes and it's different for everyone.

September

Date Night with A Difference

With the second gîte finally completed today, tomorrow will be the first working day since I arrived that Sam and I haven't been together. To celebrate another important milestone on Le Manoir's journey, Mum cooked us all a meal and it has been a lovely evening.

It was strange when Sam kissed me goodnight, though, and I watched him walk off to his car knowing that in the morning he'd be getting up and going to work with his dad. Quite frankly, it was a wrench.

As I climb into bed I realise that we've been so focused on getting the work finished that we haven't really sorted out what's going to happen next. We have become a couple and the sudden realisation that we are going to be parted hadn't really sunk in. My phone pings and I ease it out from beneath Ziggy, who has flopped down on top of it. She's so sleepy she doesn't bat an eyelid. It's from Sam and I chuckle to myself; he's only been gone half an hour.

I'm feeling sad. I'm missing my workmate, already. Guess now I'm going to have to ask you out on dates if I want to see you. Are you free tomorrow night? I'll pick you up at seven? x

A smile hitches the sides of my mouth almost halfway up my cheeks. My heart skips a beat as I marvel at the fact that we are so in tune with each other's thoughts.

Perfect. Missing you, too. Tomorrow is the first day of BRAND *new* – but it will feel strange being desk based again. Sleep well, Sam. Love you! X

As I lie here in the dark I reflect upon the fact that I couldn't imagine my life now without Sam in it. I feel relaxed instead of stressed; happy instead of apprehensive and he's the entire reason for that change. I don't need to organise every second of the future because everything will fall into place and I know that in my heart. As for my work – the more I can earn, the more time off Sam will be able to take to work on the barn. Neil and Sarah are just so delighted to see Sam happy that they'll fall in with our plans.

There was a time when I felt that maybe I was unlovable, or that I didn't deserve a grand passion that was all consuming. As if, in some way, I was flawed. Now I know the only flaw was that I hadn't found the right man and now I have.

*

'Sam has just pulled up,' Dad walks in as I'm taking my waterproof jacket out of the cupboard. 'And it's still pouring with rain.'

I reach back inside in search of an umbrella as Dad opens the door.

'Hi Sam, what a change in the weather. How was your day?'

Sam and Dad shake hands. 'Great. Spent most of it plastering a new extension. Evening, Viv.'

Mum joins us in the hallway, standing on tip-toe to give Sam a kiss on his cheek.

'We missed you today,' she adds, giving him a smile and then turning in my direction to help me on with my jacket.

'You'll need some boots, Anna,' Sam says, looking down at my shoes. 'There's a bit of walking involved.'

I shrug my shoulders. It's not exactly the sort of evening to go for a stroll but hey, it's only water.

We run across to the car, sheltering under the big umbrella and laughing like two kids. The wind is driving the rain horizontally but a quick glance at the sky shows that the clouds are moving fast and hopefully it will clear soon.

'Where are you taking me?'

A secretive smirk flashes playfully over his face and he leans forward to give me a quick kiss, before kicking the engine into life. 'It's a surprise. You'll know soon enough.'

Less than ten minutes' later Sam begins to slow the car. Looking out as he pulls in as close as he can get to the grass verge, I recognise this place. And the field of sunflowers, which have grown a lot bigger since we were last here. Their large heads seem to be smiling up at the rain. Lots of water means lots of plump, black seeds.

'I'm going to need those wellies and I know where we're heading, now.'

'Sorry about the rain but it's easing off already. Here you go.'

Sam hauls my wellington boots from the rear seat so I can slip off my shoes. I had assumed we were going out to eat so I'm a little puzzled but decide to humour him.

We follow the track round the edge of the field until we reach the old wooden stile on the other side. Then it's another track around the corn field beyond that, before we head up to the copse. The rain has now virtually stopped and Sam closes the umbrella, then links arms with me once again.

I cast my mind back to that moment when we sat together on the stone wall. We watched, entranced, as the silver blue sky turned to a deep crimson pink behind the three enormous wind turbines. With only the loud whispering as the blades turned and the low hum caught on the breeze, it had been a surreal moment. It felt special but I don't think either of us knew then quite why it felt so special. It wasn't about the setting at all, it was about two sad, lonely people starting a wonderful new journey together.

As we round the copse and stand on the brow of the hill it's like standing on top of the world. Rolling countryside, the village in the distance and across to those graceful wind turbines standing proud, transforming the turbulent wind into tranquil energy.

'It's like seeing it for the first time all over again. It's incredible to watch the rain moving across the valley and look at that blue sky, now. Everything looks and smells so fresh.' I draw in a deep breath, marvelling at the scene in front of me.

'Here,' Sam lifts me up to sit on the wall on a dry spot beneath an overhanging tree. He then levers himself up next to me. We sit for a few moments and then he turns to grin at me, reaching out for my left hand and taking it in his. Then he pulls a small box from his jacket pocket.

We're grinning at each other like a pair of school kids now and my heart leaps with pure, unadulterated joy.

'My darling Anna. The first time I brought you here we sat together on this same spot watching the sun go down. I will admit that I was a man who had lost his way. I remember wondering why I couldn't find someone just like you to make my life complete.

I still don't know what I've done to deserve this but I'm going to skip over that part quickly as I don't want you changing your mind!

'You make me want to leap out of bed each morning and build a life for us. And I will, I promise. The barn will be our dream home and I'll work day and night to make that happen. There is nothing I wouldn't do for you, to make you happy.

'When I brought you here that day, I wanted to turn my head and kiss you, so much so that it hurt. I know that bringing you here might not appear to be very romantic to some people, but I believe this was where our journey together began. And in here,' he places the small box on the wall next to him so he can touch his chest, 'I was hoping that the impossible could happen. And it did.'

His eyes search mine and they return everything and more. He nods, knowingly, and then picks up the little white box.

'Anna Lacey, will you do me the great honour of becoming my wife?'

The only sounds to be heard are the chirping of the birds and the low hum and swoosh of the wind turbines in the background. I look across at him as he turns my hand over and places the box in the centre of my palm. We both stare at it, knowing this is just the beginning.

'You're right. There is nowhere else I'd rather be right now than here, with you – rain, or shine. Perfection comes in all forms and is very much in the eye of the beholder. And this is the perfect proposal. I, too, sat there that day thinking wouldn't it be unbelievably wonderful if falling in love was as simple as two people connecting as they watch the sun go down. My head was telling me one thing and my heart another. Now it's saying "you did it, Anna, you found the one", so it's yes, Sam, you know it's yes!'

As Sam moves in for a sweet, gentle kiss on the lips I close my eyes and savour the moment. When I open them he's looking at me expectantly and I lift the lid of the box.

It's white gold, with a square diamond held beautifully in place by a four claw setting, in a twisted split band. 'It's beautiful, Sam, but it's too expensive and I don't need—'

'They told me it's a princess cut diamond. I sold the bike to pay for it and I know Granddad would be delighted to know that.'

Aww… his granddad's bike. 'But you loved that bike. It meant so much to you. I don't even need a ring!'

He looks at me, taking it from my hand to slip it onto my ring finger.

'But I love you more and I want you to know just how much.'

We sit hand in hand for a while, watching as the clouds roll away to reveal a beautiful blue sky as the sun begins to dip down towards the horizon. Life is what you make it and together we are going to make it a memorable one full of happy memories.

As the saying goes: all good things come to those who wait… and it was truly worth the wait to find my hero. One beautiful, heart stopping night has changed everything forever and I know that fate has smiled down upon us. We have each other and that's all that truly matters.

THE END

Epilogue

One Year Later

Anna sold her house to her tenant and the equity has allowed her and Sam to start work on the barn.

It will take two years to complete and they look forward to having a small and intimate wedding on the lawn in front of the barn, just as soon as they can move in. In the meantime, the caravan has been replaced with a luxury model, which Sam intends to use as his *man cave* once it's been vacated. He has already informed Anna that there will be regular Karaoke evenings. Ziggy has also taken up residence in the caravan and has settled into her new home well. She has thoroughly acquainted herself with the local mouse population, which continues to decline as each day passes.

Anna currently has a healthy waiting list of clients. Her day is split between her business activities and working alongside Sam on the renovation.

At the end of February Jack and Bella welcomed their twin boys. Bella's recent stomach flu turned out to be a little sister to complete their brood and they await her arrival, sometime in January.

Karl has recently married a high profile young model named Ariana. They are currently in the process of moving to a six bedroom house set in the middle of the rolling Wiltshire countryside. They can often be seen at A-list events and he's currently *under caution* for a fracas with a photographer, which is being investigated by the police.

Tom returned to St-Julien-de-Vouvantes to spend a weekend at Le Manoir, as a guest of Geoff and Viv's. After a memorable garden party, he spent the day with Honorine Allard, who passed away peacefully in her sleep just one month later.

Lizzie and Daniel are progressing their plans to move to France and a modest wedding will take place in the UK prior to the big move. Lizzie is going to work at Le Manoir to assist Geoff and Viv with the running of the B&B. Daniel will be taking Sam's place, working for Neil Callaghan and will be looking to widen his range of skills.

Le Manoir d'Orsenne is becoming an increasingly popular hub within the community, with regular party evenings welcoming everyone. And business, as they say, is booming.

We hope you enjoyed this book.

Lucy Coleman's next book is coming in summer 2018

More addictive fiction from Aria:

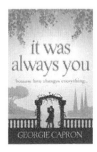 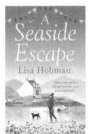 

Make your own espresso martini

You will need:

One cocktail shaker

One chilled (20 mins in the freezer) cocktail glass

Ice chips

40ml of Tia Maria

20ml of vodka

40ml freshly made, robust espresso coffee

Three coffee beans

1.   *Add an egg cup full of ice chips to the freshly made espresso.*

2.   *Add the following ingredients to the cocktail shaker in this order: Ice chips (about a handful); Tia Maria; vodka; coffee*

3.   *Shake vigorously and strain into the chilled glass. Top with the coffee beans.*

Enjoy!

Acknowledgements

Every newly published novel represents a journey that the writer has taken accompanied by a whole team of people. Together they strive to make a story the best it can be and that's a very wonderful thing. Suddenly, as a writer, you don't feel quite so alone in the process and it's a special feeling to have that team onboard, working on *your* story.

I would like to thank my agent, Sara Keane, for coming into my life at just the right time. Also, a huge thank you to the awesome Sarah Ritherdon, for reading my Christmassy manuscript on one of the hottest days in summer and feeling the festive vibe: enough to offer me a contract, which kicks off with this little journey to France, first.

Being an Aria Fiction author is such a thrill and getting to work with editorial director, Lucy Gilmour – someone I have long admired - has been a sheer delight!

I also want to send a virtual group hug to the wider team who have been involved in the process – thank you all from the bottom of my heart!

And finally, but most importantly, the readers. Your kindness in choosing my novel represents the *first* stage in the next part of my journey with Aria Fiction. In reading this I'm sending you, too, my very grateful thanks. It's your wonderful reviews that keep me writing and do get in touch via social media, as it does brighten my day. It's rather nice between long sessions of writing to engage with someone I haven't created and who doesn't only exist in my head.

For me, YOU keep it real!

Lucy x

About Lucy Coleman

Lucy Coleman lives in the Forest of Dean in the UK with her lovely husband and Bengal cat, Ziggy. Her novels have been short-listed in the UK's Festival of Romance and the eFestival of Words Book Awards. Lucy won the 2013 UK Festival of Romance: Innovation in Romantic Fiction award.

Find me on Twitter

https://twitter.com/LucyColemanAuth

Visit my website
http://linnbhalton.co.uk/

Become an Aria Addict

Aria is the new digital-first fiction imprint from Head of Zeus.

It's Aria's ambition to discover and publish tomorrow's superstars, targeting fiction addicts and readers keen to discover new and exciting authors.

Aria will publish a variety of genres under the commercial fiction umbrella such as women's fiction, crime, thrillers, historical fiction, saga and erotica.

So, whether you're a budding writer looking for a publisher or an avid reader looking for something to escape with – Aria will have something for you.

Get in touch: aria@headofzeus.com

Become an Aria Addict
http://ariafiction.com/newsletter/subsc
ribe

Find us on Twitter
https://twitter.com/Aria_Fiction

Find us on Facebook
http://www.facebook.com/ariafiction

Find us on BookGrail
http://www.bookgrail.com/store/aria/

Addictive Fiction

First published in the United Kingdom in 2018 by
Aria, an imprint of Head of Zeus Ltd

9 7 5 3 1 2 4 6 8

A CIP catalogue record for this book is available
from the British Library.

ISBN (E) 9781788541541

Aria
c/o Head of Zeus
First Floor East
5–8 Hardwick Street
London EC1R4RG

www.ariafiction.com

Made in the USA
Las Vegas, NV
17 July 2022